D1135485

Angels of Mercy

Also by Lyn Andrews

Maggie May
The Leaving of Liverpool
Liverpool Lou
The Sisters O'Donnell
The White Empress
Ellan Vannin
Mist Over the Mersey
Mersey Blues
Liverpool Songbird
Liverpool Lamplight
Where the Mersey Flows
From This Day Forth
When Tomorrow Dawns

ANGELS OF MERCY

Lyn Andrews

This edition published 1998
by BCA
By arrangement with
HEADLINE BOOK PUBLISHING

CN 4532

Typeset by Palimpsest Book Production Limited,
Polmont, Stirlingshire

Printed and bound in Great Britain by
Mackays of Chatham PLC, Chatham, Kent

This book is dedicated to Señor José Carreras and to everyone connected with the International Leukaemia Foundation which bears his name and which was established by him.

Leukaemia is a disease that knows no frontiers and does not discriminate between creed, colour, age or status. It is an illness over which Señor Carreras himself triumphed.

His recovery became an inspiration for so many leukaemia sufferers and a ray of hope for the future. It gave an equal amount of joy and relief to everyone who appreciates José Carreras' truly remarkable talent, myself included.

Lyn Andrews,
Southport 1998.

What passing bells for those who die as cattle?
Only the monstrous anger of the guns.
Only the stuttering rifles' rapid rattle.

Wilfred Owen, 'Anthem for Doomed Youth'

1912

Chapter One

'You can't wear a hat in the house!' Kate Greenway's voice penetrated her mother's reverie. 'Mam, tell her she can't wear a hat, she'll look daft.'

'No she won't. No one decent goes out without a hat, if they've got one. You'd better pin it on well, Evvie, the Pier Head can be a windy hole on a raw December Saturday,' Peg Greenway answered absently, not noticing her daughter's raised eyebrows at her failure to grasp her point.

Despite the years of hardship Peg was still a handsome woman. Physically she'd always been big-boned, but now there was more flesh on those bones. Her hair, still thick and untinged by grey, was worn in a tight knot at the back of her head.

She inhaled deeply and nodded with satisfaction at the appetising smell that permeated the kitchen, oblivious to her daughters' heated debate. She smiled as she stirred the big pan of scouse that stood bubbling gently on the open range, a smile that encompassed her seventeen-year-old twins as they took off their heavy shawls, hung them on the hook behind the door and plumped themselves down on the old sofa.

Peg thought what a fortunate woman she was. Things were far better these days with all the family working, except of course young Joe. For most of her married life she'd had to manage on Bill's small wage from the tannery in Gardners Row. It wasn't a very pleasant job and his work clothes stank but at least it was a steady wage she could count on each week. Unlike many women she knew who had to try and keep a family on whatever their men managed to earn down at the docks.

She'd not lost any of her children either and, in a city where so many died before the age of ten, it was a miracle she thanked God for every day of her life. What's more, the girls had been very fortunate where looks were concerned. It was Ma McNally, the local midwife, who had first called them 'Angels'. When she'd placed the two identical infants, tightly wrapped in towels, in Peg's arms, she'd beamed with joy.

'They're like a pair of angels, God love them. Mind, you'll have yer work cut out now, Peggy girl,' she'd added sagely as she'd busied herself collecting up the stained newspaper, old bits of towels and all the other items scattered around the front downstairs room where Peg's daughters had been born.

The name 'Angels' had stuck, for as Katherine and Evangeline had grown they were the spit of two cherubs and as alike as peas in a pod.

Peg took the big ladle from its place on the wall, stirred the stew again and smiled once more at the twins. They'd inherited none of the physical characteristics of either herself or Bill, a fact she often commented on. Their hair was not a coppery red like her own or Tom's, her oldest son, nor dark brown like Bill's and young Joe's. It was blonde – almost silver white in some lights – and it curled naturally. Nor were their eyes brown as were those of the rest of the family. They were blue. A startling, cornflower blue. 'I'll never know where I got you two from,' was often heard in number fourteen Silvester Street, though in reality both Bill and Peg knew where the twins' head-turning looks originated: his Mam. In her youth Nelly Greenway had been considered a great beauty around the Scotland Road area of Liverpool. It was a pity she'd not lived to see her granddaughters, Bill often said. She'd have been as proud of them as he was. Nelly's own daughters had died young – as had two of her sons, in the days when cholera had raged regularly through the slum-ridden city, decimating the poor who lived in conditions far worse than those that now existed in the courts and streets around Scotland Road and Vauxhall Road.

Bill was a quiet man who worked hard and left the day-to-day management of the family in the capable hands of Peg. They were proud of their family: apart from the girls, Tom was a fine lad and though young Joe was a bit of a tearaway there was no badness in him.

Peg glanced again at her daughters and felt a sense of achievement. She'd often caught her husband looking at them in the same way – the 'Angels of Silvester Street', as they'd come to be known, though, Peg thought ruefully, angels with dirty faces more often than not when they'd been growing up.

After she'd tasted the stew, Peg nodded. It was almost ready.

Kate pursed her lips in annoyance and raised her eyes to the ceiling while Evvie grinned at her mother.

'Mam, you've not been listening to a word I've said. I don't mean she shouldn't wear her hat when we go and meet Tom tomorrow. I mean she can't wear a hat for Maggie McGee's party.'

'Oh, that,' Peg replied tersely, sawing at a large loaf with the carving knife and heaping the slices on a plate.

'Well, all I can say is that Hetty McGee must have more money than sense. Fancy wasting it on a do for their Maggie an' her only seventeen. I mean it's not as though she were twenty-one, like, is it? Now *that's* a birthday to really have a do for, if you can afford it. That's the time to go to Skillicorn's for the cakes and Pegram's for the boiled ham. Not now, when that little madam is only seventeen.'

Kate and Evvie exchanged glances. Peg's views matched those of most of the neighbours. It was something the whole of Silvester Street was talking about for there was hardly ever any spare cash for such frivolities. For big occasions, like a coronation, they all clubbed together for a communal affair but most of the time everyone just managed to scrape a living.

'Mrs Holden from the shop was saying that it's a disgrace. A terrible waste spending all that money on Maggie and it will only give her more airs and graces.'

'Aye, well, Ivy Holden's got a mouth like a parish oven, but this time I have to agree with her. Get the dishes on the table, Kate. Yer da will be in any minute an' he likes his meal ready. Evvie, shift yerself, girl. Take the big jug and the bucket out to the tap, I've no water left for the kettle, and don't stand jangling with Josie Ryan,' Peg instructed, bustling about the small kitchen that also served as a living room for the entire family.

'Ah, Mam! Can't our Joe go for it? I'm worn out,' Evvie complained. Even though she was thankful to have a job, standing all day in Silcock's Feed factory was not a soft occupation.

Peg shook her head angrily. 'That little sod has scarpered again an' I told him I needed him to go down to the tap. Yer da will have to take him in hand – he's running wild. We'll 'ave the scuffers hammering on the door for him one of these days. Go on, Evvie, be quick if you want a cup of tea.'

As Evvie reluctantly fetched the jug and bucket from the dank, airless scullery Peg sighed, pausing for a moment to glance around, the Fry's cocoa tin that served as a tea caddy clutched to her chest. She didn't really have much to show for twenty-three years of marriage.

Apart from the bits and pieces in the bedrooms, all the furniture was in here. The scrubbed table stood against the window wall, with two long benches pushed beneath it. A ladder-back chair and an old sagging sofa were against the opposite wall. A food press with a mesh front, a plain dresser, two three-legged stools, all were crammed in. Rag rugs covered the floor and her pans hung above the range. Above them was suspended the slatted clothes rack that worked on a pulley and rope system, which often collapsed and festooned anyone who happened to be in the room with damp clothes. On the overmantel was a cheap clock, a couple of brass candlesticks complete with candles, a pair of china dogs and a statue of the Virgin Mary.

Peg wore herself out day after day, scrubbing and polishing, but day after day the house defeated her efforts. It was the way they were built, she knew that. They were old, some were very damp and some even looked as though they would fall down any minute, burying their occupants in debris. The kitchen floor was flagged and the chimney often smoked. There was no running water but at least they had their own privy at the bottom of the yard, an earth closet that was emptied once a week. All the houses had their share of bugs. It didn't matter how many times the Sanitary men came and stoved them, the bugs came back. Bill frequently used a blowlamp to burn them off the iron frames of the beds. The houses all needed knocking down and new ones built, but there was fat chance of that happening.

Like all her neighbours, Peg daily scrubbed the steps, the window ledges, even the section of pavement outside her door, then she went over the steps with a donkey stone.

Often she would get up off her knees in the street, her back aching, her hands raw with harsh soap and soda, and she'd glare with heartfelt venom at the clouds of smoke that poured from the factory chimneys and those of the Clarence Dock Power Station, known locally as the Three Ugly Sisters. In an hour, less if the wind changed direction, the smuts would undo all her hard work and there was nothing she could do about it. It was the same on washday. She'd cursed Tate & Lyle's sugar refinery at the bottom of Burlington Street up hill and down dale, but it didn't make the washing any cleaner.

Suddenly Kate let out a sharp cry and darted into the scullery. Peg, jerked back to reality, looked up in time to see Joe and Mickey Ryan tottering precariously on the wall at the bottom of the yard that led into the entry, or jigger as it was known. She crossed to the window and banged hard on the glass pane with the cocoa tin.

'Gerroff that wall the pair of you!' she yelled.

Kate had been quick. She'd caught her brother's jacket and had hauled him down bodily, then she marched him into the house by his ear.

Peg glared at her younger son, taking in the rip in his jacket, the scuffed boots and the woollen socks hanging untidily around his ankles, revealing dirty scraped knees.

'Just look at the state of you! I wear meself out washing, ironing, mending and scrimping so you'll have boots on your feet, and what do you do? You go playing silly beggars with that Mickey Ryan. A pair of flaming little hooligans, that's what you are! You could have fallen and broken your neck, or worse, landed in the midden! You wait until yer da gets in, Joe Greenway!'

'It wasn't all my fault, Mam! He dared me!' Joe cried indignantly, rubbing his ear but knowing that it would sting even more acutely if his da heard of his escapades. He didn't see what was so bad about jumping the jigger walls, as it was called. All the kids did it and even his da had admitted to doing it when he'd been a lad, an admission Joe looked on with great resentment, seeing that that game was now forbidden to him. Of course you could end up in Stanley Hospital with a broken arm or leg – and some of his mates considered such injuries were worth it, if it meant no school for a goodish time – but it wasn't often that that happened.

'If Mickey Ryan dared you to jump off the landing stage, I suppose you'd be daft enough to do it. Sometimes you're as thick as the wall, our Joe!' Kate remarked acidly.

'Oh, go and get yourself cleaned up and don't mither me any more tonight with your antics,' Peg said wearily. Kate was right, sometimes she wondered if Joe had any brains at all. If he had then he certainly didn't use them very often.

'There's no water. I saw our Evvie going down the street,' Joe said brightly, seeing a reprieve but totally forgetting that it was he who should have fetched the water in the first place.

Peg's temper flared again. 'Don't be so hard-faced, meladdo! Go and help her bring it in. I asked you to get it for me!' She made a swipe at Joe with the piece of sacking she used as an oven cloth but he darted past her and into the lobby, his boots clattering on the scuffed lino.

Peg shook her head and returned to her preparations. 'I'll swing for that lad one of these days, so help me I will!'

'Oh, he's not bad, Mam, he's just easily led,' Kate consoled her.

'I know, Kate. But he needs to be kept on the straight and narrow or God knows what he might get up to.'

Kate looked up from setting the table as the back yard door opened.

'Here's Da now. He's early tonight.'

'Wouldn't you just know it, when there's no water for them to get washed in and it'll take a while to boil. If that young hooligan had gone for it when I asked him to this wouldn't have happened.'

Bill had removed his boots and left them in the scullery, leaving his jacket in there too since it stank to high heaven – as Peg often commented.

Bill gave his wife a peck on the cheek. He looked tired, Peg thought.

'I'm sorry, luv, but there's no water yet. Our Evvie and Joe have gone for it and you'll have to chastise that little horror, too.'

'Now what's he done?' Bill asked wearily.

'Jumping the jigger walls, not doing what he's told, sneaking off before he fetched in the water, to start with.'

'I'm starving.'

'We all are, Bill, but there'll be no tea until you get a wash and change your clothes,' Peg stated firmly. They might not have much in material things but she did have standards.

After the meal was over, all the chores completed and Joe suitably chastened by his father, Kate and Evvie went up to their tiny bedroom. The house only had two rooms upstairs, and Tom and Joe shared the other. Peg and Bill slept in the parlour, an arrangement that grieved Peg sorely. It had been her lifelong wish to have a 'best' room. Somewhere to entertain Father Foreshaw, the parish priest, when he called. It gave you standing amongst the neighbours, but until she 'got rid of them all', as she put it, the parlour had to serve as a bedroom.

The room was cold and smelled musty, and until Kate lit the gas jet and replaced the clear glass mantle, the only illumination came from the streetlamp on the corner of Limekiln Lane. The flickering flame threw long shadows over the room.

'It's freezing in here. We should have stayed in the kitchen,'

Evvie complained, pulling the blanket from the bed around her shoulders.

'And have our Joe listening to every word and telling Mickey Ryan and then having the pair of them skitting and sniggering at me? No, thanks very much!'

Evvie sighed. Kate had always been more out-going, more confident than herself. Ideas and plans were always instigated by Kate; she just followed, usually meekly. There were occasions, though, when she did dig her heels in, if the current idea really didn't appeal to her.

Kate had wrapped the faded patchwork quilt around her shoulders and was standing by the window, looking out into the street. The rows and rows of soot-blackened terraced houses, their roofs the colour of gunmetal and shiny with the sleet that had been falling since teatime, ran all the way down to the River Mersey. It was too dark to see the river and the forest of masts, spars and funnels of the ships that crowded the six miles of waterfront.

She wanted to get away from here some day, maybe on one of those ships. She certainly didn't want a carbon copy of her mam's life. Oh, Da had a steady job – in fact he and Alf McGee, who worked for Bent's Brewery, were the only two men in the street who did – but life was still grinding hard work for Mam.

When they'd been young, Mam had gone out office cleaning in the evening to earn a few extra shillings. And that after an exhausting day at home. It wasn't unusual: all the women in the street either went cleaning or took in washing to make ends meet, except for Ivy Holden at the corner shop.

Apart from Ivy, the only woman with any status was Hetty McGee. She was a dressmaker and over the years she'd gathered a few loyal clients who paid for clothes made on Hetty's Singer treadle sewing machine that stood in pride of place in her front room, her 'Fitting Room' as she so grandly called it. With only three of them in the family there was no overcrowding in their house. The kitchen wasn't cluttered and Maggie had the enviable luxury of a bedroom to herself.

Kate sighed deeply. She wanted more from life than her mother had had but just what exactly she wasn't clear. 'You wouldn't think it was Christmas in a couple of days, would you?' she said. 'There's not a lot of "glad tidings of great joy" out there.'

Evvie looked at her sharply. 'Oh, what's up with you, Kate?

You've had a cob on all day. It's not like you to be so short with people and you nearly bit Josie's head off this morning.'

Josie Ryan didn't work with them but they all walked to the tram stop together.

'All she said was that she really liked that Frank Lynch from Athol Street.' Even as she spoke Evvie became acutely aware of the reason for Kate's bad humour. 'So *that's* what's the matter with you. That's why you were so sharp with Josie. You like him, too, don't you?'

Kate felt the blood rush to her cheeks. She should have realised that Evvie would know. They were so close that it was a wonder Evvie hadn't guessed before now. She turned back to the window and idly traced a pattern in the condensation that misted the pane of glass. 'So, what if I do? It's not a crime, is it, or a mortal sin? And he's not engaged to Josie, is he? He hasn't even asked her out yet and I hope he doesn't. I *do* like him, Evvie. Whenever I see him I feel sort of on edge, and when he looks at me my heart just turns over. Do you think . . . ?'

'What?'

'Well, is there such a thing as love at first sight?'

'I don't really know and you don't really know him. I don't think I could love someone I don't know.'

'Oh, Evvie, you're so . . . wary.'

'I'm not. I just feel as though I have to *know* someone before I said I loved them. Do you love him, Kate?'

Kate thought for a moment. 'Oh, I don't know. I think I do but what about Josie?'

'He hasn't asked her out yet but he hasn't asked you either.' Then, seeing the look that came into Kate's eyes, she added, 'Oh, all right, don't get airyated with me, too!'

'Well, don't you say anything to anyone. Promise me, Evvie, please? I'd feel such a fool. He hasn't asked me out, and if . . . if he doesn't like me —'

'Of course he likes you. I've seen the way he looks at you when we leave church on Sunday mornings,' Evvie said firmly. Josie had been her friend for years but her first loyalty was to her sister.

'Promise me, just the same?' Kate pleaded.

'Oh, all right, I promise. God's truth.' Evvie crossed herself to show she was sincere.

Kate sat down on the bed they shared, twisting a strand of hair around her finger, a habit they both had when anxious or upset. She wore her hair in a loose chignon while Evvie's was swept up into a soft roll that framed her face. It was the only way people could distinguish between them. When they'd been younger they'd often mischievously changed places, Kate saying she was Evvie and vice versa. Only immediate family didn't fall for this trickery. Mam could tell them apart just by the sound of their voices.

Kate was thinking of how Frank Lynch's eyes had swept over her with what she hoped was interest and admiration. Of course it had been after Mass and she'd been looking her best.

'I wish I had something new to wear for this party,' she said wistfully.

'Can't you afford anything? Not even a blouse?'

'How can I? We turn up our wages to Mam and I'm still paying off my Sturla's cheque with my pocket money.'

Evvie brooded in silence. She was in the same position herself. A lot of people used the 'cheque' system. It was a form of credit. You went along to Sturla's Department Store in Great Homer Street, picked what you wanted and then paid a set sum each week until it was all paid off. Often, though, the things that had been purchased were worn out before the debt was paid. She'd used her 'cheque' to buy Christmas presents. 'You know I'd lend you something if I could,' she said reproachfully.

'Oh, I know, and I suppose I'm just being daft. I mean, you can't have everything, not on what Silcock's pay us, and Mam can't sew like Mrs McGee.'

'Maybe our Tom will have got us something, something to wear, from New York.'

'And pigs might fly. We'll get the usual little bottle of some cheap scent. He doesn't earn a fortune, Evvie, and he is good to us. He's not a steward or a waiter, who at least get tips.'

Evvie nodded her agreement. Working as a trimmer in the stokehold of the *Carmania* was her idea of hell. As the ship ploughed its way regularly from Liverpool to New York and back Tom worked like a thing possessed, shovelling coal in temperatures that would make a hot summer day appear cool by comparison. It was hard and dirty work, done in shifts of four hours on, four hours off, and when he got to New York, like nearly every other member of the stokehold, he went on a drinking spree. You couldn't blame them, they had to have some relaxation.

But somehow Tom always managed to find the time to get them all the requisite little gift. It was a tradition on Merseyside that the seafarers brought home presents, no matter how small or insignificant. Tom always managed to keep a few shillings of his wages too, which was more than most of them did. He left Mam an allotment that she collected from the Cunard Building by the week. All in all, though, he could never be called well off.

'Ask him to lend you some money then, he won't mind,' Evvie suggested, for her sympathy for her sister had set her thinking of solutions.

'How can I when I won't be able to pay it back for months? No, I'll just have to make do with my blue skirt and white blouse. I'll give the blouse a dip in Robin starch and press it. That's if I can get it dry without it getting covered in smuts.' Her thoughts returned to the matter of Evvie's hat. 'And you *can't* wear a hat. You'll have to try and find a bit of ribbon or something for your hair instead. Apart from looking daft, you'll get it ruined. It'll get knocked and if you take it off someone's bound to sit on it.'

Evvie nodded. It had just been an idea and not a very good one for it was her only hat. However, she was determined to think of something to smarten up her appearance. 'I'll see if I can get a bit of ribbon and maybe an artificial flower in Great Homer Street Market tomorrow and I'll pin my hair up. I bet Maggie will have something that looks as though it's come from Cripps in Bold Street,' she added wistfully. Not only was Mrs McGee clever at sewing, she often found very ingenious ways of brightening up old clothes – a velvet trim on a jacket, a piece of pleated muslin at the neck of a dress. Maggie, too, was clever with materials, one of the reasons why she'd been accepted as an apprentice seamstress in Sloan's in Bold Street, the Bond Street of Liverpool.

'Her dress is pale green *foulé* with a narrow black stripe, trimmed with black buttons and braid. That's all I could get out of her. "It's gorgeous and it's going to be a surprise," she kept on saying. Sometimes, I really envy her!' Kate finished, trying to imagine herself in pale green, trimmed with black braid. She'd certainly catch Frank Lynch's eye in something like that.

'I know, so do I. It must be great to be able to make your own clothes,' Evvie consoled her sister, but she thought it best not to say that Josie Ryan had a new blouse, the front of which was frilled and pin-tucked and embroidered with tiny rosebuds. She'd got it cheap because there was a scorch mark on the back but Mrs Ryan had treated that with bleach until it was barely noticeable.

Evvie, Kate and Josie were firm friends and had been since they were toddlers. Maggie had never been classed as a real friend. She was that little bit younger and had been spoiled in comparison to the rest of them. She just hung about on the fringe of their group and was often a pain in the neck. However, the appearance of Frank Lynch on the scene seemed about to change things between Kate and Josie, Evvie thought, for they were both obviously smitten with him. She didn't see what either of them saw in him: he was a bit of a loudmouth and fancied himself as a ladies' man. Still, it looked as though this birthday party of Maggie's was going to be interesting to say the least. She just hoped there wasn't going to be any serious argument or irrevocable rift between Kate and Josie. It would be such a shame if they came to blows over Frank Lynch. Perhaps Josie didn't want him as much as Kate obviously did. Evvie had never known Kate to say she loved any of the other lads who'd drifted in and out of her life over the last year. Maybe it would be left for Frank Lynch himself to choose.

The front door banged shut and Evvie got up. 'That's Da off down the Royal George. I'm going downstairs before I freeze to death.'

Now that she had unburdened herself to Evvie, Kate felt better. 'I could do with a cup of tea myself and I'm going to shove a couple of bricks in the fire and then put them in this bed. It's like the flaming North Pole up here.'

Chapter Two

As Peg had prophesied, it was windy and bitterly cold down at the Pier Head that Saturday afternoon. The girls had finished work at lunch time, hastened home, got changed and, with Peg and young Joe, had caught the tram to the landing stage. Bill had to work until six o'clock.

'Hang on to your hat, Kate, we'll have to make a dash for it. They've already tied up!' Evvie cried, clutching her sister's arm, and indicating with a jerk of her head the black hull of the *Carmania* just visible between the buildings of the waterfront.

The Pier Head was always crowded. Not only was it the terminus for the trams, but it was the site of the Riverside Station, where passengers arrived on the boat trains or departed for London. There were also cars and carriages awaiting the passengers disembarking from the ships tied up at the George's Landing Stage. Cargo and luggage was also coming ashore, and drays and wagons were lined up, the huge horses waiting patiently, their heads bent against the icy blasts sweeping in from the Mersey estuary.

As quickly as they could they all threaded their way across the cobbles and between the traffic, Peg hanging on tightly to Joe's arm in case he decided to wander off on his own, for she'd never find him again in this crowd. If she didn't watch him, he'd be off messing about with the ragged street urchins, who'd have the eyes out of your head if you so much as blinked.

The two red and black funnels of the Cunarder still sent wisps of white smoke up into the sullen grey sky. Also alongside the stage was the Isle of Man steam packet *Mona's Isle*, the Dublin mail boat *Leinster*, and the Birkenhead ferry *Iris*.

'We'll never get through this lot!' Kate cried in dismay. 'We'll never find him.'

An expression of grim determination crossed Peg's face. She had no intention of letting the crowd stop her from greeting her son. 'You keep hold of meladdo here, Kate, and follow me.' Joe was shoved unceremoniously towards his sister, while Peg elbowed her way ruthlessly through the press of people.

'Mam! Mam! Over here! Here!'

Hearing the familiar voice, Peg looked up and her face was wreathed in smiles as she caught sight of Tom.

He pushed his way towards her. 'Here I am, Mam!'

The crowd parted as Peg was kissed and hugged, then Kate and Evvie in turn were caught up and swung off their feet.

'And how are my Angels? Don't you look great, the pair of you?' Tom grinned down at them. He was a younger, taller version of his father and the girls laughed, delighted he was home safe and sound for Christmas.

Joe had attached himself to his brother's sleeve. 'Did you bring me any comics? Did you, Tom? Did you? Ah, ay! You promised you would.'

'Isn't he awful, Mam? Not "Hello, Tom, how are you?" Oh, no! It's, "What have you brought me?"' Kate said acidly.

Peg held on to her hat with one hand; with the other she gripped Joe by the arm. 'Oh, you can always rely on him to make a show of you. Let's get out of this infernal crush. How they all manage to get on to the right ship at the right time beats me!'

Tom swung his canvas bag over his shoulder and pushed forward towards the floating roadway and the line of green and cream trams that waited at the top of it.

Joe looked wistfully towards the line of waiting hackneys. 'Do you think that maybe one day we might go home in one of them?' he asked, indicating the cabs. He didn't hold out much hope, but it never did any harm to ask, and if by some miracle his mam agreed, wouldn't *that* be something to tell his mates about? Comics and a hackney. They'd all be green with envy.

'Listen to him! Does he think money grows on trees or something?' Evvie laughed.

'That's because he sets no value on it. He doesn't have to slog his guts out the way I have to. Aye, and me da, too.' Tom gently cuffed his brother's head. 'He'll learn soon enough, though.'

'He'd learn a good deal sooner if he shifted himself and found something to do that would earn him a copper or two, instead of running the streets with Mickey Ryan and that lot,' Peg replied.

Joe was stung. 'I do try! Didn't Mickey and me carry all that lino for that feller in the market? All the way to Everton we had to lug it, an' all for threepence.'

Evvic laughed again. 'It's a wonder he gave you anything at all, since it was supposed to be delivered to a house in Anfield! He should have given you two a map.'

'He's about as useful as a wet *Echo*! Get on that tram, lad, and stay where I can see you.' Peg urged her family aboard the *Green Goddess*.

'I want to stay on to Great Homer Street to get a bit of ribbon,' Evvie said as Tom dug in his pocket for the fares.

'Out on the town, are we, then? What is it? A dance at the Rialto or music hall at the Hippodrome?' he queried.

'No, Maggie McGee is having a do for her birthday on Christmas night.'

'Am I invited?'

'Of course you are. Hetty knows better than to leave one of my boys out,' Peg replied, before tapping the woman in front of her on the shoulder. 'Excuse me, missus, but do you think you could lean forward a bit? That stuffed bird on your 'at is nearly poking me eye out.'

The woman glared but adjusted her large and overtrimmed hat.

'Mam! You're awful,' Kate hissed from the seat behind, while Evvie smothered a grin.

Joe's queries about the promised comics had been silenced by a handful of large, multi-coloured glass marbles, which had been surreptitiously passed to him by his older brother and which he knew would make him the envy of his gang.

'So little Maggie is sweet seventeen, then,' Tom mused.

'She's never been sweet, hasn't that one,' answered his mother. 'Hard-faced and as crafty as a cartload of monkeys, she is. It's Hetty's fault – she can see no wrong in her, and Alf's as bad.'

'Well, I suppose they think they're lucky to have her, after losing the rest.'

Peg nodded grimly. Hetty had lost three children to measles and diphtheria before she'd managed to rear Maggie.

'She's having a new frock,' Kate sighed.

'Oh for God's sake, don't start that again!' her mother complaincd. 'I'll be glad when this flaming party is over, I really will. You'd think it was a posh garden party or something the way everyone is carrying on. I don't want to hear another word about it, at least not for the rest of the way home.'

As soon as they were back Peg made a cup of tea and Kate put the flatirons to heat. Tom had taken himself off upstairs to unpack, after he'd informed them that the usual homecoming gifts would not be distributed until Christmas Day. This elicited frowns and tuts of disappointment, but he was adamant.

'Oh damn!' Peg suddenly cried, her tone irritable in the extreme.

'Now what's the matter?' Kate asked, smoothing out the old pressing cloth.

'I've forgotten to get the salt fish for tomorrow's breakfast. I must be getting old; I've got a head like a sieve lately.'

Kate didn't particularly like the fish that was the traditional Sunday breakfast in Liverpool. She was concentrating hard on getting the iron to the right temperature to cope with the neck frills of her best blouse. With its leg-o'-mutton sleeves and high collar, it wasn't the easiest thing to iron. 'Ask our Joe to go down for it, or maybe Evvie will remember and bring some in with her.'

'I never mentioned it so she won't think about it, and where has that lad got to now? Joe! Joe! Come here this minute,' she yelled, but there was silence. Joe had evidently gone in search of his mates.

'Oh, it's no use, I'll have to go myself.' She reached for her shawl but before she could locate her battered purse, Joe came bounding into the room from the yard.

'I've got a job, Mam! A regular job for Saturdays.'

'Doing what?' Kate asked.

'Well, as I was passing I just looked in the window of Steadman's. Mr Steadman came out —'

'Why were you fooling around outside the pawnshop?' Peg interrupted.

'I wasn't foolin' around, I was looking, seeing if there was anything I could afford for you for Christmas.'

Peg sighed. 'Don't be so daft, lad. Besides, you know he sells a lot of stuff off on Christmas Eve on that bit of land in Kew Street. You'd be better to wait until then – that's if you've got any money, which I doubt.'

'I will have, Mam. Anyway, he says to me, "Joe, would you like to earn threepence a week?"'

'Threepence! What for?' Kate cried.

Old Levi Steadman lived above his shop with his only son, Ben. Mrs Steadman had passed away years ago from consumption. While it was the general consensus that Levi must have a bit of money tucked away, he wasn't a man to fling it about, particularly not on ten-year-old hooligans like her brother.

'I've to set and light the fire and the gas, cook whatever he's left, sweep the kitchen and then take all the rubbish out into the yard, every Saturday.'

'You cook! You'll burn the place down!' Kate laughed.

'I won't! It'll all be ready in the pan and all I'll have to do is watch it.'

'Oh, now I see. It's their Sabbath and they can't do things like that. So what happened to that other lad who used to do it for him?'

'Dunno, but I said I'd do it. Is it all right, Mam? I mean, I won't get into trouble from Father Foreshaw?'

Peg smiled and ruffled his hair. 'No, lad, you won't. We all pray to the same God. Come on, get going if you've chores to do. I'll walk to the corner with you.'

On her way up the street, Peg passed the time of day with her neighbours.

'All ready for the big do?' Mary Ryan from number eight called as she half-heartedly swept her step for the second time that day.

Peg rolled her eyes skyward in reply and Mary nodded her understanding and agreement.

'Are you off down the market, Peg?' Vi Hawkins called. She herself was carrying a heavy hemp bag and was about to inform Peg which stallholders had bargains.

'No, Vi, I'm going last thing Christmas Eve. Better bargains then and the stuff's a bit fresher, too.' Even though there was more money these days Peg never spent foolishly and late on Christmas Eve meat and fruit and vegetables were all reduced to half price.

When she returned home it was to find Kate still pressing her blouse and Evvie begging her sister to 'run the iron over' a length of scarlet ribbon. She was surprised to see Ben Steadman sitting in the ladder-back chair by the range as though it was something he did every day of his life.

He got to his feet the minute he saw Peg. 'Dad asked me to come in and see you, Mrs Greenway,' he explained, a little abashed, thinking that maybe he'd taken Evvie's invitation to make himself at home a bit too literally. He glanced awkwardly at the figure of a woman in a long white robe, covered by a blue cloak, that smiled down from the overmantel.

Peg hung up her shawl and took the fish into the scullery. 'How is your dad, Ben?' she called. The little pawnbroker was liked by nearly everyone. He was unfailingly considerate and courteous, qualities that were admired by his customers. There was never any of the false cheerfulness or ill-disguised avarice of Jimmy Heggerty, whose shop was on the corner of Scotland Road and Martin Street.

'He's fine, considering his arthritis.'

'I'll be with you in a minute, lad. I'll just put this fish in to soak otherwise I'll be able to mend the soles of our Joe's boots with it.'

Ben smiled at Evvie, who returned his smile. She liked Ben Steadman. He was older than she and he was handsome in a dark, foreign sort of way. She didn't understand all the customs that he and his father adhered to, but he'd always been friendly towards her.

Ben looked down at his feet, a little embarrassed. He'd known Evvie all her life, and served her many times in his father's shop in years past when money had been very scarce in the Greenway household. But suddenly he'd realised that she'd grown up. It surprised him and as he'd sat and talked to her he'd felt strangely drawn to her and it was more than just the undeniable fact that she, like her sister, was beautiful. It was Evvie's quietness, her reticence that attracted him most.

Peg bustled back into the kitchen, wiping her hands on her apron. 'Right, spit it out lad.'

'Has Joe told you that Dad asked him to light the fire and the gas every Saturday?'

'Yes, he said your da's going to pay him threepence. Are you sure he's sensible enough?'

'Dad thinks so. I just came to ask you, formally, like, if you had any objections?'

'No, I'm all for our Joe earning a few honest coppers. What happened to that Vinny Brennan?'

Ben looked grim. 'He stole from us, Mrs Greenway. I'd suspected him for a while. It was just little things that kept disappearing – spoons, a vase, then a glass sugar bowl that had been Mam's favourite – but we couldn't prove it. So I watched him. He thought I'd gone out. I caught him in the act, putting a little glass salt cellar and spoon in his pocket.'

'I never trusted the Brennans meself. A shifty-looking lot, and old Ma Brennan sitting in the side passage of the Throstle's Nest morning, noon and night. Well, our Joe won't be robbing you blind, Ben, you can rest assured of that. And I'll see he doesn't go forgetting to turn up or that he doesn't burn the place down.'

'Thanks, Mrs Greenway, we're very grateful.'

'Are you going to the McGees', Ben?' Kate asked, having finally finished with the blouse to her satisfaction but holding it up for closer scrutiny.

'Yes, Dad's not, though. He gets tired so Christmas is a rest for him.'

'You don't have Christmas, do you?' Kate queried.

'No. We have Hanukkah, the festival of the lights.'

Three curious pairs of eyes were turned towards him but he suddenly felt disinclined to explain the Jewish festival to them. It would only serve to emphasise the differences in their beliefs and way of life.

'Is that what you're going to wear, Kate?' he asked.

She nodded without enthusiasm.

'Of course, anything we wear will be put in the shade by Maggie's new dress,' Evvie explained, then fell silent, intercepting a look from Peg.

Ben smiled at her. 'I always think it's not what you wear, it's the sort of person you are that matters, but you'll be the belles of the ball, both of you. Maggie can't hold a candle to you,' he said.

Evvie felt herself blushing and hoped her mam hadn't noticed.

'Oh, get off with you and your flattery,' Peg chided laughingly, but she noted the way he was smiling at Evvie. Well, that was a friendship that must definitely be nipped in the bud.

Chapter Three

Hetty McGee sat back on her heels and surveyed her handiwork with some satisfaction.

'Just a fraction more off the hem, I think.'

'Oh, Mam! I've been standing here for hours and my legs are aching,' Maggie complained, a pout on her lips and the light of mutiny in her grey eyes.

'Well, if you want to look as though you'd bought it in Blacklers, fine! I go to all the trouble to copy a Paris model gown and all you do is moan and complain! I've stood for hours in front of Cripps, memorising all the details and trimmings.'

'Sorry, Mam.' Maggie knew she really was very lucky. Mam had spent hours on this dress.

'And I should think so too,' Hetty muttered, her mouth full of pins.

The dress looked well on Maggie, she thought, but even she couldn't honestly say that Maggie was a beauty. Wearing the dress she looked quite elegant – attractive in a homely sort of way – but no amount of curling papers or tongs could induce her daughter's fine, mousy brown hair to curl, so the style Maggie had adopted was rather severe. Her eyes were definitely her best feature and if she would smile more often she would be quite passable. Frequently, though, Maggie frowned, and the lines on her forehead were already deepening.

'You know you'll have to give over frowning so much, Maggie, or you'll get wrinkles and you'll look old and sour before you're twenty-one.'

Maggie sighed deeply. She didn't want another lecture; she got enough of those at work. Mrs Sidgewick was always making snide remarks.

Three years she'd been at Sloan's in Bold Street and so far all she'd done was fetch and carry, run around the shops for trimmings, and occasionally been given some plain sewing when they were very busy. She was supposed to be watching and learning until such time as she was considered suitable to start work as a bodice hand or a sleeve hand, working towards becoming a cutter, the most prestigious occupation in the workrooms.

Her ambition didn't end there. Oh no, she had some very big ideas. Eventually she wanted her own establishment where she would do the designing and other people would do the hard work. And she really didn't want to wait for years either. She knew she was very young to have such plans but maybe that was because she was an only child and had time to daydream. But that kind of establishment cost a fortune, more than her mam and dad could earn in a lifetime, so unless she managed to find herself a husband with pots of money, there wasn't a hope in hell's chance that her dream would become a reality.

'There, that's it pinned. Now take it off while I do the hem. Won't you be the envy of the street?' Hetty smiled proudly. She wasn't blind to Maggie's faults but she indulged her because she was the only living child and very precious to both herself and Alf.

She knew nothing of Maggie's plans, but she was pleased that Maggie had chosen to follow her into dressmaking. Of course, Maggie would have the finest training and would therefore, in time, earn a good wage. She had an eye for colour and style, too. No doubt later on she would marry a good man and have children. Dressmaking was a very respectable trade and one that could be continued from her own home, should Maggie need to do so. Then she and Alf could settle back, comfortable and secure in the knowledge that they'd done their best for their only child. As she nimbly put the finishing touches to her creation Hetty was lost in her dreams for Maggie's future, a future very different from the one Maggie envisaged for herself.

In the Greenway house, Christmas Eve meant more practical matters than dress fitting. Kate decided to accompany her mother to St John's Market. She loved the market, for everyone was jovial and there was always so much light-hearted bantering and laughter between the stallholders and their customers, even more so today. Usually the Salvation Army band played carols in Church Street, too, which added to the atmosphere of excited anticipation. Evvie had been left at home experimenting with her hair and the ribbon and the wax rose she'd bought.

Peg purchased a large goose, having beaten the butcher down from five shillings to three shillings, and the hemp bag over her arm was heavy with apples, oranges, sprouts and potatoes. Kate's view was restricted by the huge armful of holly, ivy and juniper branches with which they'd decorate the house.

As they stood in Church Street waiting for the tram home, she felt exhilarated. It was a cold, crisp evening, promising a heavy frost by dawn. The sound of carols mingled with laughter and the tinkling of bells that adorned the decorated harnesses of the horses pulling the carts. From the river came the sound of an outward-bound liner's steam whistle, and she was glad that Tom was home and not having to work like a demon in that infernal stokehold. It didn't matter that she had no new dress to wear tomorrow, she thought. She felt lucky to have a happy home and a loving family.

The tram arrived and everyone surged forward.

'Yer can't gerron with all that 'olly, girl. There's no room an' you'll do someone an injury,' the conductor said, barring Kate's way.

Peg glared at him belligerently 'If you'd shift yerself, instead of standing there like a stuffed dummy in Lewis's, she could get past and put it on the parcel shelf.'

The conductor was tired and cold and looking forward to the end of his shift.

'Missus, we're full to burstin' now. They're packed in like sardines in there.' He jerked his head towards the lower deck.

'All right, we'll go up the dancers then,' Peg replied, making for the stairs to the upper deck.

'There's no room up there either, Ma. There's half the crew of the *Duchess of Richmond* up there an' they're all drunk! God knows how I'm goin' to get them off.'

The people behind were getting impatient and beginning to push forward.

'Well, they can spend Christmas in the flaming depot for all I care, I'm not getting off and neither is she. And don't call me Ma, I'm not a Mary Ellen.'

'Can I take some of the holly for you?'

Kate turned and met the dark eyes of Frank Lynch – eyes that were full of merriment. She felt her heart lurch and she blushed furiously. Oh, she felt such a fool and she certainly didn't look her best, not with her shawl pulled up over her head and her old grey flannel skirt showing beneath it

'There's still no room,' the conductor said tersely.

'You stay on, Mrs Greenway, and I'll see Kate home. If you don't mind, that is?'

Kate's heart lurched again with excited anticipation. He was actually offering to walk her home.

'I don't know about that. I don't want her walking the streets with someone I hardly know. Would you be one of the Lynches from Athol Street? Flo Lynch's lad?'

'I am.'

Peg still hesitated.

'Oh, for God's sake, missus, will yer make yer mind up? Some of us have got homes to go to!' a man shouted from the crush behind.

Before Peg could answer, Frank had helped Kate down from the platform of the tram and had relieved her of most of the greenery. The people behind Peg piled on, the conductor rang the bell with a gusto born of relief, and the tram moved off, the trolley sparking on the overhead wires.

Kate felt abashed and strangely nervous. She'd not held a conversation with him before. She glanced at him from beneath her lashes. Oh, he was so handsome. He wore his cap pushed back, revealing a shock of dark brown curly hair. His eyes were also dark and still full of amusement.

'It's a fair walk. Are you sure you don't mind?'

'No, I don't mind.'

'If you get tired, we can always get another tram, further on down Byrom Street, maybe. Would that be far enough to go?'

She wasn't quite sure if he was poking fun at her or not.

'I've often walked all the way home from town.' She drew her shawl closer to her. It was a long walk and it was bitterly cold but she didn't mind. She certainly wasn't going to pass up this opportunity. It was the first time they'd ever really been this close. It would take about half an hour to walk and surely in that time she would be able to find out if he really did like her. And what his feelings, if any, were for Josie Ryan.

'Are you getting anything special for Christmas?' he asked, after a brief silence.

Kate had been searching her mind for something to say to begin the conversation.

'No, I don't think so. What about you?'

He shrugged and grinned. 'I'm too old now for the apple, orange and new penny stuff.'

'So am I.'

'Are you going out or are you having a bit of a drink at home?'

'I'm going out, to a party in fact.'

'Anyone I know?' he asked hopefully.

He'd seen her and her twin sister many times in the past and they'd certainly grown up to warrant their nickname. He'd heard that they weren't alike in nature, though. He'd caught her looking at him with interest on the occasions when they'd been in close proximity. He'd been very flattered at first but that had changed to admiration and now he knew he wanted to hold her and kiss her and be seen with her on his arm. Her beauty and her confidence had drawn him to her.

'It's Maggie McGee's party. From down our street. Her mam is a dressmaker and her dad works for Bent's.'

'It should be a good night then, him working for the brewery and all. I don't think I know them, though. Has she got any brothers?'

'No, they died, there's only Maggie.' She knew her next remark was very bold and not quite the proper thing for a girl to do but she felt reckless. It was just the opportunity she needed. 'I can take a "guest" if I want to. Mrs McGee said so.'

'Oh, aye, and have you got someone in mind then?'

She shrugged. She was being very forward but she didn't want to appear that way. 'Not really.'

'Is this the do that Josie Ryan's going to?'

Kate looked up at him. So, he must have spoken to Josie at least. 'Has she asked you to go with her?' she said, she hoped, casually.

'No, and I don't know that I would if she'd asked, but if you were to invite me I'd come, Kate.'

They had reached the junction of Lime Street and London Road and the traffic was very congested. They stood side by side on the kerb and he suddenly caught her free hand and pulled her into the road. 'Hold tight until we get across.'

He made no attempt to release her hand once they were across the junction and she didn't pull it away as they walked along Commutation Row. She didn't notice the biting coldness of the night. She was too breathless with happiness.

'You haven't given me an answer.'

She felt herself blushing and ducked her head, the blood rushing through her veins like wine. 'Oh, all right, if you're going to be so persistent, will you come?'

He grinned down at her and, moving the greenery to his other hand, tucked her arm through his. 'That I will, Katie Greenway.'

She smiled. No one had ever called her Katie before. She hoped he would always call her Katie. It would be a special bond between them . . .

Chapter Four

At seven o'clock on Christmas night Hetty McGee looked around with satisfaction. There was nothing more she could do now, everything was ready and she'd spent a fair bit of money. She'd been saving up for six months so she didn't really mind the cost. Alf had put the big keg of beer in the scullery. The sherry and port and bottles of Yates' Australian white wine were set out on the dresser with the glasses. Not that she had enough glasses of her own – she'd scoured the street, borrowing additional suitable drinking vessels and dishes. The table was groaning with food.

She checked the table over, tweaking in several places the white sheet that served as a cloth. From Reiglers, in Doncaster Street, she'd bought small pork pies and all the cooked meats for the sandwiches. There were pigs' trotters and sheets of ribs from Sharp's on the corner of Penrhyn Street. She'd bought cakes and pies from Lunt's, things she normally would never dream of buying, but she just hadn't had time to bake for there had been two dresses for customers to finish in addition to Maggie's. Out in the yard, in a large bowl covered with a cloth, was ice cream from Fusco's. Yes, she'd certainly spent some money, but she knew it would be worth it. Not only would Maggie remember this birthday for the rest of her life, so would the neighbours.

Everything had been scrubbed and polished and her few good ornaments safely packed away. Maggie and Alf had decorated the house with holly and ivy and coloured streamers. The Christmas tree that stood in pride of place by the window in the front room was a delight to the eyes. The room had been cleared of all her sewing paraphernalia, except the machine. That had been covered with a thick chenille cloth. A piano had been borrowed from Alf's foreman. It was a bit battered and a bit tinny but no one would notice.

They'd gone to early Mass that morning and as she didn't need to buy a large goose or turkey to feed a big family, there had been no need for her to wait in line outside Skillicorn's Bakery where they let you use the ovens to cook big birds or pieces of meat early on Christmas morning.

Most people didn't eat Christmas dinner until well after three in the afternoon, for with no less than seventy pubs open along Scotland Road and its neighbouring streets, the men usually didn't get back until three. Some never made it back at all or were in such a state that eating was beyond them. She thanked God that her Alf wasn't like that. Poor Mary Ryan had a lot to put up with in that respect, she thought.

Maggie came down the stairs, holding her skirt up to avoid tripping. She felt far older than seventeen and as she'd twisted and turned before the long mirror in her bedroom, she'd gained confidence: she *did* look older. This was a copy of a dress that cost a fortune and she'd made sure everyone knew it.

'Maggie! Oh, come and see, Alf! Doesn't she look splendid?' Hetty cried.

The dress was very elegant. The high collar was edged with black braid and to it Maggie had pinned the small gold brooch, shaped as a butterfly, that Hetty had bought with the last of her savings. It had been her Christmas present. The bodice was tight and fitted, and fastened down the front with a row of shiny black buttons. The sleeves were full at the shoulder, narrowing above the elbow and tapering into a tight deep cuff, again trimmed with braid. The hemline of the skirt was festooned with three rows of braid, the top row looped in small circles. Maggie had piled her hair high on her head so the pretty jet earrings, left to her by her grandmother, were noticeable.

'How do I look, Mam?' Maggie let the skirt drop and did a slow turn.

'Like something from a fashion journal, luv!' Hetty answered, beaming with pride and satisfaction.

Alf held out his arms. 'Come here and give your old da a hug. I hardly know my girl now, she's so grown up.'

Maggie obliged and then checked her appearance again in the mirror over the fireplace. She wished Mam would let her put a touch of rouge on her cheeks and a few drops of belladonna in her eyes to make them sparkle but she'd have to resort to pinching her cheeks and biting her lips to give them more colour. She was fiddling nervously with a loose strand of hair when the first of the guests began to arrive.

* * *

Josie had called for the twins and when Kate came down to the kitchen and saw Josie's blouse her eyes lost some of their sparkle.

Peg greeted the girls. 'Now, don't you look the bee's knees, Josie! Your mam did a good job on that blouse. "Mary," I said to her, "don't go mad with the bleach bottle or you'll ruin it altogether." It's come up a treat.'

Kate felt hurt. So, *everyone* had known that Josie had a new blouse except herself. Josie hadn't mentioned it, which was unusual for she dragged her friends over to the house to see and admire every new garment. It was something they all did and now she wondered if Josie knew that Frank Lynch was going to Maggie's party.

Evvie was still fiddling with her hair. At least she had the ribbon and the rose, whereas Kate had nothing new at all.

Suddenly Kate smiled. Frank Lynch was going to the party as her guest and he'd shown by the way he'd behaved last night that she was the one he was interested in. He'd kissed her good night, just a peck on the cheek, but a kiss just the same. In fact he would be arriving any minute now.

'Evvie, leave your hair alone! You'll end up with it all falling down!' Peg admonished. Evvie had spent an hour rolling, twisting and teasing her long blonde locks around the red ribbon and placing the red rose strategically on the side of her head. She was proud of her handiwork. Evvie grinned back at her mother through the mirror.

Peg had pressed her best black dress with the bit of bcad embroidery at the neck. She'd bought it second-hand for Nelly's funeral over seventeen years ago, but as it only came out for really special occasions it still looked grand.

'Right, are we ready then?'

Kate looked impatiently at the door into the lobby. Where was he? Suddenly she had a horrible idea and her stomach felt as though it was awash with ice water. What if he didn't come? What if he stood her up? What if that kiss had meant nothing to him?

'Come on, Kate,' Tom urged. He looked very smart in a dark suit and white shirt, both of which had been purchased in New York over a period of time, although they had not been brand-new.

Kate still hung back, not knowing what to do. Fortunately her mam was giving Joe a lecture on how to behave to which everyone else added their strictures and advice. Joe was scowling, thinking he might just as well stay at home for all the fun he would have.

Peg had only just finished speaking when the sound of the door knocker echoed down the lobby.

Kate jumped nervously before going quickly to the door. Peg and Bill exchanged curious glances.

'It's not your Kieran, Josie, is it?' Peg asked. Josie's elder brother was quite taken with Evvie, she knew that, for Mary had told her as they'd walked home from church one Sunday before the holiday. He was a nice, quiet, sensible lad, Peg thought. Not a bit like his father and older brothers who managed to get paralytic every Saturday night and quite often ended up in Rose Hill Police Station, to Mary's annoyance and humiliation. No, she would raise no objections to Kieran Ryan.

As Kate entered the room followed by Frank Lynch, Peg's expression changed.

'Oh, it's you,' she said disappointedly.

'Aye, it's me, Mrs Greenway. I've come to take Kate to the party.' His gaze flitted over the room to see what effect his presence was having. He knew he looked smart for he'd encountered a few admiring glances on his way to Silvester Street. Kate and her sister looked stunning, there was no other word for it. Even little Josie Ryan looked well. He smiled to himself; he'd enjoy walking into the McGees' surrounded by such a bevy of beauties.

He addressed himself again to Peg: 'I did get her home safe and sound, didn't I, last night? It's a long walk but we didn't dawdle and we weren't too late.'

Peg ushered them all towards the door. 'Aye, I suppose you did. Well, let's get off now that everyone is here and before all the port has gone. I'm very partial to a drop of port and lemon now and then.'

As they stepped out into the street and turned to wait for Peg to close the door, Josie's face was scarlet and her lips were set in a hard, tight line. Jealousy filled her every pore. Oh, Kate was a dark horse all right. Not a word, not a single word, had she said about Frank Lynch and Kate knew she liked him. In fact she more than just liked him, she was mad about him. Hadn't she told Kate and Evvie that only the other morning? Kate had made a bit of a sharp remark at the time, but she'd not taken any notice. Oh, now she saw it all very clearly. Kate wanted him too and she'd been sly and sneaky and had somehow managed to meet him in town and they'd walked home. Kate would have had plenty of time to talk to him, to flutter her eyelashes at him and use every other means she knew to entice him, to make him forget all about little Josie Ryan. Well, this was open warfare. Kate had been one of her best friends for years and they'd shared everything, but no more. How could Kate be so nasty? If she could do something as underhanded as this, then Josie wanted nothing more to do with her.

Following the Greenways and Frank Lynch down the street Josie was consumed with anger and hurt.

Evvie dropped back to walk with her. 'I'm so sorry, Josie. It must be rotten for you.'

'Did you know, Evvie Greenway?' Josie hissed.

'I didn't know he was going to walk her home from town last night. She went out with Mam and came back with him.'

'She knew I liked him, Evvie. I told you both that I'm mad about him. She knew! She damn well knew!'

'Oh, don't let it spoil your night – or our friendship, please?'

'I'm not blaming you, Evvie, but after what she's done, she's no friend of mine now. And I'll tell you something else: I'll take him off her if I get the chance. All's fair in love and war.'

Evvie said nothing for they'd almost reached Maggie's house, but her heart was heavy.

A few yards in front of them Kate felt so happy that she could even have kissed Joe, and she never did that voluntarily. Frank walked beside her, but there was no hand holding, for Peg wouldn't allow such a liberty in public, Kate guessed, not yet anyway. Once they got inside, however, the sheer press of people and the dancing would be opportunities for greater intimacy that neither of them would pass up.

The house was already packed and the appearance of the Greenway party was greeted by cries of delight and surprise. No one would think they'd all only seen each other a few hours ago, Josie said sourly. Peg, Bill and the boys went through into the kitchen, while Evvie, Kate, Frank and Josie made for the front room. Joe disappeared to find the rest of his mates in the back yard.

Evvie caught sight of Maggie standing beside the Christmas tree.

'Maggie! Oh, Maggie! It's . . . it's absolutely gorgeous!' she cried. 'You look so grown up! You could even pass as one of those mannequins they have in the posh shops.'

'I told you it would be gorgeous, didn't I? Mam's worked her fingers to the bone over it. If I'd got it in Cripps it would have cost twelve guineas. Imagine all that money for a dress, but it *was* a Paris model gown.' Maggie smiled broadly, tossing her head to make sure everyone saw her earrings. This was praise indeed.

Josie fingered the collar of her blouse with distaste, while Evvie and Kate felt as though their clothes had come straight from Steadman's pawnshop.

Maggie's dress was more than gorgeous, Kate thought enviously.

'What about drinks?' Frank asked as Kieran Ryan joined them, accompanied by a tall, gangly lad who was very sharply dressed. 'I bet there's plenty of it with Mr McGee working for Bent's.'

'He's teetotal. Never touches a drop,' Kieran stated, thinking his own da could take a few lessons in temperance from Alf McGee.

Frank looked amazed. 'God, what a waste!'

'Can I get you a sherry, Evvie?' Kieran asked, wishing he had the easy confidence of Frank Lynch.

'That would be nice, Kieran. Who's your friend?'

Maggie had also been scrutinising the well-dressed stranger. 'You live in Hopwood Street, by the Britannia Vaults, don't you?' she questioned. 'Your Mavis works a bit further down Bold Street. I see her sometimes and we go for a cup of tea. She's younger then me, though.'

'Oh, aye. I'm David Higgins, but you can call me Davie.'

Maggie glanced at him from beneath lowered lashes and smiled. He looked very smart and he was obviously admiring her.

'Shall I get you a sherry as well?' he enquired.

'Just a very small one. I don't drink, but it's my birthday,' she said primly.

'For God's sake, we all know it's your birthday, Maggie. It's why we're all here,' Josie said tartly, glaring at Kate. It was going to be a horrible evening, she just knew it. She wished she could go home but she wouldn't give Kate the satisfaction of knowing she was upset. An opportunity might yet arise to get Frank alone.

Maggie looked hurt but Josie ignored her.

'Kate?' Frank queried.

'I'll have the same as Maggie, please.'

He nodded towards Josie. 'What will you have, Josie?'

'You'd better get her a large sherry. She needs cheering up, she's got a face like a wet week,' Maggie stated. Given who Kate had turned up with, there would be fireworks between Kate and Josie before the night was over, she was certain of it. Still, that was their affair. And it was all going very well, she thought as she danced with Davie Higgins. He'd danced with her for most of the night and had shown a decidedly marked interest. She was flattered and she liked him.

'Where do you work?' she asked.

He shrugged. 'I'm between jobs, like.'

'Like what? Have you got a job or haven't you?'

'Yes. Well, I'm starting work in Healey's Motor Car Garage after the holiday. I'll be sort of demonstrating for the customers and keeping the cars in tiptop condition. It's a great job and I won't even have to get my hands dirty.' He omitted the fact that he would spend a good deal of his time buffing and polishing.

She looked impressed. 'Can you drive one of those things?'

'Of course I can, that's why I got the job,' he lied stoutly. He'd soon learn, was what he'd told himself. It couldn't be that hard. There were even some women who could manage it. 'Of course it's only the beginning,' he hinted.

Maggie was intrigued. 'What do you mean?'

'I'm looking on it as a sort of training period, an apprenticeship, if you like. I'm going to have my own garage and my own car one of these days.'

She was sceptical. 'Oh aye, an' pigs might fly.'

'I mean it! I'll get on in life, it's just a matter of grasping the opportunities, that's all.'

She liked the way he spoke and the way he was holding her as they danced. 'Well, I'm going to have my own establishment one day, too,' she confided.

It was Davie's turn to be sceptical. 'Selling what?'

'Dresses, coats, costumes – I'll design them myself. I'm training now at Sloan's, I've been there three years. That's how I knew you were Mavis's brother.'

'And how long do you think it will take?'

Maggie shrugged. 'Oh, ages, I expect, but I've got plenty of time.'

'It's not time you need, Maggie, it's money.'

She didn't answer and he assumed that she knew where the finance was coming from. After all, she was an only child and her parents had to have a few bob to provide all this, he thought, glancing around.

As the evening went on, the more Maggie got to know him, the more she liked him. It was very unusual for any lad from this neighbourhood to have any ambitions at all. They usually took what was on offer, most following their fathers' occupations. She'd never heard anyone voice such ideas as owning a garage and a car. Well, she, too, was different. If he could sell cars, she could most certainly sell clothes she had designed and made.

She looked up at him and smiled.

'You look great when you smile, Maggie.'

She felt the blood rush to her cheeks and hoped she was blushing prettily.

'Thanks.'

'Do you believe in . . . fate?'

'Why?'

'Well, isn't it odd that Kieran asked me to come here and I . . . met you, and we both think alike. I mean about the future. I . . . I . . . I know I've only just met you but I think we were sort of made for each other.' He knew he was getting redder in the face and soon he'd probably start stammering so he plunged on. 'Do you think your mam and dad would let me take you out, Maggie? All proper and above board, like?'

She'd been hoping he'd ask and now he had he was going to do it properly. Her parents would like that.

'I'm sure they will, and I'd like to go out, Davie.'

He squeezed her hand and she smiled. She might only be seventeen but she was far more clear-sighted and determined than any of the other girls he'd taken out. And, she thought, he was right about fate, too. They were made for each other.

The party was in full swing. Everyone seemed to be having a great time, and Hetty and Alf were congratulating themselves. It had been worth all the money and fuss. Maggie was as happy as a sandboy and that friend of Kieran Ryan's seemed quite smitten with her daughter, Hetty thought. He'd been most polite and deferential when he'd been introduced and showed no signs of behaving badly, which was more than could be said for some people, the Ryans in particular . . .

Kate, too, was having a very pleasant evening. She felt as though she were floating on a cloud. She'd had two glasses of sherry and she was warm and light-headed. Frank held her very close, and he smelled of soap and brilliantine and he was so handsome and so charming. Yes, that was the word, charming. He knew exactly what to say and when to say it and she felt sure that if they'd been on their own he would have kissed her. She'd been very lucky that they'd met in town on Christmas Eve Maybe it had been fate? After all, the city had been crowded so they could easily have missed each other.

Evvie glanced at her twin, seeing the happiness in her face, observing Frank Lynch's careful attention. She herself had danced alternately with Kieran Ryan and Ben Steadman who had begun to eye each other with signs of hostility. She'd noticed that as the evening wore on, Kieran seemed to be drinking more than he usually did and that he had lost that bashful, reticent air. He was also more talkative. She inclined her head to catch his words now above the increasing volume of voices, noticing as she did so that Josie appeared to be one of the few people who weren't having any fun.

Not used to drinking anything stronger than lemonade, Josie was getting quickly and steadily drunk. She sat huddled in the corner of the front room, watching Kate and Frank Lynch dancing and getting more and more jealous and morose. Kate was sticking to him like glue. He'd not even spoken directly to Josie herself all evening. In fact, he'd not given her so much as a single glance, never mind asked her what she would like to drink. She looked up sullenly as her father weaved his way towards her.

'Here you are, girl, get that down yer! That'll put a smile on yer gob.' Matty Ryan shoved a glass into Josie's hand, but not before his wife had seen him do it.

Mary was furious. 'Give that to me. She's had enough! She doesn't need you encouraging her, Matty! A fine father you are. Can't you see the state she's in? No, you flaming well can't! How many have you had yourself? Jesus, Mary and Joseph! How I'm going to cope with the two of you I don't know. Kieran, here, lad, give me a hand to take our Josie into the yard. A bit of fresh air might do her good. Yer da can go an' jump off the landing stage for all I care.'

Reluctantly Kieran left Evvie's side and helped Mary to get Josie to her feet.

'Leave me alone, I can manage by myself!' Josie protested. She wasn't that drunk and the last thing she wanted was everyone looking at her with pity or amusement, particularly Kate. She straightened up and shook herself free of the restraining hands. 'I'll manage.'

'Look, Josie,' Kieran said quietly, 'I know how you feel. That Ben Steadman's all over Evvie. I could kill him!'

Josie ignored her brother; she didn't want his sympathy.

'Oh, please yourself!' Kieran said impatiently as Josie walked away unsteadily. He'd meant what he'd said about Ben Steadman. He had no right at all to be making passes at Evvie.

Mary made to go after her, but Kieran caught her arm. 'Let her go, Mam. She's not about to pass out. She's fed up because Frank Lynch has only got eyes for Kate.'

Mary sighed heavily and then took a swig of the sherry she'd confiscated from her daughter. 'Oh, me poor Josie, she doesn't stand a chance beside Kate.'

Kieran sullenly nodded his agreement. He had loved Evvie for months but he hadn't even asked her to walk out with him yet. He'd never managed to pluck up the courage. He'd worshipped her from afar, as his mam would say. Now Ben Steadman seemed to have captured her attention. He was only toying with her; there could never be anything between them – he was Jewish. He was just making a fool of Evvie. Oh, Kieran thought he knew very well how Josie felt. Indulging his anger, he watched Evvie talking with Ben Steadman.

Evvie could feel his hostile gaze. She liked Kieran, everyone did, but that was the extent of her feelings for him.

'Kieran Ryan is giving us looks to kill,' Ben said, reading her thoughts.

Evvie shrugged and then smiled up at him. 'I can't help that.'

'So, there's no "understanding" or anything like that between you?'

'No. Kieran's . . . he's just like our Tom.'

'I'm glad.'

She looked up at him quizzically. 'Are you really?'

'Yes, Evvie. It's strange, I've known you all my life and yet now . . . now you seem different, grown up. Special. Can you understand that?'

She felt the colour rush to her cheeks. 'I know what you mean, Ben. You've always been around – in the shop, on the street – but now all of a sudden you're more . . . interesting.'

'Only interesting, Evvie?'

She didn't know how to answer him. She was finding him *very* interesting and *very* different from all the other boys. She was also wondering why this should be so, but she felt she couldn't tell him all that. Not now. Not here.

'I've embarrassed you. I'm sorry.'

'Oh, I'm just being stupid. I'm always blushing and it makes me look such a fool!'

'No it doesn't, it makes you look even lovelier, Evvie.'

'Stop that, Ben Steadman! You'll have Mam over here wanting to know what's going on,' she laughed.

'Let's dance then, and you can say it's the heat affecting you, if she asks.'

She smiled up at him and placed her hand in his as he held her tightly around the waist and managed to find a bit of space for them. Soon they forgot all about her mam, and everyone else.

Josie found that the yard wasn't empty. Joe Greenway, Liam Hawkins and her brother Mickey were all sitting on upturned orange boxes digging spoons into a huge bowl of ice cream that Mickey swore blind Mrs McGee had given them permission to eat.

Josie didn't answer or comment. She didn't want to speak to anyone. Anger burned within her so intensely that it made her shake. How could Kate be so deliberately horrible? She knew, she bloody well knew, that *she* loved Frank. Kate was just being spiteful and nasty. She was so pretty that she could have had any of the lads in the neighbourhood with a snap of her fingers, but no, she'd wanted Frank and she'd made sure she got him. He hadn't taken his eyes off Kate all night.

She stood in a corner of the yard, her back against the wall, concealed by the shadows, and the more she thought of Kate and Frank Lynch the more ill-tempered and bitter she felt.

'Josie, are yer feeling sick?' Mickey had left the group, prompted by Joe and Liam. They wanted to know if she was going to be sick because if she was then they didn't want to be in the way.

'No, I'm not! Now leave me alone, you bloody little monster,' she yelled at him.

'I'll tell me mam you swore,' Mickey cried, before going back to the others and resuming his attack on the ice cream, half of which had already gone.

Josie stepped out of the shadows and sat on an upturned dolly tub, the cold night air stinging her cheeks, tears of self-pity and disappointment not far away . . .

'Josie? What are you doing out here on your own?'

Startled, she looked up to see Frank Lynch staring down at her.

'Oh, have you managed to tear yourself away from Kate Greenway then?' she snapped.

He looked surprised. He'd left Kate to refill their glasses and had decided it would also be a good time to visit the privy. Only the kids were in the yard, so he'd assumed.

Josie realised she was taking the wrong approach. Sugar caught more flies than vinegar did, her mam always said.

'I'm sorry. It's just too hot and noisy in there. I've a bit of a headache so I came out here for some air.'

He wasn't taken in by her lies. She was annoyed that he'd come here with Kate. He was aware that she was keen on him. She had no subtlety and on the few occasions they'd met and spoken, she hadn't hidden her interest in him. She was a mousy little thing – not bad-looking, but her prettiness dimmed beside Kate's beauty. But it wasn't in his nature to be deliberately cruel or callous; he preferred to keep everyone happy, particularly the girls.

'Can I get you anything? Shall I go and see if anyone has an aspirin?'

Josie stood up, swaying slightly. 'Oh, it's not that bad. I just needed a bit of peace and quiet.' She had him alone – the boys were out of earshot – and she was going to make the most of the opportunity. She'd never get another chance like this, not if Kate had anything to do with it. 'Do you like Kate?'

He shrugged. 'I suppose I do.'

Josie dropped her gaze. 'She tells Evvie everything, you know, and often she doesn't even have to speak. Sometimes they can read each other's minds, being twins. Isn't that creepy?'

'She tells Evvie everything?' He was startled. '*Everything?*'

'Everything,' Josie stated firmly. 'And she's as cold as ice under that sweet, soft giggly act she puts on.'

'What do you mean, Josie, "as cold as ice"?'

She felt dizzy but concentrated hard on her next words. They were so important and he *must* believe her. 'You know.' She raised her eyebrows archly. 'She gives nothing away, doesn't that one.'

Frank was bemused. He did like Josie, but Kate had captivated him and she was probably the most beautiful girl in the entire area, apart from her sister. As he'd walked Kate home last night, he'd noticed all the envious glances cast in his direction, although Kate had looked rather uncomfortable. He decided to humour Josie: she was a bit tipsy. 'And what do *you* give away, Josie?'

She threw back her head and laughed. 'Oh, that all depends on the person. If I like him the way I like you, well . . .' She laughed softly and suggestively. It was mostly the drink talking, but she didn't care.

It was enough that he was now lingering with her instead of going back to Kate, and even if he did think she would surrender herself to him, she'd cope with that situation as and when it arose.

Her ploy worked. Frank wasn't a lad who would pass up a promise of that kind. How could he when she was offering herself? he thought. He'd find a way to keep both Josie and Kate happy. It wouldn't be hard. He took her in his arms and kissed her slowly and passionately . . .

Josie's dizziness increased. She clung to him as a tide of emotion surged through her: joy, ecstasy and triumph. She'd got him! He wouldn't go back to Kate now. She clung to his lips as he pressed himself against her.

Neither of them saw Evvie standing in the open doorway. She'd come out for some air and to try to get away from the now almost open hostility between Ben and Kieran.

'You two-timing, fickle pig, Frank Lynch!' she cried.

Frank released Josie and cursed himself.

'Katie! It's not what you think! I didn't mean—' Frank started to try to talk his way out of the situation.

Evvie stepped into the yard and into the light filtering from the kitchen window.

'I'm not Kate. She's sitting in there like a wallflower, waiting for you to come back for your drink! I knew something was wrong, I just knew it.' Evvie was furious with him, remembering the rumours she'd heard about him being 'a bit of a lad with the girls' and at the same time feeling hurt for both Kate and Josie.

Josie was annoyed by both Evvie's appearance and Frank's sudden desertion. 'He's not married to your Kate, Evvie! She knew that . . . that, well, I like Frank.'

'It was a damned sight more than just "liking" him from where I was standing, Josie Ryan!'

Josie's temper flared, fuelled by drink and jealousy. Frank was hers, hadn't he just proved it? He wanted her, not Kate with her silly, simpering china doll looks. As she stared at Evvie it was as though it was Kate standing there, staring accusingly at her. 'I'll kiss who I like!' she cried, and lunged towards Evvie.

Evvie stepped back, shocked. What had got into Josie? She was usually so quiet!

Josie raised her arm and made another swipe at Evvie. 'Did you hear me, Kate? Did you? I'll kiss who I like!'

Ben Steadman had come into the yard and he looked around mystified. 'What's she doing? Are you all right, Evvie?'

'Yes, yes, I'm fine. It's Josie – she's had a bit too much to drink.'

Ben gently but firmly took Evvie's arm. 'Come inside and leave them to it. Drink affects people differently. They can totally change character.'

Josie was now crying hysterically and Frank was trying to restrain her, but she managed to break free and, rushing forward, she caught Evvie by the shoulder and began to scream abuse at her.

'Josie! Josie, stop it! It's me – Evvie. I'm not Kate! I'm not Kate!' Evvie screamed back.

'What the hell's going on?' Kieran Ryan yelled, totally misjudging the scene before him. He'd had a fair bit to drink himself and the sight of Ben Steadman's arm around Evvie and Evvie screaming at the top of her voice sent anger raging through him. 'Take your bloody hands off her!' he yelled at Ben.

'Then keep your sister under control! I'm not having her screaming abuse like that at Evvie and upsetting her. She's drunk and so are you,' Ben said quietly but firmly. 'Come on in, Evvie. They're as bad as each other.'

Kieran's fist caught the side of Ben's head and then the whole yard seemed to erupt. With a bellow of rage Ben retaliated and both Evvie and Josie began to scream, while Frank tried to intervene and pull Ben and Kieran apart. The mêlée was made worse by Joe, Mickey and Liam all prancing around and yelling, 'Fight! Fight! Fight!'

Alf McGee, Bill and Tom were first out through the door and succeeded in pulling the two combatants apart.

'All right, all right, that's enough!' Tom roared in a voice honed by the din of the stokehold.

'Evvie, get inside and tell Mary Ryan to come out here. Matty's in no state to help anyone,' Bill instructed grimly.

Tom glared at Frank. 'And you, lad, get inside too, or better still, get home! Go on, sling your hook!'

Frank made a quick exit through the yard door for Tom Greenway looked to be a bloke you ignored at your peril – the toughness of Cunard's black gangs was legendary.

'I don't know what's gone on and I don't want to know, but you'd best get back to your da, Ben, and you—' Bill turned on Kieran –

'I'd never have expected you to carry on like this. A good, quiet, steady lad I always thought you were.'

'It's the drink,' Tom stated flatly. 'Not used to it, either of them.'

Mary appeared in the doorway. 'Holy Mother of God, what's been going on?'

'Just these two having a bit too much to drink, Mary, girl,' said Bill calmly. 'Me, Alf and Tom will get Kieran home – aye, and Matty, too, if needs be, although he usually manages to stagger the last few yards. Peg will see to Josie.'

'I'll see to our Josie!' Mary said grimly. 'And by God she'll wish she'd never touched a drop by the time I get through with her!' she yelled, furious that her family had all let her down by making a spectacle of themselves in front of the entire street. 'And you, you little get! Take yourself off home before I clout you as well!' These last remarks were aimed at Mickey, who was now looking very pale and wishing he'd not eaten so much ice cream.

Bill looked at his youngest son. 'Home. Now,' was all he said, but it was enough. Joe made a speedy exit into the jigger, following in Frank Lynch's footsteps.

Bill turned to Alf. 'There's no need to ruin the party for Maggie, Alf. You get back inside and leave all this to us.'

Alf nodded thankfully. Hetty would have a blue fit if she knew there had been a fight.

'Frank Lynch, our Kate and Josie Ryan are at the bottom of this, if I'm not mistaken. Go on back in, Alf, don't spoil it for Maggie and Hetty.'

They each in turn re-entered the house, bearing their cooling anger, their shame or their bruises. Evvie rubbed her smarting shoulder, wondering what on earth she was going to say to Kate.

Chapter Five

Evvie and Peg had managed to keep the fracas from Kate by saying that Josie and the younger kids had gone home feeling ill and that someone had come for Frank Lynch. Apparently, he was needed at home urgently. Very urgently. Kate felt instinctively that something was wrong, but she didn't know what until Ben Steadman came in next day to apologise to Evvie.

'I'm sorry, Evvie, that things got out of hand.'

Evvie shot a wary glance at her mam. 'It wasn't your fault, Ben. I really did enjoy myself, despite —'

'It's Kieran Ryan who should be around here apologising,' Peg interrupted tersely, seeing that Ben had put the cat amongst the pigeons.

'What got out of hand?' Kate demanded.

'Oh, just a bit of bother at Maggie's do. Kieran was drunk and being a pain in the neck about Ben dancing with me. Then he up and belted Ben, but —'

'Kieran Ryan drunk and fighting! I don't believe it! He's so quiet!' Kate cried in utter disbelief.

'Not last night he wasn't, and neither was their Josie,' Peg stated, poking the fire in the range vigorously and wishing Ben Steadman had stayed at home, apology or no apology . . .

'What did Josie do?'

'Oh, leave it, Kate. It's all over. Let's forget it,' Evvie said wearily.

'How can I forget something I don't even know about?' Kate demanded indignantly.

'Well, you're not finding out from me,' Evvie stated firmly.

'Neither are you going round to Josie's on the bounce, milady!' stated Peg. 'There's been enough rowing and fighting to last a month of Sundays. It's over, done and dusted, and I don't want to see that Lynch lad from Athol Street around here again. Most of it was his fault and he didn't do anything to help either – just scarpered when your da and Tom went out.'

Ben looked towards Evvie again and she smiled. 'It was nice of you to come, Ben.'

'I'd better get back now.'

Much to Peg's annoyance Evvie followed him into the lobby.

'Mam, what went on?' Kate demanded. 'I know Josie was drunk and that one minute Frank Lynch was getting me a drink, the next minute he'd gone home, and now there appears to have been murder going on in the yard.'

Peg stopped picking over the carcass of the goose. She'd been putting the bits into a bowl to use in a soup.

'Josie had had too much sherry and was hanging around that lad's neck, the brazen little madam. Evvie went out and caught her and she started screaming at her. She made a swipe at Evvie, too. She thought she was you. Then Kieran belted Ben – God knows what for – and why they were all out in the yard in the first place I just don't know. Then your da and the others went to sort it out. It must have been like Muldoon's picnic out there with our Joe and those other little hooligans egging everyone on. And they'd scoffed all the ice cream between them. Hetty wasn't too pleased about that. They were all sick. Serves them right, the greedy little pigs! It must have been like a flaming three-ring circus.'

Kate shook her head, puzzled. 'Why was Josie out there in the first place?'

'Trying to get away from the sight of you and that Frank Lynch probably. This is all a storm in a teacup. I don't know, scrapping like a pair of jigger cats over a lad who's not worth the bother. Always chasing the girls, so Vi Hawkins told me. He's got a reputation for it, so it seems. You can go round and see how Josie's feeling now and make friends.'

'I'm not going over there. I'll get the height of abuse, especially if she's got a bad head. Oh, there'll be a few spectacular hangovers at number eight this morning.'

Peg wiped her hands on her apron and wagged her forefinger at Kate. 'Now look here, milady, you and Josie have been friends for years, and I don't think much of the feller that's come between you. A right fly-by-night troublemaker, and cocky with it!'

'Mam, it's not my fault if he likes me better than her and I really do like him.'

'Well, I don't! Any more than I liked that Higgins lad that Maggie seemed to think the sun shone out of or any more than I liked our Evvie making eyes at Ben Steadman. By, but she's playing with fire there. Well, Hetty said her do would be the talk of the neighbourhood and it is, but for all the wrong reasons.'

'Well, I'm not going to see Josie. How can I when Evvie caught Josie hanging around Frank's neck? I don't think the fact that she'd drunk too much was an excuse.'

It wasn't often that Kate openly refused to obey her mother but obviously Josie had been trying to take Frank away from her. She didn't care what Mam or anyone else said about Frank, she wasn't going to give him up, even if it did mean the end of her friendship with Josie.

Peg pursed her lips and frowned. She couldn't very well force Kate to go to Josie's, but it saddened her to see the end of a friendship like theirs and all over someone like Frank Lynch.

Guessing the whole sorry tale was about to be aired, Evvie had been glad to leave Kate and Mam to it. She leaned against the door jamb as Ben went down the front steps. When he reached the pavement he turned back.

'I'm really sorry, Evvie. I didn't mean to spoil your night.'

She grinned. It had been a pretty rum do one way or another, though she knew Maggie had had a nice time. Davie Higgins had asked her out, and at least Hetty and Alf approved of him.

'You didn't, Ben. I enjoyed myself, and anyway it was all Kieran's fault. I honestly don't know what's the matter with him. I'm not even walking out with him so he's got no reason at all to be jealous.'

'I didn't think you were walking out. I mean, if you and Kieran had been serious then I would never have . . . well . . .' he struggled and smiled apologetically. 'I'd best be going.'

Evvie thrust her hands into the pockets of her skirt, not really wanting him to leave yet unable to find a reason to prolong his visit.

He came back up the steps, giving in to an urge that had suddenly overtaken him.

'Evvie, would you . . . would you come out with me one night? We could go to the Rotunda, in the shilling seats, not up in the gods.'

Evvie bit her lip. She knew what Mam would say, but she did like him. He was much nicer and more considerate than the other boys, and anyway, what was so wrong in just going to the theatre once with him? 'All right, Ben, I'd like to.'

'What about Wednesday night?'

She nodded. 'I'd better meet you somewhere though. Mam . . .'

He understood. 'Outside, will that do?'

She smiled. 'Outside the Roundy at half-past seven on Wednesday.'

He smiled back, revealing strong white teeth.

'Evvie, will you shut that door? It's freezing, there's a terrible draught and the chimney's starting to smoke!' Peg yelled down the lobby.

She smiled and waved as he went down the street. Both she and Kate were going to risk their parents' wrath in the future if they persisted in seeing Ben Steadman and Frank Lynch.

She stood lost in thought. Ben was so different. He was confident in a quiet sort of way. He'd been firm and in control last night, until Kieran had lashed out, forcing Ben to act in self-defence. He hadn't been the instigator and yet he'd come to apologise. Kieran hadn't. As she closed the door, she told herself there was nothing serious in their friendship, nothing remotely serious. It *was* friendship, nothing more.

Next day, after work, when Kate and Evvie got off the tram on Scotland Road by Daly's Tobacconists, Frank was waiting for Kate. He'd only just finished work himself, she noted from his clothes. Evvie made an excuse and went into the tobacconists, which also sold sweets, so they could talk in private.

'A right flaming circus that turned out to be the other night,' Kate said irritably, remembering Peg's description of the events of Christmas night and the coolness that now existed between herself and Josie.

'Katie, I'm sorry. That's why I came to meet you, to apologise. I never meant anything like that to happen. There was so much shouting and yelling and then your da and your brother came into the yard and they seemed to think it was my fault. Your Tom looked as though he was going to brain me! I've heard all about the black gangs, so I thought I'd best leave before things got worse.'

'You could at least have had the decency to come and say good night to me.' She was trying to keep the hurt and disappointment out of her voice.

'I know. I'm sorry.'

'And is it true that Josie was all over you?'

'Katie, believe me, I didn't encourage her. I went into the yard and she was just sitting there. She said she had a headache and I asked her if I could do anything, get her an aspirin, like. Then she just threw herself at me and started kissing me. Then your Evvie came out and then . . . well, you obviously know the rest.'

Kate nodded and they walked on in silence. She hadn't spoken to Josie since the party – in fact Josie now left for work earlier and didn't walk with them. After all, Josie had been drunk; even Mam had said she was brazenly hanging around Frank's neck . . . 'Oh, I suppose I'll forgive you.'

He grinned at her, relieved. 'Would you like to go to the Rotunda with me?'

'When?'

'Oh, I thought Wednesday night?'

'Yes, I'd like that.' They'd reached the top of Westmoreland Place.

'Katie, you do like me, don't you?'

She ducked her head, feeling the blood rush to her cheeks. 'Of course I do. If I didn't I wouldn't have believed you.'

He pushed her into the doorway of the Westmoreland Arms and kissed her gently.

She felt her lips part beneath his, the world seemed to tilt and then she pulled away. 'Stop it, someone will see us and tell Mam, then I'll get the rounds of the kitchen,' she said scoldingly, but there wasn't much coldness in her voice, and her eyes were shining.

'I'll see you on Wednesday, Katie.'

'I'll meet you here. I don't think it would be wise for you to call for me, do you?'

He looked hurt. 'I thought you'd forgiven me?'

'I have, but Mam hasn't yet. Oh, she'll come round, you'll see.' She looked up at him, smiling. 'And no one calls me "Katie" except you.'

'Then let's keep it that way.'

'I'll meet you at seven.' She wanted him to hold her and kiss her again, but instead she smiled as he walked away.

'So, you've made it up then? Did he apologise?' Evvie asked, joining Kate as they walked towards Silvester Street.

'Yes. He explained, and I don't want to hear any more about it, Evvie, please.'

'I wasn't going to say a word,' Evvie said flatly, but she didn't trust Frank Lynch. She would take more convincing to believe that he had been kissing Josie against his will. 'So, when are you seeing him again?'

'Wednesday, we're going to the Rotunda.'

Evvie stopped walking. 'Oh.'

Kate turned around. 'What's the matter?'

'I'm going to the Roundy on Wednesday too, with Ben.'

It was Kate's turn now to say 'Oh'. She hesitated, then added, 'I gather you've not told Mam?'

Evvie shook her head.

'And you're not going to either, are you?'

'No.'

'Evvie, do you think you should go? I mean, I know Mam doesn't like Frank – he didn't get off to a very good start – but at least he's the same religion as me. Ben's Jewish; he's so . . . different. I mean even Protestants believe in Jesus, but Ben doesn't – and there's so many other things, too, things we don't understand or even know about, like that festival of the lights instead of Christmas.'

'I'm not going to run off and marry him, Kate! We're only having a bit of a night out.'

Kate looked doubtful. 'I won't say anything, Evvie, you know that,' she said eventually.

'Just make sure you don't, Kate, please?'

'Where are you meeting him?'

'Outside at half-past seven.'

'I said I'd meet Frank outside the Westmoreland Arms at seven.'

'At least we'll both be going out at the same time, so Mam won't suspect anything. And I think Maggie is going out with Davie Higgins. Maybe she'd call for us so's it would look better.'

'Where are they going?'

'I don't know.'

'You'd better find out. It would be a real mess if we all ended up in the Roundy. I mean, it would make a full house!'

On Wednesday Frank was waiting outside the pub and he looked crestfallen when he saw Evvie. Josie's words flashed through his mind and he wondered uneasily about the bond between the identical twins; 'creepy', as Josie had called it.

'Are you both coming?'

'No, I'm meeting someone outside the theatre. I'll walk on ahead,' Evvie said.

Frank smiled with relief. 'No need for that, Evvie. You walk with us, Katie won't mind, and I can't pass up the chance of being seen with both of you. A sort of devil between two angels, you could say,' he joked.

'Many a true word spoken in jest,' Evvie replied sharply. '*Katie* may not mind, but I do. I'll walk on. I'll see you later, Kate.'

Kate looked a little shocked as Evvie quickened her steps. Evvie didn't appear to like or trust Frank, and surprisingly it hurt. The twins' opinions seldom differed.

Evvie was flushed with exertion as she reached the round building, a famous landmark, owned by Bent's Brewery. Crowds were milling around the pavement outside, mingling with the Mary Ellens selling fruit, and buskers singing, dancing, juggling and providing a show of their own. She peered into the throng around the main entrance.

'Evvie! Here I am,' Ben called as he made his way to her side.

As she caught sight of him her blood began to race. 'Am I late? I did hurry.'

He smiled. 'No, it's only twenty past. I got here early.' All the way down Scotland Road he'd wondered whether she'd come. It was a miserable night. A fine cold drizzle made the pavements glint darkly and diffused the light of the streetlamps.

'I'm afraid our Kate and Frank Lynch are not far behind me, but we won't have to sit with them, will we?'

'Not unless he's going to pay for a private box too.'

Evvie stared up at him in disbelief. 'You're going to pay one and sixpence for a box . . . for me?'

He hadn't been intending to, but as soon as she'd mentioned Kate and Frank, he'd decided to splash out and make sure they didn't get stuck with the other two. He hadn't forgotten Frank Lynch's part in the Christmas party débâcle. 'You're worth it, Evvie.'

Evvie was mortified. 'Ben, I'm not dressed, not properly, I mean. Only toffs go in the boxes – you know, ladies in evening gowns and men in their penguin suits.'

'Only at the weekends, Evvie, and besides, you don't need an evening gown, you're beautiful. You'd look lovely in sacking.'

'Oh, Ben, stop that! I feel such a fool when people go on about me and our Kate. All that "Angels" stuff. I could murder Ma McNally who started it.'

'Well, I happen to think she was right,' he laughed.

He bought the tickets and then guided her towards the staircase, holding out his hand to assist her and she smiled shyly. He was very nice, she thought, and so considerate. He'd bought her a small box of perfumed almonds coated in sugar and she knew they cost at least sixpence. He was treating her like a queen, she thought, glancing around at the red plush upholstery, the gold-fringed drapes.

The lights dimmed, the brass rail at the edge of the dress circle gleamed, and she leaned forward, eager for the show to start. It was a strange but novel feeling, sitting up here in such style. At the party he had said she was 'special' and now she felt very special indeed.

Kate could hardly believe her eyes when she saw Ben, clutching the distinctive programmes printed especially for the private boxes, lead Evvie towards the staircase. 'He's got them a box!'

Frank peered across the crowded foyer. 'Who?'

'Ben Steadman. And he's given her a box of sweets.'

'Well, he's got the money. He owns the pawnshop, doesn't he?'

'No, it's his da's.'

'Same thing.'

'It's not.'

Frank envied Ben Steadman. It must be great to be able to afford to shower a girl with treats – it gave you prestige. And even though Kate had said Ben didn't own the shop, he was all the kith and kin old Levi had in the world, so one day the shop would be Ben's. Still, he could afford the ninepenny seats – just – and Kate had insisted on buying oranges and nuts from a Mary Ellen shouting her wares on the corner of Stanley Road.

'Frank, I don't want you spending a lot of money on me, really,' Kate said after he'd purchased the tickets.

'I would if I had it, Katie. Like Evvie you deserve the best.'

'Stop that. I know Evvie would be just as happy in cheaper seats. It's who you are with that really matters.'

He smiled down at her. 'So you won't mind just going for a twopenny sail on the ferry then, on Saturday?'

She laughed. 'No, I like the river. I like to see all the ships.' She nearly added, 'I wouldn't mind where we went, Frank, as long as I'm with you,' but she didn't feel as though she should say such a thing to him, yet.

Josie had brooded incessantly over the events of the Christmas night party. She'd felt terrible the next morning and had wished she were dead. It hadn't helped that her mam had yelled and bawled at all of them for hours on end, until her da and all the lads, including a suffering and dejected Kieran, had gone off to the Royal George for 'a hair of the dog'. She'd wished fervently that she could have gone with them.

She remembered how Frank had found her alone, she remembered him kissing her. She remembered Evvie coming out and yelling at them, but she didn't know much about what had happened after that. Her mam had enlightened her – for hours on end or so it had seemed. Now she'd heard it all so often that she ignored Mary's remarks. They altered nothing. She loved Frank Lynch and she was sure he felt the same way about her. Hadn't he kissed her eagerly and passionately and held her tightly? If he really loved Kate he would never have done those things. He would have politely told her that although he was flattered and he liked and admired her, it was Kate he loved. If Evvie hadn't come out, he'd have stayed with her for the rest of the night. Kate would have been just a passing fancy.

She'd waited at the top of Doncaster Street every night for a week after the holiday, hoping to see him. She knew he would pass there on his way home from work but she'd not seen him. So, she'd taken to hanging around Athol Street on her walk home. She'd sauntered up his street, her hopes high, ignoring the biting wind and the icy rain. But all those hopes had been dashed for she'd still not seen him. She hadn't seen Kate or Evvie either, though she was glad of this and thankful she didn't work at Silcock's. She couldn't have stuck having to work with Kate every day. She'd seen Maggie, who was so taken with Davie Higgins that she'd blossomed. This only served to remind Josie that by rights, she and Frank should now be 'walking out'.

As January progressed she made up her mind determinedly that she would just have to force the issue. She would call at his house. It was a bold, drastic step but the alternative was going into the Doncaster Arms or the White Eagle to look for him, and that didn't even bear thinking about. Besides, Mam would kill her if she found out, and find out she would.

She left it until nearly half-past six on a Saturday night. She'd spent hours getting herself ready. She'd done her hair in a new style that even her mam said suited her. She wore her new blouse and her best skirt and she'd borrowed a nice, short blue jacket from Maggie, who seemed to have enough clothes to stock a shop these days.

'It looks really nice on you, Josie. Are you going anywhere special?' Maggie had asked.

'I don't know yet. I might be, it'll be a surprise.'

'Go on, tell me,' Maggie had urged, curiosity in her eyes.

'No. I don't know . . . if —'

'You can borrow one of my hats.'

Josie was tempted. 'Really?'

'Yes. I've got a nice dark blue one that matches that jacket.'

Josie wavered.

'Go on, tell me,' Maggie pleaded. Josie had obviously fallen out in a serious way with Kate and Evvie. So now the great friendship club appeared to have broken up maybe Josie would like her to be a confidante and bosom pal.

'Only if you promise not to tell a single soul, Maggie.'

'I swear.'

'Well, I don't know where we'll be going, like, after . . . Well, I'm going to see Frank Lynch. I'm going to call at his house.'

Maggie's mouth dropped open at such forward conduct. 'No . . .'

'Oh, I'm mad about him, Maggie. He has such a way of looking at me – makes me feel special like, and I haven't seen him since your party. You understand, don't you? I mean . . . you and Davie . . .'

Maggie nodded. She was getting very fond of Davie – she saw him most evenings now. But she knew that Frank Lynch had taken Kate out on more than a dozen occasions. She was amazed that Josie didn't know – that no one had told her or she hadn't the sense enough to realise herself. It would be quite interesting to see what happened in the end, to see which one Frank Lynch would finally decide on: Josie or Kate. If she'd been a betting person she'd have put her money on Kate.

'I do know what you mean, Josie, but I think, well, I'm sure that . . . he —'

'What?' Josie demanded. She could see that Maggie was holding something back. 'Come on, Maggie, tell me!'

'I don't know if I should, Josie. I mean it might not be true.'

'Maggie, I thought you were my friend.' Maggie had never really been a close friend but Josie was determined that if Maggie knew something about Frank Lynch, she would pretend that she was a soul mate in order to find it out.

'Promise you won't get mad and yell at me?'

'I won't.'

'Well, I heard that he's still seeing Kate.'

Josie felt suddenly sick with jealousy and humiliation. While she'd been walking the streets in the cold depths of winter, he'd been out with Kate. She just hoped no one had witnessed her solitary meanderings, particularly Evvie or Kate. Evvie would be full of patronising concern, and Kate . . . well, she didn't know what Kate would do. 'Is that true, Maggie? You're not just making it up?'

'Why should I make it up? Why should I lie to a friend? Are you still going down to his house now?'

Josie was even more determined to go. 'Of course I am. I know that when he sees me and knows that I . . . I still care for him, he'll leave Kate alone. He probably thinks I've lost interest in him.'

'How can you be so certain?' Maggie was incredulous.

'I just know, that's all,' Josie snapped, but then her mood brightened. Of course, that was just it. It was so very simple. He didn't think she still cared so he'd taken Kate out on the rebound.

Now, in her borrowed finery, her heart was thudding against her ribs, her mouth felt dry and she trembled as she walked down Athol Street. She was so glad it was dark. She had to do it, she just *had* to. When she told him how much she loved him he'd give Kate up. When she told him she was prepared to show him how much she loved him, then he wouldn't give Kate another thought.

Her hand shook as she raised the door knocker, but she took a deep breath and brought it down hard. The sound seemed to thunder through the house and she stepped back a little.

The door was opened by a girl of about ten with a mass of dark curls and a red rim of jam around her mouth.

'Is your Frank in?' Josie knew her voice sounded shaky.

'What do yer want 'im for?'

She took another deep breath. 'I just want to speak to him. Will you tell him I'm here?'

The child eyed her with a mixture of curiosity and hostility. 'What's yer name then?'

'Just tell him it's Josie.'

The girl made to shut the door but Josie deftly stuck her foot in the space. She heard the child yell down the lobby to Frank and, as she waited for him to appear tiny beads of perspiration stood out on her forehead. She patted the borrowed hat to boost her confidence. She knew she looked very smart for Maggie had said so and Maggie did know about clothes.

Suddenly he was there in front of her, as handsome as ever,

his collarless shirt undone, his waistcoat open, his hair ruffled. He obviously wasn't going out. 'Josie! This is a surprise. It's nice to see you.'

'I just called to . . . to see how you are. I . . . I haven't seen you since Christmas.' She was blushing furiously, hoping he would only remember her kisses and her eager embrace and not the fracas that had followed.

'Oh, I'm great. And you, what about you?'

'Oh, I'm great, too.'

'You look very smart, Josie, very smart indeed. Who's the lucky feller?'

'Who? What?' Josie stammered.

'The lucky feller who is going to take you out tonight? You're all dressed up.'

She managed a laugh and fervently hoped it didn't sound hysterical. 'I . . . I had thought it would be . . . you, Frank.'

He came out on to the top step and pulled the door to behind him. He was standing very close to her and she started to tremble again.

She was feeling desperate. She couldn't just stand here tongue-tied, nor could she go away having said nothing about how she felt. 'You know what I said at Maggie's party out in the yard . . . before . . . before you kissed me?'

He looked bemused, thinking of how she had flung her arms around his neck. 'I remember.'

'Well, I thought we could . . . I thought you might like . . .' She couldn't go on. Waves of desire, followed by pure anguish washed over her. Why did he say nothing? Why did he just keep smiling at her in that puzzled way? Oh, he couldn't reject and humiliate her, he just couldn't!

He leaned closer and ran his finger lightly down her cheek. He wasn't seeing Kate tonight. Tom was home and it was his birthday and they were having a bit of a supper for him. He had planned to go down to the pub later, but now it looked as though something better was in the offing. No lad could pass up what Josie was offering, or at least what he deduced she was implying. He would never have dreamed that she was so forward, so bold. She'd always seemed timid, a bit shy. But that was before the party; she'd certainly not been shy then. She might need a little persuasion when the actual time came, but it obviously hadn't been just the drink talking as he'd first supposed. She must mean it if she was prepared to come knocking on his door.

'Will you come back in about an hour, Josie? Mam and Da go down to the Trinity on Saturday nights so we'll be alone then.'

'What about her – your sister?'

'Oh, don't worry about our Dotty. She goes over the road to Nelly Roach's to sleep on Saturday nights. She doesn't like being on her own in the house. We'll have the place to ourselves, Josie, just you and me. Together.' He bent down and brushed her lips with his own.

She was elated. She slipped her arms around his neck as pure joy surged through her. Oh, she'd been right to come. She *had* done the right thing. She knew she was being terribly forward, brazen even, but he didn't seem to mind.

'I like a girl who knows what she wants, Josie, and isn't afraid to say so.'

She knew she was crazy, that what she was doing was sheer madness. When she'd set out she'd had no intention of actually going through with what she'd hinted at. She'd only intended to interest him. She knew she shouldn't even be thinking about giving herself to him. He was virtually a stranger. It was wrong, terribly wrong, and a heinous sin, too. And would he still want to see her afterwards?

But her heart was thumping and she felt as though she were in the grip of a strange fever. He *wasn't* a stranger at all. He was the boy she loved. She was sure he would still love her. She'd belong to him then; he wouldn't go running back to Kate, not after what they were going to share. No, he would really be hers then. He would love her always.

As she drew away and smiled, she was so sure of herself. 'I'll see you in an hour, Frank.'

When she was halfway down the road she saw Agnes Hawkins, Vi's daughter, coming towards her.

'Don't you look great, Josie! Have you come into some money then?' she asked, taking in Josie's smart clothes and broad smile.

'Something much better than that, Agnes.'

Agnes's dark eyes searched Josie's face for some clue. 'What can be better than that, for God's sake?'

'Well, if you love someone, like, but you're not sure of him and then you find out that he . . . he *does* love you . . .' Josie shrugged.

Agnes raised her eyes skywards, 'You're easily pleased, Josie Ryan. Well, good luck, I hope it keeps fine for you – both.' But the cynical note in Agnes's voice was lost on Josie, who seemed in a world of her own.

'Oh, it *will*. I *know* it will. We really love each other.'

It couldn't really be wrong to love someone, Josie told herself. It couldn't really be so wrong to give yourself to that person. Only the Church and people like her mam and da would think it terrible, and what did they know about love? Priests didn't get married and her mam and da spent nearly the whole time yelling at each other. A warmth seemed to spread through her, followed by such relief and tranquillity. No, they could never understand true love, not in a hundred years. Frank would go on loving her and she would let him make love to her until . . . well, until they got married. That was the logical conclusion, wasn't it?

She walked through the cold dark streets, lost in a world of dreams. Dreams where she walked down the aisle of St Anthony's dressed in a long white dress and a floating veil, where Frank stood waiting for her, smiling, his eyes filled with love and admiration . . .

Chapter Six

There had only been one more visit to the theatre, for Evvie had decided it was much too close to home. After that last visit Ben had taken her hand as they walked home and she knew that she couldn't fool herself any longer that she thought of him as just a friend. If they were seen together there would be a terrible argument at home.

'Do you want to go on seeing me, Evvie?' he'd asked.

Slowly she nodded. 'Yes. What about you?'

'I feel the same way and I don't care what people think.'

'Oh, Ben, you're older than me. There's only you. You've no sisters or brothers – all this family thing and setting an example. It's different for me.'

'I know, Evvie. Things *are* different for me and yet in some ways it's harder. Dad relies on me and he's not getting any younger. There's no one to share things with and I know he wants me to take over the shop but I've other plans.'

'So, what will we do?'

'We'll have to go to places where no one will recognise us. Will you mind that, Evvie?'

'No, I won't mind, just as long as I'm with you. That's all that matters.'

'I feel the same way, Evvie. I just want to hold you and kiss you, but it shouldn't have to be like this.'

As he looked down into her eyes that were filled with love, he silently cursed fate for the accident of birth that had made their lives so different.

Evvie reached up and stroked his cheek. 'It shouldn't be, but it *is*, Ben.'

He caught her hand and kissed it, and knew that for the rest of his life he would love her and no one else.

They'd ridden the tram out to Aintree, taken the overhead railway and then the electric railway to Crosby, even gone as far as Southport. They'd walked, hand in hand, in the winter darkness along the shore at New Brighton.

Ben hated these clandestine meetings; the furtive fearful glances at strangers; the sound of a voice that made you nervous. They huddled together for warmth as well as intimacy for they were often cold. He wanted to take her to places of interest where they could enjoy themselves, where they would be warm and relaxed, not shivering and on edge. But as Evvie so often reminded him, she was in a very different position to himself. He was nearly twenty-one – a man who didn't depend on being kept by a family. In fact, he was gradually assuming an increasing responsibility for the business and he spent more and more time in the shop. Despite the need for secrecy they managed to meet regularly, usually on Mondays and Wednesdays, but never for very long as Evvie had to be in for nine thirty on working days.

'I could stay out longer at the weekend,' she said wistfully as they sat on a large boulder on the edge of the sand at Seaforth. There was no wind, the sky was bright with hundreds of stars and a crescent-shaped moon was reflected in the calm, dark waters of the Mersey. Across the river the lights on the promenade at New Brighton and the illuminated tower and ballroom twinkled invitingly. The crenellated outline of the old fort was visible and the bright beam of the lighthouse stabbed the darkness.

Ben drew her closer to him. 'Everyone is out on Saturday night and Sunday too. Wherever we went we'd be falling over people we know, on the tram or the train or the ferry.'

'Couldn't we see each other on Friday nights?' she pleaded.

He shook his head. 'No, it's the Sabbath, Evvie, and while I'm not as Orthodox as Dad, it would hurt him terribly if I were to go out.'

'I thought Saturday was your Sabbath.'

'It starts at sunset on Friday.'

'We've never spoken about religion, Ben,' she mused.

'We try hard enough not to, Evvie.'

'I know, and maybe that's wrong. Tell me about your Sabbath.'

He sighed. 'Only if you tell me about your Mass.'

She nodded and leaned her head against his shoulder.

'At sunset on Fridays, which can be as late as ten o'clock in summer, we light the candles. We say the Berachah – a prayer – over the candles, over the bread, which must be broken with fingers, not a knife, and the red wine.'

'After that is it wrong to do any work?'

'Yes. No cooking, no cleaning. There can be no music or dancing until the Sabbath ends, at sunset on Saturday.'

'So that's why our Joe goes to help?' Her brow was furrowed with puzzlement. 'But you work, and your dad used to on Saturdays.'

He smiled down at her, gently tracing the line of her cheek with his index finger. 'We have to live, Evvie. We have to earn a living to survive in a goy world. A Christian world.'

'Do you never go to the synagogue?'

'I go sometimes. For Rosh Hashanah, the New Year. I go at Kol Nidre, which is the eve of the day of Yom Kippur, the Day of Atonement.'

'What do you do when you go to the synagogue?'

'We pray, and the Rabbi reads the portion of the Torah, the sacred scrolls, that is allotted to that day or time. I used to go regularly when Mam was alive and I could always feel her watching me from the balcony to see that I behaved myself.' His voice was filled with both amusement and sadness.

'Why didn't she sit with you?'

'Because all the women and girls must sit separately from the men and boys, usually in a balcony. It's traditional. But at Mechitzah – a wedding – all the men sit on the bridegroom's side and the women on the bride's side.'

There seemed to be a lot of things with strange names but then in her church everything was said in Latin, a lot of which she didn't understand.

'But you don't believe in Jesus Christ?'

'We don't believe he was the Messiah, but he may well have been a Rabbi – a priest.'

Evvie tried to digest this for it was at odds with everything she'd been brought up to believe. She was beginning to realise just how different their faiths and upbringings were.

'Now it's your turn, Evvie.'

Evvie marshalled her thoughts. Being brought up in that part of Liverpool, Ben had seen Catholicism practised daily and already understood so much, but still, it wasn't easy to explain. There were so many complicated things like Confession, Purgatory, Limbo, Indulgences, and if she tried to explain them all they'd be here all night. 'We have bread and wine too. The bread is like a wafer. After the Priest has blessed them we believe they *are* the body and blood of Christ. At Communion we eat the bread. Well, not chew it or anything, just sort of let it . . . melt.'

Ben was finding it difficult to understand these alien practices. 'Believing it's Christ's body?'

'Yes.' She was trying to find the right words from the scriptures. 'Jesus said, at the Last Supper "Take this and eat, for this is my body." We make our First Communion when we're seven.'

'Is that why I see so many children all dressed up in white frocks and with veils and posies?'

'Yes, and we have processions on saints' days and in May, for Our Lady. Jesus's mother,' she added in case he was confused.

'The lady in the blue cloak on your mantel?'

She nodded. 'It's not really her, it's just a statue – to remind us. We don't pray to a lump of plaster, that would be like —'

'False Gods and graven images? Like in the Commandments?'

'Do you have Commandments?'

'Evvie, don't you remember that God gave them to Moses?'

She sighed deeply. 'Oh, Ben, it's all so confusing. So different and yet in some ways . . . alike.'

'I know. It's as though your faith took a different turning – sort of branched off from mine, like the Protestant beliefs branched off from the Catholic ones.' He'd been very interested in history at school and remembered what he'd learned of Henry the Eighth and the split from Rome. He eased his cramped limbs. 'I know there's lots more to your faith as well as mine, but maybe now we'll at least understand a bit more about each other?'

She gave him her hand and he helped her to her feet. They were both cold and stiff. 'But not enough, Ben.' She was now even more aware how big the gap between them was. That 'branching off', as he'd called it, had been one thousand nine hundred and thirteen years ago and that was a long, long time.

For Maggie and Davie there were no such difficulties. The more they saw of each other the more they realised they were soul mates. Maggie was ambitious, devious and could be ruthless. Davie was also ambitious, quite smart, very mindful of making the most of every opportunity that came along, although unlike Maggie he tended to daydream.

He was genuinely fond of Maggie. Oh, she wasn't a beauty by any stretch of the imagination, but she dressed well, she was neat and clean, and anyway beauty was only skin deep. Maggie's character and personality interested him more. She would go far, if given the chance, and he would be right beside her – a successful man.

Both Hetty and Alf approved of him and trusted him, and he and Maggie were allowed to sit in the 'Fitting Room' alone for an hour each night, providing Hetty didn't have a customer to attend to.

'Do they ask what we do?' Davie enquired as they sat toasting their toes by the fire and listening to the wind howling outside.

'Not really. Mam asks what we talk about.'

'What do you tell her?'

'Oh, I say we talk about people we know, about work, what's on at the Hippodrome. Things like that.' She patted his arm that was around her shoulder.

'Not our . . . plans?'

Maggie turned and looked at him squarely. He'd never said anything like this before. 'Our plans? Yours? Mine? Or both together?'

'Both together.' He felt a bit embarrassed.

'Do we have a "together"?' she asked coyly, hoping he meant it.

He was silent for a moment. He didn't want to rush things. 'I think . . . I hope we have. We want the same things, don't we?'

'I know that I want my own business.'

'So do I. And I'm very fond of you, Maggie.' He cleared his throat and swallowed hard. His mouth had gone dry. 'You're great, you really are. I don't know another girl like you. Oh, Kate and Evvie are raving beauties but they haven't got your brains or determination.'

She wasn't upset by his remarks. Kate and Evvie were exceptional. No girl in the neighbourhood could be compared to them. 'What about Josie Ryan?'

He shrugged. 'She's all right but she's very plain, you know.'

'Mousy? She could be so smart if she really tried. Anyway, she's got eyes for no one except Frank Lynch. She's a fool, a complete fool.'

'I wouldn't go as far as that, Maggie. Why do you think that?'

'You mean you don't know, Davie?'

He was mystified. 'Know what?'

'She goes round to Frank Lynch's house every week, when his mam and dad are out.'

'I thought he was Kate's feller.'

'He is. That's why I think Josie is so thick! She either doesn't know or won't face it.'

'What does she do when she goes there?'

Maggie raised her eyebrows. 'Oh, use your imagination, Davie!'

'You don't mean . . . ? Does she . . . ?'

'I don't know for certain but, well, draw your own conclusions. I mean, why else would he keep on seeing her when he's supposed to be mad about Kate? At least that's according to Kate and Evvie. Why does he never take Josie anywhere? We don't stay in all the time and neither does Kate.'

Davie digested this, thinking Maggie had a point and wasn't Frank Lynch the lucky one, squiring Kate around and then getting a bit of pleasure every week from Josie Ryan.

'Evvie goes out a couple of times a week but I don't know who with. They don't tell me things like that. They never have done.' Maggie looked pensive. 'It's strange, you'd think the fellers would be queuing up to take Evvie out. Kieran's mad about her but she won't entertain him.'

'Talking of going out, where shall we go on Saturday?'

'Nowhere too expensive. I thought you said you'd decided to start saving hard.'

'I have but you deserve a treat, Maggie. I wish I had lots of money, then I could really spoil you.'

She kissed him on the cheek and squeezed his hand. 'That's a lovely thing to say.'

'I mean it, and one day I *will* spoil you.'

'I believe you.'

'We'll be a great couple. We'll show them all around here.'

'Will we really be a "couple"?' she asked.

'You bet your life we will. A pair of toffs we'll be, Maggie, up there with the best of them and far away from Silvester Street.'

Chapter Seven

Josie stared miserably out of the bedroom window. A pair of starlings squawked vociferously as they attempted to build a nest in the broken guttering on Peg Greenway's house opposite. The sight of them only served to deepen her depression. They were building a home, of sorts, and they were building it together. Then they would rear the baby starlings and it was the way nature intended things to be done. In fact it was just the opposite to the way she had behaved, for as the wild gusts of the cold March wind shook the window pane she knew what the madness that possessed her had led to. She knew with an awful certainty that she was pregnant.

For three whole glorious months she'd lived in a dream world that had contained no other people or important decisions except those that surrounded herself and Frank. He loved her, of that there was no doubt. He hadn't spoken the actual words but she *knew*, just as she'd known after she'd shown Frank her love for him that Kate Greenway hadn't stood a chance. Josie and Frank didn't go out much, it was true. In fact if she were brutally honest they had never gone *out*. It was because money was tight, he'd told her. He turned up his keep to his mam, as everyone did, and what was left over didn't go far. There were things to buy, things he needed, and she didn't press him. Secretly she thought he was saving up, and hoped it was for an engagement ring.

At first she had been irritated and disappointed that they were really only alone together on a Saturday night when he was supposed to be out with his friends, and then she had to wait until his mam and da had gone out and young Dotty had gone over to her friend's house. Nor did she stay very long. She was always home by nine o'clock in case Flo and Bert came back early, or Dotty fell out with Nelly and came home, or his married sister, Lizzie, decided to drop in. He'd reasoned that if anyone came back and found them there would be hell to pay. She had to agree with him for she certainly wasn't going to risk losing him for the sake of an hour or two.

She turned away from the window and sat down on one of the beds she shared with her sisters. She felt physically sick – even more so than usual. She would have to tell Frank and it couldn't wait until Saturday. He'd stand by her though; he loved her. She comforted herself with that thought and felt a bit better. Why on earth was she worrying and getting herself into a state? He loved her and he'd take charge of things. They would have got married eventually, it was just a matter of doing it sooner than later. She'd go now and get it over with.

It was dark by the time she reached Athol Street and some of her optimistic cheerfulness had deserted her as she knocked on the door.

Dotty opened it and glared at her.

'Can I see your Frank, please?'

'What for? He's havin' his tea, we all are.'

'Tell him it's Josie and it's very important.'

'I know who yer are.' The child went back down the lobby and a few seconds later Frank appeared, a crust of bread soaked in gravy in his hand.

'Josie!' He was annoyed and glanced around furtively. What the hell was she playing at, coming to the door now when everyone was in? His mam knew he was walking out with Kate and she approved. She had been asking lately when he was going to bring Kate home for tea and he'd begun to realise that soon he'd have to end his fling with Josie. It hadn't bothered him greatly; he was beginning to tire of her. When he'd thought about Josie, he realised that what he felt for her was pity and contempt, not love or even affection.

Josie was too upset to notice his annoyance.

'I'm sorry, Frank, I had to come. I couldn't wait until Saturday. I've got to talk to you.'

Frank finished the bread and stepped out, pulling the door to behind him, already trying to think of an explanation to give his mam.

'We . . . we've got to get married!' She hadn't intended to blurt it out like that but she couldn't help herself.

'Married! What's up? Have you been drinking, Josie?' He was suspicious, remembering the way she'd behaved on Christmas night. God, he hoped she wasn't going to start yelling and screeching, behaviour bound to make his mam and da come to see what was going on. Maybe he should have taken her out once or twice, just to keep her content.

'Frank! I don't drink. I've not touched a drop since Maggie's party.' She was becoming desperate. 'I'm . . . I'm having a . . . a baby. We've *got* to get married.'

He just stared at her in shocked silence. It was a joke. A bad joke. A baby! Married! Married – to Josie Ryan! It couldn't be true. He'd taken care. She was lying. She was lying to trap him into marriage. Well, it was a trap he wasn't going to fall into.

'Frank, it won't be so bad. We love each other. I suppose we'd have got married eventually. Things will turn out fine, you'll see. Oh, people will talk, but let them, we won't care! We'll be so happy! We *will*!' She was gabbling and she knew it, but why didn't he speak? Why was he looking at her like that? Why didn't he take her in his arms? 'Frank, for God's sake, say something!' she choked.

Her torrent of words had battered against his ears although the only word he seemed to hear clearly and understand fully was 'married'. Oh no, he wasn't going to marry Josie, he was going to marry Kate. It was Kate he loved, not Josie. Surely Josie realised that? You didn't marry girls like Josie, you had a bit of fun with them, that's all. How was he to know she was even telling the truth? Many a good bloke had been trapped like that. How did he know it was his baby? He didn't ask her what she did the other six nights of the week and if she'd given herself so easily and so often to him, why not to others as well?

'I . . . I can't . . . I won't marry you, Josie.'

She swayed and clutched at the doorframe for support. 'Frank, you . . . you've got to!' She could barely get the words out.

'No! How do I know you *are* pregnant? How do I know it's even mine?' he hissed, glancing over his shoulder.

She couldn't speak, she was so shocked. He might as well have struck her across the face.

'We had our bit of pleasure, Josie. Don't look so bloody shocked. You were more than willing. You chased me, but it's over. It's Kate I'm going to marry, not you. I'm sorry, I never meant to upset you. I thought you understood.'

'Understood what?' she croaked.

'That you don't marry girls who . . . who let lads sleep with them before there's a ring on their finger. No one wants second-hand goods. No one wants a girl someone else has had.' He hadn't wanted to be cruel, nor have had to spell it out for her, but he'd thought she'd known the score. 'I'm not going to marry you, Josie. Go home. I'll have to go in now.' He went back inside and shut the door.

She stared at the closed door, shaking her head in disbelief. Finally she managed to turn away and walk up the street. Her head was throbbing, her legs felt like lumps of lead and she was shaking. She stopped on the corner, rigid with fear and desperation, her cheeks burning with shame, her spirit writhing under his cruel, humiliating words. She'd have to tell her mam and da now and she knew what their reaction would be.

'Oh God, what am I going to do?' she whispered hoarsely.

She walked on, head down, tears blinding her until she collided with someone.

'For God's sake, what's the matter with you, Josie?'

Agnes Hawkins pulled the folds of her shawl closer to her as she peered intently at Josie.

Josie could only shake her head.

'Has your feller dumped you?' Agnes asked bluntly. She'd not really had a conversation with Josie since that night in January. Nor did she know just who it was that Josie had been courting. Agnes never really took much notice of what most of the girls in the street did. She had her own set of friends.

Josie managed to nod.

'Don't upset yourself like this, Josie, luv. Mam always says fellers are like trams. There'll be another one along soon. Anyway, none of them are worth getting into such a state about. Do you want me to walk you home?' she added more kindly.

Josie found her voice. 'No! No . . . thanks, Agnes. I'll . . . I'll be all right.' The last thing she wanted was Agnes taking her home and going on about 'them' not being worth it. But she'd have to talk to someone soon. Maybe . . . maybe if she went to one of her friends and begged them to help her . . . Someone else's calm view would enable her to think clearly about her future. But who? Not Evvie, for she would tell Kate. Kate who Frank loved and said he was going to marry. It would have to be Maggie. Oh, she knew she'd never really thought of Maggie as a close friend, but surely Maggie wouldn't desert her? She drew her shawl tightly around her and trudged slowly back to Silvester Street.

'Oh my God! Josie, you fool! You bloody little fool!' Maggie cried when Josie had finished telling her of her plight. Her words had been jumbled and frequently choked off by sobs. At least Maggie's reaction wasn't harsh or accusing, the words spoken in a shocked but pitying tone.

'Are you sure you haven't made a mistake, Josie?'

'There's no mistake. Oh please, Maggie, help me. There must be a way out.'

Maggie felt cold at Josie's desperate words. She must be telling the truth.

'I love him, Maggie. Oh, how could he say such terrible things to me?'

Although shocked, Maggie, as usual, calmly debated the problem.

'I didn't even know you were still seeing him. I thought it was all over – not that there was much to start with. Oh, Josie, didn't you know that he's been walking out with Kate for ages?'

Josie's face drained of what little colour remained. 'He can't have been! He said he was going to marry her but I . . . I thought . . . I didn't know. I thought I was his girl!'

Maggie put her arm around her. 'Oh, Josie, you trusting little fool. He's been using you. I thought you would have known that he was courting Kate. He takes her out at least twice a week and meets her from work most nights.'

Josie felt nausea rising and a bitter taste came into her mouth. So, that's why he had no money to take her out. When he'd said he needed things he'd meant things for Kate. That's why she had had to sneak around to Athol Street on a Saturday night, like a thief in the darkness; why she'd only ever been able to stay an hour or two. Not because his parents might come back, but so he could take Kate out after she, Josie, had gone home. The sobs rose and caught in her throat and she shook like an aspen in the wind.

Maggie tried to ignore Josie's sobbing and to remember the gossip there had been in the workroom only a couple of weeks before. Gossip that had shocked everyone.

'There might be a way out, Josie,' she said tentatively.

Josie raised her head and gripped Maggie's arm tightly, the wild, desperate look in her eyes fading a little.

'What way? For God's sake tell me, Maggie.'

Maggie was having a battle with her conscience but Josie looked so awful and her plight was really terrifying. It was the very worst thing that could happen to an unmarried girl.

'I work with someone – someone much older than us – who knows a woman who . . . helps . . . girls like you. She charges, though.'

Josie's eyes widened but in their depths there was a faint glimmer of hope. 'You mean . . . get . . . get rid of —'

Maggie nodded. It was wrong. It was a terrible sin they were both contemplating committing, but what else could she do? Poor Josie, it really must have been awful for her – and to have *him* turn her away and shut the door in her face. She just wished she had Frank Lynch alone for even two minutes. She'd murder him. Well, he could just cough up the money. There was no way Josie could find the five or six guineas, and if he refused then she would warn him she was going to tell everyone in Silvester Street about him. He could find the money from somewhere. It was only right that he paid for his pleasure.

'How much will it . . . cost? I . . . I've not got much money, Maggie.'

'I don't know exactly but I'll find out. Do you really want this, Josie?'

'Oh, please. It . . . it would solve everything. No one would ever know except you, me and . . . him.' Her bottom lip trembled and she tried not to think of Frank Lynch and the way he'd treated her.

'Don't you worry about the money. *He* can bloody well cough up. It's the least he can do.' There was a harsh note in Maggie's voice that Josie drew comfort from. Oh, Maggie wouldn't stand for being fobbed off or yelled at. She was so glad now she'd come to Maggie.

'When will you know?'

'I'll ask tomorrow and then we'll sort things out, but for God's sake, Josie, don't mention me at all. It's bad enough me telling you. I'd be killed if Mam found out. In fact we'd both be killed and I mean that!' She had never been more serious in her life.

As she rose to leave, Josie was unsteady on her feet, so great was the tide of anguish that engulfed her. How could he do such a thing? How could he hurt her like this? No matter what he said he knew she loved him and she'd believed he loved her. But he'd never said those words that meant so much. Instead he'd all but called her a whore, a girl who would let any man have her. A girl who had no shame or self-respect.

Next day in their lunch break Maggie discreetly asked Vera Hepworth, who had been the instigator of the gossip in the first place, for the name and address of the woman.

'I'd never have thought you'd need something like this, Maggie,' the older woman had hissed.

Maggie had glared at her. 'I don't. I'm not that much of a fool! It's for a friend.'

'Well, swear to me that you won't tell anyone except this friend.'

'I *swear* I won't. Will that do?'

A name and address was scribbled down with a stub of a pencil on a bit of scrap paper that had been retrieved from the gutter.

That evening Maggie went over to see Josie as soon as she'd had her tea.

Josie took her upstairs to the room she shared with her sisters.

'Can you remember this, Josie, because you can't write it down. Someone is bound to see it and start asking you questions.'

Josie nodded. 'Oh, Maggie, it's something I'll never forget.'

'Right. It's Mrs Gibbons, number six Primrose Court. Primrose! A fine name to call a filthy, falling down, overcrowded court.'

Josie nodded, concentrating only on the woman's name and the number of the house.

'She charges five guineas, Josie, and you have to give it to her before . . . well before —'

'Maggie, I . . . I haven't got money like that!' Josie was stricken.

'Of course you haven't. Neither have I. But *he* has, or he can borrow it.'

Josie sat on the edge of the bed, her eyes filling up with tears. 'Maggie, I . . . I can't face going to ask him . . .'

Maggie sighed. She'd expected this. 'I'll go. And I'll make damned sure he has the money by tomorrow night. The sooner it's all over the better, so I was told.'

'Oh, Maggie, you're so good to me. I couldn't have had a better friend. Will you come back and tell me what —'

'What he's got to say? Of course I will. I'll have to go now before everyone starts asking questions. You'd better pull yourself together and go downstairs or your mam will get curious.'

Josie shook her head. She felt so much better now. She'd just have to push all thoughts of her condition to the back of her mind in case her face gave her away and Mam started asking awkward questions.

Maggie's mouth was set in a grim line as she knocked hard on the Lynches' front door, wondering just who would open it. She'd already sorted out various excuses for wanting to see Frank should it not be he. She was leaving nothing to chance in this matter. Fortunately it was Frank.

'Stuffing your face, I see, while poor Josie can't even face a mouthful of food.'

Frank went cold. God, she'd told Maggie McGee. Who else had she told?

'I won't keep you long. Josie needs five guineas and she needs it as soon as possible. Tomorrow night. Don't you start and tell me you can't afford it, Frank Lynch. You know what it's for: to let you off the bloody hook. So you can just find it by this time tomorrow.'

'How . . . how do I know she'll get it? How do I know she even needs it?' The words were out and looking at Maggie's face he wished he'd never spoken.

'You loud-mouthed, lying, cheating sod, Frank Lynch! You carry on saying things like that and I'll tell Kate all about you. In fact I think she should know what's going on.'

Frank was horrified. 'No! No, for God's sake don't tell Kate. I love Kate. I really do, Maggie!'

She just glared back, her lip curling with contempt. 'You're a poor excuse for a feller, Frank Lynch. Both Josie and Kate deserve better. God knows what either of them sees in you. I wouldn't trust you as far as I could throw you, let alone rely on you if I was in a tight corner. You'd just whine and moan and try to wriggle out of it. Just get the money.'

She turned away abruptly and left him standing on the doorstep. She meant what she'd said. Josie and Kate *did* deserve better. How could either of her friends 'love' someone like him? Josie was a fool, but Kate wasn't. Oh, 'Love is blind' must be a true saying. All Frank Lynch had in his favour was that he was handsome and had a way about him that seemed to charm some girls. But she wasn't taken in by him.

Frank stood and watched her go, his mouth suddenly dry. She was a hard little madam. She'd obviously talked Josie into getting rid of . . . it. For that he was thankful, but where the hell was he going to get five bloody guineas by tomorrow night? There was no one he could borrow it from, except his mam. He knew she had a few bob saved up for dire emergencies. This was certainly an emergency, but he couldn't approach her. No, he'd have to go to old Mr Steadman, who now and then lent money if he thought he'd get it back without too much trouble. The other moneylenders he knew charged you a terrible rate of interest. In fact it often took years to pay back and if you couldn't pay then they had people who would half kill you for the price of a few pints of ale. At least Mr Steadman wasn't like that. He'd have to go now, tonight, to avoid anyone seeing him tomorrow in the daylight. He didn't stop to tell his mam who had been at the door or why he was going out, he just grabbed his jacket and cap from the hallstand and closed the front door quietly behind him.

Arriving at the pawnbroker's, he waited until the old man had served the only customer in the shop, thankful that Ben wasn't around.

'Now, Frank, how can I help you?'

Frank looked down at his cap that he'd twisted in his hands.

'I . . . I've come to see if you could see your way clear to, er, lending me some money, Mr Steadman.'

Levi studied him. Frank wasn't the usual sort who came to borrow money. 'How much do you want and how will I know you will pay me back?'

'I . . . I . . . need five guineas, now. It's . . . it's terribly important. And I swear I'll pay you back, down to the last farthing. If I don't you can . . . you can go and ask Mam for it and, believe me, she . . . she'll kill me.'

'That's a lot of money, Frank. It must be important.' Levi thought he had guessed the reason why the lad needed it and he didn't approve at all. Life was sacred. All life. It said in the Bible: 'Thou shalt not kill.'

'It's very important, Mr Steadman.' Frank looked the little pawnbroker directly in the eye and saw there suspicion, distaste and sadness. 'I . . . I . . . wouldn't ask but . . . but . . . it's the only way. The only way to help . . . everyone, you've got to believe me.'

Levi spoke slowly. 'And will you tell your priest of this loan and why you need it?'

Frank nodded. The silence of both parties in the confessional was sacred and no priest would ever reveal such a confidence.

'And you will make reparation, should you need to?' You couldn't live nearly all your life in a Catholic community without knowing something of the religion.

Again Frank nodded.

'Then I will lend to you five guineas and you will pay me back at the rate of two shillings a week, plus another six shillings interest. I charge less than the others because I don't feel it is an honest way to earn a living. The others only care about money and they are often violent and wicked men. I care about people. I know what it is like to be poor and afraid.'

Frank was so relieved that he reached out, took the old man's hand and shook it. 'Thank you, Mr Steadman. Thanks. Oh, thanks! I'll not be late with my weekly payments, I swear.' He meant it. The loan would pay for a fresh start and no one would be any the wiser. Relief washed over him as the pawnbroker went into the back room.

He was startled when it was Ben who came back with the money.

Ben held out the coins. 'Here. Dad's had a bit of a turn. I wish he wouldn't lend money, it always upsets him.'

He had been worried when his father had come in, gone to the small brassbound casket and taken out the money. The old man looked tired and careworn and had just handed his son the five guineas without a word, before he'd sat down in the easy chair. Now Ben's face betrayed his distaste. He didn't like Frank Lynch, remembering him from Maggie's party.

Frank ignored Ben's words, took the money, nodded and left. He hadn't liked the look Ben Steadman had given him.

Frank was hovering in the lobby next evening, ready for Maggie's visit. Last night he'd told his mam a pack of lies when she'd asked him where he'd been.

He opened the door before Maggie had time to give more than one knock.

'Here, take it and for God's sake go.'

'Not a single word about Josie? How she's feeling, what she's thinking? Oh, get back to your tea, you're pathetic. Well, by this time tomorrow you'll be off the hook. I just hope you've borrowed it from one of those sharks who'll break your legs and arms if you don't pay up,' Maggie snapped at him before taking the coins and putting them in her pocket.

'How will I know . . . she . . . she—' he whispered hoarsely.

'She's been? You won't. You'll just have to wait and worry, Frank Lynch. I'm not coming back here and neither is she.' Maggie squared her shoulders as she turned away. Let him sweat, he deserved it.

'Did you get it?' Josie hissed as she opened her door to Maggie.

'Yes. For God's sake shut up about it until we get upstairs,' Maggie hissed back.

Once in the cramped room Maggie handed the money over to Josie. 'He must have gone to a moneylender. Now do you know where you're going tomorrow?'

'Yes, but aren't you —'

'Coming with you?' Maggie interrupted.

Josie nodded.

'No, I'm not. How can I? I told you we will both be killed and I'm not taking that chance. I got the money and the name and address for you. For goodness' sake, Josie, how much more do you expect me to do? I can't stay off work. Mam would go mad.'

Josie had begun to shake. She'd have to go alone. She'd been certain Maggie would go with her. But as Maggie had said, how much more help could she expect? No, it really wasn't fair. Maggie had been so good to her already.

'I'll find somewhere to hide it in here and then I'll go . . . tomorrow at dinner time. If I don't go into work in the morning Mam will want to know why. At work I'll tell them I'm not well and want to go home.'

Maggie's attitude softened. 'Everything will be all right, Josie. You'll only need a good night's rest and then . . . then things will be normal again.'

Josie nodded miserably. Her life would never be 'normal' again. She would have to stand by and watch Frank taking Kate out and, she supposed, eventually marrying her. The thought broke her heart.

The next day at lunch time she left work and got a tram to Boundary Street. She was shaking with fear. All morning she'd felt sick. She didn't need to ask where Primrose Court was, she already knew, but as she walked into the dark, dismal court with its one standpipe, its communal privies and the soot-caked, dilapidated houses, her terror grew. She wanted to turn and run, to run back to work or back home, but she couldn't do either. She stood on the dirty cobbles clutching her shawl tightly to her. She *had* to go through with this.

Number six was in the corner, the steps broken and dirty. The guttering had fallen away and the walls glistened with damp. The cotton lace curtain at the downstairs window was grey and in danger of falling apart there were so many holes in it. She knocked timidly, then louder when there was no sound from within.

Eventually the door was opened by an untidy woman whose grey hair straggled around her face. The blouse she wore might once have been white, but now it was a dirty grey colour, and over her black skirt she wore a canvas apron. She terrified Josie.

'Mrs Gibbons?'

'Who wants ter know?' It was obvious what the girl had come for. Bloody little fools they were. The married ones with large families already she could understand, but not these young girls. They never learned.

'I . . . I was told to come to you and that you'd . . . help me. I've got the money.' Josie held out the coins.

The woman nodded. 'Get inside then and be quick about it.'

The odours lingering in the lobby made Josie's stomach churn as the front door was closed behind her with a bang. Oh God, how she wanted to run away from here. Her hand went to her mouth and she balked. The woman glared at her.

'Don't you bloody well start that! I'm not cleaning up after yer. If yer sick yer can clean it up yourself. Gerrup those stairs.'

Josie's legs felt weak and she clutched the banister rail for support. It wasn't much use as most of the spindles had gone, probably burned as firewood.

Mrs Gibbons showed her into a room that contained a bed, a table and a chair. Panic rose again and she forced it down. She *had* to do this. She just *had* to.

'What will . . . happen? How will I know?' she stammered.

'Oh, you'll know, luv. It's only a few minutes of pain and it's all over. If nothing comes away, like, by the time you get home, then you'll be stuck with it. I don't do no second operations. I was a nurse before I got married an' had me own kids.'

Josie wondered faintly how any hospital would employ someone so dirty and unkempt as she sat and then lay on the bed looking up at the cracked and damp-stained ceiling.

The woman was right. She'd only felt a searing pain for a few seconds but it had seemed like an eternity.

'Just lie there for a bit, then you can go home.'

Josie closed her eyes, relaxed, and unclenched her hands. She'd left marks on the palms with her fingernails. It was over. It was all over. She felt so tired, drained and exhausted that she began to drift into a blissful sleep until she was rudely awakened by Mrs Gibbons shaking her.

'All right, it's time ter gerrup now. Yer can't stay 'ere snoring yer head off.'

Slowly and reluctantly Josie sat up and swung her legs over the side of the bed. All she wanted to do now was get back to Silvester Street. She'd tell Mam she was sick and had asked to come home. She was sure her mam would believe her; she must look terrible.

'I don't feel anything. Is that . . . normal?' she asked timidly.

'Give it a chance, girl! Get to the privy at 'ome as soon as yer can an' don't bloody panic if there's a lot of blood. It'll stop. It's normal.'

Josie's legs felt weaker as she went down the stairs. She was cold and shivering with shock and a new terror. Oh God, what did she mean by 'a lot of blood'? How much? Just what was 'normal'?

Somehow she got home and when she walked into the kitchen Mary was visibly concerned.

'Josie, luv. You look terrible. Is it the curse? Go and lie down.'

Josie nodded. Mam had unwittingly given her an excuse for the state she was in.

'I'll have to go to the privy, Mam.'

'All right, luv, then go upstairs.'

She was out there so long that Mary was worried and went down the yard and banged on the door.

'Josie, luv, are you all right? You've been in there ages. What's up? You must be frozen stiff.'

'Nothing, Mam, honestly,' Josie called back, and it was the truth. She had been there ages and nothing had happened. Nothing at all. That woman had told her if nothing happened she was stuck with it.

'Come on out, luv,' Mary called. 'I'll heat up the oven shelf an' wrap it up, and I'll go and get a drop of Indian brandy from Ivy Holden. You'll be all right.'

Josie was very near to breaking point. She couldn't stay out here for ever. She'd just have to come out and go along with Mam's bit of nursing and hope to God that *something* happened and *soon*.

She was lying in bed with her face turned to the wall, drifting in and out of a shallow sleep, when Maggie came to see how she was.

'Josie, what happened?' Maggie asked, sitting on the edge of the bed.

Josie sat up, her face pale and pinched, her eyes filled with tears of desperation. 'Nothing, Maggie! Not a thing.'

'Oh God, Josie. It's not worked.'

It was too much for Josie, who burst into tears. 'I know! I know! What am I going to do now, Maggie? I . . . I . . . can't go through it all again, even if she would do it, which she won't. She told me so. It was horrible and I was terrified, and there's no more money.'

Maggie stood up. 'Come on, get up. Get dressed and come over to our house with me. We can talk there without being afraid of someone barging in on us.'

'What will I tell Mam?' Josie sniffed and wiped her eyes with the back of her hand.

'I'll say I think a bit of quiet company will do you good and it's nice and warm in our house. It's freezing in here.' Maggie looked with distaste at the pile of old coats that were heaped on the beds, the only form of bedclothes there seemed to be. She was used to sheets and blankets and a good quilt. When it was really cold, or if she were ill, Mam lit a fire in the small fireplace. Maybe she'd light one for Josie.

Mary wasn't duly concerned about Josie going out. She was getting the tea ready, and any minute now everyone would be home and the house would be like a bear pit.

'I think you're right, Maggie. It's always freezing up there and it's nice sometimes to have a bit of comfort when you're poorly. I sometimes wish my lot would all go to hell when I feel bad.'

A few minutes later Hetty was surprised to see her daughter lead a very pale and obviously distressed Josie up the lobby.

'I've brought poor Josie over here, Mam. She's not well. You *know*, 'Not Well', and it's like a mad house over there and so cold. Can I light the fire?'

'Of course you can, Maggie. Oh, Josie, you poor thing. I'll bring you up a cup of tea.'

'No . . . no thanks, Mrs McGee. I don't think I could . . . keep it down. I've had some Indian brandy and I feel awful.'

'Oh, what we women have to go through while the men get off scot free,' Hetty tutted sympathetically.

Maggie drew the curtains across the window and lit the gas jet that was covered by a frosted glass mantle. Then she took a long paper spill, lit it from the gaslight and held it to the twists of newspaper and bits of wood that would get the fire going.

'Sit down on the bed and I'll wrap the quilt around you,' Maggie instructed. 'That fire will soon burn up and keep us warm.'

Josie glanced around. Maggie had such luxuries: wallpaper, good curtains, lino and rag rugs, proper furniture and even some trinkets. Nice clean bedding and a fire, too! She wished she could stay here all night.

'Oh, Maggie, what am I going to do?'

Maggie sat on the small stool that faced the dressing table but which she had moved closer to the fire.

'What time did you leave there?'

'I don't know. I can't remember. It was all so . . . awful. Oh, I know our house isn't as nice as this, but hers was terrible. She looked like a witch, she really did, and there was this bedroom with just a bed – nothing on it except old newspapers – and a table and chair. She . . . she had . . . things on the table, covered up so you couldn't see exactly what they were.' Josie started trembling again.

Maggie looked at her with heartfelt sympathy. As far as she could see there was no other choice open to Josie now.

'You'll just have to tell your Mam, Josie. I mean about being in . . . the "family way".'

'Oh God, Maggie! He . . . he said he wouldn't marry me.' Josie's eyes were full of tears.

'Well, he'll just *have* to, won't he? We'll both threaten to tell everyone he gave you the money for . . . this.'

'But we'll get into trouble too.'

Maggie gave it a moment's thought, then shook her head. 'We won't. He won't dare tell. Abortion's a crime and he paid for it, except that this time it didn't work. He'd be dragged off to the police station and he'd get put in Walton Jail. He won't risk that. His da would push him off the landing stage first. You know how toffee-nosed his mam is. God knows why, she hasn't got much more than anyone else around here.'

Josie's pent-up emotions burst forth in the form of gulping, noisy sobs. Maggie was right, but she certainly wasn't going to enjoy the next few hours, inevitable though they were.

'Will you . . . will you come with me, Maggie, please?'

'Just as long as there's not a single thing said about . . . where you went today.'

'Oh, there won't be, Maggie, I swear to God there won't.'

Maggie stood up. 'Come on then, let's go and face the music. It serves him bloody well right,' she said with feeling. This was going to hurt both Josie and Kate, and Maggie felt sorry for the pair of them, but she couldn't care a fig about Frank Lynch.

Chapter Eight

'Josie, in the name of God what's the matter now? You look awful!' Mary cried as Maggie shepherded Josie into the overcrowded and cluttered kitchen. 'Here, sit down, girl. There's something up. Tell your mam what's wrong.'

Josie was eased down gently into the chair by the range. Matty looked over the top of his newspaper irritably. 'A man can't get a bit of peace in his own home with all these flaming women,' he muttered.

'She's very upset, Mrs Ryan,' Maggie said tentatively.

'I can see that, Maggie. What's up with her, apart from You Know What?'

'Well, that's just it, Mrs Ryan. It . . . well, it's not . . .'

Mary looked mystified and then a horrible suspicion began to creep over her. There was only one thing that could upset a girl like this. Josie went out every Saturday night, all dressed up. She never gave a definite answer when asked where she was going or where she had been. 'Oh, just out with my mates for an hour, Mam,' was the usual reply.

Josie felt as though her throat had closed over. She just stared pleadingly at Maggie. She just couldn't say the words. Oh, it was the very worst day in her life.

Maggie sighed and bit her lip. 'It looks as though I'm going to have to tell you. She's been seeing Frank Lynch for a couple of months – well, ever since Christmas – and now she . . . she's . . . going to have a baby.'

'Jesus, Mary and Joseph!' Mary cried, clutching the table for support with one hand, while crossing herself with the other. It was every mother's nightmare.

Matty flung the newspaper on to the floor and got to his feet. 'You bloody little whore! I'll take me belt to you, you little tramp!'

Josie found her voice. 'Oh please, Da, no! No, don't! I'm sorry . . . I'm so sorry,' she cried, the tears running freely down her cheeks.

'Matty, no! Don't hit her, please!' Mary screamed, standing between him and Josie.

'You've brought shame on us an' he'll bloody well marry you! There'll be no bastards in this family! I'll not have fingers pointed at me or yer mam either!' Matty bawled.

'Oh, sweet Jesus help us! He's been walking out with Kate Greenway, too! Peg only said to me the other day that she doesn't like him, that she wished their Kate would drop him. Oh Holy Mother of God help us!' Mary was also in tears.

'Well, he can't marry the both of them! An' I'm going to make damned sure it's our Josie that the bloody two-timing little sod marries!'

Her father's words brought on a fresh bout of sobbing from Josie. Da would flay the skin off her if he knew what she'd done today, and Mam – she'd have no support from her either. She just prayed that Frank wouldn't say anything about the money he'd given her.

'It's no bloody use you sitting there howling like a bleedin' banshee, now, is it? You should have thought about what would happen before you let him touch you and put you in the club!' Matty roared, dragging on his jacket. His face, always florid due to his fondness for the drink, was now a deep shade of puce. 'By God, I'm going to kill the little bastard!'

'Matty, where are you going?' Mary pleaded.

'To find the lads and then we're going to sort him out!'

'Matty, for God's sake be careful,' Mary beseeched, but her words fell on empty air. Matty had already left in search of his three eldest sons, slamming the door so hard behind him that all the windows in the house rattled.

Mary Ryan sat down in the chair her husband had vacated and dropped her head in her hands. 'Oh Holy Mother of God, what's to become of you, Josie? I tried my best to bring you up decent. The Blessed Virgin Mary and all the Holy Saints know that I tried! Josie, how could you be so . . . wicked, so sinful? Ah God, an' all this time you've been going to Mass and confession and communion. Josie! Josie! Think of the sacrileges you've committed! I should take a strap to you meself.'

'I love him, Mam, and he loves me,' Josie lied, beyond caring about the state of her soul.

'Didn't I always tell you never to believe a word any man says? Didn't I? They'll tell you anything to get their way. Don't I know that for the truth? The black lies your da tells me when I ask for the housekeeping and he's bloody spent it . . . Oh, Josie, Josie!' Mary sobbed.

'I'll make a cup of tea,' Maggie said. It was what her mam always did in a crisis. Life was so hard for women, she thought. They always seemed to get the rotten end of the stick while men got away with murder, just as her mam had said. She looked pityingly from Josie to Mary and sighed. They were both bowed down with anguish, Josie more so than her mother. She'd been to hell and back today, while Matty Ryan was probably even now in the pub, drowning his sorrows and blustering and shouting.

Fortified by a few pints of beer, quickly consumed while he informed his sons, Niall, Pat and Kieran, of their sister's plight, Matty led them down Athol Street, grim determination and fury etched in every line of his face.

Kieran was angrier than he'd ever felt in his life before. He was thinking back to Maggie's party and the way Frank Lynch had acted. Since then he'd frequently seen Frank with Kate Greenway on his arm and yet at the same time he'd been seducing poor, trusting little Josie. He just hoped that Kate had had more sense than his sister. Niall had threatened to 'kick the bastard in the balls and ruin him', and he and Pat had nodded their approval, something he would never normally have done.

It was Bert Lynch who opened the door in response to Matty's loud and incessant hammering.

'There's no need to break the bloody door down. What the hell do you lot want?'

'Where's your lad, Frank?' Matty yelled.

'Who wants to know?'

'Matty Ryan does! Aye, and me lads here want to get their hands on him, too, for what's he's done to our Josie.'

'Eh, hang on a minute, what do yer mean?'

Matty was losing patience. 'That little bastard has put me girl in the club, that's what I mean.'

''Ere, don't you go calling our Frank a bastard. He was born in wedlock!' Bert yelled.

'And so will his baby be!' Matty roared back.

Doors were opening further down the street and curtains were twitching.

'You'd best come in,' Bert said grudgingly. Even if this wasn't true Flo would kill him for discussing it in the street with the neighbours earwigging. As far as he knew it wasn't. He'd never heard Frank mention anyone called Josie. Someone had called for Frank a couple of days ago, so Dotty had said, but he hadn't caught a name. He wasn't even sure that Dotty had mentioned one.

Frank turned very pale as the Ryans crowded into the kitchen. Oh God, she must have failed to get rid of it. And now he had to pay back the loan. If and when Matty Ryan came around, he'd planned to say he didn't believe that he was the only one she'd given her favours to. However, he'd not expected such a deputation. Panic washed over him. She must have gone straight home and told them. Not about the abortion, though. They'd all be arrested if she said a word to anyone about that. He glanced at his mam: no help there.

Bert glared at his son. 'Right, meladdo, I want some answers fast and I want the truth, too!'

'You've got our Josie pregnant and by God you're going to do the decent thing by her,' Matty yelled.

Frank felt the sweat spring from every pore in his body and the room tilted sickeningly. 'I . . . I . . .'

'Well, did you?' Bert demanded. 'Is it true? If it is you'll marry her and if not, then you can help me throw this lot out.'

'That Josie came here the other night and she comes here on Saturdays, when you've all gone out. Nelly and me have seen her.' Little Dotty's voice broke the tense silence and everyone turned to look at her.

Bert grabbed her by the arm. 'Are you telling the truth, Dotty?'

'I am, Da, honest! Yer hurting me arm.'

Bert turned to his shocked wife. 'Get her out of here, Flo. She shouldn't be listening to things like this.'

'It's true, Da, it is!' Dotty persisted, thinking he didn't believe her.

Flo slapped her hard. 'Shut up and get to bed, and don't think you can sit on the stairs listening either! Get up those dancers, Dotty Lynch, before I tan your backside until your nose bleeds!'

When Flo had closed the door on a crying, indignant and resentful Dotty, Bert advanced on his son and the look on his face petrified Frank far more than Matty Ryan's outburst had done.

'You've been bringing that girl around here and doing . . . doing . . . *that* in this house! You dirty, sly, hard-faced little sod! Messing like that under your mam's roof! On your mam's sofa or . . . by God, if you took her to your mam's bed I'll break your bloody neck!' Bert lashed out but Frank managed to duck.

'Da, I didn't! I swear it! I never meant . . . she threw herself at me!' Frank cried, backing away from the solid line of grim-faced men and wishing he had throttled his sister.

'Don't bloody lie to me. You'll marry the girl, and as soon as it can be sorted out.'

Frank was desperate, seeing ahead a future tied to Josie Ryan.

'I can't! I don't love her! I won't marry her.'

'Love! What the hell has love got to do with anything? You had your bit of fun, now you have to pay for it, never mind love or anything else,' Bert shouted.

'You can't make me do it.'

'Oh yes we bloody well can, even if we have to break every bone in your miserable body and carry you up the aisle!' Matty bawled.

Frank turned in horrified desperation to his mother. 'Mam! Mam, don't let them do this to me!' he pleaded. She'd always been soft with him, her favourite.

Flo glared at him. 'You brought this on yourself, Frank. You've defiled my home and you've probably corrupted your little sister. I don't even want to speak to you.' She turned away and Bert opened the door for her.

'Go to bed, luv, you've had a nasty shock. I'll deal with him.'

Frank knew he was beaten. He sank down at the table and covered his face with his hands. 'All right, I'll marry her. I can't fight all of you.'

Maggie had left Mary and Josie, both still in tears, to apprise Hetty of the situation. Her mam was horrified but told her to go and see Evvie while she herself went over to the Ryans' to see what comfort and consolation she could give poor Mary.

It was Evvie who opened the door to her. She was surprised to see Maggie standing there with no coat or shawl on, for it was a cold, damp night.

'Evvie, I've got to talk to you now – in private.'

'Then come upstairs. Everyone's in the kitchen.'

Maggie didn't sit down on the bed. What she had to say must be said quickly and then she'd leave. She was worn out with the events of the evening. It only took a few minutes to tell Evvie about Frank Lynch's behaviour and the situation that both he and Josie were now in.

'You've got to tell Kate before she hears it from someone else. Mam's over there now. She can keep a secret but you know what

Mary and Matty are like. It'll be the talk of the neighbourhood before the night's out.'

Evvie was stunned. 'Poor, poor Kate and poor Josie. Oh, I never liked him, Maggie, not really. There was just something about him. He was too . . . too flash, too easy with the girls. Pushy and sort of false. I never trusted him.'

'Neither should Kate nor Josie,' Maggie said flatly.

'Well, Josie's got her wish. She's got the man she wanted. I hope she's happy with him.'

'I hope so, too. She's in a terrible state and so is her mam.'

For half an hour after Maggie had left Evvie rehearsed innumerable ways of telling Kate, but in the end she knew it would be best to be blunt and to the point, though she dreaded what the news would do to her sister.

'What's so important that you've dragged me away from ironing my blouse? You know I'm going out with Frank later tonight,' Kate said irritably as Evvie drew the bedroom curtains and lit the gas. 'Is it something to do with you and Ben? Has Mam found out?'

'It's nothing to do with Ben. Frank . . . well, Frank Lynch won't be coming tonight, or any other night, Kate.'

Kate suddenly felt afraid, sensing Evvie's apprehension. 'What? Evvie, what's the matter with Frank?'

'Oh, Kate, I wish I didn't have to tell you this, but Frank has been seeing Josie and . . . well . . . he's going to marry her. He's *got* to marry her, she's . . . she's having his baby.'

Kate sat down suddenly on the bed, her eyes wide with incredulity. 'He . . . he can't, Evvie!'

'Oh, Kate, I'm so sorry, I really am, but he was two-timing you . . . both of you.' Even though she felt so desperately sorry for her sister, Evvie was also sorry for Josie. 'Oh, I hate him! I wish we'd never set eyes on him, or even heard his name!' she cried angrily, kicking the door and wishing it was Frank Lynch's head.

The tears began to trickle slowly down Kate's cheeks. She felt as though she were empty inside, empty and hollow, all feeling sucked from her.

'Oh, Evvie, how . . . how could he?'

Evvie took her hand. 'Kate, I don't know. I just don't know.'

Before either of them could speak again, Peg called up the stairs. 'Kate! Kate! Frank Lynch is here for you.'

Anger tinged Evvie's cheeks pink and her eyes became hard. 'Oh, he's got a flaming nerve! Don't see him, Kate! Ask Mam to tell him to clear off.'

Kate got to her feet. 'No, Evvie, I want to see him. I want to hear what he has to say.'

'Do you want me to come with you?'

'No. I'll be fine.'

'Kate, I know you're hurt and shocked, but don't let him . . . well, don't let him humiliate you any more than he's done already.'

'I won't.'

Evvie sat down on the bed as Kate left, and she prayed that Kate wouldn't collapse in tears, begging him to say it was all a mistake, that he wasn't going to marry Josie.

Kate and Frank walked down the street in silence. The wind tugged at Kate's shawl, the folds of which hid her face. As they reached Scotland Road she turned to him but she wouldn't look him in the face.

'Where are we going?'

'St Anthony's churchyard. It's quiet there; we . . . we can talk.'

She nodded and they walked on again in silence until they reached the church. There was a narrow dark passage between the church and the Throstle's Nest, and Frank led the way down it.

Kate stopped walking. She felt cold, icily cold, and her heart beat with slow, dull thuds. 'Is . . . is it true, Frank?'

'I . . . I . . .' he stuttered unable to form the words.

'So it is true! How could you do this to me, Frank? How could you? You swore you loved me and all the time you were —'

Frank placed his hand on her arm but she shook it off. 'Katie, I do love you, I'll always love you. Josie was . . . well, she was just a bit of . . . fun.'

Kate's eyes were swimming with tears but his words horrified her.

'Fun! Fun! Is that what you call it, Frank Lynch? I know Josie. She loved you – she wouldn't have let you touch her if she hadn't loved you. And if I had been willing to do what she did, would I have been a bit of fun, too?'

'Oh, Katie, I didn't mean it to sound like that. It wasn't serious with Josie. She kept pestering me. She came round to our house and threw herself at me. What could I do?'

'You could have had some decency and sent her home. Oh, how could you do such a thing, Frank? You can't love me or you would never have betrayed me like this.'

Frank tried again to reach out to her. 'Kate, I do love you but I've got to marry Josie or the Ryans'll kill me, all of them. You know what they're like. I've got no choice. God, how I hate them and her, too.' He meant it. Now that Kate was out of reach, out of his life, he realised just how dear she was to him. But every day for the rest of his life it would be Josie who would be by his side. Josie, who was so plain beside Kate. Josie, who had a personality to match her looks – insipid. No spirit, no vivacity, no ideas of her own. Josie, who wouldn't even think of stepping beyond the bounds of her narrow little world. Oh, he'd been such a fool.

Kate surreptitiously wiped away her tears and with a tremendous effort squared her shoulders. She had to try to come out of this with some dignity, some self-respect.

'You should have thought of all that before you had your bit of "fun", shouldn't you? I never want to set eyes on you ever again, Frank Lynch. I hate and despise you.' And, with her head high, but her heart breaking, she turned and walked quickly back towards Scotland Road.

By the time she got to the top of Silvester Street her tears were blinding her and her heart was thumping against her ribs. She didn't want to go home to face them all, to see their pity, but there was no alternative. Evvie would have told Mam by now and if she didn't return soon, Tom, Da and Joe would be out scouring the streets for her. She was so engulfed in her misery and blinded by tears that she didn't see Josie on the opposite side of the street, knocking on the door of Maggie's house.

Josie saw Kate and ducked her head. She didn't want Kate to see her. Some of her animosity towards Kate had disappeared for Frank had betrayed her too. Josie was still shocked and confused but at least he was going to marry her. Maybe in time she could forget the things he'd said, forgive the way he'd behaved. Maybe in time he would love her. She wanted to be a good wife and a good mother. It was all she had ever wanted from life but she'd never imagined it would be under these circumstances.

Mary Ryan, with a rare display of cold and bitter anger, had forbidden her husband and sons and daughters to utter a word about what had gone on in the Lynches' house.

'Hetty can keep her mouth shut, but don't you make it any worse for Josie by telling her you had to threaten to half kill him before he'd agree to marry her. She's feeling bad enough and so am I, and I don't want it broadcast to the entire street or the customers of the Royal

George either! Do you hear me, Matty Ryan? For God's sake leave us a bit of dignity!' And, because she hadn't even raised her voice, they obeyed her.

Then, urged by Hetty, Mary had told her daughter to go over and sit with Maggie. Maggie opened the front door, expecting to see her mother, returned from the Ryans, but it was Josie who stood on the step.

'Your mam told me to come. She's been great, Maggie. Mam's stopped crying now.'

Maggie took Josie up to her bedroom.

'So, will you see him? Will he be coming round?'

'No, but they were back before I left and Da said he's going to marry me. Your mam said she'd help in any way she can.'

'Where will you live?'

'That's one of the things Mam will sort out.'

'Don't you get any say in it?'

'Yes, but for now it's best that Mam does all the talking.'

'There's no room in your house for a husband and baby. You're all packed in like sardines as it is.'

'I know. We'll probably live in Athol Street. I mean there's only Frank and his sister and his mam and dad. Their Lizzie's married and lives in William Moult Street.'

Maggie sighed. It had been a long tiring day and it wasn't over yet.

'Will it be in St Anthony's or Our Lady's in Eldon Street?'

'St Anthony's.'

'What will you wear?' Maggie had quickly put the circumstances aside and was now taking a keen interest, for Josie was the first of the girls in her age group to get married, and an idea was rapidly forming in her mind.

'Oh, I don't know. I haven't had time to think about things like that, Maggie.'

'Well, you can start now. I'll make your dress, if you like.'

Josie was taken aback. 'I'd not even thought about that, Maggie. I don't think I can afford a nice dress, a proper wedding dress, I mean.'

'It needn't be expensive. Have you got anything at all saved up?

'Yes, I've nearly got fifteen shillings.'

'It's a good job you didn't tell *him* that. He'd have made you give it to him to pay for . . . today.'

'I was so upset, Maggie. You know I was nearly out of my mind with it all. I just forgot about the money.'

'Good.'

'I have been saving hard. I've been walking to work and not taking any lunch. Mam gave me the money instead. I told her I was saving up for nice clothes for the summer. I thought . . . well, I hoped that Frank would ask me to get engaged. Mam might be able to get a bit extra from Da and the lads, too.'

'I wouldn't charge you for making it, Josie, and Mam's got all sorts of bits of lace and ribbon left over from things she's made. Will you wear white?'

Josie blushed. 'I suppose really I shouldn't, but I know Mam will tell everyone that the baby was premature, so she might let me have white.'

Maggie thought that Mary Ryan was a fool if she thought anyone would believe that old excuse but she didn't say so to Josie.

'You can get a couple of artificial flowers from the market and I could make a headdress, too.'

Josie felt much better and was glad of Maggie's support. She'd been great about almost everything. It wasn't her fault that the abortion had failed. In fact, Josie thought, she was glad it had. Now she was going to marry Frank, and if she was to have a lovely dress and a veil and headdress, too, then maybe he would look at her through new eyes. 'It's really good of you, Maggie. It's so kind. I feel heaps better now.'

Maggie smiled. She seldom did anything without a purpose. This would be a test of her skills. She knew she could do it and her mam would help with the more difficult bits if need be. 'If you like I'll be your bridesmaid.'

'Oh, Maggie, will you? I don't want me sisters; they're not speaking to me.'

'And Davie will be best man if I ask him. Frank hasn't got any brothers. Has he got any mates, anyone in particular? Their Lizzie's husband?'

'Lizzie's husband, I suppose.' Josie bit her lip and frowned. 'Maggie, will you . . . will you pay for your own dress? It looks awful, me having to ask after you've been so generous.'

'Yes, I'll make it, so it won't be too expensive. What colour do you think? I suit pale green – remember the dress Mam made me for my party?'

'Isn't it bad luck to wear green at a wedding?'

'Oh, that's rubbish. Just an old wives' tale. It will be pale green and I'll do a hat or something to match. Now, stand up and I'll measure you and then we can think about designs and materials.'

Josie's eyes filled with tears. 'Maggie, you're being so good, you really are. I feel now that I'm actually going to get married. I feel much, much happier.'

'Well, what are friends for, Josie?' Maggie replied, but her mind was racing ahead. If she made a success of this venture, maybe she could think about starting her own business and to hell with Mrs Sidgewick, and Sloan's as well.

Chapter Nine

Mary Ryan took Josie to see Flo Lynch, who was as upset about the whole affair as Mary was herself. Frank was Flo's only son and she had doted on him, but after what he'd done she was very cool towards him. He had let her down badly and it would take time for her to get over that. She disliked and distrusted Josie before she'd even spoken to her, though she knew Mary Ryan's children by sight. In her opinion the girl was no good, letting Frank take advantage of her and in his own home.

It was a tense meeting. Mary had told Josie to say nothing, just to keep her head down and not fidget or snivel.

'It's a grey day for us all, Flo, that it is,' Mary said as she sat down in the chair Frank's mother indicated.

'It is but there's no changing things so we'd best get down to brass tacks, Mary.'

Mary glanced briefly around the spotlessly clean kitchen while Flo poured them all a cup of tea. The woman must spend all her time scrubbing and polishing, she thought. Josie was in for a shock if she carried on here the way she did at home. All her kids were untidy and she'd given up nagging and yelling at them years ago. You only succeeded in wearing yourself out.

'I suppose seeing as there's only the four of us here, they'd better make this their home,' Flo stated. She gave Josie a hard, speculative look as she handed her the cup and saucer. Oh, she appeared quiet enough but they were the ones you had to watch. She'd already noted the creased blouse that could have been cleaner than it was, and the part of the hem of her skirt that was in need of a stitch. Meek and mild she looked, a picture of innocence, but Flo wasn't fooled by appearances. Josie Ryan was a brazen little madam.

'That's good of yer, Flo. We're crowded out as it is. Josie, what do yer say to Mrs Lynch?'

'Thanks . . . very much,' Josie said without enthusiasm. She didn't like Frank's mam much and she could tell that the feeling was mutual. Her depression deepened.

'About the wedding?' Mary continued.

'Well?' Flo wasn't really terribly interested. She wished it was all over and done with but she cared enough not to want gossip or cutting remarks from her neighbours.

'That lot haven't got a brass farthing between them. They'll make a show of us,' had been their Lizzie's prediction. Flo'd had to agree to give them a bit of a do.

She shuddered. 'Wouldn't a family tea be a better idea and less expensive?'

Mary nodded. She knew what Flo really meant and she cursed Matty, Pat and Niall for the times they'd ended up in Rose Hill nick. 'Aye, it would. There'd be no . . . no chance for trouble to start. Josie's paying for her own dress.'

'What kind of dress?' Flo shot a searing glance at her future daughter-in-law.

'A proper one. White. Maggie McGee's making it.' Mary held Flo's gaze, her lips compressed in a tight thin line, defying Flo to object.

'Right.'

'Maggie will be bridesmaid. She doesn't want 'er sisters an' I don't blame 'er.'

'Someone will have to go and see Father Foreshaw.'

'He'll want to see them both,' Mary stated grimly. And wouldn't the pair of them get a good tongue-lashing, too. She ignored the sniff that Josie was unable to suppress.

Josie was fighting a hard battle with her tears, a battle she was losing. Oh, this was terrible. This was not the way it should be at all. They were both discussing and deciding things as though she wasn't even in the room, never mind allowed to express an opinion or an idea. Oh, she wasn't looking forward to coming to live here. She wiped her tears away with the back of her hand and sniffed again. Both her mam and Flo Lynch glared at her and she hung her head, her misery complete.

'You and me had better go with them,' Flo said, and Mary nodded her agreement. By telling glances and brief nods the two women silently agreed to keep Josie and Frank apart, or at least not to leave them alone. They wanted no arguments, no protestations, no accusations. They had enough to put up with as it was.

The wedding was arranged for the second Saturday in April as Maggie said she couldn't possibly get the dresses done any quicker.

As it was she would have to stay up half the night. Hetty had agreed to help. Her sympathies were with Mary, not Josie. After all, the girl was getting the man she wanted. Poor Mary Ryan had enough to cope with in life with a drunken husband, two sons who were determined to better their father's performance at consuming ale, those three lazy daughters who should have long since been married and off her hands, and that young tearaway Mickey. Was it any wonder she had little time or inclination to keep her eye on Josie? Kieran was the only one in that house that poor Mary could be proud of, and he was following Evvie Greenway around with his heart on his sleeve and she didn't appear to notice him.

'Just let this be a lesson to you, Maggie,' Hetty had said curtly as she cut out the green taffeta for Maggie's dress. It was a remnant in two pieces that didn't quite match but with skilful cutting that would hardly be noticed.

'Mam, what a thing to say! I'd never let Davie do anything like that. He'd get his face slapped if he tried, but he's got too much respect for me.'

'That's good, Maggie. When you get married I want you to have a decent home of your own. I don't want you moving in with your in-laws or even with us, although we have got the room. A young couple need time on their own, to adjust. Marriage is not a bed of roses.'

Maggie had said nothing. If and when she married Davie, it wouldn't be a hole-and-corner affair like Josie's. No, it would be very grand and she would have a nice little house of her own. She intended to do things properly. Josie Ryan was a fool if she hadn't even known Frank was still seeing Kate. In fact she hadn't been able to see further than the end of her nose, she was so besotted.

Maggie warned Josie not to ask Evvie to the wedding, for it would be bound to cause more ill feeling, she being Kate's twin.

Peg, however, had agreed to go, out of deference to Mary. Peg was also thankful that Frank Lynch would now be out of Kate's life for good, and the way he'd carried on he was certainly no loss. She was worried about Kate. She was so silent and withdrawn, but wasn't that only to be expected? she asked herself. The way he'd hurt and humiliated Kate would put you off men for life, she'd said to Vi Hawkins as they'd walked home from the market.

'Aye, she's had a lucky escape there, Peg. I can't say I like the lad much and if I was Josie I wouldn't trust him. He's two-timed her once.'

'Well, a wife and baby should sort him out. I hate to say it, Vi, but I hope it will teach Kate to be more careful, more choosy in future. I'll be glad when it's all over and done with. Our Kate will get over it.'

The sun shone brightly in the cloudless blue April sky as Josie and Matty were driven the short distance to the church. Kieran had paid for the hackney carriage as a wedding gift and Josie had been over the moon. It meant that she didn't have to walk all the way as many girls had to do. Had things been different, had she been engaged for a proper length of time, she wouldn't have minded the walk. She would have enjoyed showing off her dress and seeing the looks on the faces of all the neighbours. But things were far from normal. Gossip and speculation were rife and so she was thankful for the hackney. The rest of the family, and Maggie and Davie, had made their own way to the church. Alf McGee had provided another hackney for Maggie and Davie.

Josie was happier than she'd been for weeks, though she was dreading living with her in-laws. But today was her day.

Maggie had excelled herself and the dress was gorgeous. They'd bought white taffeta, cheaper than satin, from the wholesaler that Hetty patronised, and they'd got a discount too. Maggie had advised her against frills and flounces as she was small and slight. 'You don't want to look like an overdressed china doll, do you?' It had been more of a statement than a question. So, the dress was cut plainly with a high neck and long sleeves, the cuffs and collar decorated with tiny bows of white ribbon. Hetty had shown Maggie how to let broad bands of ribbon into the short train. Tiny white wax flowers had been bought from Great Homer Street Market and these Maggie had fashioned into a circlet with wire and blue ribbon. Maggie had also pleaded with her mother to let Josie borrow her own lace veil.

'That covers the something old and borrowed, your dress is new and there's bits of blue in your headdress.'

'Oh, Maggie, I look . . . I look . . . so . . .' Josie searched for words as she stood in Hetty's front room and gazed rapturously at her reflection in the long mirror.

'You look gorgeous and he'll be made up with you,' Maggie said with satisfaction. It was partly true: Josie did look lovely.

'You look great, too, Maggie. You were right, green does suit you.'

Maggie's dress was similar in style to Josie's, with bands of ecru lace at the neck and cuffs. She had covered a wide-brimmed hat in the same material, and had added cream-coloured flowers and ribbon. It all looked very stylish and far more expensive than it really was. They both carried small posies of spring flowers.

The church was half full and Maggie couldn't disguise the triumph in her eyes as she noted the admiring and surprised looks they both received as they walked down the aisle. And the look on Davie's face made her positively preen. Even her mam had admitted that both dresses were a triumph and proved to everyone that Maggie had real talent and style.

'Well, she certainly looks very well,' Peg whispered to Vi Hawkins.

'She does, but who let Maggie wear green? It's bad luck.'

'Oh, don't be daft, Mam, that's rubbish. Maggie is certainly clever. She made Josie's headdress and her own hat, too. I'd never have thought of putting those colours together,' Agnes whispered enviously. If she ever got married, she'd certainly ask Maggie to make her dress. It hadn't cost a fortune either, so she'd heard.

'She takes after Hetty for that,' Vi said sagely.

Suddenly Agnes pulled at her mother's sleeve. There seemed to be something wrong.

'Mam, Mam, where's Frank? Where's the bridegroom?'

Vi stood up and searched the faces of the group now huddled at the bottom of the altar steps. The parish priest, in his white and gold vestments, was looking far from pleased.

'Oh God Almighty, she's right, Peg. I saw Mary go over to Flo but I didn't take much notice. He must have done a runner.'

She'd barely finished speaking when Matty Ryan and his sons, followed by Bert Lynch and Lizzie's husband, strode back down the aisle, their faces wearing the same grim determined expression.

'Why didn't you watch him, you bloody idiot?' Bert stormed at his son-in-law as they left the church.

'I thought you were. Our Lizzie was mithering something shocking about me bloody collar.'

'Well, we'd better go and look for him, the bloody little coward. He's not making a show of me and our Josie.' Matty was livid. There had been snide remarks passed in the pub over the last few days.

'He's done that already,' Lizzie's husband said morosely, and received a black look from his father-in-law for his pains.

'Where the hell do we start?' Pat Ryan asked. 'He could be anywhere.'

'We'll split up,' Bert said. He couldn't believe that *no one* had seen

Frank slope off but then everyone had been totally engrossed in their own affairs and Lizzie's fussing had got them all worked up. Oh, when he got his hands on his son he'd kill him, bringing more shame down on them, especially Flo. She was still trying to come to terms with having Josie Ryan living with them.

'You'd better go back inside and tell our Josie and yer mam to go home. If we find him today we'll be bloody lucky,' Matty instructed Kieran, who reluctantly went to impart this news to his already sobbing sister.

They reasoned that the most likely place Frank would head for was the docks or the Labour Pool at Man Island and try to get a ship. So Matty and Bert said they would take the Pool and the rest of them would take the docks.

'It'll be like looking for a needle in a bloody haystack,' Matty muttered as he and Bert broke into a run for the tram stop.

'There's never a bloody one when you need them,' Bert said, peering down Scotland Road.

'There's one coming now, Da,' his son-in-law replied.

'I wish it would get a bloody move on,' Matty said.

As the tram drew to a halt they caught sight of Alf McGee crossing the road and coming over to them.

'Where the hell are you lot going? You're supposed to be at a wedding.'

'We are but the little sod of a bridegroom has scarpered.'

Alf's forehead creased in a frown. 'I've just come from the Pier Head, had a bit of business to do at the Royal Liver Friendly Office. I could have sworn I saw him going for the Isle of Man boat, but then I thought it couldn't have been him, he was getting married.'

'The Isle of Man boat?' Bert queried.

'Definitely. Apart from the ferry it was the only ship tied up there.'

'Then get on, you lot,' Bert instructed.

'I'll come back with you,' Alf offered, thinking of poor Mary, and poor Josie, abandoned at the very altar rail.

Pat Ryan and Lizzie's husband, being younger, raced from the tram across the Pier Head and down to the landing stage where the *Lady of Man* was still tied up. By the time the rest of them arrived it was to see Pat arguing with an official of the Isle of Man Steam Packet Company.

'Look, here's me da; he'll tell you. This feller won't believe us.' Pat turned to his father.

Bert interrupted. 'If my lad, Frank Lynch, is on that bloody boat I want him off it – now!'

'We're ready to sail.'

'Well, you can bloody well wait for five minutes.'

'How old is the lad?'

'He's under the age of consent if that's what you mean. He can't do anything without my permission and he's not going to the Isle of Man leaving his girl at the altar.'

The official looked at the six men, shrugged and ran his finger down the passenger manifold. 'Lynch, F.'

'That's him!' Matty cried.

'All right, you've got five minutes. This is the mail boat, in case you've forgotten, and interfering with His Majesty's mail is a criminal offence.'

'Oh, shut up. Five minutes won't matter. It's April, not bloody December. The weather's fine; you can make it up.'

Frank looked over the side and saw them. The wave of blind panic washed over him again – the trembling, breathless, unreasoning panic that had made him give his family the slip and make a break for freedom. All through the night he'd lain awake, imagining what life would be like with Josie, and as the hours lengthened his panic had grown. He *couldn't* go through with it. He *hated* Josie. It was Kate he loved and Kate he'd lost for ever.

He'd washed, shaved and dressed in silence, feeling as though he was going to prison rather than church. As the time drew nearer he'd sidled closer and closer to the back door. His mam and Lizzie had the place up and no one saw him leave. He'd just fled, with no idea of where he was going or what he would do. When he'd reached the Pier Head he'd seen the *Lady of Man* tied up and he'd gone and got a ticket. A one-way ticket. He'd find work there, he'd survive, and they wouldn't think to look for him so near to home. They'd think he'd signed on for a ship going somewhere far, far away.

Gradually the trembling had slowed, his heartbeat became regular and he'd sat in the saloon for a while feeling very relieved and thinking he'd made just the right decision where to run to. Then, as it neared sailing time, he'd gone up on deck for some air.

'Oh Jesus, Mary and Joseph!' he stammered as he saw the group of six men at the bottom of the gangway. He was unable to let go of the rail. It was as if his fingers were welded to the metal. He wanted to run, jump over the side and swim – or even sink

– but his hands and his feet had let him down. He couldn't move an inch.

'You cowardly little bastard! Did you think you could leave our Josie in church?' Matty roared as he saw Frank clinging to the rail, his face ashen.

'I . . . I . . . can't . . .' Frank couldn't get the words out.

'You bloody well *can* and you bloody well *will*. Haven't you disgraced your mam enough?' Bert yelled at his son.

Except for Alf McGee, they were all oblivious to the interested crowd that was gathering around them.

'It's no use yelling and bawling at him,' said Alf. 'Just get him and us off this bloody boat and back to the church.'

'You're right, Alf,' Bert conceded, and Matty nodded.

So surrounded by the six men Frank went down the stairs to the saloon and then the gangway, like a prisoner going to meet the hangman. He felt physically and mentally battered.

Josie had sobbed all the way home while Maggie fumed in silence and Mary called Frank Lynch all the names she could think of to a tight-lipped, red-faced Flo.

'This is getting us nowhere,' Peg said flatly.

'Come on to my house,' Hetty said.

'I want to go home!' Josie sobbed.

'I don't blame you. Oh, the nerve of him after all the work I've done on these dresses.'

'Maggie McGee, that's quite enough of that. There are far more important things on our minds than dresses,' Hetty rebuked her daughter sharply.

Maggie tutted.

'Hetty's right. Maggie can take off her hat and you can take off your veil for a while,' Mary advised. She felt heartbroken for her daughter but Josie's sobs were grating on her shredded nerves.

'What if they . . . if they . . .' Josie choked.

'Just stop that, Josie!' Mary snapped.

'It's all right, Mary, luv, you're upset,' said Hetty. 'I'll make us a nice cup of tea and I baked a Sally Lunn. I'll cut it up and butter it; you must all be starving.'

'Mam, if we have that we won't be able to go to Communion.'

Hetty glared at Maggie. She, and she suspected all the others apart from Josie, knew that the men hadn't a cat in hell's chance of finding Frank Lynch.

'Get out the cups, saucers and plates, Maggie,' she instructed.

As Josie sat in Hetty's kitchen, still in her finery, clutching a cup in both hands, she couldn't believe what had happened. She'd hoped that when he'd seen her in her wedding dress he would have tried to love her just a little bit. But he'd run. He'd run away from her. The whole neighbourhood would know that he'd jilted her, that he found the thought of marrying her so awful that he hadn't been able to stand it.

They'd finished their tea and the buttered slices of fruit cake, but the time dragged on and the case clock on Hetty's overmantel marked the hour and half-hour with tinny little sounds. It annoyed Hetty so much that she got up, took it down and consigned it to the draining board in the scullery. No one wanted to be the first to suggest that they all go home and get changed. Hetty sighed. Seeing as she'd invited them here she supposed it was up to her to make the suggestion but just as she was trying to choose her words the sound of the door knocker broke her concentration.

They all looked at each other apprehensively. Hetty went to answer it.

She returned with Father Foreshow.

'Josie, child, put on your veil and dry your eyes. The Nuptial Mass will start in fifteen minutes.'

'Father, did they . . . have they . . . ?' Mary stammered.

'They did so. He's over at the presbytery now with the men.'

'Oh, thank God! My prayers have been answered.'

'Indeed they have, Mary. Now, ladies, will you please put on your hats and let's make as good a fist of it as we can.'

There was no note of relief or happiness in his voice. He'd spent ten minutes with the extremely reluctant bridegroom, pointing out where his duties lay.

Kate had had a miserable day. Evvie had insisted that they both go to town and treat themselves to something new.

'What for?' Kate had asked.

'Well, to . . . to cheer ourselves up. I mean, winter is over now, it's spring. Soon we'll be able to go out without a coat or shawl.'

'Evvie, I'm not really in the mood.'

'Neither am I, Kate, but we have to get away from here.'

So they'd gone and they'd looked at the new spring clothes displayed in shop windows, but neither of them had any real interest, and Evvie had bought only a pair of stockings before they'd caught a tram home, Evvie wishing she'd suggested a trip by ferry to New Brighton instead. The weather had been nice enough.

'Was it really bad, Mam?' Evvie asked after Peg had told them of the fiasco and Kate had gone straight upstairs.

'It was a flaming disgrace, Evvie. I was heart scalded for poor Mary – aye, and for Flo Lynch too. She'll give Bert and that dimwit of a husband of their Lizzie's a right ear-bashing for not making certain that Frank got to the church and stayed there. It's not much to ask, after all. I don't know how their Lizzie came to marry someone as thick as him. It's been an exhausting day, Evvie. Go on up to Kate now. She'll need you.'

Kate was sitting on the bed just staring into space.

'Are you all right?' Evvie asked, sitting down beside her and feeling despondent. She often became a mirror for Kate's emotions and she knew Kate reacted in the same way. It was something to do with being identical twins, Mam had tried to explain years ago.

'I'll manage now that's over.'

'Well, it really seems to have been awful. Poor Josie, and then Frank having to be dragged off the Isle of Man boat.'

'Don't Evvie, please.'

'I'm sorry.'

'I know he was forced to marry Josie, but to do something so cowardly, so despicable . . . I'm beginning to go right off men.'

Evvie shook her head but didn't speak.

Everyone would say he wasn't worth crying over, Kate thought, but she was trying to understand how he must have felt. It was herself he loved and she loved him. He must have been so desperate to do such a thing. He'd run, hoping to get to the ends of the earth, she surmised, rather than have to marry Josie, and had he remained free there would always be a chance that some day in the future he could come back and marry her. But would she want him? At that exact moment she really didn't know.

On Monday morning Kate was glad to get to work.

'There's something wrong with you, Kate. I've noticed it over these last weeks. You seem preoccupied and not like your usual lively self,' Doris Kay, her supervisor, remarked.

They'd taken their lunches to the packing area. No facilities were provided so everyone tried to find a quiet corner, no matter how dusty or cold it was.

'Oh, they've been the worst weeks in my life.'

'Why?' Doris looked concerned.

Kate sighed. It would be good to unburden herself to someone outside the family. 'You know the lad I was walking out with?'

'Frank Lynch?'

Kate nodded and swallowed hard. Oh, it hurt so much just to mention his name. He really wasn't the fly-by-night, the Jack-the-lad everyone made him out to be. At least he'd not been like that when he was with her. He had a caring, quieter, even gentler side to him that people seldom saw – mainly because he didn't want them to see, so he'd told her. His reputation was a useful cover for what he really felt about many things, herself included.

'He . . . he got married on Saturday.'

'He WHAT?'

Kate nodded. 'You heard me, Doris.'

'Who did he marry? I thought it was going to be you – in time, of course.'

'Josie Ryan. She lives opposite to us.'

'But why? I mean, did you know? Did you have a row with him?'

'No. It would be easier to bear if I had. He . . . he'd been seeing Josie as well as me. She . . . she's . . . going to have a baby, so he *had* to marry her. It gets worse, Doris. He almost jilted her at the altar rail. He ran off and no one noticed until Josie arrived.'

'Oh, that's great, that is,' Doris said acidly.

'Her da and brothers and his da and Mr McGee caught him on the Isle of Man boat and forced him back home and to the church.'

'God help poor Josie then. So, he was two-timing you?'

Kate nodded miserably. 'I . . . I . . . feel so unhappy. What has life to offer now?'

'A great deal more than he could offer you. Would you want to be stuck at home with a baby?'

'I'd not thought about it like that.'

'And I suppose Josie didn't either. I know you won't think so now, Kate, but if that's the way he carries on, you're better out of it.'

'I know, and I know I should think I've been lucky, but I . . . I . . . love him. There's a side to him that . . .' She couldn't go on.

'Oh, it's typical, Kate. Men control our lives one way or another. We've no say and won't have until women's rights are taken seriously.'

Kate sighed. 'I can't see that happening. You grow up, get married, have kids, and spend the rest of your life looking after them and the house, and it's what most women expect.'

'We've not much choice. It's get married and look after a family or be an old maid and look after your mam and dad and old aunties and uncles—' Doris suddenly realised what she'd said. 'Oh, Kate, I'm sorry. I didn't mean to be so tactless.'

'I know.'

'Oh, I know there are a few women with education and work like men, but not many. Men get the really good jobs. Given the choice I wonder what most women would want.'

'To . . . to get married, I think. Most girls don't have much education and you need that to get good jobs. Marriage is the only choice but it's what we look forward to.'

'But there are hundreds of women trapped in terrible marriages, Kate. Look at Mary Ryan for one, and she's not on her own around here.'

Kate was thoughtful, interested in spite of the way she was feeling. 'So, what can be done?'

'All women should join the Suffragist movement. If everyone did then men would soon have to change their ideas.'

'You mean the suffragettes?'

'Yes. I'm a member.'

'I thought it was only posh ladies who joined that.'

'No, working women, girls like us, can join. In fact they welcome us with open arms. It doesn't matter what class we come from, we're all sisters in the fight. It does help to have educated women, though. I mean, they speak so well and people take notice of them. There's a big meeting at the end of the month, why don't you come with me?'

'Me?'

'Yes. The world's a flaming mess and it's men who are to blame. Emmeline Pankhurst has just been sentenced to three years in prison.'

Kate looked horrified. The Pankhursts were ladies. 'What for?'

'Incitement to arson. Trying to set fire to the Prime Minister's house. No one will take us seriously so we have to resort to things like that.'

'Oh, Doris, my da would kill me.'

'You don't have to tell him. Oh, come on, Kate. We need more members. All your friends could join too. It'll make you look at things in a different light.'

Kate smiled sadly. 'You mean it will take my mind off Frank Lynch.'

'What's so bad about that?'

'I'll think about,' Kate promised.

On her way home she debated it with herself. It would be an interest. It would take her mind off . . . things. It wasn't fair what men were allowed to get away with. But what would Mam say? She'd have to tell her. And what about Evvie? Should she tell her? Oh, she just couldn't make up her mind. She'd have to give it more thought.

That evening after work she got off the tram and walked along Scotland Road. As she drew close to The Plough, nicknamed The Widows, she could see a man and a woman arguing. The man was 'Tip' O'Connor, one of Matty Ryan's less salubrious drinking companions. He was unshaven, bleary-eyed and his clothes were filthy. Nelly, his wife, was urging him to come home. It was an all-too-familiar sight. The O'Connors were the poorest of the poor, due to his fondness for the drink. Everyone tried to help Nelly to keep her and her kids out of the workhouse.

'Bloody leave me alone, woman. Bloody leave me an' gerrof 'ome!' Tip bawled, lashing out at Nelly, catching her a hefty blow, which sent her sprawling on the cobbles.

Kate ran and helped her up, anger bubbling up in her.

'You leave her alone, you flaming bully! Leave her alone or I'll call the scuffers, so help me I will!' Kate yelled at him.

Tip spat, turned away and staggered down the road as Kate looked pityingly at Nelly.

'Are you all right, Mrs O'Connor?'

'Aye, girl, thanks.'

'Why don't you just leave him? I'm sure you'd be better off. One of these days he's going to kill you, Mam says.'

'And where would I go with six kids and only our Lizzie old enough to work? And he takes the wages off her. It would be the workhouse, and it's only thanks to yer mam, God bless her, an' the other neighbours that we're not in there now. I can usually manage to get a couple of coppers off him, even if it does cost me a black eye and a few bruises.'

Kate dug into her pocket and handed a threepenny bit to Nelly.

'Here, take this and get yourself and the kids something to eat. But let him flaming well starve.'

'God bless yer, Kate. I'll get to the chippy now. God luv yer, Kate Greenway.'

Kate watched her go. If she needed anything to make up her mind about going with Doris, that encounter with Tip and Nelly O'Connor had just provided it.

Chapter Ten

Kate watched the sun, a huge ball of red fire, slip down behind the wall of the back yard. She shivered a little as the chill of the early spring evening dispelled the residue of warmth the rays of the sun had created. She had felt so claustrophobic in the house, so stifled in the cheerful fuggy warmth of the kitchen. The fire burned in the range winter and summer, it being the only source of heat and needed for cooking and hot water.

She felt so miserable, so utterly desolate. Mam had said it would pass, that time was a great healer, but what did Mam know about broken hearts and betrayed trust and love?

She'd heard all the details of Josie's wedding. She'd gone on an errand for Mam to the corner shop, which had been full at the time, and she had stood at the back, listening with horrified fascination as Ivy Holden regaled all her customers with every detail, adding pertinent and sometimes acid remarks of her own as embellishments. In the end Kate had run out and gone home before anyone saw her, before she was subjected to curious and pitying stares. Mam hadn't been annoyed with her. She'd just sent Joe down instead.

The pain tore at her raw emotions again. There were times when she hated Frank for what he'd done, but mostly she felt weighed down by a terrible sense of sorrow and loss. It should have been she who had made such a grand entrance into St Anthony's in what Ivy Holden had described as a 'wonderful creation' of Maggie's. Frank should have been waiting for her at the altar steps. Oh, would the pain and all the images conjured up by the gossip she'd overheard ever fade? At least Josie had gone to live in Athol Street. At least she didn't have to see either Josie or Frank entering or leaving the Ryans' house opposite. Mam had pointed that out to her as a blessing and she was grateful for such small mercies.

The yard door creaked on its hinges and she looked up. Dusk was falling and the yard was mostly in shadow.

'Evvie, is that you?'

'Hush. I don't want Mam to see me.'

Evvie had hoped that by sneaking in through the scullery her absence would not have been too marked. She and Ben had taken the tram to Otterspool and had walked along the Cast Iron shore, known locally as 'the cassy'. There weren't many isolated beauty spots in Liverpool, where they wouldn't run the risk of being recognised. Of course there were the parks where they occasionally strolled, but they were favourite places for courting couples, many from Scotland Road.

'She knows.'

'Knows what?'

'That you've been out with Ben, that you've been seeing him a couple of times a week.'

'Oh, no! We've been so careful.'

'Madge Hartley saw you and so did Jessie Blackstock.'

Evvie's chin jerked up determinedly. 'That pair of jangling busybodies.'

Kate looked sadly at her sister. 'Evvie, please don't get too involved with Ben. It can't come to anything and I don't want you to feel . . . well, to feel the way I do now.'

Evvie took Kate's hand. 'Oh, Kate, I'm sorry. Sometimes I wish that Maggie had never had that party; it's done so much harm. But I *am* involved with Ben, I can't help it and neither can he.'

Tears welled in Kate's eyes but before she could speak, Peg's voice carried clearly from the scullery.

'Evvie, is that you?'

Evvie sighed. 'Yes, Mam.'

'Well, get in here now, I've a few things I want to say to you, milady. And, Kate, you come on in too, luv. It's cold out there now. You'll catch a chill.'

Both girls reluctantly went into the house.

Evvie noted thankfully that both her da and Tom, currently ashore, were absent and that Peg was in the process of ordering Joe to bed.

'I think I'll go up too, Mam. I've got a headache,' Kate said, not feeling up to coping with what she knew was to follow. She couldn't back Evvie up in this as she had neither the emotional strength, nor the conviction that what Evvie was doing was right.

Peg eased herself down on the bench by the table and poured herself a cup of tea, not looking forward to what she must do.

Evvie stood twisting a strand of hair around her finger.

'Well, milady, what have you got to say for yourself? Where have you been?'

Evvie knew it was useless to lie now. 'To Otterspool.'

'Who with?'

'You know who with, Mam. Ben. Ben Steadman.'

'Evvie, for the love of God, what's the matter with you, girl? I'm not going to start yelling and bawling at you but have some sense. Use your head, not your heart. He's Jewish and you're Catholic, nothing can ever come of it. You must know that.'

'But, Mam, I . . . I . . . won't give up going to church or anything like that.'

'Too right you won't, and he won't give up going to the synagogue.'

'He doesn't go very often.'

'That's not the point, Evvie. He's not going to give up his faith, is he? He's a good boy. Don't think I don't like him – I do – but he's not for you and never can be. Put a stop to it now, Evvie, before you both get hurt. Listen to your mam. I know: I've had more experience of life. Kate will get over Frank Lynch and you'll get over Ben Steadman. You'll both look back one day and be thankful that you made the right decisions. Except that Kate's was made for her.'

Evvie was twisting her hands together. Every word Peg had said was true, she knew that, but she couldn't do it, she just couldn't. She knew now that she loved Ben. 'Mam, please . . .'

Peg got to her feet and put her hands on Evvie's shoulders. 'It's for your own good, Evvie. Give him up.'

'Mam —'

'I don't want to hear another word. I've kept it from your da up till now, but if it goes on, then he'll have to know – and from me, before he hears it from someone else.'

Evvie dropped her head so her mother wouldn't see the tears in her eyes.

'Go on up to bed, Evvie. Have an early night and sleep on it. It will do you good and in the morning you'll see things in a different light. Go on, girl.'

Peg watched her daughter walk out of the kitchen and her heart was heavy. She'd promised herself she wouldn't shout and she hadn't. What she'd done was all for the best. She'd spoken the truth when she'd said she liked Ben Steadman, which was more than she could say about Frank Lynch. She wished that the entire Lynch family, including Josie, would emigrate to somewhere like Australia, but even that wouldn't be far enough in her judgement. Every time she looked at Kate she felt as though she could cheerfully stick a knife into Frank Lynch.

She sighed heavily and looked up at the statue on the mantel. 'Oh, Holy Mother, it's not easy, is it? Do you ever stop worrying about them? I suppose I should count my blessings, but please, let the pain ease for Kate and let Evvie see sense,' she prayed.

It wasn't as if Evvie had no one else. Kieran Ryan was eating his heart out over her and he was a good, steady Catholic lad. She prayed that Evvie would see sense and also realise how much Kieran loved her.

But maybe, Peg thought, the time had come to give her prayers a bit of a helping hand. She would seize the moment! She sent Joe, who had secreted himself under the table to read his comic, over to Mary's with the request that she wanted to see Kieran as soon as possible. Joe had heard Evvie and his mam arguing but he'd taken no notice.

'What does she want me for?' a mystified Kieran asked him.

''Ow do I know? All she said was, go and get him. She'd forgotten I was supposed to be in bed an' I was reading me comic. When I said she was always goin' on about me not readin' enough, I gorra clip around the ear!' Joe glared up at Kieran. He didn't like Kieran much; he was quiet by his standards.

When Kieran and Joe reached the Greenways' house, Peg instantly sent her son off to bed and then told Kieran to sit down.

'I know it's getting late but I want to talk to you, lad,' she said, settling herself in the armchair.

'What about?'

'Our Evvie.'

Kieran gulped. 'What about her?'

'I know you love her, Kieran, and I approve, so does her da. You're a good, steady lad. Your Mam can be proud of *you*, at least,' she added, thinking of Mary's other sons. 'Nothing would please your mam more than to see you and our Evvie walking out, she's told me so.'

'I . . . I'm glad. I really do love her,' Kieran answered earnestly.

'Then do something about it. Oh, I know she can be a stubborn little madam at times, so you'll have to be firm with her.'

'That's easier said than done, Mrs Greenway,' replied Kieran, ruefully. 'How can I be "firm" with her when she won't even go out with me?'

'You've got to keep asking and asking. Wear her down. Persevere, lad. I know she's fond of you, and Bill and I will do our bit to help.

She'll see sense,' Seeing the look on Kieran's face, Peg added kindly, 'You're only young, the pair of you. Take my word, she'll come around.'

'Does Evvie . . . is she really fond of me?' Hope was surging through him.

'Yes, she is. I'm her mam and I *know* these things. She won't admit it and she'll carry on being pig-headed, but she can't keep that up forever.' Peg spoke firmly but she was thinking of Ben Steadman. Evvie had kept *that* up and kept it secret.

'You take my advice, Kieran. Never give up. You've got the patience and the strength. You're a fine-looking lad, you're honest, hard-working, loyal, generous. What more could any girl want?'

Kieran got to his feet, more hopeful, more confident and now somehow stronger. Evvie did care for him. Her mam was bound to be right on that. He'd persevere. He'd never give up no matter how long it took. Now he was determined that someday he'd marry Evvie Greenway.

The following day after work, as the twins were walking home from the tram stop on the corner of Scotland Road and Wright Street, Kate decided to broach the subject of her conversation with Doris.

'I'm sick of that place, the dust, the smells. Wouldn't it be great to work in a shop?'

'Yes, and when the weather gets warmer the smells get worse.'

Kate shrugged. 'Are you still going to go on seeing Ben after what Mam said?'

Evvie bit her lip. 'Yes, it's not that easy to give him up. You should know how I feel, Kate.'

'What we both need is something to take our minds off things.'

'Like what?' Evvie asked without much interest.

'I'm going to a meeting in Crane's Theatre in two weeks with Doris Kay.'

Evvie pulled a wry face. 'A meeting? What kind of a meeting? It doesn't sound much fun.'

'It's not meant to be fun. It's deadly serious. It's about women's rights.'

'Women's rights!'

'Yes. Oh, come with me? Doris says we'll understand that things can change. That men won't be able to control our lives for much longer.'

Evvie was thinking more of Kate than herself. Maybe if Kate

had something else to think about it would be easier to forget Frank Lynch.

'Come on, Evvie, give it a try, please?'

It didn't sound very appealing, Evvie thought, but then it would be better than having to sit at home brooding, Kate over Frank Lynch and herself over Ben Steadman.

Mam watched Kate all the time and was always trying to get her to eat and smile. Mam, Da and even Joe went to great lengths to try to cheer her up, Joe only doing so at Mam's instigation, and, she suspected, as a result of bribery.

'All right, it's better than sitting at home, I suppose.'

'I'm not saying I'll join any society.'

'Neither am I. It's just to see what it's like – what they have to say.'

The day of the meeting arrived.

Peg was working her way through a pile of mending, wondering just how Joe managed to get such enormous holes in his socks, but was relieved that both girls had plans to go out.

'We're going into town to a meeting,' Kate informed her.

'A meeting? What meeting?'

'Oh, it's all about women and politics,' Kate replied vaguely, hoping Peg wouldn't pursue the issue more deeply.

'What do you want to go getting mixed up in things like that for?' Peg asked, concentrating more on threading her darning needle.

'We're not getting mixed up in anything, Mam. It's just a night out, a bit of a break. It'll be . . .' Kate searched for the right word, 'interesting.'

Peg had raised her eyes to the ceiling. Well, it was no worse than seeing the pair of them moping about. But if there was any nonsense out of them about 'Women's rights', she'd soon put a stop to it. It was a disgrace the way those ladies were carrying on. Having demonstrations and protest marches, saying terrible things about the Prime Minister. With their backgrounds and breeding they should know better. And these days they were filling the heads of good working-class girls with their nonsense too.

The hall was crowded to capacity and Evvie was surprised to see a lot of girls and women from her own class mingling quite freely with women who were real ladies. The ladies were distinguishable by their expensive clothes, in the height of fashion.

They were all wearing sashes and rosettes of purple, white and green.

'I've brought two of my friends, Miss Devonshire. This is Kate and this is Evvie,' Doris said, introducing Kate and Evvie to the well-dressed young woman who was sitting at a table by the door.

'That's wonderful, Doris. Kate, Evvie, you are very welcome here. We don't hold with segregation; we are all sisters united in a common cause. There's no need to feel ill at ease or daunted in any way. Here, let me give you these.'

As Dahlia Devonshire reached out to pin a rosette on her jacket, Evvie backed away.

'Oh, we haven't come to join, miss, we've just come along to . . . to see what it's all about.'

Dahlia Devonshire smiled. 'That's all right. We hope that after this evening you will join us, but have these anyway.'

Both Kate and Evvie submitted to having rosettes pinned on, then they followed Doris to some vacant seats.

Kate glanced surreptitiously at the girl sitting next to her. She wore a costume of dark blue corded velveteen, her reddish brown hair was covered by a large and expensive hat and her hands were encased in soft kid gloves. Kate looked down at her own work-roughened hands and felt very uncomfortable.

'Hello, I'm Cecile Chapman.'

The hazel eyes smiling into her own were full of warmth and Kate smiled back. 'I'm Kate, Kate Greenway, miss.'

'Oh, please call me Cecile.' She had caught sight of Evvie. 'Why, you're twins!'

'Yes, we've come with a friend.'

'Ah yes, Doris, isn't it?'

Kate was amazed. Didn't Doris feel out of place with all these ladies who seemed to know her so well?

There was no time for further conversation for the meeting was being called to order by a handsome but formidable-looking woman standing on the stage at the further end of the hall.

The speakers were introduced and both Kate and Evvie became engrossed as, one after another, girls and women took the stage to inform and urge their audience to a campaign of civil disobedience.

When at last it was over, Doris turned to the twins. 'Well, what did you think? Now do you understand?'

'I understand in one way, yet I don't in another,' Kate mused.

'What on earth do you mean by that?'

'I can see that things need to be changed, but I don't think they will be, not for a very long time.'

'Well, I don't approve of it at all. It's no use giving the likes of us the vote, we don't understand the first thing about politics and I don't want to. Women were meant to have children and that means having a home and looking after it and the children. Men are the breadwinners,' Evvie stated firmly.

'Oh, don't be so old-fashioned, Evvie Greenway! You know as well as I do that Mam and most of the women in the street go out to work, or have done.'

'That's because they *had* to, not because they *chose* to. They needed the money to keep the family out of the workhouse. Half of this lot here have never known what it's like to be hungry, cold and desperate to know where the rent is going to come from. Most of them here have never had to work and half of them have probably never even cooked a meal.'

Kate got impatient with her, something she rarely did.

'Didn't you understand anything? If women get the vote eventually we can change things for *all* women, the poor ones as well. How many families would be better off if the man didn't spend his wages in the flaming pub? They're *his* wages, he can do what he likes with them: drink them, gamble them or spend them on other women, and the wife has no say. She can't stop him. She can't stop him from belting her either. Look at poor Nelly O'Connor.'

'But how is getting the vote going to stop all that?'

'Women would have *rights*, Evvie. A whole lot of opportunities would be opened up for all women if they were seen as people in their own right and not appendages of their husbands.'

'Oh, it's all right for these posh women. They marry rich men so they don't lack for anything. They can afford to stay at home, in luxury, and with someone to do all the housework and look after the children. No wonder they want "rights". They're just bored with nothing to do all day. They want to be able to use those "rights" to occupy themselves.'

Kate was exasperated. 'Oh, I give up! You just can't see it, can you, Evvie?'

'No, I can't and I don't understand you, Kate.'

Kate had been thinking of Josie and Frank. It was painful but she had to admit that Frank had wronged both Josie and herself and yet it was both she and Josie who were suffering because of him. She'd heard that Josie wasn't happy and at first she'd thought 'serves her right' but after listening to these women tonight her attitude had begun to soften.

'Take you and Ben, Evvie. If Da finds out, he'll forbid you to even set foot in Steadman's ever again and you'll have no choice but to obey him.'

'That's different, Kate. That's all to do with religion and you know it.'

'You're missing the point. What about . . . me and Josie and . . . *him*. He's the one who did wrong, but it's Josie and me who have to suffer. Men seem to get away with murder.'

'I don't think he got away with anything. He had to marry her.' Evvie had had enough. 'Oh, Kate, let's go home. All this arguing is giving me a headache. Don't let's fall out over all this women's rights business.'

'I'm not falling out with you, I just *can't* understand you, Evvie, that's all. I— Well, I think I might join.'

'Kate, you're mad!'

'No, Evvie, she's not,' Doris chipped in. 'We *have* to get a vote, a say, in how *our* lives are controlled.'

'Mam is going to be livid and so is Da. If you want to join, Kate, it's your own affair. I won't tell Mam but just keep me out of it.' Evvie was upset. It was the first time in their lives that they'd disagreed so strongly.

There appeared to be some confusion at the entrance to the hall and the women at the front were remonstrating with people outside.

'What's the matter now? Oh, we'll just have to push our way through the crowd,' Evvie said irritably.

They did manage to get to the doors only to find their way barred by a small crowd of men and boys who were jeering and shouting.

Evvie glared at Doris. 'Oh, I've had enough of this. I must have been mad to let you talk me into this. Look at that lot. Half of them are drunk and the rest are just hooligans.'

Two ladies were calling for the crowd to disperse and a third had managed to push her way through and was talking to a policeman, who was standing on the corner with his arms folded, just watching.

The abuse was getting worse.

'That flaming scuffer isn't going to do a bloody thing to help. We're going to have to manage by ourselves,' Doris yelled above the din.

As Evvie pushed and shoved her way through, giving as good as she got in the way of abuse, she thought grimly that being born and brought up in Silvester Street did have some advantages. They only understood abuse, did this lot. Those well-brought-up ladies with high ideals couldn't cope with men like this. But what else did they expect – setting themselves up as rebels and always going on about being strong and courageous? They'd started doing awful things like trying to set fire to the Prime Minister's house, for God's sake. Men would lose all respect for them if they carried on like that. She could see Doris ahead of her, lashing out at a youth in a greasy cap and dirty white muffler. She hoped Kate was behind her.

Kate had managed to get as far as School Lane using the same tactics as Doris and Evvie, but she'd been jostled and had lost her hat. She leaned against the sooty bricks of the wall and tried to catch her breath and gather her thoughts. If she walked down School Lane and cut across Manesty's Lane, she could get out on to Paradise Street, near to the tram stop. Evvie would have to make her own way home for she certainly wasn't going back to find her.

She had just turned into Manesty's Lane when she felt uneasy, and turning quickly she was certain she saw someone in the shadows. She walked on, hastening her steps. Again she heard the scuffling and turned.

'All right, come out here where I can see you,' she yelled.

To her horror three lads emerged from the shadows. They were all scruffy, well built and menacing.

'It's one of them suffrage women, lads. Look at 'er, all tarted up with the ribbons an' all.' The bigger of the three was within arms' reach now and Kate felt paralysed with fear. There was no one in sight and Paradise Street and safety seemed so far away. She'd never reach it.

'What's that word they always use, Dermot, la?'

'Lib— Liberated,' one of the others replied, stumbling over the half-remembered syllables.

'That's it. I suppose it means that yer want us to take liberties with yer.'

He leered at Kate and she turned her head away in disgust at the smell of beer on his breath.

'Look at 'er, all prim an' proper.'

Kate suddenly found her voice. 'You lay one hand on me an' I'll belt you an' I'll scream blue murder, too!'

'Oh, she's no lady. She speaks like us,' the one called Dermot laughed.

'And I can fight like you, too, lad!' Kate cried, and lashed out as hard as she could, catching the youth a hefty swipe across the face.

'Yer bleedin' little cow!' he bellowed.

As dirty hands reached out and grabbed her, Kate began to scream and fight, kicking and scratching.

'Shut 'er up, for God's sake!' one of them yelled and a hand was clamped over her mouth. She bit hard into a finger and had the satisfaction of hearing a yell and a curse. She was frantic for she was being dragged down to the cobbles and hands were tearing at her skirts. Her strength was beginning to give out and she knew she was no match for all of them. She intensified her screams.

A cloying blackness, heavy with the smell of sweat, tobacco and beer, was threatening to overwhelm her, when suddenly she heard running feet and another voice: a man's strong, authoritative voice. It was a few seconds before she realised that her attackers had fled. She raised herself up on one elbow, feeling dizzy, then struggled to pull down her skirt and petticoat, both of which seemed to be twisted up around her waist. Her shoulder hurt and she realised she must have hit the cobbles hard. Her nails were broken and bleeding and other small scrapes and scratches were beginning to smart.

'Here, let me help you. Are you badly hurt? Did they . . . ?'

A young man was looking down at her. She gasped and jerked back.

'Please, don't be afraid of me. I won't hurt you. I heard your screams and I saw them attacking you.'

Kate now saw the gun in his hand and uttered a cry of fear.

'I didn't intend to use it. It doesn't work, you see. It's not loaded, honestly.' He put it back in his pocket and reached down.

She took the outstretched hand and slowly got to her feet. 'Thanks.'

'Did they . . . hurt you? Shall I call a policeman?'

'No, no, I'm not hurt and they didn't . . . well, it was a good job you came.' She brushed down her skirt. 'Thanks again.'

'Oh, I'm Charles Wilson, by the way. And I'm glad to be of help.'

She noticed now that he was well dressed – nothing overly expensive, just good and sober, and he looked kind.

'I'm Kate, Kate Greenway.'

'Let me take you for a cup of tea – you've had a nasty shock – and then I'll see you safely home, if I may?'

Kate nodded. 'I'd love a cup of tea, but I'll be fine on my own. Getting home, I mean.'

'No, I won't hear of it. But let's find a café or something first.'

They sat in the Carter's Rest Café in Paradise Street, so named because it was most frequently patronised by carters on their way to and from the docks. It was also the only one open. Charles Wilson brought two teas to the scrubbed table.

'Here you are, Miss Greenway. Drink it up while it's hot.'

'Thanks. You don't need to call me Miss Greenway. Kate will do.'

'I see you are a suffragette.'

She realised that the rosette was still pinned to her jacket. 'Not yet, but I'm very interested. I went to a meeting just to see what it was all about. There was some trouble outside, a crowd, and I got separated from my sister. I hope she gets home in one piece.'

'I don't think she would be molested on a main road. Where do you live?'

'Silvester Street. It's not that far away.'

'I live in Litherland. I belong to a club of firearms enthusiasts. We meet once a month. I collect guns, old ones. That's why I had this.' He laid the pistol down on the table and she could see that it was old and rusty, something that hadn't been evident in the darkness of Manesty's Lane.

'Oh, I see.' Kate had almost finished her tea and was feeling better. He was quite good-looking, she noticed, with light brown hair and hazel eyes. She judged him to be about twenty.

'I must look a terrible sight,' she said, inspecting her crumpled clothes.

Charles smiled at her, thinking she looked far from terrible. She was beautiful, really beautiful. 'I don't think so. You are very . . . er, lovely, Kate Greenway.'

Kate blushed and started to get up. 'Well, thank you, for . . . for being there and for the tea.'

Charles got to his feet.

'Really, there's no need to see me home,' Kate insisted. 'It's not far to the tram stop, just across the road really.'

'I wouldn't dream of letting you go home alone.'

Kate managed a smile. 'I must look dirty and very untidy; you won't want to be seen with me.'

'Don't be ridiculous. You've had a very unpleasant shock. You can't go home on the tram. We'll get a hackney cab.'

'No, I can't appear in a hackney, Mam would have a fit.' She could well imagine what Peg would say if she arrived at the door in a cab with a strange young man and looking the way she did.

'Well, I can drop you off at the top of your road or somewhere nearby. I won't take no for an answer, Kate,' he said gently

Kate didn't argue. She still felt shaky and bruised. She didn't feel like having to suffer the stares and comments she knew her appearance would excite on the tram, so she nodded her acceptance. Besides, she instinctively knew Charles Wilson wouldn't harm her.

Chapter Eleven

Kate had joined the suffragettes and had attended every meeting and rally throughout the summer months. Charlie, whom she saw regularly, didn't agree with her views but had agreed to respect them and not inform her parents of the various demonstrations she attended, but he knew it would only be a matter of time before someone saw her. He thought she was just taken by a new and different idea and he looked on benignly because he loved her.

The wild October wind tugged at Evvie's shawl as she walked back from the corner shop with the starch she needed for her blouses and the 'Dolly Blue' bag that Mam added to the rinsing water and which she swore helped to make the whites look whiter. She ducked her head as she drew level with Steadman's shop, glad of the deepening dusk. She was forced to look up on hearing her name called aloud and saw Levi Steadman standing in the doorway.

'Evvie, can you spare me a couple of minutes of your time?'

She bit her lip but nodded, hoping Mam wasn't looking out of the window. With a heavy heart and growing apprehension she followed Ben's father into the room at the back of the shop. She had a good idea what was about to happen.

'Ben has gone into town,' Levi explained in reply to the quick, searching look she cast around the room.

'Oh, I see.'

'Sit down, Evvie.'

'No, if you don't mind . . . I can't stay long, Mr Steadman. Mam wants these things.'

'She is going to do the washing at this time of day?'

'No, she . . . she just wanted them in. What did you want to see me about?'

'You know what, child. Your mother and father, they don't know? They don't ask?'

She shook her head. 'Mam thinks it's all over. Da never knew.'

'Then don't upset either of them, Evvie. They don't approve and neither do I.' He sighed heavily. 'It's not because I don't like you, Evvie. You're a good girl, but you're a goy.'

'I know what that means.'

'Ben has talked to you about our faith?'

'Yes.'

'Then why do you both carry on?'

'Because . . . because . . . I love him.'

She followed his gaze to a sepia-tinted photograph of Ben's mother.

'I know about love, but there are some things that even love can't survive.'

She looked down at the faded carpet and wondered if he was going to tell Mam and Da.

She looked so miserable that Levi faltered. Oh, there had been cases of Jewish men and women marrying out of their faith, but like the Catholic faith, it was forbidden. 'Evvie, don't go on deceiving them or yourself.'

'Will you tell them?'

'No, not yet. I don't want to cause trouble, but Ben and I, we argue about it all the time. It won't work. It can't work. Your parents are good Catholics, I know that, and I'm an Orthodox Jew even if Ben isn't. Would you cut yourself off from your family and your Church? Would you ask Ben to do the same thing? He is all I have, Evvie.' His glance again rested on the smiling face of his dead wife.

She felt so guilty and confused and yet she knew he was right. She didn't know if Mam and Da would disown her but her Church would. And he was saying that the same thing would happen to Ben. She looked at him pleadingly.

'I . . . I only know that I love Ben.'

'Evvie, why make so much misery for yourself, for Ben, for everyone? I don't want you to be hurt. I look at you now and I see the tears in your eyes, but time will heal. Forget Ben.'

'No, I can't.'

He shook his head sadly. She was so young and young hearts healed quickly, but she would never believe that. The pain she was feeling now would be nothing to that she would have to bear from a family and a community who would almost certainly shun her. He knew Ben wouldn't suffer to the same extent, he also knew Ben wouldn't stop seeing her, so all he could do was to try to persuade her to end this disastrous liaison. He didn't want to use emotional blackmail but it was for her happiness in the long term.

'Please think carefully, Evvie, about all the people you will hurt and disappoint. Can you deliberately make so many people miserable?'

She couldn't stand any more. She burst into tears and ran from the room, through the shop, into the street and collided with Kate.

'Evvie, what's the matter? Mam sent me to look for you. What were you doing in there?'

Between sobs Evvie told her.

'Oh, Evvie! Wipe your eyes or Mam will know.'

'I can't help it. What am I going to say to her?'

'Oh, say you've got something in your eye or . . . or that Mrs Holden was peeling shallots to pickle and sell and the whole place reeked of them. Here, have my handkerchief. Do you think he'll tell?'

'I don't know. He said he didn't want to cause trouble, but he made it sound so terrible.'

Kate looked at her sister with sadness. There were thousands of Catholic boys in this city, and Evvie had to go and fall in love with Ben Steadman. 'Maybe . . . maybe you should think about it all,' she said gently. Evvie's love was as impossible as her own but at least Ben wasn't married and about to become a father.

'How can you say that to me, Kate? I love Ben.'

'I'm sorry, but I don't want you to get hurt.'

'That's what Ben's da said, but if I give Ben up it will be worse.'

'Oh, it's such a mess. Such a flaming mess. Don't start crying again, Evvie.'

'Then don't you turn against me.'

'I'm not. I won't, you know that. Let's go home before she comes looking for us both and then the fat will be in the fire.'

Evvie didn't tell Ben of her conversation with his father. The last thing they wanted was to force the issue and if she told Ben and he got angry with Levi, it might just make Levi forget about not wanting to cause an open rift with her mam and da. She had to put the whole episode firmly out of her mind. She *had* to, it was the only way to cope, but she was glad that winter was approaching and, with the darker evenings, she would be able to see more of Ben.

They had arranged to meet on the second Wednesday night in October, but she needed an excuse.

'Oh, please, Kate? There's no other way I can get out. If you say we're going out too, Mam won't be suspicious.'

Kate turned away from the small mirror on the bedroom wall and looked with concern at her sister. They were both in the process of getting ready to go out and freshly ironed blouses and skirts were draped carefully over the wooden clotheshorse in the corner of the room.

The little room held more in the way of luxuries these days, paid for out of their own pockets and bought second-hand. There was a single wardrobe and a chest of drawers that held all their clothes. On top of the chest was a jug and bowl set, decorated with a blue and white willow pattern. Alongside it was a small wooden box that held the few trinkets they possessed and their hairbrushes. On a small, flowered, china tray, chipped a little around the edges, were the hairpins not in use. Bright rag rugs were scattered on the floor and a blue and white cotton counterpane covered the bed. On top of the wardrobe reposed two hatboxes that had seen much better days, but had only cost two pence each. Their working clothes were neatly folded on a narrow wooden stool set under the window. It was more cramped than it had once been but neither of them minded that.

'You know what she said, Evvie, about the last time we went out.'

'Oh, that awful meeting!'

They could both remember the tongue-lashing they'd received after arriving home that April night. Hence the alibis Charlie now provided for Kate whenever she went to a suffragette meeting.

'Oh, please, Kate. The nights are darker; it won't be so hard. We always go to the music hall or the moving pictures more in the winter and you know I hardly saw Ben through the summer, it was just too risky. It was light until nearly half-past ten some nights.'

Kate took her blouse from the clotheshorse and put it on. She frowned, concentrating on fastening the rows of tiny buttons on the cuffs.

'Evvie, what are you going to do about Ben? It's a week now since you had that talk with his da and it's ten months since you started going out with Ben.'

Evvie fastened up the last curl and secured it with a hairpin. Her reflection stared back at her. The blue eyes mutinous, the chin raised determinedly. 'So? You've been seeing Charlie Wilson for five months and you keep telling everyone it's not serious.'

'Oh, that's different. I do like Charlie very much. He's kind and considerate and has such good manners and he is understanding about me belonging to the suffragettes, but I'm not head over heels in love with him. It's just a sort of . . . affection and I know he feels the same way about me.'

This wasn't strictly the truth, she thought. It was true on her part, but Charlie loved her – he told her so often – though he'd not once tried to overstep the bounds of propriety.

They usually met in town but he had come to the house a few times. They hadn't been successful visits for everyone had seemed ill at ease, except Joe, who wouldn't feel ill at ease anywhere, neither in Buckingham Palace nor a zoo, she'd remarked acidly to her mam after Charlie's last visit. They all knew that Charlie was a cut above them.

'For God's sake, the lad's an articled clerk. He'll be a solicitor one day. I work in a tannery, Tom slogs out a living in a stokehold and you two are factory girls. He's more than just a cut above us, he's way up on the social ladder,' Bill had once stated. On these visits Charlie himself had been quiet, sensing the uneasy atmosphere. At her remarks about Joe, Peg had shaken her head and seemed to be thinking of something else.

'You can't disapprove of Charlie, Mam. What is there to object to?'

'Did I say I objected to him, Kate?' Peg had demanded.

'No, but you don't look overjoyed about it.'

'Oh, I've other things on my mind, Kate. Besides, it's not serious, is it?'

'Of course not, Mam. I don't intend to . . . well, to be so trusting again.'

Peg had nodded and the subject had been dropped.

Kate realised now that she'd changed – grown up. She certainly wasn't the silly girl she'd been a year ago. She was more serious, quieter, more sceptical, although she knew Peg wouldn't agree with that. Mentally she shook herself out of her reverie and, seeing that Evvie was still looking obstinate, decided not to pursue the subject of just how serious her relationship with Ben was. 'So, where are you going tonight, Evvie?'

'Only for a sail to New Brighton. We'll have a bit of supper and then come back. At least no one knows us over the water.'

'What time will you be back? I'll have to meet you at the top of the street.'

'Oh, about ten.'

'That's too late. You know Mam insists we be in at half-past nine on working days. There'll be a row.'

Evvie pursed her lips. 'Oh, all right. A quarter past nine at the top of the street then.'

'Just make sure you're there. I'm not telling any more lies for you, Evvie.'

'Oh, don't be so miserable, Kate.'

'I'm not. Just don't be late.'

The chill of autumn was in the evening air but Evvie and Ben hardly noticed it as they stood on the ferry's upper deck for it had been three weeks since they had been alone together. It was worth sacrificing the warmth of the saloon downstairs for the privacy afforded by the open deck. A low mist hung over the oily grey surface of the river but the lights and the skeletal outline of the tower could be clearly seen against the dusty indigo of the sky.

'We'll just go for a walk along the promenade then have a drink before we come back to the ferry.'

Evvie rubbed her cheek against the rough tweed of Ben's jacket sleeve. 'Fine. I . . . I want to talk to you.'

He looked down at her upturned face and smiled. She was beautiful but she was also very sweet, generous, good – and oh, he could find a hundred other adjectives to describe her. He loved her. 'What about, Evvie?'

'Oh, not here, Ben.'

'Why not here? There will be lots more people around when we get off the boat.'

Something was troubling her, he could see it in her eyes. His heart plummeted. Had she found someone else? 'What's the matter, Evvie, is there someone else? I don't suppose I have any right to complain if there is, after all —'

'No, Ben, there's no one else, you know that,' she interrupted, placing the tips of her fingers on his lips. 'You know, Ben, that I —'

He gently kissed the palm of her hand. 'I love you, Evvie. I've loved you for months.'

'I know. Oh, Ben, I love you so much that sometimes it hurts, but —'

'Evvie, don't say it, please. I know what you're thinking, but I *won't*, I *can't* let you go.' He pushed the memories of the frequent arguments with his father from his mind. He didn't want to hurt Levi but he had to realise that he was a man now. He wouldn't need Levi's permission to do anything and he'd told him so.

'Ben, I don't know how long it will be before Mam and Da find out. We've been lucky so far. Do you think your da will say something to Mam?'

'No. It's not his way of doing things. He won't deliberately cause arguments or trouble. He's a pacifist. He came from Estonia when he was ten. All his family had been murdered, except his zayde – his grandfather. They came to Liverpool together on a cargo ship. Zayde started a "safety box" scheme with the sailors at the docks. He rented them a box for their money and valuables. When they came ashore they got drunk and were always robbed blind by the crimps and prostitutes. He kept their money safe and word quickly got around that he was to be trusted. He bought the shop the year before he died.'

Over the years it had been an often repeated story and he remembered his mother telling it to him. He looked wistfully across the darkened river. She'd had a gift for storytelling.

'No, Dad won't tell them but he doesn't approve. He's threatened me with lectures by Rabbi Neiland and with Kaddishim.'

'What's that?'

'It really means prayers for the dead – mourning prayers.'

'I don't understand.'

'It also means that he will consider me dead. He'll cut me off, throw me out. To him I will be dead.'

'No! Oh no, Ben!'

'It's all right, Evvie, he won't do it. It's just a threat. We've been careful, Evvie and if we go on being careful they won't find out. The winter is before us – short days, long nights.'

Evvie was trying not to be swayed by his words. It was inevitable that someone must see them soon and she dreaded to think what would happen then.

'Evvie, I love you and that's all that matters. Don't think about the future, think about now.'

Evvie knew she'd lost the battle with her head; her heart had won again. 'Oh, Ben, hold me, hold me tightly,' she whispered.

'I love you, Evvie, and I always will,' Ben murmured before pressing his lips hungrily against hers.

In the darkened lee of the squat funnel that had hidden him from view, Kieran Ryan watched them. He felt sick. He shouldn't have followed her, then he would never have known for certain that it was Ben Steadman that Evvie was seeing.

He balled his fists in the pockets of his jacket. All summer she'd refused every offer he'd made to take her out. Each time her refusal, delivered in an offhand yet not deliberately cruel manner had hurt him deeply. He wished he had a more forceful personality, that he could use fancy words to flatter and persuade her, but it was no use. He wasn't that kind of a person. Eventually he'd guessed there was someone else. There had to be, for she did go out and she'd never looked lovelier. She seemed to have bloomed, to be filled with happiness, a love of life. It shone in her eyes and he saw it in all her movements. Now he knew it wasn't just a love of life, it was a love of Ben Steadman.

Jealousy twisted and knotted his guts. He should have known that it would be Steadman even though there had been nothing in their everyday behaviour to arouse suspicion. They stopped and passed the time of day when they saw each other on the street or in the shops, but he hadn't seen them talking together for more than a few minutes at a time and no one had mentioned a word about them – obviously because no one knew. Oh, they'd been clever; clever and underhand. Kate must know, but she wouldn't tell on Evvie, they were too close for such a betrayal. But why Ben Steadman?

Surely Evvie must realise that she could never marry him? Kieran had not trusted Steadman since the night of Maggie's party and now his hatred deepened. There could be only one thing Ben wanted of her. So far he obviously hadn't satisfied his lust, for that's all it was. It wasn't love. He'd marry a Jewish girl eventually – she'd probably already have been picked out – but in the meantime he was just amusing himself. Obviously Evvie had had the sense not to degrade herself so far, but for how much longer? He was holding her so closely that there wasn't an inch between them.

What should he do now? Kieran asked himself. He had to protect her from both herself and Ben Steadman. He could tell Mr Greenway or Mr Steadman or both. That would bring the plaster falling down around their heads – aye, and he'd enjoy seeing the look on Ben's face, too. But what would Evvie think of him then? Would she turn on him? Would she say she hated him and never wanted to see or speak to him again? He couldn't bear that. He didn't want to risk any chance he may have of winning her affection, no matter how slight that prospect looked right now.

Maybe if he just confronted her, he could perhaps talk some sense into her. Maybe she wouldn't be so ready in future to come sneaking out to meet Ben and maybe in time she'd lose interest in him altogether. It was better to confront her first, he decided.

He was cold and even more depressed by the time he got back to the Pier Head. He'd decided not to follow them once they reached New Brighton. It was pointless and he couldn't bear to watch them together for any longer. So, he'd stood for hours and searched the faces of the passengers as they'd left the boats. He'd lost count of the ferries that had arrived and departed, but he was certain he hadn't missed her.

He spotted Ben Steadman first and drew back into the shadow afforded by the iron columns supporting the overhead railway that crossed the section of road at the top of the covered gangways that led up from the landing stage where the ferry had disgorged its passengers. He watched them kiss briefly and then they parted company. Steadman walking away towards the Albert Dock and Evvie across to where the trams stood waiting.

He quickly caught her up. 'Evvie! Evvie, wait!'

Evvie's heart dropped like a stone as she turned and saw him. 'Oh God, don't let him have seen us,' she muttered. She'd have to think of something to say and quickly. 'Kieran, where have you been? You look half frozen.' It was the truth; he looked perished with cold.

'Never mind about me, Evvie. I . . . I want to talk to you.'

She ducked her head so he wouldn't see the panic and fear in her eyes. The last thing she wanted was a shouting match aboard a tram.

'All right, let's walk for a bit then.' She quickened her steps until she'd crossed the Pier Head and was in the shadow of the Liver Buildings, on top of which the Liver Birds stared, unseeing, across river and city.

She was racking her brains furiously. 'I . . . I went over to see a girl I work with. You don't know her, she lives over there.' She jerked her head in the direction of the river. She knew it wasn't much of an excuse.

'You don't know anyone who lives in New Brighton, Evvie. It's too posh. Birkenhead, maybe, but not New Brighton.'

'I do. Not everyone over there is wealthy,' she snapped. That had been a mistake. She thought frantically. She should have said her friend was in service over there. But that wouldn't have rung true either. He'd only want to know how she knew someone who lived and worked over the water.

Kieran caught her arm. 'Evvie, don't tell me any more lies. I know. I saw you with him, with Ben Steadman.'

She could think of nothing to say at first, she just stood staring up at him.

'Well, can't you say anything, Evvie?'

'Yes, I can. How dare you follow me, Kieran Ryan? How could you be so . . . so underhand?'

'Me, underhand! How long have you been sneaking off to see him?'

'That's none of your business.'

'It is, Evvie. Can't you see he's only using you? He only wants one thing from you. He knows he'll never marry you. He can't.'

'Stop it, Kieran. Stop it. You're jealous, you can't think straight because your mind is so twisted. I love him and he loves me and that's all that matters.'

'No, Evvie, it's not! He doesn't love you, he only says he does. He knows your da and the lads would kill him if he came round asking them if he could marry you – that's if Levi didn't kill him first. He knows that's something he'll never have to do and so he's stringing you along.' Kieran's pent-up anger, love and jealousy obliterated his shyness and he plunged on, all his reticence forgotten. 'I love you, Evvie. I've loved you for ages. I'll always love you and I won't be afraid to go and ask your da if he'll let you marry me.'

'Stop it, Kieran! Stop it!' Evvie cried, not caring if anyone heard her.

'Then give him up, Evvie, please.'

'I can't. I won't. Oh, Kieran, if you love me you must understand how I feel about Ben.'

'I can't understand and I can't stand by and let him make a fool of you the way Frank Lynch made a fool of our Josie – aye, and your Kate.'

She ignored the comparison. 'Oh please, Kieran, don't tell on me,' she implored.

He remained silent, the force of his emotional outburst spent. It was as though all the words he had wanted to say had dried up and been blown from his mind like dust and dead leaves. He couldn't speak.

'Please, Kieran. You know I've always been . . . fond of you. Please do this for me? Please don't make me miserable, don't hurt me by telling on me. He does love me, he isn't using me, he's never even tried to do anything more than kiss me.'

He found his voice. 'Stop it, Evvie. I don't want to hear any more.' The words were shouted aloud and his voice was harsh with pain.

'You won't tell?' she pleaded, reaching out to take his hand.

Kieran backed away. He wasn't sure what he believed any longer; he didn't know what he would do.

'Kieran?'

'I don't know, Evvie. I just don't know,' he cried, before he turned and ran towards the line of waiting trams.

Evvie watched him go with tears in her eyes. What would he do now? He was so full of envy and yet she knew he did love her. Would he keep quiet because of that love? Oh, it wasn't fair that she should even have asked him to. She'd hurt him – she'd seen the pain in his eyes and heard it in his voice – but she'd never meant to. She was fond of him in the way she was fond of her brothers. He was kind, gentle and thoughtful but she didn't love him. She walked slowly in the direction he'd taken, her heart full of misery and gnawing fear. Only time would tell what Kieran decided to do.

Kate and Charles were waiting at the top of the Silvester Street. Charles looked annoyed but Evvie was past caring.

Kate was concerned. 'Evvie, what's the matter? Kieran Ryan's just got off a tram and nearly knocked us flat he was in such a tearing hurry, and he didn't apologise either. He looked terribly upset.' Kate had a suspicion that Kieran had seen Evvie and Ben, and the look in her sister's eyes confirmed it.

'He was probably drunk,' Charles said tersely.

'Not Kieran. His brothers, yes, but not him,' Kate replied.

'Did he say anything?' Evvie asked, her voice shrill with fear,

'No. Didn't Kate just say he didn't even apologise?' He was fed up waiting around in the cold and he didn't approve of Evvie's relationship with Ben Steadman. It was futile. It annoyed him that it encroached on his time with Kate, which was short enough as it was. Nor did he like Kate becoming embroiled in an affair that was bound to end in disaster and tears.

'Charlie, we'd better go now. Mam will go mad if we're late. Thanks for a lovely evening. Will I see you on Saturday?'

'Of course. We'll go to the Empire if you like.' His petulance disappeared as Kate smiled and kissed him on the cheek.

'That would be great. Good night, Charlie.'

He tipped his hat respectfully, 'Good night, Kate. Good night, Evvie.'

Evvie's reply was barely audible.

'You look as though you've seen a ghost. He saw you, didn't he? Kieran, I mean.' Kate had linked her arm through Evvie's.

'He followed me, Kate. He followed me. I can't believe he'd do such a thing.'

'Oh, Evvie, he's mad about you, you know that. He's always asking you out. He's been hanging around like a moonstruck calf for nearly a year but there's none so blind as those who don't want to see, as Mam would say.'

'Kate, I've never encouraged him and I never thought he'd do something like this.'

'He obviously realised you were seeing someone. What did he say?'

'Oh, a lot of nonsense about Ben just using me. I begged him not to tell anyone he'd seen us together. I told him I loved Ben and that he loved me. I pleaded with him, Kate.' Evvie was near to tears again.

'And he didn't say yes or no?'

'He just ran off.'

Kate looked anxious. 'Then we'll have to wait and see. You'd better warn Ben, though, in case he does decide to tell someone.'

'How? If Kieran sees me near Ben I don't know what he'd do.'

'I'll have to tell him then. I'll make some excuse to go and see him and I'll warn him. He does realise that I know?'

Evvie nodded. 'Oh, Kate, thanks. I'll just have to pray that Kieran won't betray us, that's all.'

Kate looked at her sadly. 'What good will praying do, Evvie? How can you ask Jesus Christ to help you go on seeing someone who doesn't believe in Him? Oh, I'm not criticising – I know how you feel about Ben – but I don't think prayers will help much. They'd be pretty pointless. None of us round here have managed our lives very well so far, have we? Mam and Da will kill you if they find out about Ben —'

'Josie's made a real mess of her life,' Evvie interrupted.

'That's her own fault. Then there's me and Charlie.'

'What about you and Charlie? I thought everything was fine.'

'It is, but he keeps on at me about meeting his parents.'

'Don't you want to?'

'I don't know, Evvie. Sometimes I think I do and then other times, well, I think they'll take an instant dislike to me.'

Evvie looked amazed. 'Why?'

'Because of the way I speak and where we live, what Da does and what I do for a job. Charlie's more than a cut above me, Evvie. You know how awkward everyone is when he comes here, but it'll be ten times worse for me at his house.'

'You shouldn't think like that, Kate. Charlie doesn't or he wouldn't still be walking out with you. Go and see them.'

'Oh, I don't know. I don't even know if . . . well, if I love Charlie enough to marry him – that's if he is intending to ask at all.'

'You still love Frank Lynch, don't you?'

'I don't give two hoots for Frank Lynch.'

'You do, I know you too well, Kate. You're my twin sister, for heaven's sake. No one knows you better. You do love him.'

'Well, there's nothing I can do about it, is there, Evvie? He's stuck with Josie and the baby, so shut up about him, please. I'm trying to forget him entirely.'

'I'm sorry, I didn't mean to upset you.'

Kate sighed. 'Oh, I know, Evvie.'

Chapter Twelve

Hail, mingled with sleet driven by a bitterly cold November wind, rattled against the windows as Josie watched the fingers of the clock on the mantel move slowly, very slowly, towards a quarter past ten. She glanced across at her mother-in-law with pent up annoyance. Even though Frank took little notice of what she had to say, he would usually listen to his mother.

Flo sat in an upright, ladder-back chair by the range, her back ramrod stiff, her hands busy with her knitting. She hardly ever smiled, at least not these days. Josie assumed her mother-in-law had once been young and cheerful, but now she frowned constantly and her voice was always sharp. Flo had resented and disliked her from the first day she'd met her. There had been no attempt to welcome the new Mrs Lynch and as the months progressed, Flo's attitude had hardly changed at all. Except that over these last weeks she'd turned on Frank for showing her up in front of the neighbours just when she'd thought that the gossip was dying down.

Josie glanced at the clock whose tinny ticking was the only sound in the room, apart from Flo's knitting needles. He was obviously going to come in drunk again. Those couple of half-pints he had on his way home had gradually become pints, then four or five, and then six or seven. She shifted awkwardly in the chair, trying to adjust the cushion at her back, her own knitting abandoned, lying on the bulge that was her stomach. She wasn't much good at it anyway. There seemed to be too many holes and dropped stitches and she was always having to ask Flo to help, which annoyed them both.

She'd be glad when it was all over, for she felt ugly, bloated and utterly miserable. Oh, how long ago it seemed since that day in April when she'd walked up the aisle, knowing she looked beautiful. 'Pctite' Maggie had called her. All her hopes had been dashed for Frank had made it clear that he didn't love her. And that had been when she'd at least had a small claim to being attractive, if not beautiful. These days he seemed unable even to bear the sight of her, which was why, as the weeks passed, his sojourn in the pub lasted longer and longer. When she thought about things deeply, which she tried hard not to do, she felt hopelessly trapped.

She didn't want this baby. She'd only voiced this dreadful thought once to her mam, and Mary Ryan had been appalled and horrified.

'Don't ever let me hear you say such a thing again, Josie! Not to want your own baby is sinful . . . it's wicked. You should be down on your knees thanking God for the new life that's growing inside you.'

She'd hung her head and not replied, for what could she say? That Frank didn't love her? That Flo didn't like her and made it abundantly clear in a hundred ways every single day? That she was eighteen and her life was over? That she was tied for ever to a man who despised her and that she'd be a skivvy for the rest of her days? There was nothing for her to look forward to, no love, no happiness, no fun. No, she dare not say anything more to her mam; she'd never understand. Mam hadn't had much out of life herself and her attitude was that you had to make the best of things and thank God for all blessings, no matter how small.

Josie occasionally saw Maggie, Evvie and, more rarely, Kate. She didn't belong to their circle any more. They were all free spirits and how she envied them. Once she'd seen Kate on the arm of a young man who didn't live in the neighbourhood. That had been obvious from his clothes and the fact that he wore a hat, not a cap. All her former friends looked so young, so carefree and so slender. She'd always thought of Maggie as plain, but no longer. She was always smartly dressed and in the latest fashion, and was so full of confidence. She knew Frank often saw her brother Kieran in the pub, and as unlikely a pair of friends you'd ever see. She knew why Kieran often joined Frank: they were drowning their sorrows; Kieran because he loved Evvie, who wouldn't give him a second glance, and Frank because he loved Kate. That was about all they had in common, but the knowledge just served to hurt her even more.

The sound of the key turning in the lock of the front door interrupted her brooding and she looked across at Flo, who sighed and got to her feet.

'I'll get his meal, though it'll be dried up. It's a shocking waste of good food.' Flo took the two plates, between which the meal was sandwiched, from the top of the pan of simmering water that had been keeping it warm. She looked without much pleasure at the now dried-up potatoes and mince that had earlier constituted an appetising shepherd's pie.

'I don't want me tea!' Frank announced from the doorway, swaying slightly.

'I'm not throwing more good food away, Frank Lynch. You'll eat it and like it,' Flo said grimly, slamming the plate down on the table.

Frank became belligerent. 'It looks like a plate of mud. Bloody filthy mud.'

'Well, if you came home at a decent time it wouldn't look so awful. Meat is too expensive to waste and so is your mam's time and effort making it,' Josie snapped.

Frank was trying not to look at her. He hated her. She sat there like a huge, fat rabbit. Yes, that's what she reminded him of with those soppy big eyes, brown hair and that ugly brown dress. And she was always whinging and whining. It was all her fault that he couldn't face the future without a drink in his hand. It was the thought of being tied to her for ever that drove him to the pub every night. He hated coming home now. There was nothing to come home for; even his mam had turned against him. Whenever he saw his da there was an argument, and as for Lizzie, his married sister, and young Dotty, he hated them both but particularly Dotty.

'I said, if you came home at a decent —'

'I bloody heard what you said, Josie,' he interrupted. 'Stop bloody nagging.'

With an effort Josie got to her feet for, unusually, Flo hadn't attempted to reprimand him for swearing. 'Don't you swear at me, Frank Lynch. I won't stand for it!'

'I'll say what I like in my own house. It's *my* home. *I've* always lived here, *you* haven't. You're like a leech, do you know that? Living off me, off Mam. Sitting on your backside all day like lady bloody muck, being waited on; getting decent food, not that pigswill I have to eat.'

Josie's cheeks burned with anger. 'It's not my fault I can't work. It's not my fault I'm having a baby, it's yours. And I hate living here. I hate having to put up with her glaring at me all day. You all hate me. That Dotty roots through my things and your Lizzie treats me like dirt.'

'Who was it who came knocking on the door, offering herself like a common tart? You threw yourself at me, what was I supposed to do?' Frank yelled.

'I loved you. I loved you then. I must have been mad, but I did,' Josie sobbed, unable to hold back the tears any longer. She could feel Flo's eyes boring into her back.

'Oh, shurrup. That's all you ever do, bloody whinge and whine. You've got a decent home here, better than that pigsty you came from in Silvester Street.'

Josie's nerves snapped and she lunged at him, raking his cheek with her nails. 'I hate you! I bloody well hate you!' she screamed.

Frank roared like a wounded bull. 'You bitch! You bloody little bitch!' He raised his arm, but Flo caught it and shoved him back against the wall.

'Oh no you don't, meladdo! I don't think much of her and I don't like what she's doing to you, but you don't raise your hand to any woman in this house. Get up to bed and sleep it off before your da comes in, because if he knows you're drunk again, he'll throw you out. He's had enough and so have I. Who do you think keeps her? You booze most of your wages away, so your da has to keep you both.'

Her outburst silenced Frank, who made his way unsteadily into the hall.

Flo turned to Josie, who was sobbing noisily. 'This is all your fault. There used to be none of this drinking and swearing and shouting. He hardly touched the drink before he got mixed up with you. This was a peaceful house, a happy respectable house, until you brought shame on us all.'

Josie had snatched her shawl from behind the door. 'I'm going home to me mam. I won't stay here, I won't. I don't care what anyone says, not even Father Foreshaw!' Suddenly a pain tore through her and she gasped and clung to the back of a chair. 'Oh God, I think I've started.'

'Are you sure?'

'Yes. Oh, the pain!'

The anger left Flo's eyes to be replaced with concern. 'You'd better get to bed. I'll come up with you. He's going to have to sleep it off down here – that's if Bert doesn't pitch him out into the street.'

'I'm going home!' Josie cried hysterically.

'Don't be so stupid, Josie! You can't go home now.'

The fierce cramp had caused Josie to slump forward on to the chair. 'I want to go home. I want me mam,' she sobbed.

'You'll be a mam yourself before this night's over. So pull yourself together, girl, and get up those stairs.' Flo got her to her feet and pushed her forcibly from the room, and, still sobbing, Josie half walked, half crawled up the stairs.

Josie's son was born just after one o'clock the following morning and as the midwife placed the little bundle in her arms, she felt the pain and exhaustion fall away. It was replaced by an overwhelming surge of love and pride. She didn't need Frank any more. This tiny scrap of humanity belonged to her and he would love her, even if no one else did.

'What are you going to call him, Josie?'

She looked up at her mother-in-law and was amazed to see the softness in her eyes. 'Matthew Albert after me da and Mr Lynch.'

A ghost of a smile hovered around Flo's lips. 'Can I hold him?'

Josie was too tired to carry on the feud. She passed the baby to his grandmother and was astonished to see Flo smiling and stroking the tiny cheek with a finger. From somewhere far away she heard the voices of the midwife, Bert and Dotty but she couldn't hear what they were saying, nor did she care, she thought as sleep overtook her.

On the following Saturday, as Kate got off the tram, she almost collided with Maggie, also alighting. She hadn't seen her on the journey, she must have been on the top deck, Kate surmised.

'What's up with you, Maggie?' Kate asked. 'You've got a face like thunder.'

'And so would you have if you'd had to put up with what I've just been through. A fortnight! A whole flaming fortnight I'd spent on that flaming toile, as well as my other work, and Mrs flaming Sidgewick says, "It's not right. Take it apart and start again, Miss McGee."'

'What's a toile?' Kate asked.

'It's a sort of dress pattern made out of muslin. You use it for fittings before the proper material is cut out. There was nothing wrong with it. She just hates me. She can't stand it because she knows I've got talent and more style in my little finger than she'll ever have. And as it's getting near to Christmas we've all been working like mad, staying late, too, with no extra pay. That's why I didn't finish at lunch time today.'

'Calm down, Maggie. Can't you just take no notice?'

'I can't, and her days of having a go at me with her nasty remarks are over. I told her what to do with her toile, and her flaming job as well.'

'Oh, Maggie! You didn't?' Kate cried.

'I did.'

Kate stared at Maggie incredulously. Everyone had to put up with moaning overseers and snotty blockermen, as foremen were known because of the bowler hats they wore. Maggie must be mad to have chucked up a fine apprenticeship at a posh place like Sloan's. 'What's your mam going to say?'

'I don't know yet, do I?'

'She's not going to be very happy, Maggie.'

'I don't care. I've got plans.'

'Well, I'll leave you to it. I've got other things on my mind.'

Maggie shrugged. She too had important matters to think about, one of which was to convince her mam that she hadn't made the greatest mistake of her life.

Hetty looked up from the skirt she was pinning. 'Maggie, what are you doing home? I thought you were going to be at work until six o'clock?'

'Mam, put that away. I know you're in a rush to finish it, but I want to talk to you. I'll put the kettle on.'

Hetty's forehead creased in a frown but she began to fold the material. Oh please God, don't let Maggie have got the sack, she prayed silently, following her daughter into the kitchen.

Maggie had hung her coat up and placed her hat on the dresser. She was always very careful with her clothes; she knew just how much work went into making them.

'What have you done?'

'I've left.'

Hetty sat down suddenly. 'You've done WHAT? Are you mad?'

'No, Mam. I just couldn't take any more from that woman. She's picked on me ever since I started there. She's made my life a misery for four years. I'd finished the toile. I'd done it exactly as I'd been taught, as she and you had shown me, and she said, "Take it apart and start again, Miss McGee." Mam, that was two weeks' work and there wasn't a thing wrong with it. It was perfect.'

'Maggie, oh, Maggie, what am I going to do with you? Why didn't you say something to me? I would have gone and spoken to her. Well, to someone anyway.'

'They wouldn't have listened to you, Mam, and you know it. They'd have looked down their noses and backed her up.' Maggie passed her mother a cup of tea.

Hetty took a sip of the scalding liquid. 'Oh Lord! What will you do now?'

'I've got it all worked out, Mam. I've been thinking about it for months. I just needed a bit of a shove, a reason to start, and this is it.'

'Start what, in the name of heaven?'

'My own business. You said yourself I did a grand job on Josie's wedding dress and my own dress. I want to design and make wedding dresses and bridesmaids' dresses.'

Hetty shook her head. 'Maggie, there's a big difference between dressmaking and making special dresses like that. They have to be perfect in every detail and stitch. It's not easy and you don't have the experience or, more to the point, the customers.'

'And I'm never going to get the experience at Sloan's, not for years and years, and I know I *can* do it, Mam, and you'll help me. I'll get customers. I'll advertise.'

'Maggie, you're not even eighteen years old until next month. For something as important as a wedding dress, your customers would want you to be older, so they feel confident you have the experience. What I am going to tell your da I don't know – giving up an apprenticeship like that for all these . . . daydreams.'

'It's not a daydream, Mam. I can do it.'

'Well, you'd better do a good job at convincing your da for you haven't even convinced me yet.'

Maggie held her hands towards the fire in the range. 'Look, I'll make some sample dresses out of cheap material – they won't cost much – then I'll have something to show my prospective customers. They can touch and examine, even try it on if they want to, and I'll draw other designs in a book. Word of mouth is the best form of advertising, you always say, but I'll put a piece in a newspaper.'

Hetty shook her head. Maggie had it all worked out in her head, but would it work in practice? 'You can't make a living just doing wedding dresses. You won't have one of those to make every week or so.'

'But I'll do the bridesmaid dresses as well.' Maggie sensed a softening, a faint sign of enthusiasm in her mother. 'I'll be able to help you with your work, too, Mam. That should give you more time. Look at you – you have enough to do for Christmas without rushing, staying up half the night, finishing dress orders for Christmas. I'll make sure all you have to worry about are the household chores.'

Hetty reflected on this. It would be nice to have a bit of help, especially at the busy times. 'Well, you'll have to talk to your da, Maggie. He's the one who is going to have to support you until you start earning.'

'Oh, I'll convince him, and it won't be long before I start to make money,' Maggie replied confidently.

Davie was calling on his way home from work as he did a couple of times a week, and Maggie was glad of that. He was usually full of ideas and he had ambitions of his own. He wanted his own garage but needed capital. He would require premises in a good location, he'd told her, and to buy at least two cars as demonstration models. The commission on the sale of cars was very good, but he'd need to invest anything he earned buying more cars and it would all cost a lot of money to set up.

His father had told him he was mad, that he'd never get his hands on money like that, but Davie ignored him. Cars and a garage of his own were things he cared passionately about. It was a dream that nothing could make him abandon.

'I'll show him, Maggie,' he'd said. 'I'll show everyone. I'm not going to be polishing cars and rattling off the sales patter all my life, earning money for someone else to spend. It's going to be my money and I'm going to have all the things my governor's got. Then we'll see who's mad.'

He was saving hard and was learning everything he could about the cars he helped to sell, and he was keeping his eye open for suitable premises, just in case he had a stroke of good fortune. It was his enthusiasm and ideas that had fired Maggie's own imagination.

Fortunately this evening he arrived a full half-hour before her da was due in.

'I had an early finish tonight. The governor was feeling generous; he's out to some big do at the Exchange Hotel. By, he certainly lives the life of Riley.'

'I've left Sloan's,' she announced bluntly. 'I want you to help me talk to Da.'

He wasn't surprised. As far as he could see Maggie would never make her fortune in the workrooms at Sloan's and she was very clever with materials and such; he'd never known anyone like her. She was also spoiled, and had a fiery temper, particularly when she was thwarted, but she had a determination that matched his own.

'I'd just about had enough of Ma Sidgewick, the old witch.'

'Look, let's go for a bit of a walk, let your da have his tea in peace. Tell your mam to say you're out with me. She needn't say anything about you leaving.'

Maggie nodded and went to inform Hetty. Davie would have plenty of ideas to convince her da. He hadn't thrown up his hands in horror and told her she'd done the wrong thing. He was practical and ambitious, both traits she admired in him. She was also learning that he could be manipulated.

When they returned, their cheeks rosy from the cold wind, Alf had finished his meal and was reading the *Echo*. Hetty gave them a quick smile.

'I could certainly make short work of a piece of that pie, Mrs McGee,' Davie said, his eyes fixed on the remaining half of an apple pie Hetty was about to place in the food press.

'Haven't you had any tea, lad?' Alf asked.

'Not yet.'

'Maggie, what's the matter with you? Haven't you even let the lad go home for his tea? He must be starving. Where's your manners?'

'It's not her fault, Mr McGee. I was the one who suggested we go for a walk. I wanted to talk to her.'

'It *was* my fault, Da, and it was me who wanted to talk to him.'

'Oh, aye?' Alf lowered his paper. They were up to something, the pair of them. He could see it on their faces.

'Da, I've got a plan,' Maggie began.

'This is going to cost me money, Hetty, I know it.' Alf smiled at his wife and was surprised to see she looked serious, concerned even.

'She's gone and left Sloan's, Alf. But before you go off the deep end, just listen to what she has in mind.'

Alf bit back the retort that had sprung to his lips. 'Well? It had better be good, Maggie.'

'I want to start up on my own, Da. I can do it. Everyone admired poor Josie's wedding dress so that's what I want to do. I'll specialise,' Davie had told her to say that, it sounded impressive, 'in wedding and bridesmaids' dresses. I'll advertise at first. I'm going to make some sample dresses and do a portfolio,' another of Davie's words, 'of designs.'

'She could really make a go of it, Mr McGee. She's got great ideas and she'll do well. We've talked about it. She could have her own workrooms and shop – in time, of course.'

'And I could include hats and headdresses and even shoes and gloves. Everything could be bought in one place, instead of having to trail around all the shops looking for hats and shoes and things that all match. Mam could even work for me, doing dresses for mothers and relations – that's if she wanted to,' Maggie added hastily.

'And what are you going to do for money for these sample dresses and port – portfolios?' Alf stumbled over the unfamiliar word.

'I've got a bit saved up and I could help Mam with her work. She won't need to stay up half the night finishing the Christmas orders now. I'll help her and in the new year I'll make a start on getting myself organised, and finding customers – clients,' she corrected herself. Davie had said clients sounded better.

Alf shook his head. It was a gamble, of course, but obviously Hetty had pointed out all the pitfalls to her. Maggie worked hard and was talented, and if she did make a real go of it then no one would be more pleased and proud of her than he.

'All right then, give it a try, but if it doesn't work you'll have to get a job, Maggie, and that certainly won't be easy, you having walked out from Sloan's.'

'It will work, Da, I *know* it will, and I'd sooner serve behind a stall in the market than go back to Sloan's.'

Alf sighed. It didn't seem five minutes since they were in the midst of the preparations for her seventeenth birthday party, and yet a year had gone over and here she was, nearly eighteen years old, full of ideas and enthusiasm and about to start her own business.

Chapter Thirteen

On the Saturday before Christmas Evvie was helping Peg with the baking. It was something she enjoyed and she hummed to herself as she rolled out the floury lumps on the scrubbed board placed on top of the table. Kieran Ryan had said nothing, something she would be eternally grateful to him for. She and Ben had stopped seeing each other for two whole weeks and they had both waited on tenterhooks for the storm to break. It hadn't and so their relationship had resumed.

'You sound happy,' Peg laughed. She was rubbing flour and fat between her fingers. 'Although you haven't improved since you were little. Look at you, flour up to your elbows, on your face, and you've even got it in your hair.'

Evvie laughed as Peg started to spoon out the rich mixture of fruit and candied peel into each cup of pastry, frequently glancing at Joe, who would stick his finger in the jar if she didn't watch him, and God alone knew where his fingers had been. He was coming up to eleven, but *he* hadn't improved much, she thought grimly.

'Oh, now who's that?' she cried as the sound of the door knocker echoed down the lobby.

'I can't go, I'm covered in flour,' Evvie cried.

'Oh, blast! I'll have to go, but keep an eye on meladdo here. I don't want him poisoning us all by sticking his filthy fingers in the mincemeat.'

Evvie raised her eyebrows and looked questioningly at Joe as the sound of voices in the lobby grew louder and then Peg ushered a police constable into the room.

'What's the matter?' Evvie asked fearfully.

Peg sat down at the table, the baking forgotten.

'Oh, this is going to be a fine Christmas for us. It's your sister. I've warned her, I've pleaded with her, your da's threatened to give her a good hiding, but she just wouldn't listen. Did you know, Evvie, about this latest carry on?'

'What carry on, Mam? What has Kate done, for God's sake?'

'She's been arrested, that's what. She was with those flaming women.'

Evvie bit her lip. She knew nothing about all this. Obviously Kate had kept it from her, knowing she'd try to persuade her against taking part in whatever it was she'd done. But arrested . . . It must be something really awful.

'I'll get my coat, Mam.'

'I'm sorry, miss, there's no visiting. It's not a nursing home or hospital we're running. Law enforcement is our business. I just came to inform your mother and now I'll be off.'

Evvie stared at Peg as she dropped her head in her hands.

'Oh, God help us, I'll never be able to hold me head up in this street again.'

Kate had deliberately not told her sister about the sit-in at the town hall. It wasn't that she didn't trust Evvie, but she was afraid to put such a worry on to her sister's shoulders. She already had enough to contend with over Ben Steadman and Kieran Ryan.

She'd felt very apprehensive as she'd met Doris and they'd walked up Dale Street to the town hall. She'd never taken such an active part as this before.

'There's nothing to worry about. We aren't going there to smash the place up or burn it down, Kate.'

'I know. Cecile Chapman explained it all. It's a part of the civil disobedience thing. We're just going to sit there peacefully, but won't someone try and put us out?'

'Very probably. Didn't you ask Cecile that?'

'No.' Over the months Kate had struck up a friendship with Cecile, the only daughter of a man who owned a shipping company, who had threatened to cut her off completely if she fell foul of the law. It would be the last straw; he'd already been far too tolerant with her. He was an important man and she had embarrassed him too often. Their backgrounds couldn't have been more different but they found they got on well together, after Kate had lost her initial awe of Cecile.

When Kate and Doris arrived there were crowds of girls and women milling around the building until Miss Devonshire raised her arm and everyone fell silent.

'We will enter in twos and threes, ladies. There will be no pushing or arguments. The main purpose of this exercise is *peaceful* demonstration.'

Kate took a deep breath and linked arms with Doris and Cecile.

She'd never been inside the building before and she marvelled at the splendour of the place. There was gold leaf on almost everything.

'I've never seen anything like this,' she said to Doris.

'Neither have I. They do themselves proud, don't they? All men, of course. The only women they probably allow in here are the cleaners.'

By now the whole entrance hall was filled with seated girls and women, many of whom were chatting quietly or gazing around them in wonder. It wasn't long before the Deputy Mayor arrived and requested them to leave.

'Otherwise I will be forced to call in the police to have you ejected. You have no business in here.'

'I expect your wife does, though, accompanying you, of course,' a cultured voice called out from somewhere behind Kate.

'Will he bring in the police?' Kate asked nervously, a nervousness she lost when she saw the determination on Cecile's face. If Cecile was prepared to risk everything, and she had so much more than herself, then Kate felt she *had* to take what came.

The police arrived, all huge men, and the sergeant who seemed to be in control asked once more if they would leave.

'I'm sorry, officer, but we can't comply with your demands,' Dahlia Devonshire said calmly.

The sergeant nodded and then the whole place seemed to erupt. It was nothing less than a police charge, but without batons, Kate thought, as she was wrenched by her shoulder away from her friends. She was pushed, pummelled and had her hair dragged by the officer, who towered over her and who had a neck like that of a bull. She was shaken, bruised and yet strangely angry as she was pushed violently down the town hall steps, landing on her knees.

'Leave me alone! Leave me alone!' she screamed at the policeman as she struggled to get up. A sharp jab from his heavily booted foot sent her sprawling again. Her cheek came into contact with the cobbles and she yelled out in pain. Then she was hauled roughly to her feet and tossed into the waiting black Maria like a rag doll. Her head hit the side of the van, the pain seared through her, and she began to cry.

'Kate! Kate! Don't get upset. It will only give them more satisfaction.' Cecile put her arm around her. She herself was hatless, her face was streaked with dirt and her hair was straggling and slipping from the pins that held it.

'Where . . . where's Doris?'

'I don't know. Maybe she's in another van; maybe she managed to get away altogether and I don't blame her. There is absolutely no excuse for treating us so badly. They enjoyed it. They damned well enjoyed it.'

Through her tears Kate saw the indignation on her friend's face and she marvelled at Cecile's courage. Scuffers had never respected the likes of her or Doris, but they should certainly have respected someone of Cecile's standing.

At least it wasn't far to Police Headquarters in Hatton Garden, just a few yards down Dale Street, she thought, trying to compose herself and wipe her eyes with the torn and dirty hem of her skirt. Everyone crammed into the van was in a similar state – factory and shop girls, even ladies and gentlewomen. She'd heard a rumour that Lady Constance Lytton had been in the town hall and they'd treated her just the same way, and she was the sister of an earl.

Kate climbed stiffly out of the van that had turned into the big yard at the back of the building, and was thrust in the direction of a small back door.

'There is no need to use such force, Constable. I can assure you we are not going to run away.' Cecile's voice was quiet but sharp.

'If I had a daughter like you I'd take my belt off to her – carrying on like this and you a lady. Well, no doubt your father will have something to say as well as the Magistrate,' came the disapproving reply.

'Are they going to lock us up?' Kate demanded, clinging to Cecile's arm. Now she was really scared and the police officer's words about Cecile's father had made her think of her own da. He would kill her. She began to tremble.

She gave her name and address to a grim-faced desk sergeant and then was led down a narrow staircase into a corridor that was tiled both on the walls and floor and was cold and damp A door swung open and she, Cecile and five other women were shoved inside. Then the heavy door closed with such a loud thud that she burst into tears again.

'Kate. Oh, Kate. Don't get upset. They'll leave us here all night. They think that will terrorise us and that we'll be so broken and upset that in the morning when they charge us we'll be so sorry we will go quietly home and not do such a thing again. Well, we'll surprise them. If Emmeline Pankhurst can stand prison and Lady Lytton can stand force feeding, then we can stand a bit of rough handling and a night in a cell. It's not so bad; we're all together.'

'But it's all such . . . such a nightmare, Cecile. You make it sound so easy and maybe you're strong enough and rich enough not to be afraid of your father, but I'm not. I'm not rich, I'm afraid of Da, and this will hurt my mam terribly and shame the whole family. I . . . I . . .' Kate broke down. She had never expected it to end like this. She was shocked, afraid, cold, and aching from her fall. How could these ladies cope with it all? She'd heard about force feeding and it was terrible. A suffragette in prison couldn't cope with the other female prisoners because they were usually common criminals, although she'd heard that some of them had even got fellow prisoners to call for votes for women.

Cecile made hushing, soothing sounds and at last Kate's tears stopped.

'That's better. Now I suppose we had better try and get some sleep, make the best of it. It's only for one night. They can't hold us for longer without charging us and that would mean extending the writ of habeas corpus. They'll charge and sentence us tomorrow morning.'

Kate had never had a worse night in her life. It was ten times worse than the night she'd found out that Frank was going to marry Josie. She was terrified of going to prison and it took all her self-control to stop her from breaking down and crying hysterically.

When at last she heard the clanking of keys and the sound of heavy footsteps, her fears claimed her and the tears filled her eyes. She bit hard into her bottom lip. She mustn't cry. She couldn't let them see her crying, not when everyone else was so calm. The others were all trying to tidy themselves up, to smooth and pin up hair, wipe their faces with dainty scraps of cotton and lace that served as handkerchiefs. She borrowed Cecile's and did the best she could but she still must look awful. She knew she must have bruises all over her face, the result of being sent sprawling on the cobbles.

With Cecile she stood in the dock and heard a policeman inform the Magistrate of her name, address, occupation and the charges against her. 'Disturbing the peace and obstructing a police officer in pursuit of his duties.'

She gripped the rail so tightly that her knuckles were white. She was shaking like a leaf and couldn't stop the tears. Oh, this was terrible. Terrible. She felt little more than a common thief or prostitute and how long she would get in prison she didn't know.

Cecile stood beside her, calm and composed. There were too many of them to stand in the dock separately otherwise the hearings would last all day.

'Sir,' said Cecile with dignity, 'may I speak for Katherine Greenway? She is an uneducated girl and this is her first offence. I would like you to take into account some mitigating circumstances.'

The Magistrate looked coldly at Cecile. He knew exactly who she was. He had dinner with her father once a month at the Lyceum Club at the bottom of Bold Street.

'Very well, proceed.'

'Katherine is the daughter of hard-working, law-abiding, church-going parents who know nothing about her activities with us. She has never in her life committed the slightest offence. I persuaded her to join us and to accompany us to the town hall yesterday. The blame is entirely mine and I am willing to pay the price for us both.'

Kate sobbed quietly. Cecile was offering to do her share of time in prison as well as her own.

There was silence for a few minutes and then the Magistrate nodded slowly.

'On this occasion I will dismiss her conduct but only if she will swear to be bound over to keep the King's peace. Miss Greenway, will you do that? Swear on the Bible to keep the peace?'

Kate could only nod as a clerk placed a heavy, leather-bound Bible in front of her.

Cecile took her shaking hand, placed it on the book and whispered, 'Raise your right hand, Kate.'

Kate did so, repeated the words of the oath and was then dismissed, but before she was allowed down she took Cecile's hand.

'Oh, God bless you, Cecile.'

Cecile smiled back. 'You've nothing to be ashamed of, Kate. Our day will come and I hope you'll remember my words.'

Tears filled Kate's eyes as she was led down but relief was mingled with a new fear: that of her da's anger.

He was waiting for her in the court's cold, bare entrance hall and one look at his face turned her legs to jelly and made her stomach turn over. Never in her life had she seen him look like this.

'Take my arm, Kate, leave me some dignity.' His voice was cold and hard as she took his arm.

All the way home on the tram he was silent and she knew she must look terrible because of the curious stares she was subjected to. When they alighted he led her up the back entry, ashamed to walk up the road, and once the back door had slammed behind them he pushed her into the kitchen with fury in his eyes.

'Oh Mary, Mother of God! Look at the state of you!' Peg cried, jumping to her feet, as did Evvie, horrified by her sister's appearance. She too had had no sleep for, as she'd tossed and turned, she felt Kate's fear and, strangely, on occasions some of the aches too.

'Never mind the state of her. She was damned lucky she didn't end up in Walton. That lady, Cecile something or other, spoke up for her, one of the scuffers told me.'

'Oh God Almighty, Kate, what possessed you?'

'Mam, I . . . I didn't know! They were terrible to us. It was them, we were peaceful, I swear we were.'

'You've done enough swearing for a while, girl. You've gone against everything we told you, everything we've taught you. Decent young girls don't join organisations like that. I hate to do this, Kate, but you'll have to be punished.' Bill began to unbuckle his belt.

'No! Oh no, Da! She's sorry, I know she is. She'll never do it again. Hasn't she suffered enough, been punished enough? She's covered in cuts and bruises. Please, please, Da, don't beat her,' Evvie begged, tears streaming down her cheeks.

Bill hesitated, then looked at his wife.

Silently Peg shook her head and he nodded.

'I'll not hit you this time, Kate, but I want you to swear you'll have nothing to do with them ever again.'

'Da, I . . . I've already sworn that on the Bible in . . . in court. And I'm sorry, so sorry that I've caused you such worry.'

'We believe you. Now, Evvie, take her upstairs while I make your da some breakfast. He's been down at Hatton Garden since before seven o'clock.'

Evvie led her sister upstairs. 'Oh, Kate, you did mean it, didn't you?'

'Of course, Evvie. But I feel awful – I don't mean about the cuts and bruises. I'm a coward. Oh, Evvie, they are so brave, and all I could do was cry. No one else did. Cecile spoke to the Magistrate and asked to serve my sentence as well as her own. Otherwise I'd have gone to jail and I . . . I couldn't have stood that.'

'Well, I suppose she's used to it and she can afford to.'

'No she can't. Her da has threatened to throw her out.'

'She'll have money of her own hidden away somewhere. She won't starve. God knows what Charlie will say to all this.'

It was something Kate hadn't even thought about but just now she was too exhausted and beaten to care.

Silvester Street was almost deserted by midnight on Christmas Eve. All the shopping, cooking and cleaning had finally been finished and those who were tired out with the preparations were either in bed or dozing before the kitchen range. The younger element were at Midnight Mass.

Evvie, accompanied by a very chastened Kate, Tom, who was home on leave, and Kieran Ryan, walked through the cold streets together. Maggie and Davie walked a few paces behind. They were all thinking of what had happened to them in the past year.

Evvie was thinking of Ben and trying not to be too downhearted because there was no excuse for them to be together over the holiday. There were no parties this year. The Steadmans didn't celebrate Christmas, so there was no legitimate reason for Ben to come to their house or for her to go to his.

'You can't go and wish someone "Happy Christmas" if they don't believe in it,' Kate had advised.

Kate thought briefly of Josie, Frank and little Matthew, then turned her thoughts to Charlie. He'd asked her again to go home with him. He had suggested Boxing Day, but again she'd got cold feet and had made an excuse. He'd looked annoyed but had not pressed her about it.

Kieran trudged along beside Evvie, torn between love and the nagging desire to tell her mam and da about Ben Steadman and so bring the affair to an end. But every time he saw Evvie he felt he couldn't hurt her like that. Maybe in this next year something might happen to drive Evvie and Ben apart.

Maggie was full of plans and ideas, and was chattering on excitedly. Davie was thinking about his own future and wondering where he could get his hands on more money. If Maggie's business took off he certainly didn't want to appear to be lagging behind her. After all, he'd been the one who had encouraged her. Oh, wouldn't they show everyone when they were both successful and rich? Naturally, they'd get married. He loved Maggie and she loved him, but they were both level-headed. 'Eighteen going on twenty-eight', was how Hetty described Maggie. Maggie wanted a nice house in a good area of the city, fine clothes and maybe even a maid to do the heavy housework. He, too, wanted a grand house, smart clothes and a fancy car. The only trouble was, all that would cost a fortune, so how could he get the money to get started on the road to success? How could he get more money now?

The others had crossed Scotland Road but Davie held back, having caught sight of a lad he was at school with.

'What's wrong? Why haven't we crossed over? We're going to be late and we'll never get a seat,' Maggie said irritably.

'That's Tommy MacNamara. He was in my class.'

Maggie scrutinised the burly figure that was approaching them. 'Well, he looks as though he's done all right for himself.'

Davie concurred. Tommy did look well. The clothes were a bit flash but they were new. At school the boy had been a real dunce. 'Tommy Mac! Don't you look great?'

'Davie Higgins, I 'aven't seen you fer years. What are yer doing now?'

'I'm a motor car salesman – great job, it is. Oh, this is Maggie McGee, we're walking out.'

Maggie nodded at Tommy, taking in every detail of his clothes. They were stylish but of inferior material and not very well finished off either.

'I work with our kid an' his mates now. It's the gear. Our kid's gorra motor car,' Tommy said proudly.

Davie was incredulous. 'Where the hell did he get the money for that?' He was amazed. Big Kevin Mac, as Tommy's older brother was known, with a motor car!

'Does he drive it for someone else?' he went on. 'Does he get paid? Is it his job?'

'No. I told yer, Davie, it's 'is, he bought it. Oh, 'e's gorris finger in all kinds of things. He's dead smart, is our kid —'

'What do *you* do?' Maggie interrupted. It was the first time she'd heard of anyone in this entire area owning a motor car. There were a few motor lorries but definitely no cars.

Tommy shrugged and pushed the black homburg to the back of his head. 'Oh, this an' that.'

Davie had a sudden inspiration. 'What about going for a bit of a bevvy one night, Tommy, after Christmas, like?' If the MacNamaras had money, and it looked as though they had, then he was going to find out where it came from and maybe get some of it himself. 'See you outside The Widows on Sunday night, about eight?'

'All right, Davie, la, I'll see yer then. 'Appy Christmas, an' ter you, Maggie.'

When they had at last crossed the road Maggie turned on Davie.

'What did you want to go and do that for? He's as common as muck. Fancy wearing a waistcoat like that, it was terrible. And I didn't like the way he kept leering at me.'

'Oh, he's all right, Maggie, there's no harm in him. It was a pretty awful waistcoat but did you see the watch chain? Gold, it was, and you can bet that the watch attached to the end of it was gold, too. I asked him for a drink because they've obviously come up in the world. He never had a pair of boots to his feet when he was at school and the backside was always hanging out of his trousers. Now he's sporting gold watches. If they've got money I want to know where it comes from and maybe get a bit myself. I could do with a lucky break. I save as hard as I can but it's not growing very fast.'

'Well, take care. He looked like a real thug to me.'

'He's a big soft dope, Maggie. Stop worrying. Come on, Kieran's waving to us to hurry up.'

Chapter Fourteen

It was the second week in February when Maggie got her first customer, or client as she insisted on calling Miss Beatrice Holland. She'd worked hard all the previous month, and even Hetty had to admit that the two dresses she'd made were very professional, as were the drawings carefully stored between stiff pieces of card. She'd made the dresses in completely contrasting styles. One was very plain, well cut and with the bare minimum of trimmings. Not everyone wanted, or indeed suited, frills and furbelows, Hetty had advised. The other dress was very fancy, with ruffles, ribbons, lace and even some tiny wax flowers. Maggie had also made headdresses, circlets with flowers and ribbons, and Hetty had been cajoled into lending her veil, for demonstration purposes. Maggie had promised to treat it very carefully.

She had placed a small advertisement in the Liverpool papers, but had been worried about the location of her business.

'What's wrong with Silvester Street? My ladies have never complained about coming here,' Hetty had replied indignantly when Maggie had voiced her fears.

Maggie looked perturbed. It was Davie, as usual, who had pointed out that it was not the most fashionable area of the city, nor was the exact address particularly salubrious. 'Well, I don't suppose there is much I can do about it. I'll have to hope my clients won't be put off. But later on, if everything goes to plan, I'll be able to afford premises in a good area.'

Hetty had tutted and shaken her head.

Maggie was very deferential but enthusiastic with Miss Holland and her mother, who'd accompanied her. As she'd opened the door Maggie had seen the older woman sniff with distaste as she'd looked up and down the street, noticing the women standing on their doorsteps, the younger children with dirty faces, playing in the street or sitting on the kerb with their feet in the gutter. Still, there was nothing she could do about it yet. However, there was no shabbiness or dirt about Hetty's front room, still called the Fitting Room. In fact

Maggie had persuaded her father to give it a coat of paint and make a sign and attach it to the door.

'I can make any of these designs in any fabric you wish, Miss Holland. Would you care to try one of my sample dresses? I'm sure they'll fit you.'

Miss Holland had opted for the more ornate dress while her mother leafed through Maggie's portfolio of designs.

'Oh, this is just gorgeous!' Miss Holland was entranced and Maggie knew there would be no point in showing her anything else.

Mrs Holland nodded approvingly. 'It does suit you. Now about the cost, Miss McGee . . .'

'That depends entirely on the material you choose, madam: taffeta, satin, duchess satin, corded silk, ottoman silk or georgette over taffeta. Personally I would advise, if I may, duchess satin. It drapes well, yet it is stiff enough to take all the trimmings without the material sagging. It does, of course, give the appearance of being a far more expensive dress than will in fact be the case.'

'And how much will the cost be, Miss McGee?'

'Three guineas. My prices are very competitive.'

Mrs Holland nodded her agreement.

'I can show you designs for bridesmaids' dresses, too.'

Miss Holland was still twisting and turning and admiring herself in the long mirror.

'Why don't you try these on, just to give you an idea of the whole effect, while your mother looks through my portfolio?' Maggie suggested, arranging a headdress and Hetty's veil over Miss Holland's dark, straight hair.

'Oh, do you make the headdresses, Miss McGee?'

'Yes, if they are required, but not veils. Not yet,' she added to herself.

'What do you think, Mother?'

'And the cost of the headdress?'

'Five and sixpence, madam.'

When they had left, Maggie hugged herself and did a little jig around the kitchen. 'That's her dress and headdress, two grown-up bridesmaids and two small ones, with hats for the older ones and circlets for the little ones. I've arranged times and dates for all the fittings. That's nineteen pounds and thirteen pence, Mam!'

'And a lot of hard work, and don't forget you've got to buy the materials and trimmings first.'

'I'll get them on your account at the wholesaler's, then I'll pay you.'

'I'm just warning you not to get carried away and think it's a fortune. Half of it will go on materials.'

'I know, but I'll still have nearly ten pounds. Ten whole pounds, Mam.' Maggie executed a few more steps, avoiding the furniture.

'Don't go and spend it all, Maggie. I don't want to put a damper on your spirits, but she might well be the only customer for now. It might be a few months before you get any more enquiries.'

'Oh, I'm going to save as much as I can. I mean to have my own workrooms one day. You should have seen the look on her mam's face as I opened the door. I just wish all those kids hadn't been out.'

Hetty shook her head. 'Maggie, I won't have you turning into a snob. This is your home and you've nothing to be ashamed of.' She didn't want to discourage Maggie but she knew her daughter was looking at life through rose-tinted glasses.

'Mam keeps saying, "Be careful, Maggie. Don't be too hopeful, Maggie." I could cheerfully scream at her sometimes,' Maggie confided to Davie one evening. She was tacking rows of dainty ruffles on to the train of Miss Holland's dress. Davie was busy with a pair of pliers and florists' wire, making the two circlets for the young bridesmaids, which Maggie would cover with ribbon and decorate with flowers.

'When is the big do then?'

'The sixth of March at St Mary of the Angels, Fox Street.'

'The friary? Well, I hope everyone admires the frocks.'

'Oh, Beatrice Holland's already told me that she's described it to her friends, and Constance, one of the bridesmaids, is engaged and she said to me, "It's so nice to have someone young making your frock, not some old harridan who thinks anything modern is shocking." She particularly liked the plain sample, and I told her it would really suit her, with maybe a little bit of trimming. She's so . . . so big that lots of frills would just make her look awful. I didn't tell her that, of course.'

Davie laughed. 'You're a good businesswoman, Maggie. You know you should have a label to sew in them, like they do in Cripps and Sloan's.'

Maggie laughed. 'I was only thinking the same thing, and I should have some business cards printed, too.'

'What will you put on them?'

'Oh, the usual, "Miss McGee, Specialist Seamstress" and the address.'

'You can't put all that on a label. On a card yes, but not a label.'

'No, I suppose not.'

'You need something short and snappy and yet . . . classy-sounding.'

'Like what? There's not much you can do with Margaret. Meg, Maggie; Peg, Peggy . . .' She pulled a face. 'Definitely not classy. "Miss Margaret" is the best I can think of and it's still very ordinary.'

'What about "Margo"?'

'Where on earth did you hear that?'

'I can't remember. How about, "Designed by Margo" for the label?'

She looked thoughtful and then repeated it twice. 'Yes, I like that.'

'Then when you are really successful, people will be clamouring to have their dresses "Designed by Margo".'

'And you'll be able to tell one of my dresses just by the style. I think I'll put something on every dress I make so it can be recognised. I know, I'll have a tiny bow of blue ribbon on the inside of the cuffs.'

Davie sighed. She was bursting with ideas. She seemed to dream them up with no effort at all. She was definitely going to make it while he was still only thinking about his ambitions. Still, his meeting with Tommy Mac had been interesting and he was seeing him again soon.

'I'm having a drink with Tommy Mac again tomorrow night. You don't mind, do you?'

'No, I'll be working on this. Mam is being really good. She's cutting out and tacking up for me, and she said if I get really stuck, she'll do the straight seams as well.'

'By this time next year, Maggie, you could well have your own premises and girls to work for you.'

Maggie looked dreamily into the future. 'Yes, wouldn't that be something, and wouldn't it make them all sit up and take notice around here? It's going to be very hard work, Davie. Won't you mind not seeing so much of me?'

'Of course I won't mind, Maggie. We've got years ahead of us, and once you get established you won't have to do all the hard work yourself. I'm not having my wife working her fingers to the bone. No, you can just, well, keep your eye on things. Do the buying, things like that.'

She smiled at him. They had their future all worked out.

Davie smiled back yet he felt disgruntled. It was all right talking big like that, but so far he hadn't been able to take one tiny step along the road that led to his own grand design.

'All gas and gaiters' his da described him frequently. He'd taken no notice but then he'd overheard a conversation between Alf and Hetty one evening. He'd gone to bid them good night as he always did but the door was open a crack and he'd heard Alf say, 'I worry about that lad, Hetty. I think he's aiming too high – all this car and garage business. It's not like our Maggie, starting up in a small way.'

'I thought you were glad he has ambition?'

'I am. I just hope his ambitions don't overstretch his brain.'

'Oh, Alf, what a thing to say!' Hetty had cried.

'I'm not being unkind, Hetty. I like the lad and they'll make an ideal couple. I just think he's aiming too high and there's plenty of others – his da included – who think the same way. He has got a decent job, after all. Why reach for the moon?'

He was thinking along much the same lines while staring moodily into his pint in the saloon bar of The Widows, waiting for Tommy Mac.

'What's up with yer? You've gorra gob on yer that'd stop the Liver clock. I can't stay long, I've gorra date with little Lizzie O'Connor.'

'I didn't see you there, Tommy. I wouldn't have thought she was your type.'

'She's all right is Lizzie. Mind, I've bought 'er a few good frocks an' things. She's got nothin'.'

'Won't Tip pawn them?'

'No, 'e bloody won't. I've 'ad a good talk with 'im an' 'e was almost sober at the time. I told 'im I'd purra lip on 'im if 'e did. I'm not 'avin' Lizzie upset.'

'What's your poison?' Davie asked.

'I'm spittin' feathers. Giz a drop of der crater. Best Irish, please, Freddie, la,' Tommy addressed himself to the bartender.

'That's a bit heavy, isn't it? I haven't come into a bloody fortune.'

'If yer going ter get all airyated, I'll pay me own whack.'

'No need for that, I'm not skint yet. It's no good for you, though, isn't that.'

'Sez who? Me owld girl has a drop every night and she's as fit as a fiddle, an' me granny's nearly ninety an' she swears by it.' Tommy tossed the whiskey back in one gulp. 'By, that warms yer up.'

Davie remembered Ma MacNamara well. She was famous for her propensity to outdrink all the customers of The Grapes at the junction of Scotland Road and Edgar Street, which was why Tommy had never had a decent rag to his back until recently and probably why he seemed so protective of little Lizzie O'Connor.

Davie looked his friend up and down. 'Is that another suit?'

'Yeah, it's the gear, isn't it? I got it in London Road. It's bespoke, an' all,' Tommy said proudly.

'Have you robbed Martin's Bank or something? Where's all this cash coming from, Tom?'

'I told yer, I work for our kid.'

'But you never told me what you do, or what he does either.'

Tommy glanced around furtively and then jerked his head in the direction of some empty seats in a corner under the window.

'I told yer, he's gorris finger in lots of things. Buyin' and sellin', sort of lookin' after people, an' gamblin'.'

'On what?'

''Orses.'

'That's against the law – well, outside the track it is. Is that what you do? Are you a runner for your Kev?'

'As well as some other things. Moving things, organising the carts and lorries an' things.'

Davie looked sceptical. He doubted that Tommy Mac could organise anything to save his life.

'He could put a bit of work your way, if yer like?'

'Doing what?'

'You know, what I just said. He's always lookin' for fellers to 'elp out, like.'

'Be a runner?'

'Keep your bloody voice down.' Tommy looked around uneasily.

'How could I do that? I'm in the garage all day.' Davie had lowered his voice to a whisper.

'Yer 'ave people comin' in an' out, don't yer?'

'Not that many, and besides, what if they grassed me to Mr Healey? Not only would I get the sack I'd be hauled up before the Stipe an' all. Use your sense, Tommy.'

'I don't mean ask yer posh customers.'

'Well, who then?'

'People must be comin' in all the time.'

'For what?'

'Deliverin' things, cleanin' the windows, brushin' the pavement outside, takin' the rubbish away, lots of things. An' word would get round and you'd gerra lorra customers.'

'How will I explain that lot trailing in an' out all day?'

'Is that Healey feller there all day?'

'No, he goes out quite a bit and when he is in, he sits in the office. God knows what he does, but there's a fire in there. It's just muggins here who has to stand in the garage and freeze.'

'There yer are then. You could tell people business between, say, twelve on' two, dinner time, like. Does he go out then?'

Davie nodded. It was very risky. 'How much . . . er, how much does he pay, your kid?'

'Sixpence a punter, and a bit of a bonus if yer do well an' don't rob 'im blind.'

Davie did some quick mental arithmetic. Even if he only had five punters a day, keeping the number small, that would be half a crown a day, six days a week. That was fifteen shillings a week! It was certainly tempting.

'He's dead smart, our kid. He knows that his blokes run the risk of being nicked by the scuffers an' brought up before the Stipe an' that they won't grass on 'im, so 'e pays well.'

'He . . . he expects us to get caught?'

Tommy shrugged. 'Yeah, everyone does in the end. But you're smart, Davie. You'd 'ave a great setup.'

'For a couple of coppers a week I suppose I could pay a kid to keep an eye out for me.'

'I'd 'ave snatched yer 'and off for a few coppers when I was a kid.'

That was indeed the truth, Davie thought, remembering Tommy's background.

'After a bit, he might let yer in on sellin' stuff, too.'

'What stuff?'

'What would yer like?'

So that's the way the wind blew. Pinching stuff to order, probably from the docks. 'Er, no thanks, Tommy. Nothing like that.' Running a book for Big Kevin Mac was bad enough without getting involved in fencing stolen goods. But fifteen shillings a week, clear profit, was very tempting, and that would only be with just five punters, which was very insignificant. No one would notice five spread out over a couple of hours. With double that number he could earn thirty shillings, but having ten people traipsing in and out was too risky. Even with five his savings would grow in leaps and bounds. Well, he was always telling Maggie to grasp the opportunities, so why not take his own advice?

'How does he get away with it? Don't the scuffers know? Don't they come chargin' in mob-handed?'

'I told yer, 'e's dead smart. 'E buys some stuff, dead legal, like, so it's a proper business. They did come once, all wavin' papers with the blue duck on them, search warrants, like, but our kid 'ad shifted the stuff an' 'e keeps receipts for everythin' else. Are yer in or not then, Davie?'

'Well, count me in, but only for running. Nothing else.'

'That's what they all say ter start with, then they get greedy. You're smart, Davie, and yer honest. You and our kid would gerron like a 'ouse on fire. You could make a fortune. You could buy that judy of yours a good ring, an' a big 'ouse.'

'Just running for now, Tommy.'

'All right. I'll 'ave a word with our kid and then I'll meet yer in 'ere at the weekend and gerrit all set up.'

As he walked home that night, Davie pondered how he was going to tell Maggie what he was about to embark on. She wouldn't be happy about it, that he knew for certain. Indeed, he was still doubtful himself, but he kept thinking of his savings and how little there was of them currently. He wouldn't tell her the truth, but he'd have to tell her something; she wasn't a fool. He'd always been good at figures. He'd say that Big Kevin Mac was looking for someone to help do his accounts and would pay. He couldn't tell her how much, though. No one paid fifteen shillings a week for something like that. And besides, Big Kevin Mac wouldn't commit anything to paper, it was too incriminating. He wasn't what you would call clever, but he was sly and cunning.

'I wouldn't have thought someone like that bothered with accounts. I wouldn't have thought someone like Kevin MacNamara could even write his name, let alone add up!' Maggie remarked caustically when Davie told her of the offer of extra work.

'Oh, he's not that bad, Maggie. He's not as dense as Tommy and he's looking for someone honest.'

'That's a joke. All the MacNamaras are up to their eyes in skulduggery. It's well known. One or other of them is always being carted off by the scuffers.'

She was right. The MacNamaras were a big, loud-mouthed, obstreperous family who were frequently being brought up before 'the Stipe', as the Liverpool Stipendiary Magistrate was known. Ma Mac, her mother and her sisters all spent more time in the pub than they did at home, and so the kids had all been left to bring themselves up. Consequently they were all villains in varying degrees. There wasn't a single one you could describe as law-abiding or industrious. Idle, devious, and vicious, yes, but honest – no.

''E's in Walton an' 'as been fer years. Best bloody place for 'im, the idle, thieving sod. I'm sick of 'im an' his bloody kids,' was the stock answer Ma Mac gave to anyone who happened to enquire as to the whereabouts of her husband.

Davie pulled himself out of his reverie when he realised that Maggie was speaking to him.

'Are you really going to work for him?'

'Maggie, I need the money. I've got to earn more if I'm ever going to start up on my own. You're going to be way ahead of me. I'll still be saving up in ten years' time when you've got fed up waiting for me and moved to Abercromby Square, or somewhere like that. And no one's going to say that Davie Higgins is being kept by his wife.'

'Well, as long as they don't involve you in whatever it is they get up to. I'm not having people point at me and say, "She's walking out with that Davie Higgins, who was involved with Big Kevin Mac and got arrested."'

'Maggie, don't make a big drama about it. It's only a couple of shillings a week extra, and I won't get involved with the MacNamaras,' he replied emphatically.

Evvie hated Sunday afternoons. She glanced around the kitchen and sighed with boredom. Da was dozing in the chair. Mam, after the dinner dishes had been washed and put away, had an hour or two to herself and was leafing through an old copy of the *Illustrated London News*. Maggie bought the popular women's journals for her clients to read, should they have to wait for any reason. When the magazines became too dog-eared they were passed on to the neighbours. They usually ended their days being torn up, twisted into balls and used to light the fire.

Kate was out with Charlie Wilson, and Joe was with Mickey Ryan and Liam Hawkins at Vi's house, where they were supposed to be learning their catechism. The Bishop was due to pay a visit to St Anthony's next month and they were all to be confirmed.

Evvie didn't see Ben on Sundays. It being a very quiet day for them, he always took his father to the Jewish Cemetery in Lower House Lane where Mrs Steadman was buried.

She saw little of her friends. Josie had her hands full with Matthew and Frank, and besides, she'd grown away from them all. She seemed older nor was she interested any longer in the things they talked about. Instead, her conversation was always to do with Matthew or Frank or her mother-in-law.

Maggie was so busy that she hardly ever went over the doorstep these days, except to go for materials. Maggie was doing very well, for spring was a popular time for weddings.

'Can I have a look at that when you've finished with it, Mam?' Evvie asked. There wasn't anything else to do.

Peg looked up. 'There's some nice things in here. Maybe Maggie would consider making you something.'

'She won't. All she's interested in are wedding dresses. It's all you can get out of her these days. She's a real pain in the neck, always going on about silk ruffles and lace inserts. I mean, I like clothes but she's so . . . so involved . . .'

'It's a pity you two don't have some kind of talent. Never mind, I suppose when the time comes she'll be more than glad to do your wedding dress and Kate's. It's a pity Charlie hasn't got any sisters to be bridesmaids but Kieran's got three besides Josie. I suppose she could be a matron of honour, though.'

Evvie raised her eyes to the ceiling in annoyance. 'Mam, will you stop it! I'm not going to marry Kieran, ever. I just don't love him – and as for our Kate, well, I don't think she'll end up marrying Charlie either.'

Peg ignored Evvie's remarks about Kieran. She was saying a novena to St Jude – everyone's last resort after all other saints had failed. He was guaranteed to intercede for what were considered 'impossible causes' and if Evvie and Kieran were not an example of an 'impossible cause', then she didn't know what was. The lad was still mooning over her yet Evvie obstinately refused all his offers.

'Why do you think Kate won't marry Charlie? She's mad if she doesn't. I mean, he's a real gentleman, lovely manners and not short of money either. He's got a good job and her life would be a bed of roses compared to mine – compared to anyone's in Silvester Street.'

Evvie was sorry she'd brought Kate's name up. She certainly wasn't going to tell her mother that in her opinion Kate still loved Frank Lynch. 'I don't know why.'

'Then why did you say it?'

'I think she feels she's not good enough for him, or his family.'

'She's a well brought-up girl and he'd go a long way before he found another one as lovely, except for you.'

Evvie sighed again. Mam would now go on about how fortunate they both were – how they all were – never having known real poverty, never having lived in the terrifying shadow of the workhouse. In Peg's eyes real poverty was what Nelly O'Connor lived in: no money for anything, not food nor coal nor clothes, let alone furniture and bedding. Nelly's kids slept head to tail on a straw mattress covered by old clothes, little more than rags. They were dressed in the serviceable but ugly clothes provided by the scuffers, who paid into a fund to provide the desperately poor with items of clothing and boots. The clothes were of stiff, hard corduroy, in a uniform colour, and marked so they couldn't be pawned. Some days water and a crust of stale bread was all Nelly could give her kids. That was real poverty, Peg often said.

Before Peg could launch into a full tirade there was a knock on the back door and Evvie jumped up to open it, thankful for any diversion to alleviate the boredom.

'It's Mr Steadman, Mam,' she said, ushering Levi into the kitchen. Her heart was beating with odd jerky movements and her mouth felt dry. He must have changed his mind. There must have been an argument and he'd come to demand that she stay away from Ben.

'Levi, I thought you'd gone to the cemetery. Don't you go to Ada's grave on Sundays?'

'Not today, Mrs Greenway.' He was a very formal man who adhered to old traditions and he always addressed his neighbours and customers by their full title, even though he'd known most of them for over twenty years. He looked uncomfortable and Evvie clenched her hands until her nails were digging into the flesh. Oh, this had to be it.

'Sit down, Levi. Would you like a cup of tea?'

'No. No, thank you, but it's kind of you to offer. I . . . I . . .' He looked from Peg to Bill, who'd woken from his doze, and back to Peg.

Evvie couldn't breathe.

'What's up?' Bill asked. 'You look as though you've something on your mind, man.'

Peg shot a suspicious glance at Evvie. Evvie didn't see it for her eyes were riveted on the slightly stooped figure of Ben's father.

'I have. I . . . I wish I didn't have to come here and say what it is I have to say.'

'Then get on with it, man. Let's hear it,' Bill urged, not unkindly.

'Yesterday morning I left a five-pound note, folded up, on top of the dresser. I left it for Ben to put in the cash box while I went to shul – the synagogue. Ben says he never saw it, that there was nothing on the dresser. I asked him, late in the evening, you understand, had he put it away safely?'

Bill looked stern. 'What are you saying, Levi?'

'I have to say this, but I am so sorry. Joe – he is the only other person who comes into the house on Saturday.'

'Joe? Holy Mother preserve us!' Peg cried in horror.

'Where is he?' Bill demanded.

'Over at Vi's, learning about confirmation.'

'Evvie, go and get him, now, this minute!'

Evvie didn't pause to put on a jacket or even her shawl. This was bad enough, but at least it wasn't the end for herself and Ben.

She gave neither Joe nor Vi any explanation except that he was wanted urgently at home. As soon as they both entered the room, Peg caught Joe by the shoulder.

'Mr Steadman here is missing a five-pound note. What do you know about it, meladdo? And I want the truth.'

'Nothing, Mam. I never saw any money.'

Bill looked grimly at his younger son. 'It was folded up on the dresser, Mr Steadman said. Did you see it, Joe?'

'No, Da. I swear I didn't see anything on the dresser.'

'All right, tell me what you did yesterday at Mr Steadman's house.'

'Only what I always do. I stoked up the fire, I put that stew in the oven to cook for their tea, I set the table, took the rubbish into the yard, an' I lit the gas, same as always. Da, I never saw any money, never mind a fiver. I know what they look like. Da, I swear I never saw one. Honest to God!'

'Did you go in there on your own? You didn't have Mickey or Liam or anyone else with you?'

'No. Mam would half kill me if I let them in. She told me that ages ago, didn't you, Mam? You said no one except me had to go in. It was very private.'

'Joe Greenway, I'll give you the hiding of your life if you're lying to me,' Peg threatened.

'I'm not, Mam, I'm not! I never took anything! I didn't!'

Peg bit her lip and shook her head and addressed herself to her husband. 'He's a right little hooligan at times, but he doesn't lie or steal, Bill.'

Bill too was perturbed. 'Are you certain you left it there, Levi? Sometimes I forget things I've done, or meant to do and not done them.'

'No, I remember it for certain. It was torn on one corner, that I remember.'

'Have you had a look around?' Peg queried.

'I have searched, Ben has searched – his eyesight is better than mine. We find nothing. I'm sorry. It's a lot of money to lose, more than I take in a month.'

'Joe, I'm going to ask you once more and then we're going round to see Father Foreshaw,' Bill said. 'You can come with us too, Levi.'

Joe was now in tears. 'Da, I didn't take it! I didn't an' I'll tell Father Foreshaw the same thing an' I wouldn't lie to him, would I? I'd have to tell him in confession and he'd know I'd lied.'

'But he wouldn't be able to tell us what you tell him in this confession, that I know,' Levi said.

'What he means, Levi, is that he can't tell the priest a barefaced lie in front of us, and have Father Foreshaw find out later.' Bill was now beginning to lose his patience. 'I'm sorry, Levi, but I think you are mistaken. I also think you'd better find someone else to do your chores on a Saturday. I'm not having my lad talked about in the same breath as that Vinny Brennan who *did* steal from you. I'd advise you to go home and have another good search. Now, if you don't mind, this is our day of rest, and I would like to do just that. Rest.'

Levi left and Evvie let her breath out slowly. She didn't honestly believe that Joe would steal, but five pounds was a big temptation to anyone. Peg was saying the same thing to Bill.

'Maybe he put it there deliberately, to sort of test Joe.'

Peg was outraged. 'But why now? Our Joe's been going in there for over a year.'

'Mam, I didn't take his rotten money,' Joe sobbed.

'It's all right, lad, your mam and I believe you. The old fool has probably put it somewhere else and forgotten where.'

'Well, in future any dealings with them will be strictly business and unless anything terrible happens, we don't need to pawn things these days, so that's the end of that. We'll have nothing more to do with them,' Peg announced firmly.

Oh, this just made things even worse, Evvie thought. But surely Ben didn't believe Joe was a thief? He just couldn't . . .

By the following Sunday evening Evvie was frantic. She hadn't seen Ben for a week and hadn't been able to get a message to him either. They were all forbidden to have anything to do with the Steadmans. Kate knew how she felt, but Kate couldn't help her. The only thing she'd been able to suggest was that Evvie write to Ben and post the letter, or that Maggie be coerced into helping, but Evvie wouldn't drag Maggie into the affair in case she accidentally let something slip.

When Peg ushered Ben into the kitchen, Evvie stifled a gasp, amazed to see him.

'Mr Greenway, Mrs Greenway, I'm here to apologise. Dad was mistaken. Well, he wasn't mistaken really, he *did* put the money on the dresser, but then someone came into the shop and he must have absent-mindedly put it back in his pocket. He had his best suit on and didn't find it until today. He's so upset, he can't face you, so I . . . I said I would come. We both apologise for accusing Joe.'

'I should think so, too. The poor lad has cried himself to sleep for nights on end.'

'We really are very sorry, Mrs Greenway. Is there anything we can do to make amends?'

'No, nothing, thanks. But Joe won't be coming back so you'd better get someone else for Saturdays.'

Ben nodded. He felt terrible about the whole affair and the worst thing was that he couldn't tell Evvie just how bad he felt. 'May . . . I have a word with Evvie, please, Mr Greenway?'

Evvie gasped. What did he think he was doing? Was he mad?

'What about?' Peg asked.

'I wanted to ask her advice about . . . about a present. A birthday present for a friend, a lady. I . . . I don't know much about these things.'

Peg raised her eyebrows but nodded and Evvie followed Ben into the yard.

'Ben, have you lost your senses?'

'Evvie, I'm sorry, I really am. It's such a mess, all of it. I told him to have another search before he came accusing Joe. I begged him, but he was adamant that he'd left the bloody money on the dresser.'

'Well, it's all over now. It means that I can't just nip in to see you, and neither can Kate. What are we going to do, Ben? I haven't seen you all week.'

'I know, Evvie. Can you meet me at the Pier Head on Tuesday night?'

She nodded. 'What time?'

'Say eight. It will be dark by then.'

'I'd better go back in before she comes out after me. You didn't really believe that our Joe . . . that he stole it?'

'No, Evvie, of course I didn't. I thought he might have brought someone in, one of his mates, but I was wrong. If I've hurt you, Evvie, I'm so sorry.'

'It's all right now. Go on home. Mam'll be peering out from behind the curtain.'

'See you on Tuesday, Evvie,' Ben said, but she'd already turned and gone back indoors.

'Well, what was that about? What present? What lady friend?'

Evvie felt weary. She was sick and tired of all the subterfuge but now was not the time to make a clean breast of anything, and she had an answer ready. 'A birthday present for someone called Rebecca. She's twenty-one. Now can we just let things drop, please?'

'Evvie's right, this whole affair is best put behind us,' Bill agreed.

Ben and Evvie went for a sail on Tuesday. It was a pleasant spring night with very little wind and the river looked like smooth pewter-coloured velvet, with only the bow wave of the ferry breaking the surface.

'From now on we'll just have to make arrangements from week to week and pray that nothing happens,' Ben said as she leaned closely against him.

'Oh, Ben, it's just getting worse and worse.'

'It's not easy for me either, Evvie. Dad knows, your parents don't. Last week he'd arranged a meeting with Rabbi Neiland, in our house. I didn't know anything about it. I had them quoting the Torah, chapter and verse at me for over an hour.'

She looked up at him, her eyes troubled. 'What did you say?'

'I told them, time and again, that I loved you; that I wasn't going to give you up.'

'Oh, Ben, how much longer can we go on like this? Why does everyone have to get involved? Why can't they just leave us alone? We don't argue over religion, so why do they?'

Ben sighed. 'Evvie, it's not just religion – on its own, I mean.

Being Jewish is not just belonging to a religion, it's a way of life. It's traditions that have been passed down for thousands of years. Something you are born to.'

She could understand that. In a way being a Catholic was the same. You were baptised almost as soon as you were born, and until the day you died you remained a Catholic, even if you did lapse or never set foot in a church except for christenings, weddings and funerals.

'Oh, I feel so miserable and I should be happy. It's the first time I've seen you for a week.'

'Don't be unhappy, Evvie, please. Let's just live for now, not tomorrow.'

She didn't answer, she just raised her face to his, letting his lips banish the doubt and anguish from her mind.

Chapter Fifteen

Bill had not had a very satisfactory evening. He'd gone into town to meet Billy Brindley, an old friend who knew someone who could possibly get Joe an apprenticeship at Cammell Laird's, the shipyard on the opposite bank of the Mersey, in Birkenhead. Joe had two years still before he left school, but these things took time and know-how. Or rather time and who you knew. He didn't want Joe to end up on the docks or be slaving away in the atrocious conditions in the stokeholds of one of the hundreds of ships whose home port was Liverpool. He wanted better things for Joe. Oh, the lad was a bit of a tearaway but no real harm in him, as that episode with Levi Steadman's money had proved. Joe deserved a chance in life.

Bill had thought that Billy Brindley would have been more forthcoming – promising to speak to his contact, possibly arranging a meeting between Billy, Billy's mate, Joe and of course himself. But no, that had not transpired.

'I'll have a word in the right ear,' was the only firm promise he'd managed to extract from Billy Brindley. It had been a total waste of an evening. He could have been relaxing, reading the paper with his feet up on the fender. It would have been cheaper, too, for he would have saved the tram fare and the money spent on drinks. Peg would be very disappointed. He stared out aimlessly through the window of the tram at the darkened streets. There was money in this city if you knew where to look for it. It wasn't all slums and factories. There were good-class areas – West Derby, Walton, Aintree, Allerton – and there were fine buildings that had cost a fortune, built by the men who'd made their profits from the river and its ships, and in the bad old days from slavery.

He got off on the corner of Scotland Road and Wright Street and began to walk home, trying to formulate in his head the words that he would use to explain things to both Peg and Joe. Not that Joe would be too disappointed – he wasn't looking forward to work of any kind. He'd have to shape himself soon, would that lad, and start to grow up.

*   *   *

Evvie had begged Ben to get the tram with her. They usually parted company at the Pier Head, but tonight she wanted them to spend as much of their precious time together as they possibly could.

'We can walk down the back jigger. No one will see us,' she'd replied when he'd suggested that as they couldn't walk openly down the street together he got off the tram a few stops earlier and walked the rest of the way. She wouldn't hear of it.

'Who is there to see us in the dark? There's no lights in the jigger. Everyone will be indoors and all the kids will be in bed.'

And so he'd agreed.

It was dark, very dark. The only illumination came from the dim lights in the upper storeys of the houses. The yard walls obscured the kitchen windows of the houses of their neighbours. They didn't even heed the rubbish underfoot. Evvie clung to his arm tightly.

'You'd better go in now, Evvie. They'll be wondering about you.'

She'd told them she was going over to help Maggie. She did do this sometimes, sitting for hours making lengths of ribbon into bows that Maggie would sew on at a later date. It saved Maggie much of her precious time and she was glad of the help. She also paid Evvie a penny a dozen. There were risks attached to this alibi, of course, but they were marginally less than those posed by some of her other excuses. Mam seldom went to Hetty's house for anything and Maggie was always too busy to be popping in and out of the Greenways' house.

'I know they like you to be in for half-past nine and it's nearly that now,' said Ben.

Evvie sighed. 'Oh, Ben, just a few more minutes.'

She slid her hands around his neck, her fingers stroking the dark curls and he drew her closer and kissed her, his kisses more urgent because they were the last he would have until next week.

Bill almost fell over them in the dark. He'd come down the jigger to avoid meeting any of the neighbours. He wasn't a man who went out much in the evenings and someone would be bound to see him, remark on the fact, and ask where he'd been. It was that sort of street and he didn't feel like broadcasting private family business to the entire neighbourhood. Nor was he in any mood to chat amiably to anyone after his wasted evening.

'Sorry, I didn't –' he began to apologise but his eyes had now become accustomed to the darkness. 'Evvie? Is that you?'

Evvie managed to stammer, 'Yes, Da.'

And then Bill realised who it was that his daughter had just been clinging to. 'You! Evvie, get in the house this minute! And you, you get out of my sight before I give you the hiding you deserve!' he roared.

Evvie fled and Bill followed her. The yard door slammed in Ben's face and he groaned aloud. Why had he listened to her? He should have known better. Poor Evvie, there'd be hell to pay now.

Peg looked up in surprise from her mending. 'You're in a rush, Evvie . . .' Her words trailed off as Bill, with a face like thunder, followed his daughter into the kitchen.

Peg jumped up, the work basket and its contents spilling on to the floor. 'Bill, what's the matter?'

'I'll tell you what's the matter, girl! I've just caught milady here in the entry, hanging around the neck of Ben Steadman!'

Peg's eyes widened. 'Oh, Evvie!'

There was nothing Evvie could say in her defence, nothing her da would take much notice of by way of an explanation.

'So, how long has this been going on, you deceitful, lying little madam? Over at Maggie's my bloody foot!'

'Da, I . . . I love him and he loves me,' Evvie cried.

'Love! Don't be such a bloody little fool, Evvie. He's after one thing. You'd have ended up like Josie and there's no way he would marry you, nor would I have given my permission. I asked how long it's been going on?'

'For . . . for a long time.'

'How long?' Bill yelled.

'Over a year.'

Peg covered her face with her hands. 'Oh, dear God, Evvie! Didn't I tell you months and months ago to get rid of him?'

'Mam, I couldn't. I really do love him. It's not fair that I can't tell everyone. It's all to do with religion and that's not right.'

'Don't you tell me what's right and what's wrong, Evvie Greenway. It's more than religion, it goes deeper than that. The gap is too wide for you to cross, and besides, they had the nerve to come in here and accuse your brother of stealing.'

'Da, please . . .' Tears were pouring down Evvie's cheeks.

'Has he taken advantage of you?'

'No. No, I swear he hasn't. He loves me.'

'I don't want to hear that word again, Evvie. You've lied to your mam and me and you've involved your sister and your friends in your deceit. It's over. Finished. Do you know what would happen if you married him? You'd be excommunicated. Do you really understand what that means? You'd be denied the sacraments. If you were dying you'd be refused Extreme Unction. You'd be refused the right to confess and be absolved, your soul would burn in hell. Your children would be unbaptised and if they died, and so many do, then heaven would be denied them. The Church would cast you out and so would many other people. Your friends, relations, neighbours would turn away from you. Is that what you want, Evvie? Do you want to break your mam's heart and mine?'

Evvie was sobbing but was looking to Peg for some sign of pity or understanding.

Peg, though, was too shocked and hurt to offer comfort. Why in the name of heaven had Evvie persisted in seeing him? Surely she realised that everything Bill had said was true? She knew her Catechism and the Church's teachings.

'I should take my belt to you, but I won't. You are *never, ever* to see Ben Steadman again, Evvie. I forbid it. I forbid you to go anywhere near either the shop or the house. It's over. If you flout me, Evvie, then much as it would hurt me, I'll turn you out on to the street. By God, I mean it and I'll make sure the whole Parish knows the reason why, including Father Foreshaw.'

'Oh, Da, please. Please, I love him.'

'Evvie, get to your room!' Bill yelled, completely losing his temper.

Evvie threw out her hands in the age-old gesture of appeal but Peg only shook her head and there were tears in her eyes.

'Evvie, get to bed. You've hurt us, girl, you've hurt us both. You knew it could never be, yet you went on defying us and lying to us. Oh, Evvie, it's going to be a long time before I can forgive you and a long time before I'll ever trust you again. Get upstairs.'

Evvie fled.

Bill sat down and undid his collar stud while Peg wiped her eyes with the corner of her apron. 'Oh, Bill, I hate to see her so upset,' she sniffed.

'I don't know what's come over her. She's always been the quiet one, with more sense than our Kate. She must have known there was no future with him. There was too much . . . difference.'

'Oh, I blame him. He's older and should have known better.'

'I can't believe how . . . devious she's been. Over a year! How can you keep something like that quiet? Why didn't we suspect? Someone must have seen them.'

Peg didn't reply. There had been times when she'd had her suspicions, but Evvie and Ben had been so crafty, so clever. 'I'll make a cup of tea.' She patted Bill's shoulder. 'It's for the best, luv.'

He nodded. 'It's been one of those days, Peg. I could get nothing much out of Billy Brindley – nothing you could pin your hopes on – and then I walk slap bang into those two. I'm worn out with the worry of them all.'

Peg sighed, she knew just how he felt.

The room was chilly but Evvie didn't even notice. Nor did she care that she was creasing her good skirt. She threw herself on the bed, her whole body shaking, and sobbed brokenly. 'Oh, Ben! Ben!' she cried into the pillow. 'I love you. I'll love you until I die. There'll never be anyone else. Oh, Ben! It's all my fault. I should have listened to you.' Within minutes the pillowcase was soaked with her tears.

When Kate arrived home she looked at the strained faces of her parents and knew instantly that something was terribly wrong. 'What's the matter?'

'You should know what's the matter, Kate Greenway. You lied for her while she went off to see him. You're almost as bad.' Bill's tone was harsh with anger.

'Oh God, you caught her,' Kate said in a choked whisper.

'Don't you dare to take the Lord's name in vain in this house!' Peg snapped. 'Why did you do it, Kate? Why shield her, lie for her? You knew nothing could ever come of it. She was just cheapening herself.'

'Mam, I'm sorry, I knew that what she was doing was wrong, but somehow I couldn't hurt her or see her hurt. She's my twin sister, she's like a part of me.'

'I don't want to hear all that nonsense. You're as much to blame. If you hadn't covered up for her it would have ended long ago. I'll not forget your part in this, Kate.'

'Mam, it's not nonsense and anyway, she'd have found some way of seeing him.'

'Well, you're going to have to live with the consequences now, Kate. You'd better get upstairs as well, before I really lose my temper. Dear Lord, what a family. What a trial you all are,' Bill said sadly, passing a hand over his furrowed brow.

Evvie was still sobbing in the darkness when Kate opened the bedroom door. She sat down on the bed and gathered Evvie in her arms. 'Oh, Evvie, I'm so sorry. I'm so very sorry. I know how you feel and I never wanted you to be hurt the way I was. At least Ben loves you and was faithful to you. At least he didn't betray you.'

Evvie raised a tear-stained face. 'Kate, don't say, "I told you so." Please, please don't say that to me.'

'I won't. What happened?'

Evvie was a little calmer, but tremors still shook her body. 'It was all my fault. I was so stupid, so bloody stupid. If we'd have parted company at the Pier Head like we always used to do . . .' A fresh wave of sobs choked off her words.

'Why didn't you?' Kate asked gently.

'Because . . . because . . . since that business with our Joe I hardly see Ben. I said no one would see us if we walked down the back jigger and no one did. And then Da, he bumped into us.' She dissolved again into tears on Kate's shoulder.

'I've lost him, Kate. I've lost him and it's my own fault. Da said he'd throw me out on the street if I ever see Ben again and he meant it. Where would I go? How would I manage? He said he would tell everyone and you know what that would mean. No one would help me. Oh, Kate, I love him so much. What can I do?'

Kate shook her head. Evvie's words had reopened the wound in her own heart, bringing back memories that she'd tried so hard to obliterate. 'Oh, Evvie, there's nothing you can do. It will get better, the pain, I mean. Believe me, it will ease. It won't go away for ever but in time you won't feel as lost or miserable.'

'I will! I will! How can you say that, Kate? You still love Frank, I know you do.'

'Evvie, don't torture yourself or me. Neither of us can have the man we really love, so we've both got to try to accept it and get on with life.'

'I don't want to, Kate. I haven't got a life without Ben. There's no reason for anything.'

'Stop that, Evvie! Stop it!'

Evvie couldn't speak. Her heart felt as though it had been smashed into little pieces and she couldn't see a future without Ben. She didn't *want* to see a future without him. Kate held her tightly while Evvie cried out her pain and Kate's eyes were full of tears. Tears for Evvie and Ben. Tears for herself and Frank.

Levi was sitting reading in his armchair. His eyes were screwed up in concentration despite the spectacles perched on his nose. He could see by the look on his son's face that trouble was brewing. 'So, what happened to you?'

'Mr Greenway caught Evvie and me and . . . well, that's it.'

'I told you to leave the girl alone, didn't I? Rabbi Neiland told you. We both begged you, but no, you know best. Well, now it's over, thank God. I can sleep at night now. Your mother can rest easy in her grave. It would have been kinder for you to tell Evvie a long time ago that it was over. You were selfish. You thought only of yourself. Not of Evvie, not of me nor your poor mother. She must have been spinning in her grave.' Levi sighed 'It's for the best.'

'Don't lecture me, Dad. I feel bad enough already.'

'You'll get over it. You marry a Jewish girl and forget little Evvie. Oh, I know she looks like an angel, I know that's what they call her, but she's not for you, Ben.'

'I'm going to bed, Dad. Is there anything you want before I go up?'

'Nothing, but thank you. Go and get some sleep.'

The old man watched him leave the room. He was sorry for the boy because he was hurting now, but God was good. It was all for the best. Now he could approach Mrs Myers, the Matchmaker. She would find a girl for Ben. After all, he'd met Ada through the Matchmaker and they'd been happy. Young people had no sense. They needed guidance and the experience of older heads.

Chapter Sixteen

Kate was becoming very perturbed. Ever since Christmas Charlie had been pressing her to meet his parents. Now he was harping on it every time they met. She felt that she couldn't unburden herself to Evvie; it would be tactless and hurtful for Evvie was still very miserable. She'd thought of mentioning it to Mam, but was dubious about that course of action. She knew her mam didn't have any real objections, she said she liked Charlie, but there was something in Mam's attitude that she couldn't quite put her finger on.

'Kate, please come. I don't see what you're so afraid of.'

By the end of May she'd run out of excuses. Now she sat waiting until it was time to go out to Litherland. She'd dressed with care, not wanting to appear too ostentatious.

'Demure, that's the look you want to aim for,' Maggie had advised. These days everyone went to Maggie for advice on how to dress. Kate had bought a pale blue and white striped dress that was trimmed with blue braid around the small, shirt-style collar and cuffs. It had a broad belt with a plain blue buckle, but there was no other embellishment. Her hair had been neatly pinned up and she wore a straw-boater-type hat with a blue ribbon around the crown. She'd also bought a pair of white cotton gloves, first to hide her work-roughened hands and secondly because Maggie said they were something no well brought-up girl would be seen without.

'You look very nice, Kate.' Bill smiled at her, his eyes full of pride and admiration. 'Very . . . what's the word I want? Genteel, that's it. I read it somewhere.'

'Demure is what Maggie said.'

'Aye, that as well.'

'You don't think I look too prim and plain?'

'You could never look plain, Kate. Dress you in sackcloth and ashes and you'd still be a beauty, and Evvie, too.'

She was exasperated. 'Oh, Da, you know what I mean.'

She still didn't know if she was doing the right thing. She was very fond of Charlie but was that enough of a foundation on which to build a life together? It would be a good life, if you considered material things. There would never be a shortage of money; she would want for nothing. She would have nice clothes, her own well-furnished house, but it wouldn't be in this neighbourhood. It would be somewhere where there was never any necessity to visit shops like Steadman's. Somewhere where, if you wished it, groceries and meat would be delivered and the bill settled promptly. Somewhere where you never asked to have things 'on the slate', but where a monthly account was the standard and highly acceptable practice.

'You'd best be off, Kate, you'll be late,' Peg instructed. She wasn't at all sure that this was a good idea. There just didn't seem to be that vital spark between those two, and then there was the difference in class. That could be as insurmountable as a difference in religion.

Kate grimaced before kissing her parents. 'Wish me luck.'

'Oh, get off with you, girl, you don't need luck,' Bill smiled. 'They'll be made up with you.'

She would have to get the tram and then the overhead railway to Seaforth Sands Station where Charlie would meet her. Then they'd get another tram up Crosby Road South. She was lost in thought as she walked towards Vauxhall Road. As she turned the corner opposite Telary Street, she came face to face with Frank Lynch. It was the first time she'd ever been in such close proximity to him since before he'd been married.

'Frank!' He looked older and careworn. He'd lost that boyish, devil-may-care attitude.

'Kate, er . . . it's nice to see you.' He felt his heart turn over, he'd almost forgotten how beautiful she was. And she looked so cool and fresh in that dress. Her hair beneath that smart hat framed her face like a ribbon woven of silver and gold thread. He noticed that she was wearing gloves. 'Are you going somewhere special?'

There was no one about. No one she could look to for diversion or deliverance.

'Just to meet some . . . people. How are you, Frank?'

He shrugged.

There was an awkward silence that threatened to lengthen, so she spoke. 'How are Josie, and Matthew?'

'Oh, he's a grand little lad.' Frank's eyes lit up for a second. Then the light died and his features registered bitter discontent. 'It's a pity I can't say the same for Josie.' He was mentally contrasting Kate with his wife. There was no comparison. Josie was dull, miserable and dowdy, a perpetual look of disenchantment and annoyance etched on her face.

Kate didn't reply.

Suddenly Frank reached out and took her hand. 'Kate, I hate her! I can't stand even to speak to her these days. She trapped me and she does nothing but moan and whinge all the time. My life's hell. It's you I loved, Kate. You I should have married and I still love you.'

She snatched her hand away as though she'd been burned. 'Frank, stop it! You're not being fair to . . . to anyone. Not me, not Josie, not yourself nor Matthew. What's done is done, Frank.'

He would never get another chance like this.

'It needn't be, Kate,' he pleaded.

'No, Frank! You're a married man, besides —'

'You've got someone else, haven't you?' His tone was bitter. 'That posh feller I've seen you with. Is that where you're going now, to meet him?'

'Yes, I'm going to meet Charlie and his mam and dad.'

Frank looked beaten and she wanted to cry out to him, to comfort him and hold him.

'So, you'll marry him?'

'I . . . I don't know.'

'Do you love him, Kate?'

'That's none of your business, Frank,' she replied gently.

'Do you?' he pressed.

'I'm . . . very fond of Charlie.'

'That's not the same thing, Kate, and you know it. I still love you, Kate, do you . . . do you still love me? Don't lie to me, Kate, please? I've paid, over and over, for my mistake with Josie, and I'll have to go on paying for the rest of my life, so don't lie to me, Kate.'

'Frank . . . I . . .' She was searching for words, struggling to buy time.

'You do! You do, Kate! You can't hide it from me. Say it, Kate! Say it.'

She turned and ran, praying he wouldn't follow her. She hadn't trusted herself to speak because she knew the truth; he had forced her to face it. She did love him.

On the short tram ride to Clarence Street Station, she'd calmed herself down, adjusted her hat and made sure no wisps of hair straggled loosely.

What use does loving him make? she asked herself as she walked up and down the platform waiting for the train. The platform was raised high above the street and the docks and she was glad of the cooling, refreshing breeze coming off the river. There is nothing either of us can do about it. Frank can't leave Josie and I won't start seeing a married man.

So, what are you going to do about Charlie? her conscience probed. You'd be a fool not to marry him, but could you live a lie for the rest of your life? Could you hurt him? In time you might even make him as miserable as Frank is now. Is it fair to Charlie? Is just stringing him along fair either?

She had no more time for these deliberations for the box-like train rattled into the station.

He was waiting for her when she alighted at Seaforth Sands.

'Kate, you look lovely – as always.'

She smiled at him. 'Oh, Charlie, you always say that.'

'It's because it's true.' He drew her hand through his arm. 'It's not far to walk to the tram.'

It seemed like miles and all the time she felt her stomach churning as though a million butterflies were flitting around inside her.

When they at last turned into Elm Drive, it was just what Kate expected: very solid-looking houses in a very respectable street. All the houses were red-brick Victorian villas, their paintwork clean and immaculate, brass knockers and letter boxes shining. Crisp white lace curtains covered the windows and every one was fronted by a neat little garden, enclosed with clipped privet hedge.

'Here we are.' Charlie opened the door and then took her hand.

She took a deep breath. She'd never felt so nervous in all her life as she followed him down the hallway. It seemed dark, but this may have been because it had been so bright outside. The Anaglypta that covered the walls up to the dado line were painted chocolate brown. Above it the walls were papered, the paper a cream background with brown scrolls all over it. The doors were varnished and grained. The room she followed him into was very bright in comparison as the sun streamed in through the bay window.

'Mother, Dad, this is Kate.'

He resembled his dad, she thought, as she smiled and shook his father's hand. It was a firm handshake and his eyes were kind. As soon as her eyes met those of his mother she knew instantly that she didn't like her. She was also aware that the feeling was mutual. There was no handshake either.

'Kate, do sit down. Charles is always talking about you, and now, at last we meet you.' Roberta Wilson waved a hand towards the sofa.

Kate sat down gingerly on the edge of it. It and the other chairs in the room were covered in a plum-coloured, damask-like material. The drapes were of the same colour. On the mantelpiece were fine china ornaments and photographs in silver frames. Covering the empty fire grate was an ornamental screen. There were small tables set around the room, each bearing an array of ornaments: porcelain figurines, alabaster boxes, vases of flowers. The carpet was very rich and oriental-looking. Kate felt totally out of place. Panic began to rise in her as she contrasted all this with her humble home. Charlie's father looked kind but his mother was taking in every detail and was no doubt making mental notes for future reference.

'We'll have tea in a few minutes, shall we?' Roberta Wilson looked at her husband with raised eyebrows.

'Whenever you wish, my dear.'

Kate felt beads of perspiration dampen her forehead. Suppose she dropped something on the carpet? Suppose she dropped the whole lot, cup and saucer? Did she leave her gloves on or take them off? She hadn't asked Maggie about that. She realised that Charlie's mother was speaking to her.

'I'm . . . sorry . . . Please pardon me.'

'I was saying, you work for Silcock's, so I understand?'

Charlie glared at his mother and his father gently shook his head in mild reproof but Roberta ignored them both. Oh, she could see what Charles saw in the girl. She *was* a beauty, but that accent! You certainly knew exactly where she came from as soon as she opened her mouth. He'd never be able to take her anywhere, well, anywhere decent that is.

'Yes. I don't suppose it's much of a job really, but . . . well, it is work.'

'Not everyone can afford to stay at home, Mother. Not everyone can have the plum jobs either.' Charles's tone was curt.

'Of course I understand that, but, well, perhaps something in a shop would suit you better, Kate? Much less, how shall I put it . . . demanding?'

She didn't know what she was expected to say and so she looked at Charlie for guidance and some form of deliverance.

'Shall we have tea now?' Mr Wilson interrupted. 'It's very warm outside. It's quite a long journey and you must be thirsty, my dear.'

Kate smiled at him with heartfelt gratitude. Charlie's mother had risen and so she also started to get to her feet.

'Can I . . . can I help?' she offered, praying her offer wouldn't be taken up. She knew nothing of the ritual of afternoon tea – something else she should have asked Maggie's advice on. Maggie always made sure her clients had a cup of tea and a biscuit before leaving or while designs were being discussed. She'd bought a lovely china tea set from Stoniers specially for such occasions and she'd also acquired a book on etiquette. They only ever had the thick white mugs at home.

'No, of course not, dear. There's nothing to help with. Frances will bring it in.'

Kate noticed that Roberta had risen only in order to pull a cord that hung beside the fireplace. She felt her cheeks burn with embarrassment. Oh God, they'd got a maid! Why hadn't he told her? Why hadn't he ever mentioned this Frances to her?

'Frances just comes in occasionally; she's not even part time.' Charlie was trying to put her at her ease, but she was beyond that now. She felt about six inches tall.

A girl, older than herself and dressed in the standard uniform of a parlour maid, brought in the tray and placed it on a low table near Mrs Wilson. She disappeared and returned with a three-tiered adjustable, mahogany cake stand on which there were plates of tiny sandwiches of white bread, and small cakes. Kate was desperately praying that her hands wouldn't shake when she took the proffered cup and saucer. It was so delicate and light that she felt it might disintegrate at the slightest pressure.

'We'll all feel better for a nice cup of tea,' Mr Wilson said encouragingly and she tried to return his smile but it was as though all the muscles in her face had frozen.

She never wanted to have to go through such a humiliating and agonising ordeal ever again, she thought as Charlie took her back to the station. He was insisting on seeing her home all the way to Silvester Street.

'Please, Charlie, I'll be better on my own, honestly I will.'

'Kate, what would your mother and father think of me?'

'They wouldn't think anything, Charlie. That's the difference between us – one of them, anyway. She hated me and I felt awful the whole of the time.'

'She didn't, Kate. It's just her way. You'll get used to her, in time.'

'Why on earth didn't you tell me about her, that Frances?'

'I didn't think it was important enough. She doesn't come in all the time. Not even once a week. Just for special occasions. I don't even look on her as a maid. Mother does, but to me she just helps out. That's why I didn't mention her.'

Kate shook her head sadly. 'Oh, Charlie, it won't work. I'm sorry, I should have let you go a long time ago. I've not been fair to you.'

'Kate, you don't mean that?'

'Yes, I do. It's better if I don't see you again. I . . . I'm fond of you, Charlie, but I don't love you, and I'll never fit into your world, never. I'd just be an embarrassment to all of you.'

'Oh, Kate, please don't think like that. Don't let her attitude influence you. Father liked you and you liked him, didn't you?'

'Yes, he's very nice, but your mam's attitude hasn't got much to do with it, except that it's opened my eyes. She just pointed out something I should have seen months ago. We come from two different worlds, Charlie. We'd both end up miserable. I couldn't live . . . live like that.'

'But, Kate, you're used to mingling with ladies like Cecile Chapman. You were a suffragette, you coped with the class distinction.'

'That was different, Charlie. I . . . I never went home with Cecile. I never met her or any of the others socially.'

'Kate, please just think about it? Don't make any hasty decisions. I know you're upset now. Wait and think about it. It *can* work. I love you, Kate. Let's not see each other for a while, say two weeks? You'll have time to think more clearly. Please?'

She felt so miserable and so very sorry for him. 'All right, Charlie, but please let me go home now? It's so hot, my head's absolutely thumping.'

He kissed her on the cheek as the train arrived.

'Remember, two weeks, Kate,' he called

She raised her hand in a wave and then slumped back against the seat. She just wanted to go home.

When she got in she threw her hat and the now grubby gloves on the table.

'Well?' Bill asked concernedly.

'Oh, it was awful. I've never felt so . . . so small in my life before!'

'Why? Sit down, luv, and tell us what's the matter.' Peg guided her to the sofa.

'I felt so out of place, Mam, and she didn't like me the minute she set eyes on me. Probably even before that.'

'What's the matter with you? You look grand to me.'

'I didn't like her either, Mam. She was so . . . snooty. She just looked at me as though I was some kind of . . . of . . . creature that had wandered in. It was a lovely house, expensive furniture and carpets. China ornaments and silver photograph frames and tea. Oh, Mam, I could have murdered Charlie because they even have a maid and he'd never mentioned her. His mam got up and I thought she was going into the kitchen to make the tea, so I offered to help. Oh, I wished the floor would have opened up and swallowed me. You should have seen the look she gave me. She was just pulling the bell for this Frances person. She called me "dear" but she meant it to sound like "bitch", I know she did.'

'What did Charlie say?' Peg demanded.

'Oh, he was annoyed with her, I could see that, but he didn't think Frances was worth mentioning. She only comes in now and then and for special occasions. Oh, this afternoon was a "special occasion" all right. She was making sure I knew how different they were from us. His da was very nice to me, but I couldn't live like that, Mam, and she'd expect me to. She'd be forever on my back. I . . . I told Charlie it was all over. That I was sorry I've hurt him, but —'

'Kate, don't you think you'd better think about this more carefully? You were upset. When you've calmed down maybe things will look better.'

'Da, that's what Charlie said. He wants me to have a break. He said he'd see me in two weeks.'

'Well, maybe he's right.'

'No, Da, it won't work. Apart from everything else, I don't love him. I'm fond of him, but it's not the same, is it? I'd only end up making everyone's life a misery.'

In her heart Peg knew Kate had made the right decision so she said nothing, but when Kate had gone up to get changed, she shook her head. 'Now we'll have the pair of them as miserable as sin. Oh, why can't our Evvie love Kieran, and why can't Kate meet someone she really loves from her own class?'

'You don't think she's still carrying a torch for Frank Lynch?'

'I hope not, but even if she is, what good would it do her? Oh, I don't know, Bill, when you've nursed them through all the illness when they're little, and got them reared and working, you'd think your troubles would all be over, but they're not. You just swap one set of worries for a different set.'

'Things will work out, Peg, don't worry about those two. Angels lead charmed lives.'

'Maybe angels in heaven do, but these two of ours here below don't seem to share that good fortune.'

Chapter Seventeen

Maggie staggered along under the weight of the shopping she was carrying: three brown paper parcels and two rolls of what appeared to be material.

'Maggie, here, girl, let me take those before you do yourself an injury. You can hardly see where you're going,' Tom Greenway called to her. He liked Maggie even though she was a tough, hard-headed little madam at times and bossed Davie Higgins around like nobody's business.

He'd been to sign on again. His trips were short – he was only away for two weeks at a time – but, like all the other seamen, at the end of the voyage Tom signed off and then when the next trip came up, signed on again. It was the way the system worked, no matter how long you'd worked for the same shipping line.

Tom had met Brid O'Hare on the tram, a girl he'd known for years, and he'd asked her to go out with him that evening. She was good company, though a bit flighty, but as he wasn't ready to settle down yet, that didn't really matter.

Maggie was very thankful to see Tom and Brid now. 'Oh thanks, Tom. My arms are nearly broken with the weight. I should have had it all delivered. I had to go myself otherwise Mam would have forgotten something or got the wrong shade of ribbon, and anyway, I couldn't have expected her to carry this lot and she's busy with the housework.' Her eyes lit up with pride. 'I've got some really wonderful news.'

'What is it? You look like the cat who got the cream.'

'I've got my first really big commission.'

Tom looked puzzled. 'What's that when it's at home? I thought it was something you got in the army?'

'Don't you know anything, Tom Greenway? It's an order, an advance order.'

'What's so special about it?' Brid queried. She'd known Maggie from their school days.

'It's only for Miss Heller. Miss Elizabeth Heller.'

'Who's she?' Brid couldn't think of anyone of that name.

'Of Heller's Furniture Emporium on County Road. Her wedding's to be a very grand affair at St Mary's, Walton-on-the-Hill. She's having six bridesmaids and two little flower girls.'

'Sounds more like a May Procession,' Tom muttered *sotto voce*.

'And she wants only the best of everything. I made a dress for someone she knew and she came straight to me rather than go into town. Fancy, she chose me over all the shops in Bold Street! She said she'd heard how good my portfolio was, she came and looked through it and then asked if I'd design something especially for her! Me dream's out! Once this gets around I'll really be in business.'

Brid was incredulous. 'Won't all that take a long time? I mean, there's only you and your mam and that's nine dresses!'

'I'm going to have to get someone to do the straight seams and an experienced bodice hand.'

'You mean you're going to employ people, Maggie?' Tom was now as amazed as Brid.

Maggie nodded, her eyes shining. 'I know a couple of girls I used to work with at Sloan's who would be glad of the extra money. They could do the work at home. That's why I had to go into town myself for this lot. I had to choose very carefully, get exact matches in lace and ribbons and buttons, besides all the taffeta and crepe de Chine. I must have been mad to try and get it all home on the tram, but I'm anxious to get started on it and it would have been Monday before they could deliver. She's having sweet-pea shades for the bridesmaids: pink, lilac, a sort of misty, bluey purple, and deeper shades for the underskirts. Oh, I'm really going to enjoy making all of them.'

'Does Davie know?' Tom asked. 'I mean about taking girls on to work for you?'

'He knows about the commission but I haven't told him yet about everything else. If Miss Heller recommends me then I'm going to have to start looking for workrooms.'

They had reached Maggie's house and Tom handed over all the parcels. 'Well, good luck with it all, Maggie.'

'Thanks.'

Brid smiled. Maggie was certainly someone special in this neighbourhood.

'Why don't you and Davie come to the Rialto with us tonight? We're going dancing. It'll do you good to get out, Maggie – a last fling before getting stuck into all that work.'

Maggie considered it and then nodded. Yes, she and Davie would go out with them. It would be a sort of celebration and she liked Tom and Brid.

'We'll call for you at half-past seven then,' Tom said before turning to cross the road.

'Fancy that. That plain little mouse having her own business, employing people, having workrooms. Oh, she'll go far, will Maggie. Miss Morgan at school used to say she wished everyone had the same outlook on life and work as Maggie McGee.'

'They both will,' said Tom. 'That Davie's full of big ideas too. Going to have his own car and business although I don't see much sign of either yet.'

Davie called to see Maggie at lunch time, as he usually did on Saturdays. Hetty always made him a 'doorstep' with cheese or ham for a filling. Maggie was full of her good news and as he sat listening to her plans for the future he felt resentful. She was racing ahead of him. He could see it was all falling into place. She'd soon have her own workrooms, her own staff, her prestige and her own money while he . . . well, his dream was still just that: a dream. He did have more savings now. Big Kevin Mac's money was very handy, but he was careful not to risk his job by having more punters. Too many people coming in and out and Mr Healey would want to know what was going on.

'You're not listening to a word I've been saying, Davie Higgins!'

'Sorry, Maggie, I've a lot on my mind just now.'

'Maggie, for heaven's sake let the lad have a bit of peace,' Hetty said laughingly, although she sensed that Davie's lack of interest was caused by envy. She would have to have a word with Maggie and tell her not to make too much of things. All men had their pride and it didn't do to wilfully hurt or undermine it. Women shouldn't appear too successful. Her own business had never been a challenge to Alf. He had always been the breadwinner, and more importantly, seen to be such.

'I said, what time will you be here this evening? I promised Tom Greenway and Brid O'Hare that we'd go to the Rialto as a sort of celebration. They're calling at half-past seven.'

'So, what time do you want me here then?' Davie queried.

'About a quarter past seven. I've some work to do this afternoon.'

'That's enough about work for one day, girl. Go and make this lad a cup of tea. He's got a job to do as well,' Hetty said tartly.

Davie's resentment grew. All afternoon he was lost in thought.

Maybe it was time to take the plunge, and go and see Big Kevin Mac about 'buyin' and sellin'', as Tommy put it. He'd only had one potential customer all afternoon, A toffee-nosed, supercilious old buffer who had insisted on being dealt with by Mr Healey, or 'the Proprietor', as he'd demanded. It was the last straw. He wasn't going to stay here for ever, bowing and scraping. He'd go and see Big Kevin Mac before he went to Maggie's.

After enquiring at the house in William Moult Street, and being informed by an untidy woman of uncertain age that ''E's at 'is office, a big place at the back of Vandries Street,' he'd made his way there.

It was a pleasant June evening and Davie felt better, more confident. You had to take chances if you wanted to get on in this life, especially if you weren't born with a silver spoon in your mouth. Even more so if you had the bad luck to be born in a slum area. He knew he'd done well by a lot of folk's standards, but then so had the MacNamaras.

The 'place' at the back of Vandries Street was near its junction with Waterloo Road, which bordered the Dock Estate. It was a dark, decrepit old warehouse, which looked to have been abandoned. It also looked unsafe. Inside it was dark, dingy and smelled musty. It was full of crates and boxes covered by tarpaulins. There was also a cart and a motor lorry, Davie noticed as his eyes became accustomed to the gloom. The 'office' was no more than a cubbyhole at the back.

He threaded his way towards it for there was a crack of light showing underneath the badly fitting door. He knocked and without waiting for an answer opened the door wide.

Tommy, Big Kevin and two other men were all bending over a desk that was covered with money. Five-pound notes were spread across it in neat piles. He'd never seen so much money.

A huge hand shot out and grabbed him by the throat. 'Who the 'ell are you?'

'It's all right, he's one of me mates.'

He was released and he gasped for air. The three older men looked at each other and Davie felt a chill run down his spine. They all looked like hard, violent men who were no strangers to prison. Big Kevin Mac began hastily collecting up the money but Tommy still clutched a note which he proceeded to hold up towards the gas jet. 'It's dead good this, Kev, ain't it? Yer can't tell it from a real—' He got no further. His brother snatched the note from him and cuffed him hard across the side of the head. 'You an' yer bleedin' big gob! Yer as thick as pig shit, an' if yer wasn't me brother I'd stop yer gab fer good!'

Tommy rubbed the side of his head ruefully and glowered. 'I'm goin' ter tell the owld feller the way yer treat me!'

'An' what is 'e going ter do about it, stuck in bloody prison? That's where we'll all end our days, yer soft get, if yer don't keep yer gob shut! Can 'e be trusted?'

Tommy nodded.

Davie stood very still and silent as though watching a scene from a play. It wasn't proper money, it was forged. So that's how Big Kevin Mac came to have a car and flash clothes and gold watches. This was really serious stuff, no petty crime like running a bit of a book, selling a bit of dodgy merchandise – dealings that were so commonplace in this area that they were almost considered as acceptable occupations by some people. Not by the scuffers, of course . . . But this – oh, this was anything up to twenty years' hard labour in jail.

'What do yer want?' Kev barked.

'I . . . I . . . came to ask about a bit of buying and selling, like. I won't say anything. I'm no scuffers' nark. I won't grass.'

'Well, I ain't got no stuff fer you to sell just now, so clear off. Stick to yer 'orses.'

'I could do with the extra cash, like.'

Kev looked thoughtfully at one of his henchmen, who shrugged. 'I might 'ave something next week. If yer keep yer mouth shut.'

'I will. I swear to God I will!'

'He's a good skin, is Davie. Yer can trust 'im; one of me best mates, he is.'

'I hope 'e's got more bloody brains than you 'ave! Come back next week, la.'

Davie turned to leave, disappointed and yet still shocked by what he had seen.

'You keep yer gob shut!' the older of the two heavies growled at him. 'An' just so yer'll remember, 'ave this.'

Pain exploded in Davie's knee and his legs buckled under him. 'My knee! Oh God, you've smashed my knee!' he screamed, writhing on the floor.

'What did yer do that for? He's me mate! Tell 'im 'e can't go round kickin' me mates,' Tommy roared at his brother.

'Then get yer "mate" out of 'ere and fast. I can't stand 'ere all night. I've got places ter go, fellers to see.'

Tommy half carried Davie out and into the street. 'I'm dead sorry, Davie, honest. I didn't know Lol was going ter to do that to yer. 'E's a real bad 'un, that Lol. It don't do ter cross 'im.'

'I didn't. Oh God, Tommy, the pain! The pain! I can't walk. Take me to the hospital!'

'I can't do that, Davie. They'll ask all kinds of questions, like how did yer do it an' what I had ter do with it. I'll get yer an 'ackney. Go 'ome.'

'I can't bloody well walk, Tommy! Jesus! It's agony, it's pure agony!' The pain was so intense that he was almost crying.

'All right, I'll come with yer.'

'Take me to Maggie's house. If I don't turn up she'll get mad.' He knew it was no use going home. His mam would have hysterics and his da would rant and rave. He was always moaning at him for something, always saying he'd come to a bad end.

'All right, but I'm not goin' in, mind.'

Maggie was ready and waiting impatiently, peeping out from behind the curtain, watching for him to turn the corner. She was mystified when she saw the hackney come down the street, wondering who was coming home in style. A hackney cab was hardly ever seen in this area. When it stopped outside the door, she pulled the curtain right back to get a better view. As she watched Tommy alight and then almost carry Davie out, she ran straight into the hall calling for Hetty and Alf.

'If that Tommy Mac's got him drunk I'll kill the pair of them! I'll flaming well kill them! He can just take him back to wherever it is they've come from while I've been sitting here waiting.'

Her anger died as she realised that Davie was not drunk but hurt. His face was almost grey with agony.

Hetty and Alf both went to help Tommy.

'What happened? Davie, what happened?'

'It's his leg, Hetty. Here, lad, grab hold of me, and you, whatever your name is, get the other side of him. Let's get him inside.'

'I can't, I've got ter get back ter me mam, she's sick,' Tommy lied. There was no way he was going to get involved here. Maggie's da looked like someone who would call a scuffer at the drop of a hat. He hurriedly got back into the hackney.

'Oh, go to hell, Tommy Mac. It's the only place fit for you, you useless sod! A sick mam my foot! Drunk, yes, sick no!' Maggie had her arm around Davie, trying to support him. Every movement, every jar, made Davie scream with pain.

'Oh, Da! What can we do?'

'Hospital. Stanley Hospital, that's where you're going, Davie. Hetty, go and get Bill Greenway and a couple of the Ryan lads.'

'Davie, what happened?' wailed Maggie. 'Oh, I wish to God you'd not got mixed up with that Tommy Mac. They're all thugs. His da's in Walton. What have you been doing? You haven't got mixed up with all of them, have you?'

'Maggie, can't you see the lad's in no fit state for a bloody interrogation? You'd be better saving your breath for going round to tell his mam and dad. We can sort everything out later, when he's had his leg seen to and he's not in so much pain. Go on,' Alf urged.

Maggie pursed her lips tightly as Bill and Tom, Kieran and Matty Ryan came running up the street. She knew he'd been up to no good with that Tommy Mac, she'd just known it. Trouble followed that lot wherever they went. She felt desperately sorry for Davie, but she'd get to the bottom of this if it was the last thing she did, and she'd put a stop to Davie's friendship with Tommy Mac. With friends like that, you didn't need enemies.

The two weeks were up and Kate had done a lot of thinking before she'd finally made up her mind. She wasn't looking forward to this meeting but she dressed with care just the same. Knowing she looked nice would give her confidence. Oh, she knew people thought that because she and Evvie were attractive they were full of self-confidence, but neither of them really was. Self-consciousness was more like it.

Charlie was waiting for her at Seaforth Sands Station when she alighted. He looked so smart in his lightweight suit, fresh white shirt and brown and tan tie. His shoes shone and he wore his Panama hat at just the right angle.

His eyes lit up at the sight of her. She always looked so radiant.

'Kate, I wondered if you'd come.'

'I said I would and I don't break promises if I can help it.'

'Shall we walk to the park or is it too far?'

'No, it's not far.' She was thankful for the extra time. She'd go over it all again in her mind.

They walked in silence down the platform and steps, and along the road to Victoria Park.

'Shall we sit here, Kate? It might be cooler.'

She sat down on the bench that was half shaded by a large laburnum tree, and clenched her hands tightly in her lap. This was going to be so hard, so very hard. She really didn't want to hurt him.

'Have you thought about . . . us?'

She nodded. 'I've thought about nothing else, Charlie, and I can't

. . . I'm so sorry but I can't go on seeing you. It wouldn't be fair. I know I said that last time but I still mean it. I . . . I don't love you, Charlie. I'm fond of you but that's not enough for a successful marriage. I've seen what happens when one person doesn't love the other. Marriage is hard enough, Charlie – a whole lifetime together – so you need to love each other very much or it all goes wrong and you end up hating each other.'

'Kate, I could never hate you.'

'Oh, Charlie, don't say things like that.'

'But I mean it.'

'I know you do, but it's over, Charlie. Oh, I never wanted to hurt you. It's all my fault. I should have said something before you got serious. I'll never forgive myself for that.'

She got up and he followed suit, gazing down at her, the hurt and misery clear in his eyes.

'I'll never forget you, Charlie, and maybe . . . maybe if I'd met you a couple of years ago things might have been different, I don't know.'

She extended her hand. She was not going to use those tired old words. They *couldn't* part as just friends.

He surprised her by taking her hand, raising it to his lips and kissing it. Oh, he had such manners, such delicacy. Tears sprang to her eyes.

'Goodbye, Kate. I can see that nothing will change your mind and thank you for being so . . . honest. Many a girl wouldn't be.'

'Thanks. I . . . I'd better go now. I've a letter to finish, to Cecile.'

'You do know that she's in prison? I saw it in the newspaper. There was quite a big piece about it – "City fathers shocked, etc", "Examples must be made, etc".'

'Yes.' She paused and looked him squarely in the eyes. 'And but for her I would be in prison. It was the sit-in. I didn't like to tell you before in case you were angry, but I was arrested too.' She smiled sadly. 'You see, Charlie, you would be marrying a criminal. Your mother would have ten blue fits.'

Although taken aback by her words he smiled.

'You're not a criminal, Kate, any more than Cecile Chapman or Lady Constance Lytton are. Kate, you feel completely at ease with Cecile, who is obviously a very wealthy young woman, and yet not with me.'

'Charlie, it's not the same. I don't have to love Cecile. She's a friend. I would have to love a husband.' Things were becoming complicated and she drew back.

'Goodbye, Charlie, and thank you.'

He stood and watched her walk away and knew that as long as he lived he would always love her.

When Kate arrived home and had gone to take off her hat and the good dress, Evvie followed her.

'Was he upset?'

'Yes, but he's too well bred to make a scene. He just kissed my hand and said, "Goodbye". Oh, Evvie, I feel so awful. I *know* I would have had a wonderful life. I *know* he'd love me for ever, but I just couldn't do that to him.'

Evvie nodded her agreement. Kate had made the right decision. She just wished she could give up Ben so easily.

Chapter Eighteen

Davie stared up at the clear, blue August sky from which the sun beat down relentlessly. It was so hot. There wasn't even a breath of air, he thought irritably. It added to his misery. He was able to get about now, using a stick, but it had been a long, painful recovery. He'd lost his job and his other source of income. He hated Big Kevin Mac with a passion but he also feared him.

He'd had endless questions fired at him – from the doctors at the hospital, from Maggie, from his da, from Alf – but he'd told no one the truth. He'd not said a word about the forged money, knowing that that would mean risking severe injury or 'an accident', possibly a fatal one. He'd told Maggie that he'd had a difference of opinion and a bit of a set-to with Tommy's brother, and he'd stuck to the story for his da, to make things easier. Only one set of lies. Both Maggie and Alf had wanted to go to the police, but he'd managed to persuade them not to.

He sat gazing morosely at the back yard wall. It had been a miserable summer and not just for him. During his enforced idleness he'd taken to reading the newspapers. 'God knows why I even bother, everything is so bloody depressing,' he'd often said to himself. The prospect of war was growing, it seemed. Both Britain and Germany had been rapidly increasing their fleets. The world's biggest ship, the *Bismark*, had been launched in June, and the Archduke Franz Ferdinand had been assassinated in that month too, but as he understood neither the politics nor the implications of what was going on in foreign countries Davie didn't take a lot of notice of the 'scaremongering', as his da called it.

He'd read that the Kaiser had now taken offence at Britain's suggestions to mediate between the already warring factions. The Austrians had taken courage from that and had already declared war on Russia. The Tsar had ordered the mobilisation of his armies, and Germany and France had responded with orders to their own troops. The headline in today's paper read 'Will Britain Fight?' He threw the paper down in disgust. If there was a war he'd bet his life the army wouldn't take him, nor was it any use having big ideas and ambitions. What money he had managed to save was quickly being used up and what he would do when that supply was gone didn't bear thinking about. Maggie, however, was doing very well. She'd found workrooms in Faulkner Street in one of the large houses. Slowly the wealthy merchants were moving away from the district. A few years later it would become an exodus, but it was still a good area.

Maggie now employed two girls, one an experienced cutter and the other a bodice hand. She also sent work out. She wasn't even nineteen and yet her reputation was growing amongst the young, smart set. Maggie was mature for her age, at least in business matters. She'd told Davie how one of her clients had said it was so nice to have someone of your own generation to design and make your special dress, someone who was young and yet very astute. They'd both had to look the word up in the dictionary. Maggie was already talking about looking seriously at millinery, veils, gloves and shoes.

He got to his feet with difficulty, grimacing slightly. He was fed up and bored just sitting here. He'd go round to the Royal George and treat himself to a pint and he'd need it by the time he got there. Maybe there would be some lively company, too. It was August Bank Holiday Monday and many people had gone out for the day, but not he, nor Maggie either. She had a big order on.

By the time he arrived at the pub he was sweating profusely and the effort of his exertions showed clearly in his face. None of the lads he knew was there. A few of the older men stood around in groups, and Matty Ryan, Bill Greenway and Alf McGee appeared to be having a serious conversation.

As he caught sight of Davie, Alf looked concerned. 'Davie, lad, you look all in. Sit down. You shouldn't have come so far by the look of you. Will you have a pint?'

Davie nodded his thanks, both for the offer of a drink and the chair Alf had pulled forward for him. 'I thought maybe Pat or Kieran or Niall might have been in.'

'No, they've other things on their mind and so have we.'

'What things?'

'War, Davie. It looks as though we can't escape it, now that the Kaiser has declared war on the Tsar. The Royal Navy's been mobilised.'

'I know. I've just been reading about it all in the paper.'

'Our Tom said town is full of navy reservists. He's gone to join the

Royal Navy. His mam doesn't know yet, so if you see her, Davie, don't say anything, for God's sake.'

'Aye, my lot can't wait to join up,' Matty added. 'It might do them some bloody good. A bit of discipline never hurt anyone.'

'They're all hot-headed, Matty, but I've got to side with them over this.'

Alf looked thoughtful. 'I can't see why they didn't all get together and sort it out between them.'

'Between who?'

'The King, the Kaiser and the Tsar. They're all cousins, Matty. The old Queen, God rest her, was their grandma, all three of them.'

'It's gone beyond a family bust-up, Alf.'

'What I'm saying is it shouldn't have been let get beyond a family row and this Government has been too taken up with Ireland and all this Home Rule business.'

'So that's what I'm supposed to go home and tell my lads? It's all off, and them raring to go,' Matty said, thinking how a statement like that would be received in their house.

'What they don't seem to realise is that in a war people get killed and wounded, that's all I'm saying. They just don't think that far ahead.'

'No one will stop them now, Alf, and you've got to agree that it's a just cause. If the Kaiser takes over Belgium and France, will we be next?'

The three men nodded silently, absorbed in their own thoughts. Davie sipped his beer but he didn't enjoy it. It tasted bitter suddenly. He would be left behind. When they all went marching off to war, he wouldn't be with them. He'd not be able to share their experiences. Neither the army or the navy would take him, not with his bad leg. It was something else to add to the store of hatred that was building up against Big Kevin Mac.

Kate and Evvie were sitting on the front step that evening. It was cooler than being in the house or even the back yard, where the walls trapped and held the heat. Peg had both the front and back doors wide open to catch any bit of breeze there might be. It was sultry. 'Headache weather', Peg called it, adding that a good storm would clear the air and make life easier for everyone. It was so hot at night that no one slept well.

As it began to go dusk Agnes Hawkins joined them and a few minutes later Maggie appeared with her sewing basket under her arm.

'It's a bit like when we were all kids, remember? We'd all sit on the steps or on the kerb under the lamp.'

Evvie drew aside her skirt so Maggie could sit down.

'I'm tacking this bodice and I can do it out here just as well. It's so hot inside the house, my head is throbbing.'

'How are you going to see to tack?' Agnes queried.

'The lamplighter will be here soon. I'll wait.'

'How's Davie? I saw him this afternoon. I think he'd been to the pub.'

Maggie shrugged. 'He's about the same really, Kate. It is getting better but slowly. I still don't know whether to believe him about him having had an argument and that Kevin Mac kicking him. Now he's upset that he'll miss all the excitement with this war business.'

'Oh, aye. It's all our Tom's gone on about since he got home. I'm not supposed to tell you, but that's where he went this afternoon, with half the crew of the *Carmania*. I can't see them being able to sail unless they can sign on another crew. I bet they are all celebrating somewhere.'

'So where exactly did they go?'

'To join the Royal Navy. To sign up.'

'What about Brid O'Hare?'

'Oh, that was over ages ago. You know what she's like, a different feller each fortnight.'

'Won't your mam have a fit?' Agnes asked.

'She won't when Da and Tom get through explaining everything to her,' Kate stated.

'I wish someone would explain everything to me, Kate. I don't know how we've managed to get involved. I don't understand anything about politics or foreign archdukes and tsars and emperors,' Maggie said.

'It'll be all over by Christmas, so Da says,' Kate added. 'That's why our Tom rushed off.'

'And that's why Davie is so fed up. I wish old Harry would get a move on, I'm wasting time.'

As Maggie spoke the rotund figure of the lamplighter could be seen down the street. As the lamps were lit they threw out a circle of brightness into which moths and other winged insects were instantly drawn.

'We've been waiting for you, Harry. Maggie can't see to do her sewing,' Evvie called to him.

As he lit the gas he smiled at them. By, they were a pretty group of girls, he mused to himself. No need for posh frocks for these Liverpool lasses. Like a posy of flowers, they were, and with their whole lives before them. 'Now don't get on yer high horse. I'm a bit late tonight. People keep wanting to stop and talk.' His expression changed. 'It's all this business about war. Oh, I can tell you a thing or two about war. I had a bellyful of it in South Africa. I fought the Boers, an' a tough bunch they were, too. It's not all drums an' bugles an' God Save the King – or Queen as it was then. There's not much glory in it but try telling that to the fellers around here. They can't wait to go. They think it's going to be a flaming picnic. An' here's another lot who can't wait to go an' fight Kaiser Bill.'

The little group looked in the direction he indicated. Four figures were making their way down the street from the main road.

'It's our Tom and the three Ryan lads,' Kate said as her brother, Kieran, Niall and Pat drew closer.

'Well, we're in. All of us. Signed on the dotted line,' Tom announced proudly.

'And sworn to fight for King and Country,' Niall added.

'I hope it keeps fine for yer all, lads,' old Harry said tartly, before he moved on down the street.

Kate looked up at Tom. 'So you really have gone and joined up?'

'I have, Kate. They're going to send for me soon. I'll be off to Chatham. They've joined the King's Liverpool Regiment,' Tom informed his sisters, jerking his head in the direction of the Ryan boys. 'Our Joe's really fed up because he's not old enough.'

'Then you'd better get in and tell Mam. She's not going to like it.'

'Have you told your mam yet, Kieran?' Evvie asked.

'No, I think she had an idea though.'

'She won't know herself with you lot out of the way. The house will be empty and a sight tidier too,' Maggie commented.

'And she'll be better off. She won't have you eating her out of house and home.'

'Well, let's go an' tell her the good news then,' Pat urged.

Kieran desperately wanted to talk to Evvie, but he certainly wasn't going to ask her to come for a walk with him in front of everyone.

As the three Ryans crossed the road and Tom went inside, Kate sighed, thinking of Charlie. 'I wonder if things will change.'

'Of course they'll change, they'll have to.'

'How, Maggie? We won't have to do anything, will we?'

'I expect we'll just have to wait and see, Kate. Was that thunder?'

'I hope so or we'll not get a wink of sleep tonight. That bedroom is like an oven.'

Peg was not happy although Bill and Tom tried to to lessen her worries.

'It will be over by Christmas, luv, and as for Tom here, well, there's no need to worry there. We've got the biggest and best fleet in the world and have had since Nelson's day. He probably won't even see a German ship.'

'Well, I can't help it. I'm bound to worry, aren't I? There are lads who are going to get hurt. Mary Ryan isn't too happy either, even though it will mean less work for her and more money in her purse. Have they actually said it's on?'

'You mean has war actually been declared? No, but it could be tonight or tomorrow. But they've got to get organised first, Peg. The lads have all got to be trained and that takes time. They may not even see a single shot fired in anger. It might all be over before they're ready.'

'Maybe and maybe not,' Peg answered.

Bill's theory proved correct. War was declared on Tuesday, 4 August and the call to arms brought hundreds of thousands of boys and men flocking to recruiting offices all over the country. Lord Derby raised three whole battalions of the King's Liverpool Regiment, known as 'Pals' because they all worked together and lived in the same neighbourhoods. But there were no uniforms and no weapons and training was on a daily basis in the parks throughout the city, until things became more organised.

Tom was sent for three days later. The Royal Navy was well equipped and proud to live up to its name of the senior service. The Greenways all went to Lime Street Station to see him off. The station concourse was crowded with men, all sailors and their families.

'Will they give you a ship straight away?' Kate asked.

'I don't know. I suppose so.'

'You will write and let us know what's going on?'

'Of course I will, Mam. Well, I suppose I'd better get on the train and see if I can get a seat. It's a long journey.' Tom shook his da's hand and Bill beamed back at him. It was a fine thing to have such a grand lad going off to fight for all that was right.

Peg kissed him and then hugged him and then she stepped back as Kate and Evvie said their farewells. Tom punched Joe playfully on the shoulder. 'You'll have to give Mam and Da a hand. You have to take my place here. I'll be back soon and I want to hear what a good lad you've been.' Joe gently punched his brother in return, but he stood a little straighter at Tom's words.

'I don't want it to be over soon. I want it to go on until I'm old enough to join up. It's not fair. You lot are going to get all the fun.'

Peg turned on him. 'Joe Greenway, that's a terrible thing to say! You can get round to confession when we get back, talking like that.' She was only just holding back the tears, She *was* proud of Tom but it didn't stop her worrying and wondering when she would see her eldest son again.

'Trust you to say the wrong thing,' Tom muttered to Joe.

He waved to the little group as he made his way towards the crowded platform and they all stood and waved back until finally he was lost to sight in the crowd.

The following evening Evvie was startled to see Peg usher Ben into the kitchen. Her mother's lips were set in a tight line of disapproval. Bill looked up from his newspaper and instantly a frown creased his forehead.

'All right, before you get all airyated, Bill, let the lad have his say.' Peg folded her arms across her chest and stood waiting for an explanation from Ben.

'Mr Greenway, Mrs Greenway, I'm sorry to intrude. I know I'm not welcome, but do you think I could take Evvie out for an hour? There are special circumstances and I won't be troubling you again after tonight. I'm off to Grantham in the morning for training. I joined up before war was declared. I could see it coming.'

He looked pleadingly at Bill, and Evvie held her breath. Silently she begged Bill to agree. If Ben was leaving Liverpool tomorrow then she desperately wanted to have some time with him.

'Evvie?' Bill asked quietly.

'Please, Da?'

'All right then, but just an hour. I want you back in here at nine.'

She got up, took her hat from the shelf and pinned it on, looking at neither her mother nor father.

The weather was still fine and it was a pleasantly warm evening.

'Where would you like to go?' he asked when they were out of the house.

'I don't know. Somewhere near, we haven't got long.'

'Stanley Park?'

'We'll still have to get the tram.'

'Well then, do you just want to walk?'

'No, there are too many people around and too many people nosing out from behind their curtains. It had better be Stanley Park.'

They caught a tram but during the journey they were both silent as if afraid to speak to each other in public, frightened of breaking down and clinging to each other.

The park was far from empty; it was too fine an evening for people to stay indoors. There were quite a few men carrying on their training manoeuvres in their own time. The flowerbeds were a riot of colour and the rays of the now setting sun caught the dome of the bandstand, tinting it gold. They finally sat down on a gentle rise overlooking the boating lake.

'Why did you volunteer so quickly, Ben?' Evvie asked quietly.

'There didn't seem any point in staying around, not for me anyway. And, like I told your da, I could see it coming.'

'I thought . . . I thought you might have . . . found someone else.'

'Oh, they've tried, Evvie. They've tried very hard and they mean well. No less than three eligible young ladies have been found for me by Dad and Mrs Myers, the Matchmaker.'

'Do you still have them? Even now, in this century?'

'Yes, it's part of the tradition, the custom.'

'Oh yes, the "traditions".'

'Evvie, don't be bitter, please.'

'I'm sorry, Ben. I didn't mean it. They'll not let me see you again, you know that.'

'I know, but I couldn't go without talking to you, Evvie. I still love you.'

This was too much for her. 'Don't, Ben, please!' She tried to get to her feet but he caught her arm and pulled her back.

'Evvie, don't run away from me.'

'I've been trying so hard to forget, Ben, and it hurts.'

'I didn't mean to hurt you, Evvie. I just wanted you to know that I love you and that that's why I'm going.'

She was a little more composed but her hands shook. She clasped them tightly in her lap. If she were to touch him, she would be lost. 'I'd be lying if I said I don't love you, Ben, but I'm trying to come to terms with knowing that I'll never be able to be with you.' She swallowed hard. 'What . . . what will you do after the war is over? Da says it will be over soon, probably before our Tom gets properly trained.'

'I don't want to come back to Silvester Street, Evvie. Can you understand that? I can't live all my life in the same street, the same neighbourhood and never be able to even speak to you. I've been thinking for a while about starting my own business. I have got some savings and Dad says he will put some money into it too.'

'What will you do? Open another shop?'

'No. I want to go into upholstery, soft furnishings. Styles and fashions will change, Maggie knows that, and not only in clothes but in houses and furniture, too. There is a place for furnishings that are moderately priced yet of good quality, somewhere between what you see in the very grand houses and what can be bought in the markets and the really cheap shops.'

'So, you'll leave Silvester Street?'

'Yes, hopefully I'll move to Chester. As a shopping area it's growing and gaining prestige.'

'What about your da?'

'He'll come with me, so he says, now at any rate. He'd like to retire.'

She shivered as though a chill wind had suddenly sprung up and she was trying not to think of the years ahead. Years without him . . . 'Then I won't see you . . . ever . . . again?' The words stuck in her throat and the tears were stinging her eyes.

'That was the general idea, Evvie. I can't go on all my life loving you, living almost next door to you, and knowing you can never be mine. That I can't even touch you or kiss you.'

'Oh, Ben, I feel so . . . so . . . miserable. Everything is . . . hopeless.'

'Maybe you should marry Kieran, Evvie. He does love you and he's good and kind and —'

'Stop it!' she interrupted. 'How can you say that?'

'Because I don't want you to waste your life. I don't want you to become an old maid because . . . because of me.' He leaned forward to kiss her but she pulled away.

'No, Ben, please, don't! I couldn't stand it. I'd break down. I would just want to run away with you. Anywhere, somewhere where we could be together.'

'Maybe we should have just done that a long time ago, Evvie. Maybe we just didn't love each other enough to ignore everyone else, what they felt, what they believed in.'

She fought down the sobs, but she couldn't stop the tears. 'And now it's too late. I'll never see you again.'

'No, but I'll write and tell Dad to at least let you know that I'm safe.'

Evvie nodded, glad that dusk was falling rapidly and that people were leaving. She blinked hard, trying to clear her vision. Soon the park keeper would be locking the gates.

Ben helped her up and bending, he gently kissed her forehead, steeling himself against the urge that made him want to hold her for ever. It would be utterly selfish, he told himself. To give in to his desire now would be the most hurtful thing he could do to her. He delved into his pocket and brought out a cameo ring that had belonged to his mother.

'Evvie, take this. I want you to have something to remember me by. It was my mother's.'

Evvie let him place the ring on her finger. On the third finger of the right hand, not the left. Tears welled up in her eyes and she could only nod her thanks.

Ben took her hand and they walked in silence towards the gates and home.

Chapter Nineteen

Desolate though she was, Evvie knew as soon as she opened the door to Kieran that this time she couldn't refuse his request to take her out.

'Come in, I'll get my hat. I won't be long.'

When Peg saw him come into the kitchen, smiling, while Evvie searched for her hatpin, she sighed with relief. At last. At last Evvie hadn't refused him. Maybe now her prayers would be answered. She'd been uneasy the whole of the time Evvie had been out with Ben. She'd even wondered if Evvie would come back at all. What will I do if they've gone and eloped? she'd asked herself, but she needn't have worried. Evvie had returned. She'd been very quiet and subdued, and Peg could see she'd been crying. Nothing had been said by either Evvie, Bill or herself, and Evvie had gone straight to bed. Peg hadn't questioned her at the time, because if she were really honest she didn't want to know the answers. Besides, Evvie would probably tell her in time; despite that affair over Ben Steadman they still had a close relationship. Maybe Ben had urged her to see Kieran, perhaps that was it.

'Bye, Mam.'

'Bye, Evvie. Bye, Kieran,' Peg called, thinking it was a pity it had taken a war to make Evvie realise how Kieran felt about her.

'Where are we going?' she asked when they were out of the house.

Keiran shrugged. 'You choose.'

'Oh, I don't mind, anywhere except Stanley Park.'

'What about Lester Gardens?' He took a deep breath. 'I . . . I want to talk to you, Evvie.'

She knew what was coming and she was already trying to form the words in her mind, words that would let him down easily.

It was only a short tram ride. Lester Gardens were set between Archer Street and Furness Street at the bottom of Royal Street. It was a pretty enough place, she thought, and it was quiet, despite the fact that it was surrounded by buildings. Or maybe because of it. People went to the parks because they were large open spaces.

There was a bench set in a small arbour festooned with roses that had been left to revert to briar, and she wondered why she hadn't suggested to Ben that they come here. It was much more private than any park.

Kieran had been rehearsing what he would say to her for days but he was still very reticent. He hadn't felt at all nervous when he'd gone and joined up, but then he'd had Niall and Pat with him and a lot of other lads he knew.

Evvie decided she would have to break the silence. 'Kieran, thanks for . . . for not telling on me.'

'I was going to a couple of times, but in the end I just couldn't hurt you, Evvie.'

'It's all over now, I suppose you know that. I suppose the whole neighbourhood knows.'

Kieran felt so relieved that he could have jumped for joy. 'No. No, Evvie, I didn't know. I hoped that it was, but . . .' In the past Josie had been his source of information concerning Evvie, but since she'd got married she hadn't seen much of her former friends. He left the rest of the sentence unsaid, wanting to know more, yet not wanting to ask directly.

'He came to see me, the other night. He wanted to see me before he left for Grantham.'

Kieran didn't speak.

'He . . . he won't be coming back to Silvester Street after the war. He's going to start his own business, in upholstery. He and his da will be moving away to Chester.' She wondered why she was telling Kieran all this, but it only seemed fair to give him all the facts.

'They'll sell the shop?'

She nodded. 'I think I've been so unfair to you in the past, Kieran. What I'm saying is that for Ben and me, it's over. We can never be together, but I still love him, Kieran, and I suppose I always will.'

All Kieran's well-rehearsed speeches fled from his mind. 'Evvie, you'll change. In time . . . maybe you could . . . well, you could love me.' He knew he sounded a fool, stuttering and stammering like that, but he just couldn't help it and he couldn't stop now. 'I want to marry you, Evvie. I've always loved you, you know that.'

This was exactly what she had feared. 'Oh, Kieran, I wish I could love you. You really deserve to be loved. You're so kind and gentle and . . . good. Any girl would be happy . . . to have you as a husband.'

'Any girl except you, Evvie?'

'I don't want to hurt you any more than I've already done, Kieran. I don't deserve your love. I can't lie and say I'll love you or that I'll marry you. We would only end up tearing each other to pieces, like Frank and your Josie.'

'Evvie, it wouldn't be like that. Frank doesn't love Josie, but I do love you. I'll be a good husband.'

'Stop, Kieran, please! I . . . I can't marry you. I'm very . . . fond of you, but that's not enough.'

'It is for me, Evvie,' he pleaded.

She got to her feet and looked down at him sadly, the tears not far away. She'd meant everything she'd said to him. He was so loyal, so devoted. Oh, why was she being so cruel to him? She could never have the man she loved so why couldn't she accept Kieran's love? He would be good to her. 'Oh, Kieran, maybe in time. I don't know.'

He jumped up and caught her hands. 'Will you think about it, Evvie? I wouldn't rush you in any way. When the war is over – will that be time enough?'

She swallowed hard. What had she done? She couldn't hurt him now. 'I'm not promising anything, Kieran. Now, I feel as though I won't love anyone again. It hurts too much. Maybe I'll always feel like this. Maybe I won't.'

'I won't mind, Evvie. I'll wait until you know. I don't mind how long it takes. I've waited all this time; even another couple of years won't matter.'

She couldn't see his face, her eyes were filled with tears. What had she done? She hadn't meant to give him any false hopes. She'd heard the joy in his voice. 'Please, Kieran, don't press me. Don't hold me to anything. Don't make me say things or promise things I don't mean.'

When he spoke the eagerness, the hope, had gone and it drove the knife deeper into the awful wound of guilt.

'I won't, Evvie. But I'll write to you, will that be all right? You won't mind if I write?'

'I won't mind.' She wondered how long she would feel like this. How long would it be before he finally gave up all his dreams? Would she have changed even in six months? Would he have changed? She doubted it. She couldn't ask Mam's help or even Kate's. Kate had lost the man she loved and yet had ended her affair with Charlie because she couldn't love him or fit into his world. At least Kate had been honest with Charlie.

Josie had just put Matthew down to sleep and she smoothed away a strand of dark hair that clung damply to his forehead. It was still so warm, she thought. He didn't need any covers over him yet. She'd come up later when it had become cooler.

She could hardly credit that nine months had passed since she'd had him, or how much her life had changed. He was the centre of her world for she and Frank hardly exchanged a word these days. Flo had become more amiable and Josie had found her sympathetic when asked for advice. She spent part of her day round at Mam's but there was so much noise, so much confusion and clutter, that she was always glad to get back to Athol Street.

She wasn't used to such untidiness now. Mam had absolutely no system at all for anything. She did wash on Monday, but it still all seemed to be hanging around the house for the rest of the week. As for cleaning – well, Mam's idea of that was 'a lick and a promise'. Nothing was ever done methodically or thoroughly, the way Flo cleaned. Josie knew there were corners in her mam's house that hadn't seen a sweeping brush or a mop for years, and God alone knew what lived under the scullery sink or under the stairs. She really didn't blame Mam too much. She must have got very disillusioned years ago, Josie reasoned, what with her da and all the lads traipsing in and out all times of the day and night, dumping clothes everywhere and clumping through the house in their dirty working boots. Flo would never allow either Bert or Frank beyond the scullery door in their working clothes. At Flo's house things were put away, if not immediately then within a couple of hours. Nothing was ever left neglected for so long that its owner gave it up as lost, and was surprised when it was discovered, months later.

The door slammed downstairs and her brow creased in a frown. Couldn't anyone close a door quietly? She didn't want Matthew awake. It was probably Dotty. She did it on purpose, the nasty little madam. Oh, but she'd got the measure of Dotty. She'd caught her one day rooting about in one of the drawers of the chest in their bedroom. She'd given her a hefty clout, something she'd been asking for for a long time. 'And you go whinging to your mam and I'll tell her what you, Nelly Roach and Tilly Barton were up to in Holden's shop. I saw you putting halfpenny liquorices in your pockets.' After that Dotty had been very wary of her.

The baby hadn't stirred so she went downstairs. There was no sign of Dotty but Frank and Flo were in the kitchen and Frank was actually smiling. In fact he was grinning.

'You look like the Cheshire Cat from out of that book,' Josie remarked tartly.

Flo looked far from happy.

'Well, I've got something to grin about for a change, haven't I?' He felt happy, elated, interested in life – feelings he'd not experienced since before he'd married her.

Josie looked at Flo questioningly but there was no response from her mother-in-law.

'What?'

'I've joined up.' He felt proud to be able to say it and he squared his shoulders and straightened up.

'Is that all? At least it will keep you sober. We might even get a regular wage out of you.'

'Josie, is that all you've got to say?' Flo demanded.

'What else am I supposed to say? He doesn't care a fig for me or Matthew and you know that. It doesn't matter, I don't care, I've got my baby.'

'I do care about Matthew, you lying bitch.'

Josie rounded on him. 'Don't you call me a bitch! You don't care. You never take him out, you never play with him. You never buy him things.'

'That's because you always make damned sure he's in bed when I get home, and I do buy him things – or I would if I had the money to spare.'

'You've money to spare for ale. The state you come home in you don't know what day of the week it is. Do you think I'd leave my baby in the care of a drunk? He's mine, Frank Lynch. It's *me* he loves, and he'll go on loving me but he'll grow up hating you, I'll see to that.'

'Listen to her, Mam, just listen to my so-called bloody wife! Well, it's you I'm getting away from, Josie. I can have a normal life, with some excitement, some future. I can do something useful and I'll be as far away from you as possible. And if you try and turn Matthew against me, I'll kill you, Josie, and by God I mean that!' He snatched up his jacket and cap.

'And now I suppose you're going to do what you usually do, get so drunk you can hardly walk home. Oh, a fine soldier you'll make, Frank Lynch! All the Huns will have to do is wave a bottle at you and you'll give up.'

'I hate you, Josie! I wish . . . I wish a bloody tram would run over you!'

'Stop that! Stop that, Frank! It's downright wicked to say something like that!' Flo cried.

The front door slammed so hard that the cups on the dresser rattled and from upstairs came the fretful cry of a baby whose sleep has been disturbed.

'Now look what he's done.'

'Josie, you're a hard-hearted little bitch,' Flo snapped.

'Am I supposed to fall on his neck? Am I supposed to thank him for ruining my life? What kind of a life will Matthew and I have with him? If it wasn't for you and Mr Lynch we'd be in the workhouse now.'

'Josie, he could be wounded or . . . or even . . . killed.'

Josie was unrepentant. 'And I'm supposed to go after him and say, "Frank, I'm sorry, I don't want you to go"? You heard him. He hates me enough to wish me dead. I won't be a hypocrite and lie to him. You tell him how upset you are. You pray for him because I won't. Now, I'm going to have to get Matthew back to sleep and if Frank comes in and starts banging around, I'll bloody kill him myself.'

All the pleasure, the comradeship, the sheer enjoyment of joining up had gone. She'd managed to spoil even that, Frank thought furiously as he strode down the street. She was a bitch, a nasty, conniving bitch, saying she'd turn his son against him – and she'd do it, too. Well, when the war was over there would be some changes in Athol Street. He'd throw her out, send her packing back to that midden, number eight Silvester Street, but not with Matthew. He'd get advice, legal advice. It would cost but he wouldn't mind that. He would save up. Out of the seven shillings a week the army would pay him, he'd send five home to his mam and he'd save the other two. He'd get his bed and board and his uniform, he didn't need much else. They'd start training soon and this would be the last night he'd drink himself into oblivion. He had a purpose in life now and he would be away from Josie.

As he turned towards Hopwood Street his spirits rose. He was free, almost. He'd be away from Mam and Dad too, for they both disapproved of the way he behaved these days. They just couldn't understand how bad life had been. To hell with them all. He'd be with the lads, with all his mates, and there'd be great goings-on. This war couldn't have come at a better time. He'd thought his life was over, that excitement, hope and purpose were dead, but he'd been wrong. No, things were looking really great.

He decided he'd go to the Royal George and see Kieran Ryan, so he carried on along Latimer Street and turned up Silvester Street.

As he neared Holden's shop Kate came out. She hadn't seen him and had turned away to walk home.

His spirits rose even higher. 'Kate! Kate, wait!' he called, breaking into a run.

Kate's heart dropped. She couldn't ignore him. She couldn't pretend she hadn't heard him. It was too late, she'd already turned around. If she started to run now, she'd look such a fool.

'Kate, I wanted to see you.'

'How are you, Frank? How are Josie and Matthew?' She kept her voice controlled. She remembered that she'd said the same things to him last time they'd met.

'Matthew's fine.' He ignored her reference to his wife.

'I'm on my way home.'

'Walk this way with me, Kate, please?' He indicated the entry that ran behind the houses.

'It's out of my way, Frank, and Mam is waiting for this stuff.'

'Kate, please. I want to talk to you before I go.'

'Go where?'

'I've joined up.'

She nodded. She knew she was being foolish but if he was going away . . . well, what harm could a few minutes cause? Evvie had had an hour with Ben Steadman. She walked beside him up the narrow cobbled way until he stopped.

'You know that Tom has gone to Chatham. Kieran, Pat and Niall Ryan have joined up and gone to Prescot to train. So have Georgie and Fred Hawkins. Ben Steadman's gone to Grantham; he'll be one of the first to go to the front.' She was gabbling on, trying to postpone the inevitable.

'I know all that. I'll be going to Prescot myself. Kate, you remember what I said the last time I saw you? When you were going off to see that Charlie Wilson?'

'That's all over, Frank.'

'I know. Kieran told me. Kate, will you write to me?' he pleaded.

'Frank, please . . . you're married. Mam would murder me if she found out. You can't write to me either, Frank. You must understand: you're a married man, there can't be anything between us.'

'I'm going to leave Josie after the war. Well, I'm going to make her go back home.'

'You can't do that!'

'I'm going to. I hate her, Kate. I can't stand the sight of her.'

'Frank, it won't help. You still won't be free. You promised "until death do us part."'

'We can go away somewhere, Kate. I'll take Matthew and we can go somewhere where no one will know us.'

'Frank, stop it! Stop it! It's just a crazy idea. I couldn't do that to Josie or to Mam and Da. I couldn't do it, Frank – not even for you.' She was praying that no one could hear them – that no one was in the back yards behind the walls.

'But, Kate, I love you and you love me. I know you do, otherwise why did you give that Charlie up? He had everything to offer you.'

She had her back to the entry wall and she was shaking. He caught hold of her shoulders and pulled her towards him.

'Kate, Kate, I love you.'

Her resolve was slipping away. He was going to war and she didn't know when she would see him again. Nor would she know how he was faring for there could be no letters. She raised her face to his and closed her eyes. She didn't care who saw her, she just wanted these few precious minutes with him.

He held her tightly, all his love and longing surging through him. She did love him. She'd gone on loving him all this time. 'Oh, Kate, Kate,' he whispered, kissing her cheeks, her forehead.

The touch of his lips sent tremors through her and she felt weak and dizzy. 'Frank, why did you ever betray me? I love you. I've always loved you.'

He kissed her then on the lips and her mouth opened like a flower beneath his. Time seemed to stand still. The noises of the street faded, caught and held somewhere beyond the fragile bubble of ecstasy that enclosed them both.

When at last she drew away she buried her face against his shoulder. 'Oh, Frank, how am I going to go on now? How will I know where you are, what's happening to you? I can't spend my days and nights not knowing. I'll go insane.'

He cast about frantically for a solution. 'I'll write to Davie Higgins. He can pass the letters on to you.'

'How?'

'I don't know, Kate, but there's no one else, is there? I'll find a way, I swear I will. Oh, Kate, I love you.'

'I love you, Frank, and no matter what happens, I'll go on loving you.'

He tried to draw her closer to him again but she pulled away.

Reality was encroaching on the dreamlike trance that had held her. 'Frank, I'll have to go or Mam'll send someone out to look for me. Take care of yourself, please.'

He released her, those few precious moments over. 'Oh, Kate. We'll find a way to be together after the war, I swear it. Will you write to me?'

She nodded, then, placing her fingers on her lips, she blew him a kiss and turning, ran into Silvester Street and towards home.

Frank watched her and sheer joy filled him. Oh, life was sweet now, he thought. In a matter of a few hours it had changed completely and for the better. He felt he could face anything and anyone now. She loved him and when the war was over they'd sort something out, even if he had to drop any claim to his son.

'Where have you been? I'd given you up for lost and your da's waiting for his cup of tea. A nice state of affairs when a man can't have a cup of tea because his daughter's been jangling.'

'Sorry, Mam. I just didn't realise the time.' Kate ducked her head as she passed Peg the tea and sugar she'd been sent for.

Bill didn't notice anything amiss. He was concentrating on writing a letter to Tom.

'You can put your bit on the end of that, Kate,' Peg instructed, making the tea.

'He's got a ship, HMS *Victorious*,' Bill informed her.

'Oh, that's great, Da. Where's Evvie?'

'Upstairs, putting away her clothes,' Peg supplied.

As soon as Evvie saw her sister she knew something had happened. 'What have you been doing? Your cheeks are pink and your eyes look all . . . glassy.'

'I met Frank Lynch as I was coming out of Holden's. I couldn't avoid him.' Kate sat down on the bed and began to pick at the coverlet.

Evvie folded her stockings and closed the drawer. 'And?'

'And he's joined up.'

'And what else, Kate?'

Kate sighed deeply. 'Oh, Evvie, I couldn't help it. I let him kiss me and . . . and I told him I love him.'

'You let him kiss you in the middle of the street! Kate, are you mad? Someone will have seen you. Mam will be livid.'

'It wasn't in the street, Evvie, it was in the entry. What was I supposed to do? He's going away and I do love him.'

'Oh, I know, Kate, but what will happen now?'

'Nothing. He was talking about leaving Josie after the war. Of taking the baby and running off with me.'

'Dear God Almighty! Kate, you didn't agree to go, did you?'

'No. He can't do it. I won't let him. It would kill Josie and we'd never be happy. At least I wouldn't. It was a mad idea. Oh, Evvie, I just don't want to think about the future. All that matters is that I love him and he loves me. That will have to do for now.'

Evvie nodded. She'd felt the same way all those months she'd been seeing Ben. 'Live for today' had been her motto then. She also knew that like her love for Ben, Kate's love for Frank had no future.

'I said I'd write to him and he said he'd write to me. He's going to see if Davie will pass his letters on to me. There's no one else he can send them to.'

'Do you think it's wise to write at all, Kate?'

'Isn't Ben going to write to you?'

'No, there'd be no point. It would only make things worse, more painful. We both agreed on that. But I will write to Kieran.'

'Is *that* wise?'

'It's fair. I said I'd write. I haven't promised anything more.'

'Oh, Evvie, what are we going to do? It's so . . . so crazy, all of it. Why can't life be uncomplicated?'

'We've just got to make the best of it, Kate. We've got to grow up. Maybe that's what's the matter with us both. We need to look at things more seriously, get rid of all the daydreams and face reality, be more practical. "What can't be changed must be endured", isn't that one of Granny Greenway's sayings? Still, we've got a while before we both have to make decisions.'

'Maybe the war will go on for a long time. Maybe we'll not have to decide things for ages. Oh, Evvie, I know it's wrong, but it's the only thing I can think of that will keep me sane.'

Evvie shivered. 'Don't talk like that, Kate. We don't know what the future will bring.'

'Sorry, it's just how are we both going to cope with the future?'

'I saw something in the paper last night. They were asking for girls and women to join a new nursing thing, the Voluntary Aid Detachment.'

'We don't know anything about nursing.'

'I know, but we could try. It would be *something*, Kate, something to help, and it might take our minds off . . . things.'

Kate nodded. 'Where do they say you've to go?'

'Walton Hospital.'

'Do you want to go, Evvie?'

'I think so.'

'All right, we'll go and see what it's all about after work tomorrow.'

Chapter Twenty

They went the following evening after work. When they got off the number thirty tram at Rice Lane they looked across at the huge, soot-ingrained building with its tall square clock tower.

Evvie said, 'It looks a bit . . . well, a bit —'

'Grim,' Kate finished.

'It used to be the workhouse, so Mam told me,' Agnes informed them. She had joined them after hearing of the plans as she'd met them on their way home from work.

They walked tentatively into the main reception area and it did indeed look grim. The walls were half-tiled in white and the area above the tiles was painted a dark green. The floor, too, was tiled.

'That's for the bugs. Bugs don't like green paint,' Agnes said sagely, pointing to the wall.

'God, Agnes, you're full of sweetness and light, aren't you?' Kate said.

It was she who first approached the nurse on duty, seated at a large desk at the far end of the room. Wooden benches placed in rows filled the rest of the room and they were empty.

'Excuse me, but is this where you come when you want to join up? The Voluntary Aid Detachment, I mean?'

The nurse looked up. She was in her thirties, Kate thought, and she wore no wedding or engagement ring. Her starched apron crackled when she moved and her equally stiff cap and cuffs were pristine.

She stood and smoothed down her apron.

'Yes, it is. I'll go and fetch Sister Williams. She'll deal with you. I thought we were finished for the day. Everyone else came in a steady stream throughout the day until six o'clock.'

Kate was becoming irritated by the woman's attitude.

'Well, we work during the day.'

'Exactly what kind of people came "throughout the day"?' Agnes asked.

'People who don't need to go out to work. It is the *Voluntary* Aid Detachment, you know,' came the sarcastic reply.

'Yes, we do and we're *volunteering*, so can we see someone, please?'

Evvie looked down at her feet. What the woman was saying was they didn't want factory or shop girls. She felt acutely embarrassed and the smell of carbolic and ether was making her feel a bit sick.

The nurse left them.

'Isn't she a bitch! God, I hope they're not all like her, otherwise I'm going home. "People who don't need to work", if you don't mind!'

'Well, I'm not stopping either if they are, Agnes,' Evvie replied.

'Oh, take no notice,' Kate said, looking around her. The building's former use seemed still to hang over it and she shivered, thinking of all the misery the inmates had suffered within these walls.

Only the Sister returned and they were all glad when she greeted them civilly.

'I hear that you all want to volunteer but that you work during the day.'

'That's right, Sister.'

Sister Williams' gaze swept quickly over them, not indicating in any way that she was aware that identical twins stood before her. The more composed and confident girl in the blue and white dress, with a blue ribbon around her straw boater, seemed to be their spokeswoman.

'Then let me take down some details, although I can see that I'm going to have to duplicate yours.' She smiled at the twins and drew a large ledger from a drawer of the desk.

'Excuse me, Sister, but will we be able to continue working? You see, Mam still depends on our money for the housekeeping.'

'I don't see why not, at least while you are training. After that you'll have to give in your notice because you'll be going to France.'

After she'd taken their details she sat back in the chair and looked up at them.

'This is not a rest home or a convalescent home. Your training is going to be very hard work and something quite different from your current employment. It's true that most of the girls and women who have volunteered so far come from very different backgrounds from yours, but we're going to need nurses. Training you should take years, not months, but I don't have time for that. I just wish that we had been given more notice. Training could have been well under way by now.'

'I know, Sister,' Kate said quietly. 'I write to a girl – well, she's a lady – and she has been keeping me informed.'

'Indeed? And what would her name be?'

'Chapman. Cecile Chapman.'

'Lady Cecile Chapman? She's in prison.'

Kate became confused. Why hadn't Cecile told her that she was a titled lady, like Lady Lytton? And Cecile had been so nice, so caring and so brave. Kate was even more ashamed now of her weakness. Cecile – Lady Cecile – would have been out by now if she hadn't been serving the extra time for herself. She didn't think that now she could write to her friend in the same easy way. Somehow the class divide had opened up in front of her again.

Sister was waiting.

'I know she is,' Kate replied.

Sister's expression hardened. 'Then you are a suffragette?'

'I used to bc but not any longer. Not after the town hall sit-in. I got into serious trouble with my da over that.'

'He sounds like a sensible man. I don't hold with what they are doing – burning down buildings, chaining themselves to the railings of Buckingham Palace and the like – but they have got a point and I think this war could be useful, no matter how short everyone thinks it's going to be. There are women taking the place of men already and doing the job better.'

'Is . . . is there anything we need to bring, when we start, I mean?' Evvie asked.

'No, just yourselves. We provide a uniform which you will have to pay for, not all at once though. Will you be able to come every night?'

'Yes, Sister, and at weekends.'

'Then I'll expect you to be here by seven at the latest tomorrow evening.'

Sister Williams watched them as they left. Those two were so identical that they must have caused havoc at school when they were younger, she thought. Tomorrow she would ask them to wear a red and a blue ribbon respectively so they could easily be identified. She certainly had no intention of spending time asking them who they were.

After a week Evvie was sorry she had volunteered. The sickening antiseptic smell greeted her at the door and the work was hard – very hard – and quite revolting at times.

'I thought we were going to be trained as nurses, not employed as flaming domestics,' Agnes complained as they were all scrubbing the wooden tables in the kitchen.

'So did I,' Kate agreed. 'I think we all know how to scrub a table. We've done enough of it at home.'

'Maybe because we come from Silvester Street she doesn't think we do it.'

'Evvie, don't start that again. We are all as good as the others who come in the daytime. It's something Cecile taught me – not to be afraid of people who have got more than us or who are better educated.'

'Have you seen what's next?' Agnes asked, jerking her head to indicate a work sheet that was pinned on the wall.

'What?'

'The Sink Room.'

Kate pulled a face. 'Oh God. Isn't that where they keep bedpans and things like that?'

Agnes nodded. 'On my half-day off I came down here and I was talking to a girl who was in service and had joined with the lady she worked for. It all sounded pretty awful but maybe she was just trying to upset me. She obviously thought she was better than me because she worked in a big house in Rodney Street and I only work on a fruit stall in the market.'

When they progressed to the Sink Room it was far worse than Evvie had expected.

'Oh, Kate, it's horrible!'

'You'll get used to it. Stop moaning, Evvie. And stop talking or Sister'll be in on top of us with more instructions.'

Everything in the Sink Room had to be scrubbed: shelves, tables, bowls, sinks and rubber sheets. Urinals and bedpans were stacked on the shelves, with their covers, and the trainees were instructed on their use and their cleaning. There was a big sack of what looked like straw in one corner and Evvie had examined its contents.

'What's this stuff for? It's like they make coconut matting from.'

'I don't know, Evvie.'

'We'd better ask.'

Sister Williams came in to see that work was progressing to her very high standards and that there was no idle chatting or gossiping.

'Sister, what is the stuff in the sack for, please?' Kate asked. 'We've never seen anything like it before.'

'It's called "two". It's hemp and you take a large handful and stuff it into the handle of the bedpan.'

'I'm sorry to be so ignorant but what do we do with it then?'

'It's used instead of toilet paper. To be blunt, it's to wipe the behinds of patients.'

They all blushed furiously. Oh, they were used to certain things, living as they did in such overcrowded conditions, but they'd never had to do anything like this before. It sounded awful.

'You dispose of it in that bin there. It's taken away and burned. Then you throw the rest of the contents of the bedpan down the sluice.' She pointed to a big sink with huge brass taps. 'And then you scrub out the bedpan and its cover. Does that answer your question, Nurse Greenway?'

Kate gulped. 'Yes . . . yes, thank you, Sister.'

'Oh, and when you get some minutes to spare take some bandages and linen home with you.'

Evvie felt as though she didn't want to know what they were for.

Seeing their mystified faces Sister explained, 'The bandages are for rolling. They've already been washed and dried. The linen is for shrouds. I presume you *can* sew. They require only straight seams.'

When she'd gone Agnes turned to Kate. 'Mam will go mad if I tell her I've got to make shrouds. You know how superstitious she is. She'll not have them over the doorstep, or me either. I'll be sitting in the yard sewing them.'

'Well, I've got to say I never thought we'd have to do something like . . . that. It's all pretty awful, but I suppose it's part of the job. But shrouds!'

'You're here to work, not to complain and gossip,' came a sharp voice from the other side of the door.

'She's got eyes in the back of her head,' Agnes hissed, raising hers to the ceiling.

'I think I'd sooner stick to the table scrubbing,' Evvie whispered.

When they told Peg about the duties they'd learned of that day she was horrified.

'Jesus, Mary and Joseph! I thought this nursing was a good idea, but bedpans! Expecting decent young girls to do and see . . . things like that. It's disgusting.'

'Mam, we'll have to get used to it. When we're sent to France we'll be looking after soldiers who can't get up and walk to the toilet.'

'Kate, don't! It just doesn't bear thinking about. Young girls and soldiers! Oh, Mother of God!'

'Mam, how do you think some of the others feel – girls and women who have never had to share a privy at the end of the yard, or a bedroom even? It's going to be worse for them.'

'I just don't know what the world is coming to. I know that Miss Nightingale changed nursing but I wonder if it was really worth it.'

'Mam, don't be so old-fashioned. That was the Crimean War, this is 1914.'

As the weeks passed they progressed to what Kate called 'real nursing'. They learned about morphine, ether and paraldehyde, which had a foul smell and was used for insomnia. They were taught how to dress wounds, use a thermometer, check a pulse and give an enema.

'When are we going to get time to write up those notes? I don't understand all those big words,' Evvie asked one night on their way home. She was very tired. They all were. They were tired when they got home after a day's work and now they had to spend every evening and weekend at the hospital.

'None of us understands anything properly, Evvie, we haven't got the education. But for God's sake ask, or I'll ask, what it all means. She's not that bad, isn't Sister Tutor. Not compared to Sister Williams, who's a real battleaxe.'

Sister Tutor had a porcelain figure of a human being covered with little hooks and a box of small pieces that fitted on to the hooks. The bits were shaped like the heart, the liver, the kidneys, and numerous bones. She also had a skeleton and the very first time she saw it Evvie had let out a shriek. She'd received a very sharp rebuke and stern words about being 'grown up'. They were supposed to make notes and learn them, but it was hard, especially when you were so tired. They'd managed to club together to buy a second-hand copy of *Taylor's Manual of Nursing* and *Black's Medical Dictionary*, and the latter was pored over every day and was even taken to work to use in the lunch break.

Maggie thought they were all mad.

'Why did you have to volunteer now?' she asked. 'Why didn't you wait? They might not need you even, and you're half killing yourselves going to Walton every night, your half-day *and* every weekend.'

'The lads that are training in the parks after work could tell you why, if you want to know, Maggie,' said Kate quietly.

'That's different. If you wanted to do something, why didn't you volunteer to give up your jobs and get new ones? Ones that the men used to do – clerks, shop assistants, things like that?'

'Nursing's more use,' Kate said flatly, and Maggie gave up.

* * *

By Christmas it was obvious that the war wasn't going to be over quickly. As early as 23 August, the British Expeditionary Force was in retreat and Mons had fallen. Casualties were heavy. By September, German troops had advanced deep into France. They had overrun Rheims and were pushing on towards Paris. In Belgium Liège had fallen and only the depleted Belgian army stood between Brussels and Antwerp. The British Expeditionary Force and the French army were holding south of Paris, and news was beginning to come through of a new type of warfare. The Germans had miles of deeply dug trenches and there was fighting from Belgium in the north to Alsace and Lorraine in the south. Herbert Asquith, the Prime Minister, called for fifty thousand more troops to join the British army.

All the local boys had gone to either Prescot or Knowsley Hall, where they were in training, and from where they would eventually go to France. Except for Tom, who aboard *Victorious* was away at sea, though just quite where he was the Greenways didn't know.

On 20 March there was a huge march past of all the Liverpool regiments and Lord Derby took the salute on St George's Plateau. Everyone had gone to see the boys, everyone except Davie.

Davie sat in his room, the old tin box that held his money on his knee. There were only a few coins left now. His hatred of Big Kevin Mac was so strong it tasted like bile in his mouth.

He was broke, all his dreams and ambitions were as dust under his feet. He was crippled, useless, no one wanted him. Not Mr Healey, not the army. Even Maggie, in time, might think she was better off without him. Big Kevin Mac should pay, he thought. He should pay for what he'd done, for the life he'd ruined.

'Davie! Davie, are you up there?'

It was Maggie's voice. He sighed heavily, heaved himself to his feet and made his way slowly and awkwardly down the stairs.

Maggie could see by his face that he was upset. 'Where is everyone?'

'Gone into town to watch the bloody parade.'

'Davie, don't swear.'

He sat down on the sofa and she sat beside him and took his hand. 'Don't be upset. I hate to see you like this.'

'How can I help being upset? I should be down there marching along with them, with all my mates.'

'Yes, and some of them are going to die and some are going to be wounded and maimed.'

'Just like me, but at least they'll have suffered in a good cause, an honourable cause, and people will feel sorry but proud of them.'

Maggie sighed. Sometimes now it was so hard to see what she'd seen in him. He'd changed, through no fault of his own, but she *did* love him.

'I'd sooner have you here and alive, Davie, than in a hero's grave. Stop it, for heaven's sake. Try to look on the bright side. You'll get work. Someone is going to have to take all the jobs the men have left.'

'Aye, women and girls and men like your da and mine – old men, too old for the army or navy. I don't want to be pitied by old men. He's robbed me, Maggie. Big Kevin Mac has robbed me of my chances, my future.'

She squeezed his hand. 'Oh, Davie, I know how much you wanted your own business and a grand life, but we'll manage. You'll get a job soon.'

'What kind of a job, Maggie? I'm never going to have my business now and I'm not going to live off you.'

'Did I say you were?'

He didn't answer her. She was successful, she had her own money now, it was easy for her to say 'we'll manage'. He had his pride.

'Davie, pull yourself together and stop brooding. It won't help.'

'Oh, for God's sake, Maggie, stop preaching at me. What am I supposed to do?'

'I'm sorry.'

'No, I'm sorry. You've taken the time to come here and all I do is yell at you. God, but I wish I could get my hands on that bastard.'

'You should have gone to the scuffers.'

He nodded thoughtfully. 'Maggie, I didn't tell you the whole truth. It wasn't Big Kev who did this, it was one of his mates, someone called Lol.'

'Then why didn't you tell someone?'

'That's not all, Maggie. I'd been working for him.'

'I know. You'd been doing his books.'

'No, I'd been running a book for him. He paid me fifteen shillings a week and I'd gone to see him about, well, about getting more work.'

Maggie's eyes were wide with amazement. 'Are you mad?'

'Let me finish, Maggie. I needed the extra money badly. You were racing ahead and I was just lagging behind, getting nowhere.'

'As if that mattered, Davie Higgins.'

'It mattered to me, Maggie. It mattered a lot. I . . . I was going to ask him if I could sell some stuff for him. To earn more money.'

'To get yourself arrested, you mean.'

'When I went into his office, Tommy was there and two other fellers. Hard cases they were, real hard cases.'

'So, what did he say to you? What did that flaming Tommy say?'

'Nothing, they . . . they were all counting money. I don't know if I should tell you this, Maggie.'

Her eyes had a hard glitter in them. She was going to get to the bottom of this once and for all. 'You might as well, because I'm not going home until I've heard everything, even if I have to stay here all night.'

Davie knew she meant it, and anyway he was sick of brooding over it.

'Like I said, they were counting money. I'd never seen so much money in all my life. All fivers, piles of them.'

'What had they done, robbed a bank?'

'No, it was forged. Tommy was holding a note up to the light and he said something about it being as good as the real thing. Big Kev belted him and told him to shut up.'

Maggie was appalled. 'Oh God Almighty, it gets worse!'

'Then he told me to keep my gob shut. I swore I would and then, just as I was going, this Lol kicked me.'

'So that's how common trash like that can afford motor cars and gold watches.'

'I couldn't go to the scuffers, Maggie.'

Maggie was deep in thought, her eyes narrowed, the crease between her eyebrows deeper.

'What's the matter? Are you shocked?'

'Of course I'm shocked, but I've thought of a way to stop their gallop and benefit you, too.'

'How?'

She looked at him steadily. 'Blackmail.'

'God, Maggie, they'll kill me.'

'No they won't. Not if you do it properly. Right, listen to me, Davie. You write to that Big Kevin Mac – I presume he can read – saying that you're going to the scuffers. Say that you're going to tell them everything, all about the forged money, the stolen stuff, the gambling, unless he pays you . . . say three hundred pounds.'

'Maggie, I couldn't do that! They really would kill me.'

'They won't lay a finger on you. How much do you reckon there was?'

'I dunno, maybe two hundred.'

'Right then, say you want two hundred.'

'But, Maggie —'

'Will you stop that? Sometimes I wonder why I bother at all. You're not very smart at times, Davie. All you have to do is write everything down on a piece of paper, put it in an envelope and give it to me. On the outside of the envelope you write, "To be opened by the Liverpool City Police should anything happen to me." In your note to that shower of thugs, you tell them about the other note and say that if anything happens, even the slightest hint of a threat, then that letter goes straight to Hatton Garden. You don't need to say who is keeping hold of it – or maybe you should.'

'No, Maggie, I'm not putting you in danger. I know them, they'd beat you up, or your mam and da, or all of you, and they'd ransack the house until they found it.'

'Then take it to a solicitor and tell them that too. They won't dare to touch you, Davie, and you'll have the money.'

Davie looked at her with amazement and awe. He'd thought his dream was dead, but now there was hope again. 'Maggie, you're the smartest person I know. Any other girl would have had hysterics or even fainted, but you – you just used your brains.'

She smiled at him. 'And that's why we'll get on, Davie. You and I.' Her brow creased in a frown.

'What's the matter now?'

'Maybe you shouldn't open a garage, Davie. I mean, they'd know. They would find some way of, well, smashing it up.'

'Would they dare?'

'I think they might try. Perhaps you'd be better waiting for a while. Oh, and tell them you want it all in pound notes. I wouldn't put it past them to try to pay you off with forged fivers.'

'I'll write the letters now.'

'Post theirs and I'll take the other to a solicitor in town tomorrow. Tell them to send that useless gobdaw Tommy round with the money.'

She sat and watched him as he wrote. She felt no qualms of guilt, only proud satisfaction. Oh, Davie had been a fool, but in her opinion people like the MacNamaras should have been drowned at birth; the world would be a better place without them. Well, that Lol, whoever he was, and Big Kevin Mac could pay up handsomely for what they'd done to Davie and to herself. His health and wellbeing affected her, too. She smiled grimly. He'd thought he was so cunning, so crafty, did Big Kevin Mac. It was a pity that he'd never know he'd been outsmarted by a girl of nineteen.

As she walked home with the letter in her pocket Maggie met Josie. She was carrying the baby, her shawl wrapped around them both. She looked ten years older than she really was, Maggie thought. She made no attempt to smarten herself up, her hair was greasy and straggling and her clothes were creased.

'Have you been into town, Josie, to see the big parade?'

'No, I went round to Mam's but they were all out. I expect that's where they've gone.'

'Isn't Frank with the other lads, marching down Lime Street?'

Josie shrugged. 'I suppose so. Flo and Bert have taken Dotty. I expect it will all be over now.'

Maggie decided to change the subject. 'Matthew's getting big now, isn't he?'

Josie's face became animated. 'Yes, he's sixteen months now. He can't half get into mischief, too.'

Maggie wondered why on earth the child wasn't walking instead of being carried. He must be heavy and Josie was so thin she looked as though a gust of wind would blow her over. She was overprotective, wanting to keep him a baby for ever, was what she'd heard her mam say about Josie.

'I've just been round to see Davie,' she added, not wishing to hear a catalogue of Matthew Lynch's escapades.

'How is he? Is he getting on any better now?'

'A bit.'

'It was shocking what that Kevin Mac did to him.'

'I know, but don't worry about Davie, he's got a good head on his shoulders. He'll do well, you'll see,' Maggie smiled smugly.

Josie turned away. Out of the corner of her eye she'd seen Agnes, Evvie and Kate coming down the street.

'Wasn't it great, Josie?' Agnes called, and Josie knew she couldn't escape now.

'She hasn't been. She didn't want Matthew getting crushed,' Maggie answered by way of an explanation, even though Josie hadn't given her a reason for not attending the parade.

Josie cast her a grateful look. You could always rely on Maggie to come up with a suggestion and quickly. She wished she was that clever herself.

'Well, it certainly was a sight. The bands were playing, everyone was cheering and singing, his nibs was up on the plateau, taking the salute . . .'

Josie was trying not to look at Kate.

'Give him here, Josie. It's ages since I had a cuddle.' Agnes held out her arms and Josie passed Matthew to her.

'Josie, he weighs a ton! You're going to do yourself an injury carrying him around all the time. Who's a big boy now?' She cooed to Matthew. 'Give Aunty Agnes a kiss.'

Maggie raised her eyes to heaven. 'She's just practising, Josie, for when she has one herself.'

'Well, that won't be for a long time, will it? I haven't even got a steady feller and everyone is going off to war. Still, we're going to do our bit, too.'

'Oh, you mean all this racing off to Walton at every opportunity? They haven't started recruiting girls yet, have they?'

'Don't mock, Maggie. They may want you one day. We've joined the Voluntary Aid Detachment,' Evvie informed Josie.

'To do what? What do they mean by "Aid"?'

'Nursing,' Agnes replied, handing Matthew back to his mother.

'You don't know the first thing about nursing, any of you,' said Maggie, who still didn't see the point.

'But we are learning, Maggie. And soon they're going to have to start asking more and more women to take the men's jobs an' all. In fact Lord Derby said something like that in his speech. He asked for "ladies", mind, to work in the shops, filling the men's jobs.'

'I'd sooner work in a shop than go nursing.'

'I'd sooner do anything than work in Silcock's,' Kate replied with feeling.

'Well, I've got my business to see to and I'm busy, too. Lots of girls are rushing to get married before their fellers go off.'

'You might have to give up your business, Maggie.'

'Never! Who said that?'

'No one, but you might be needed for something else,' Evvie ventured.

'Like what?' Maggie demanded.

'Oh, I don't really know yet. It was just a thought.'

Josie had said nothing. At first she'd been taking in the details of their clothes, comparing them with her own, comparing their lives with her own. She had Matthew and she wouldn't say she wished she'd never had him – he was her life – but when she saw them all together, she longed for her freedom. The freedom from worry, from her desperate existence with Flo and Bert. The freedom of being able to work, earn money of your own that you could spend how you liked. She had very few clothes. Frank gave what money he had to his mam. What she had and what Matthew had had been bought by Flo and they were all second-hand. Occasionally her mam gave her a shilling or two, when she could spare it, which wasn't often. Then she bought things for Matthew, never herself.

Maggie had always had far more clothes than anyone else and she was generous about lending them for special occasions. Josie often thought it was Maggie's aim in life to smarten up all the women in the street. Her clothes were very stylish, the material good quality. These days Maggie never went out without a smart hat and gloves – leather gloves in winter, cotton in summer, and in all shades. Today she was wearing grey. She wore a well-cut costume in grey wool, a white blouse underneath the jacket, with a cameo brooch at the neck. Her hat was dark grey velour but trimmed with bands of pale grey and white ribbon, and her gloves were grey leather.

Kate and Evvie wore coats – Evvie's dark blue, Kate's brown. Evvie's hat was also blue and sported a large blue flower. Kate's was cream, trimmed with a huge bow of brown ribbon. Agnes also wore a coat, but it was three-quarter length, her black skirt showing beneath it. The coat was red, as was her hat, a colour that suited Agnes. None of the clothes was expensive except for Maggie's. Cheap and cheerful, Agnes called them, but at least they'd been bought with their own money and chosen by themselves, not picked up from a second-hand shop, taken home and passed over without a word.

Josie didn't envy them going to be nurses. She had experienced childbirth, and that was a messy affair, and she knew about babies and all the unpleasant chores that went with them. She hadn't minded with Matthew, but she couldn't do it for other babies. No, nursing wasn't a job she'd choose. But shop work, that was something else.

When she'd left school it was something that hadn't even been considered. You had to be good at arithmetic, look smart and talk, if not what could be called 'posh', at least speak better than any of the girls she knew. But now things were different. As Agnes said, someone would have to step into the jobs the men had left empty.

'Did they say which shops or when?' she ventured.

'I suppose they meant all shops. I don't know when, though,' Agnes answered.

'Are you thinking of working, Josie?' Evvie asked.

'How can you with him?'

'Mam will mind Matthew for me, Agnes, if I ask her. Or Frank's mother.'

Kate winced at the mention of his name on Josie's lips. She pretended to peer down the street, unable to bear to think of Frank and Josie together. Josie hadn't even been to see the parade.

'Well, you can't go looking for work dressed like that, Josie.' Maggie as always was appraising everyone's dress and in her opinion Josie looked like the rag picker's daughter.

'I used to have some nice things.' Josie thought wistfully of the white blouse with the rosebuds embroidered on the front. She wasn't going to admit that she'd not had anything new since her wedding dress.

Maggie sighed. 'If you decide to go and look for a job, I'll lend you an outfit, and for heaven's sake, Josie, do something with your hair.'

Agnes came to Josie's defence. 'Maggie, stop being so flaming bossy. She hasn't got hours to spare sitting in front of the mirror, titivating herself up. She's got a baby to see to, remember.'

'I'm sorry, I didn't mean to sound bossy. It's just that I always seem to be looking at people and thinking how they *should* look, instead of how they actually *do* look.'

Evvie laughed. 'It's a good job you're not going to come with us. You'd be redesigning the uniform and giving lectures on How to Make the Best of Yourself.'

Maggie smiled good-naturedly. She didn't mind what Agnes said, what any of them said. It paid her to be objective; it was her business to see that all her clients looked elegant and beautiful. And at the end of the day, she had the last laugh. She guessed she had more money in her savings bank than any of them, and when Davie got his windfall, she had plans for that, and they didn't include opening a garage.

'I'd better get back. Matthew will be wanting his tea soon,' Josie said reluctantly.

'Remember, Josie, you come and see me before you go looking for work,' Maggie called, as she joined Agnes, Kate and Evvie, who had started to walk up the street.

'Do you think she'll get taken on in a shop?' Evvie asked Agnes.

'She's got to get her mam or Mrs Lynch to mind the baby first, and I don't think that's going to be easy. Her mam never went out to work, even though they could have done with the money. Said she was too worn out seeing to them all, but she was no more worn out than my mam or your mam, Evvie. And as for old misery guts Lynch, she definitely won't approve. She never went out to work either. I've heard Mam say they live on the smell of an oil rag in that house,' Agnes said tartly.

'Well, I hope she does get a job. She's had a rotten time,' Maggie said.

'It was all her own fault, Maggie. She knew what she was doing,' Evvie replied.

Kate said nothing.

'She's made her bed, et cetera, et cetera,' Agnes added.

Maggie sighed. 'I know, but I still can't help feeling a bit sorry for her.'

Chapter Twenty-One

On the following Monday Josie went round to see her mam. No one was home but Josie let herself in. She settled down to wait until Mary returned from wherever it was she'd gone. The front doors were always left open for no one had much to pinch and besides, anyone caught stealing from their neighbours was subjected to summary and very rough justice. The police were never called.

The house seemed strange now all the boys had gone, she thought, glancing around Mary's still untidy kitchen. Mickey was at school and her sisters were at work. She gave Matthew the little brass bells – bought for Mam years ago by Kieran – to play with. She opened the kitchen window a bit to let in a breath of fresh air. The room was very stuffy and the odour of damp wool was strong and cloying.

She'd been awake half the night thinking of what to say to both her mam and Flo. Now she went over it again and again in her mind until she heard footsteps in the lobby.

'I swear that woman gets worse. She was giving out the full details of Mabel Parkinson's confinement and I only wanted a bit of bacon and sugar. Put the kettle on, Josie, luv.' Mary dumped the bits of shopping on the table, after making space for them by a quick swipe of her arm that sent mugs and plates further up the table. She looked with disgust at the dirty dishes left after breakfast. 'I can never get to the end of the damned dishes.'

Josie pushed the kettle on the hob. 'You should make them all put their dishes in the scullery before they go out.'

'There'd be a flaming riot if I did that.'

'Mam, you've made a rod for your own back. All these years you've waited on them hand and foot. Make our Rose, Maureen and Sall do more for you. They don't do a tap.'

'They go out to work.'

'So what? It wouldn't hurt them to wash the odd dish or make the bed.'

'Oh, I couldn't put up with all the moans and complaints. It's easier to do it meself.'

'Oh, well, you sit down and I'll make the tea.'

'Take those bells off him, Josie. I've got a headache as it is.'

'He'll only kick up more, Mam, leave him.'

Josie poured the tea and handed her mother a cup. 'It seems strange without all the lads.'

'It's quieter, I'll say that much. And I've more money in my pocket. They send money home instead of drinking it. Mind, I have the devil of a time with yer da sometimes. He says he should have more now that I've got six of them paying up. He's forgotten I've still got him, Mickey and the girls to feed. He wants to keep all his wages, if you don't mind. The flaming cheek of the man! Still, I suppose I should be thankful he hasn't decided he doesn't need to work at all. "Mary," he says, "I'm getting too old for humping cargo around." Too old! He never did much when he was young and fit. I told him I was getting too old to be doing all the housework and his flaming meals. That shut him up.'

'Mam, I want to ask you something.'

Mary looked questioningly over the rim of her cup. 'What?'

'I was talking to Agnes and the others yesterday, and they were saying that women are going to have to take the jobs the men have left. They're looking for shop girls now and I thought maybe I'd go and see what I could get.'

'What about meladdo, here? Who's going to see to him? Here, give yer nan those blasted bells and have this instead.' Mary dipped a crust in sugar and handed it to her grandson, who immediately put it in his mouth.

'Mam, I wish you wouldn't do that. He gets all sticky.'

Mary tutted. 'You should stay at home, never mind thinking of going out all day and dressing yourself up. I've never had much in the way of clothes. It was hard enough keeping you lot in them, and in boots.'

'Mam, I won't be just dressing myself up. If I work I can buy all the things I want to get for Matthew. I won't need to rely on her or him. I won't have to see things, clothes and toys, and wish I could buy them for him. Please, Mam, will you look after him?'

'Have you asked Flo? Have you even mentioned it to her?'

'No, I thought I'd come to you first.'

Mary bit her lip and looked askance at her daughter. You couldn't fathom young girls at all today. They never seemed to be content with their lot, always wanting something else.

'You've got the time, Mam,' Josie coaxed.

'I haven't. Even with the lads away I still don't seem to have a minute to myself. Look at me now. Monday morning and I'm sitting here with you and the washing not even started.'

'Oh, never mind about the flaming washing. I'll give you a hand with it. Will you mind him, Mam, please? It won't be just for me, it will help the war effort. Evvie, Kate and Agnes are training to be nurses. I can't do that, but I could work in a shop.'

Mary pursed her lips. Thus appealed to, what could she say? No one was going to accuse her of not doing her bit towards the war effort and she with three lads in the army. 'All right, but you'll have to give me something, and you'll have to pick him up on time. I've still got the others coming in for their meal.'

Josie hugged her. 'Thanks, Mam. Come on, let's make a start on the washing, then tomorrow I'll bring him round and then I'll go into town and see what I can get.'

Flo was far from happy at Josie's piece of news. 'I don't approve of women going out to work, Josie, unless they are desperate.'

'Maybe you don't, but I'm sick of being stuck in here all day, of never having any money of my own. And I'm sick of looking like a walking rag bag.'

'Josie, I know you and Frank are not happy, but you've got to think of Matthew.'

'I am. I'll be able to buy him toys and clothes.'

Flo could see the girl had her mind set on this course and the thought of not having her moping around all day was very tempting. She'd have the house to herself for a change, and neither of them would be so much of a burden financially.

'Well, if you're dead set on it, Josie, you go, but I'm not having my grandson dragged around to Silvester Street every morning and then back again at night. It's unsettling for him and your mam's got enough to do as it is.' What she meant was that she couldn't bear the thought of her grandson being let loose in Mary Ryan's far from spotless house.

'You mean you'll look after him?'

'Yes.'

'I'll pay you.'

'I don't need paying, he's my grandson. And besides, Frank sends money home.'

'But I'll have to give you something. You've kept me all this time.'

'Then just give me what you used to give your mam.'

Josie could hardly believe it. She'd prepared herself for a battle royal, certain that Flo would raise a terrible fuss. Things were certainly looking up. Of course, she'd feel terrible leaving Matthew. If he cried and clung to her skirts she'd be dreadfully upset, but she couldn't pass up this wonderful opportunity. If she were honest, she was glad Flo had offered to mind Matthew. He'd be better off than with her mam. She'd wash her hair and go to see Maggie tonight and borrow something to wear.

That evening Hetty opened the door to her.

'Josie, come in. Maggie said you might call. She'll be in any minute now. Will you have a cup of tea?'

'No, thanks.'

'How's Matthew?'

'He's great. I'm going to try to get a job tomorrow. Ma-in-law is going to mind him.'

The girl looked so drab and down-trodden, Hetty thought. 'I think it will do you the world of good, Josie. You're not even twenty and you look as though you've the cares of the world on your shoulders. Oh, here she is now.'

Maggie smiled at Josie and her mam. 'So, you've sorted everything out, Josie?'

'Yes. Frank's mam is going to see to Matthew.'

Maggie raised her eyebrows. 'Really? That's a turn up for the book. Well, let me have a quick cup of tea and then we'll see about something for you to wear.'

Five minutes later they were up in Maggie's bedroom.

'You've lost weight,' Maggie stated as she critically appraised Josie's slight figure.

'I know, but I've never really been bonny.'

'Being skinny doesn't suit you. It makes you look old. Here, try this on.'

Josie took the navy and green tartan dress from Maggie and slipped it over her head.

'It's not too bad. A bit loose in the bodice but that won't show. Put this jacket over it.'

Josie pushed her arms into the sleeves of the navy-blue jacket Maggie held out.

'Fine. Now for a hat.'

Josie was flabbergasted by the size and variety of Maggie's wardrobe. 'Maggie, I've never seen so many clothes!'

'I make them myself. It's so much cheaper and it means I can buy more expensive materials.'

Josie's newly washed hair was tucked up in a loose chignon. Maggie placed a wide-brimmed, navy-blue felt hat over it, tilting it one side.

'You see, it's a . . . transformation. Some decent clothes, a hat and nice shiny clean hair and you look a different girl.'

Josie could only nod. The woman she saw in the mirror was a stranger. Oh, she'd not looked so smart, so . . . elegant, since her wedding day. She'd be bound to get a job looking like this. Already she felt younger and far more confident.

'You'll be able to buy some new clothes with your wages.'

'Oh, Maggie, you're so generous. You don't know how much this means to me.'

Maggie did. Having your own money made a lot of difference and looking at Josie now she felt sure she could have got herself a good respectable man if she hadn't been married to that deadbeat Frank Lynch.

Josie was loath to take the outfit off but she didn't want to take up any more of Maggie's time. She'd not even had her tea yet.

'Wish me luck tomorrow?' she asked earnestly as Maggie showed her to the door.

'Don't worry, you'll get something. Go for the bigger shops first.'

'I will, thanks. Goodbye, Mrs McGee,' she called as she stepped out into the street with new purpose and determination.

It was a pleasant evening and Davie and Maggie sat in the back yard on a bench. Hetty's yard was never full of rubbish, it was swept regularly and everything had a place. The tin bath hung on the side wall, the mangle and dolly tub stood against the opposite wall. The privy had been given the first of its twice-yearly coats of whitewash and lime, and a big tin of Jeyes Fluid stood by the door. Hetty even had some flowers, primulas, in a trough Alf had made from bits of wood. Their pale lemon petals stood out against the background of soot-coated bricks.

'Did Tommy say anything to you?' Maggie asked in a low voice. They'd come to sit out here purposely, giving the excuse that they might as well make the best of the lovely evening, after the miserable winter weather.

'Nothing. He looked scared.'

'Did you say anything to him?'

'Only that I was sorry for him. He was just trying to help me when all is said and done. He just handed me the parcel, and went off. Lizzie O'Connor was waiting for him on the corner although I hardly recognised her. She was looking very smart. Well, for her, that is.'

'Well, good riddance, I say. I wish to God you'd never met up with Tommy Mac again. Have you counted it?'

Davie nodded. 'It's all there. Two hundred pounds in one-pound notes.'

'You see, Davie, it worked. It couldn't fail. They knew they'd get twenty years in Walton if you told the scuffers and they're terrified now because of the letter. Solicitors and lawyers put the fear of God in them.'

'But I worry about you, Maggie. They may try to do something.'

'They won't. They know you'd never stand for it. Oh, let's forget about the MacNamaras. Where have you put the money?'

'It's still in the parcel, under my bed.'

'Don't you think it would be safer in a bank?'

'I don't like banks. They ask all sorts of questions.'

'They don't. Da went with me to Martin's Bank in Victoria Street and I opened an account.'

'You've got your business to see to.'

'You don't *have* to have a business.'

'I know, Maggie, but I'd feel safer knowing just where it is.'

'What will your mam say when she cleans under your bed?'

'She doesn't do that often and I'll move it.'

'All right. What are you planning to do with it?'

'I thought I'd look at some premises.'

'I'd wait a bit, let the MacNamaras settle down. They might all have to go in the army, which would be a blessing.'

'Aye, then they wouldn't be nosing around and I could get started. Oh, Maggie, I can't believe it. All that money. It's like backing the winner of the Grand National or coming into a fortune.'

'It's not. You earned that money, Davie. Think of all the pain and suffering you went through. Think of all your savings – That hard-earned money that you wanted for your business, all gone to pay for your keep. It's . . . it's like compensation, Davie, that's what it is.'

Hetty's voice calling for Maggie interrupted their conversation.

'Maggie! Josie's here again. She's brought you some sweets as a thank you.'

Maggie got to her feet. 'The daft ha'p'orth! She's going to try to get a job tomorrow and I lent her something to wear. She's got nothing decent of her own and she looks such a mess that no one would let her through the door, let alone consider her for a job.'

'You're very generous, Maggie.'

'I'm not. I made her wedding dress and that got me started. Without Josie I'd be working in some miserable, low-class workrooms for a pittance. I'd never have got on. I owe Josie a favour.'

'This house is like a morgue. I can't get used to having them out all day and night, with only Joe to torment me,' Peg said to Vi. She'd asked her in for a cup of tea, having met her in the market.

'I know, and the place doesn't get in a mess either, although our Liam still manages to litter everywhere with clothes and bits of wood and paper. His excuse is that he's trying to make a model of one of those aeroplane things.'

Peg shuddered. 'No one will ever convince me that those contraptions are safe. If God had meant us to fly He'd have given us wings. Deathtraps, that's what they are. Kate and Evvie are so tired when they come in they just fall into bed. I don't know about nursing, all they seem to be doing is skivvying: scrubbing floors, making beds, washing out bedpans. Seeing men undressed and having to help them with their . . . toilet.' Peg shuddered.

'Our Agnes says much the same. I think it's awful, the jobs they have to do and she says this Sister Tutor, whatever she does, has got a down on her. Meself I think our Agnes's too much of a daydreamer. She never concentrates properly. It was the same when she was at school. She's got brains, she just can't be bothered to use them.'

'How is Josie Lynch getting on with the job in Blacklers? She was lucky to get that. Mind you, she smartened herself up a bit.'

'She's loving it and so is Flo. She has all day to spoil the baby, Josie's not under her feet and there's more money coming in.

'Has Mary got over the cob she had on over Flo minding Matthew?'

'Oh, aye. I can't see what she had to moan about. Flo's got more time and room, and her place is like a little palace. I've never been in, mind, but I've heard people say it. And you're right, Josie's smartened herself up no end. She used to be so dowdy. You've got to admit, Vi, that she let herself go after she got married. She's still only a bit of a girl.'

At the sound of the front door being opened, Peg looked at the clock. 'Holy Mother, is that the time, and me sitting here jangling and Bill's tea not even started.'

Vi hastily gathered up her own bits of shopping. 'I'd best get back home meself.'

Bill looked grim as he nodded to both Vi and his wife. He had a copy of the *Echo* in his hand. 'Have you seen this?'

'Seen what?' Peg asked.

'There's been a heavy attack on an inbound convoy and the escort ships.'

Peg crossed herself. 'Oh, Lord help us.'

'There's not really much detail, but it says that possibly three merchant ships and one escort ship have been lost.'

Peg had sat down and she gnawed her lip with anxiety. 'Does it give *any* names? Any names at all?'

'No, luv, it says full reports will be available from the Admiralty tomorrow but the relatives will be informed first. As soon as possible.'

Vi patted Peg's arm. 'I'll go round to church tonight, Peg. There's a special rosary at eight.'

'You go with Vi, luv, and take our Joe and the girls with you, I'll stay here,' Bill offered, his glance straying worriedly to the newspaper once more.

There was no taking the tram to Walton that night. On their way home from work Kate and Evvie saw the headlines of the newspapers that were being read on the tram. There was quite a lot of speculation too amongst the passengers, all of whom declared that the Admiralty wanted to do something about the Germans and their bloody U boats, and quickly.

'Oh God, I hope they're right about the Admiralty doing something,' Evvie said as they alighted. 'Those horrible grey boats just lurk under the water like some kind of huge fish, trying to drag the ships down.'

'I wonder, does Mam know yet?'

'We'll find that out in a couple of minutes. Perhaps Da's home already and has told her,' Evvie said, fear in her eyes.

Seeing the anxious look on their mother's face as they entered the kitchen and seeing the newspaper in Bill's hand, they knew the speculation about the convoy was true.

'Oh, Da, what does it say?' Kate pleaded.

'Not much. I've read every line of it but it's only vague reports.'

'So no one knows how many ships have been . . . damaged?' Kate just couldn't say the word 'sunk'. Each time she heard of a ship – any ship – being sunk it sent a shiver down her spine.

'No, luv, and maybe that's for the best . . . in some ways.'

'I'm going to Our Lady of the Angels in Fox Street tonight with Vi. I'm taking our Joe.'

'We'll come too, Mam. They can do without us for one night. I'll explain to Sister tomorrow.'

Peg had never prayed so hard in her life before. In between each 'Our Father', 'Hail Mary' and 'Glory Be', she begged God to have spared Tom. The church was packed for there were many men from Liverpool who sailed regularly in the convoys. Even Joe seemed subdued.

Kate and Evvie spent most of the time with their hands covering their faces and neither of them could concentrate on the formal prayers. One plea went round and round inside both their heads: 'Please God, don't let him have been drowned. Don't let him have been killed.'

When the prayers were over, they went and lit candles before the statue of the Virgin Mary. All three stood with their heads bowed, each of them feeling the fear gnawing at them. They all wanted to *know*, to hear some news, anything about the tragedy.

At last Vi came and pulled at Peg's sleeve.

'Come on home, Peg. You can't stand here all night, luv.'

'Mrs Hawkins is right, Mam. Let's go home,' Evvie coaxed.

They spent the return journey in silence, each engrossed in their thoughts. Peg opened the front door quietly and slowly and Evvie clutched Kate's hand. She didn't want to go in and yet she felt compelled to. She couldn't just turn and run from the nagging fear. As Peg reached the kitchen door her chest felt as though her heart was about to burst through her ribs, her hand shaking on the handle.

As soon as she opened the door and saw Bill she knew. A telegram lay on the table in front of him.

'Oh no! No! Bill, not Tom! Not my lad!'

He put his arms around her and she could feel his shoulders shaking. She couldn't take it in. Not her tall, handsome, laughing lad. Gone.

'Did they say . . . how?' she managed to whisper.

'Torpedoed. Please God it was quick. There were no survivors from *Victorious*.' He eased her down in the chair by the range, and handed her the telegram.

She read the first few lines: 'The Admiralty regrets that Able Seaman Thomas Albert Greenway . . .' Then she let it fall to the floor and covered her face with her hands and sobbed.

Joe tugged at Bill's sleeve and the tears were coursing down his cheeks. 'Da, is . . . is our Tom . . . ?'

'Aye, Joe. Tom's . . . gone. God have mercy on his soul.' Bill pulled his youngest son to him and held him.

The girls had their arms around each other, Evvie sobbing quietly, Kate just shaking her head as tears coursed down her cheeks. Tom, who had always been so good to them, bringing them little gifts. Tom, who was always happy when he was home. He'd never sail from the Mersey ever again and they'd never go to see him off or welcome him home.

'Oh, Kate, why him? Why our Tom?'

'I don't know, Evvie. There will be hundreds asking that question in this city tonight,' Kate choked. She couldn't comfort Evvie with any more words, nor herself.

Bill at last made a move. 'Come on, son, let's get you to bed now,' he said to Joe. 'Evvie, Kate, make a pot of tea.' He glanced at Peg but she was just staring into space, the tears falling silently down her cheeks.

'Mam, do you want a cup of tea?' Kate asked, trying to fight back the tears.

'No. No, luv, but thanks.' There was a note of despair in Peg's voice.

'Then Evvie and I will go to bed too, Mam.'

Peg nodded and Kate put her arm around her twin's shoulders, the same sharp pangs of grief filling them both.

When they'd all gone Peg looked up at the statue her mother-in-law had given her so long ago. Oh, never in her life had she dreamed that she'd lose one of her boys like this. He was the first in the street to go to war and the first to be killed, and now he had no grave except the sea. 'Oh, take care of him, Holy Mother. Take care of him,' she sobbed.

When Bill came down he put his arms around his wife.

'The poor little lad says he's going to make a parcel of all his comics, marbles, candy wrappers. He said he's going to keep them for ever.'

His words brought on a fresh surge of tears and they clung together for support in this, the worst day in their lives.

They were not yet to know that *Victorious* had been hit midships bv two torpedoes. Her back broken, she'd gone down in eleven minutes. Three merchant ships, the *Hampshire*, the *Beaver Lodge* and the *Braemore* – a tanker carrying petrol – had all been lost. But HMS *Flint* managed to limp home despite the jagged-edged hole in her stern. She was a Corvette and rode light in the water, a fact her Captain thanked God for. The first torpedo had missed her completely, the second had caught her stern as she'd been rising out of a trough, her bows well clear of the water. Had she sat low like *Victorious* they would have been hit below the water line, and 752 men would have lost their lives that day.

Josie conveyed the sad news to Stanley Jeffries, a colleague, as they sat in Lyons Corner Cafe in Ranelagh Street.

'I'm sorry to hear that, Josie. They said in the paper that *Victorious* was blasted by two torpedoes. They never stood a chance and neither did many of the others. The *Braemore* exploded in a huge fire ball. Those men were the most vulnerable and the most courageous. They all knew from the start what would happen if they were hit. At least it would have been instantaneous.'

Josie nodded. 'I'd known Tom all my life and he was a great lad. Always cheerful, always generous. Unlike my husband,' she ended on a bitter, resentful note.

'Your husband's in the army, isn't he?'

'And he can stay there too.' She'd never discussed him or her marriage before strangers. 'Frank and I . . . we don't get on. We never have really.'

'Oh.' He fiddled nervously with the teaspoon.

Josie suddenly felt very weary of pretending as she had to do when her workmates asked about Frank – polite but not what you could call sincere enquiries.

'I was very young.'

'You're very young now, Josie.'

She smiled. 'I don't feel it, but I was only eighteen when I had Matthew. Frank and I, it was . . .'

'Convenience?' he suggested seeing she was struggling. He'd already guessed the truth.

'I suppose you could say that. It was a mistake, Mr Jeffries. A terrible mistake. He hates me, he said so often.'

'Oh, surely not, Josie?'

'It doesn't matter. There have been times when I've hated him too. He wasn't . . . the person I expected him to be. He . . . he was courting someone else, one of my friends, at the same time. I suppose I should have known but I didn't.'

'He was two-timing you?'

'Yes.' She felt the blood rush to her cheeks, remembering Frank's cruel words when he'd turned her away from the door, refusing to marry her.

'Josie, I don't like to see you upset and I don't know how he could have done such a thing to you.'

'You've never seen Kate – the other girl. She's a real beauty.'

'Beauty is in the eye of the beholder, so they say.'

She smiled. 'He should have married Kate. It was her he loved, not me, and I think she still loves him. It doesn't matter now.'

'You could get a divorce if you really felt you couldn't spend the rest of your life with him.'

'Oh, I couldn't do that! I'm a Catholic and besides, there's Matthew to think of. Frank *is* his father.'

'It seems so tragic to waste your life, Josie.'

She had begun to gather up her jacket and bag. 'I know, but things are much better than they used to be. He's away – his mam and I get on much better now. I have Matthew and my job and my friends.'

'I hope you consider me one of them, Josie?'

'Oh, I do. You are the first man who has ever been considerate and sympathetic to me. I . . . I really do think of you as a friend.'

'Then can we drop this Mr Jeffries? It's Stanley.'

'Oh, I couldn't call you that.'

'Not during working hours, of course, but at . . . other times.'

She wondered whether there would be 'other times'. He was a very kind man, but he was so much older than she.

He helped her on with her jacket and held the door open for her, thinking sadly that friendship was all there ever could be between them. She was so much younger and bound for ever to another man by vows that were stronger than any chains.

By October Josie's relationship with Stanley Jeffries was blooming. He treated her as no one else had ever done, with respect and deference and also almost like an equal. He made her feel that she was a person of some standing. All her life, and especially since she had married Frank, she'd been made to feel useless: plain, dowdy, only fit to work as a skivvy. It was true he was older, and she was still a married woman, but it did no harm. It wasn't as though she was madly in love with him.

At the beginning of October too the girls' training was finished; they had two weeks' leave and then it was off to France.

'I'll never be able to say the names of these places,' Kate said, poring over the letter they'd both been given. 'Boulogne, Pont Rémy, Vignacourt, Albert —'

'Well, you'll remember that one,' Peg interrupted.

'Just hold on, Mam, I haven't got to the last one yet. Hébuterne.'

'How do they expect you to speak to those people?'

'Mam, they're soldiers.'

'I don't mean them. I mean the others, the people who live there, God help them. Stuck in the middle of a battlefield.'

'Well, we're not going to look after them, just our own lads,' Evvie replied.

Now that the time had actually come to go to the front she was excited and apprehensive. Sister Williams had given them all a lecture, telling them of the conditions and the types of injuries they would face. Evvie had said nothing on the way home that night. She'd thought of Ben Steadman. He'd been one of the first to join up and he was fighting in France. What would she do if she saw him? How would she be able to stand it if he came in badly injured? How would she be able to stand it if any of the lads came in wounded? Later she'd voiced these thoughts to Kate.

'Evvie, don't you dare go getting cold feet now. We leave soon, for God's sake. If we do have to . . . to nurse anyone we know we'll do it professionally, just like Sister Williams told us to do. You have to put your own feelings away. You're a nurse first and foremost. Oh, you'll be all right. It's just nerves. We've never been anywhere, never mind a foreign country.'

'I know. I'm just being plain stupid.'

When the time came to go to Lime Street Station for the train they were all nervous.

Maggie went with them, for even though she thought they were a bit too quick off the mark, rushing off to volunteer, they were her friends.

There were other girls and young women at the ticket barrier. They all wore the dark green coat and 'pork pie' shaped hat as Maggie called it.

'God, isn't it awful?' she'd exclaimed when she'd first seen it.

'It doesn't look too bad if you shove all your hair underneath it,' Kate had replied, demonstrating the fact by pulling the hat with the narrow strip of brown leather and silver badge down over her forehead. Beneath the coat they wore the grey dresses and white aprons that had a red cross sewn on to the bib. Their starched caps and cuffs were in their cases.

Peg was in tears. Every night she still wept for Tom. She felt that if there was a grave, a headstone, it would help her in her grief. But thank God there was no danger of losing her girls. They would be working well to the rear of the front line.

'You'd better get a move on or you'll not get a seat, although half of this lot will have First Class tickets judging by the state of some of the clothes their families are wearing,' Maggie said.

There were hugs and kisses all round, and finally they went through the barrier, turning to wave just as everyone else was.

'You feel as if there should be a band and a few dignitaries to see them off,' Vi Hawkins said, feeling a little disappointed.

'They're nurses, Vi, not soldiers,' Peg said with a note of relief in her voice.

Chapter Twenty-Two

The Channel crossing wasn't too bad for the time of year. Although everything was grey, Agnes remarked morosely.

'The sky's grey, the sea's grey, even our uniform dresses are grey.'

'Aren't you a happy little soul? Don't start already, Agnes, for God's sake,' Kate said impatiently. They were all weary.

'It was just a remark. I wasn't complaining.' She lowered her voice. 'There aren't many working-class girls on board, though, are there?'

'No, I'll give you that. They're all quiet and well bred,' Evvie said, jerking her head in the direction of the girls and women who sat or stood in little groups.

The ferry was also carrying soldiers.

'I wonder whereabouts all these soldiers are going?' Evvie mused.

'Same place as us, I should imagine,' Kate answered. 'Evvie, what's the matter? You're not a bit happy or enthusiastic.' Kate felt her sister's mood.

'Oh, I suppose I'm just a bit nervous. Wondering what we're going to. Wondering if any of this lot —'

'Stop it, Evvie! You can't start off by wondering how many of these lads are going to be killed or wounded.'

Agnes raised her eyes to the ceiling. In her opinion Evvie Greenway would have been better in a shop or munitions factory. She might look like her twin but she certainly wasn't like Kate in nature.

'Just try and get some sleep. I heard one of the soldiers say it's like going on a neverending journey to get to the front.'

They did their best but Kate was already worried about Evvie. None of them knew exactly what lay ahead, in spite of their briefing by Sister Williams. Hearing about places and conditions was a far cry from actually being there and witnessing such things. She just dozed, as did most of the men, except for a few who were playing cards, and pitch-and-toss, which though a form of illegal gambling was tolerated. The men had to do something to keep themselves occupied.

Neither of them saw much of Boulogne, except the supply stores, and the horses of a cavalry unit and the rail yards. The train, pulled by a massive steam engine, that was to take them on the third leg of their journey was waiting.

'Isn't that huge? Our engines aren't that big.'

'Then let's hope it gets us there sooner than ours did getting us to Folkestone,' Kate replied acidly. That part of the journey had been very, very tedious.

They were shepherded on by a Senior Nursing Sister, Sister Caldwell, who had come to meet them.

'There is to be no mingling with soldiers. It's a long tedious journey so I'll distribute some sandwiches and some drinks, also some bandages that need rerolling.'

'Oh, not more flaming bandages!' Kate groaned.

'At least it'll keep us occupied and we are going to get something to eat and drink. I'm starving. We've had nothing since we left Folkestone.' Evvie tried to sound enthusiastic.

The train eventually left and finally Sister Caldwell arrived at the compartment they were sharing with two girls from Birkenhead and one from Anfield. The Sister was carrying sandwiches, drinks and bandages in a huge canvas bag.

'How long will it be before we get there, Sister?' Kate asked

'It depends on what the state of the tracks and the roads are like. The towns and villages we pass are in a bad way. Some are little more than mounds of rubble. The soldiers will march the last bit of the way. Don't expect to see much "countryside" – grass, trees, birds – that sort of thing. We'll be passing through places that have been fought over and hard won.'

'We were told something of the conditions before we left, Sister,' Kate said.

'That's as may be, but the real thing is ten times worse.' She looked from Kate to Evvie.

'Names?' she demanded of Kate and Evvie.

'Kate Greenway.'

'And Evvie Greenway.'

The older woman nodded curtly. 'Becaue it's so hard to tell you apart, from now on to all medical staff and patients you will be called "Nurse G1" and "Nurse G2". You can stitch labels to your dresses.'

'I don't much fancy being called Nurse G2. I feel like a parcel or something.'

'Shut up, Evvie, you're getting to be a real pain,' Agnes said, beginning to roll the long piece of cotton into a neat roll.

'Well, I *don't*!' Evvie replied mutinously.

As they passed through Abbeville, Pont Rémy and Corvie they were shocked by what they saw. Houses, shops, churches were all damaged, some beyond repair. There seemed to be men, artillery, ambulances, horses, mules and wagons everywhere. And everywhere there was mud.

'Oh, isn't it terrible? Fancy those poor people having to live in the middle of all this.' Evvie pointed to the scene beyond the window.

'From what old misery guts said, it's going to get worse,' Agnes said, referring to Sister Caldwell.

It did get worse. When the train had slowly chugged its way to Albert they all got off and were told to wait for the lorries to take them on to Martinsart, Englebelmer, Auchonvillers and finally Hébuterne.

They were all silenced by the devastation they'd seen in the villages they passed through; even the town of Albert bore the scars of heavy artillery fire. It was so hard to believe that once these had been peaceful old farming communities. Now they resembled demolition sites.

'Is there anywhere in this flaming country where there isn't any mud?' Kate asked the soldier who was helping her board the canvas-sided lorry.

'No, it's bloody everywhere. Sorry, my tongue just slipped, lass.'

'Where are you from?'

He grinned. 'Not far from where you've come from. Ormskirk.'

'I've heard of it but I've never been there.'

'Well, when this lot is over you'll have to come and visit me.' He laughed and then looked taken aback as Evvie placed her foot on the tail board.

'There's two of you! Isn't this my lucky day?'

Evvie laughed, too. 'We've got to stitch labels on us so we can be recognised. What's your name?'

'Tom Ormesher. What's yours?'

'I'm Evvie and this is my twin, Kate Greenway.'

'Good luck to you both and if I see you again, we'll have a drink together.'

'Sister will kill us if she hears talk like that! Do you want to get us kicked out before we've even got to the hospital?' Evvie laughed.

They were bumped, shaken and thrown violently from side to side as the lorry travelled the rutted, muddy lanes and they were glad of their heavy coats. It was freezing and they kept their hands in their pockets.

By the time they arrived at Hébuterne it was nearly dark and they were cold, hungry, thirsty and aching all over. It looked just like all the other villages they'd passed, the shells of buildings, blasted trees, abandoned vehicles and mules, wagons and guns bogged down in the cloying mud.

Sister Caldwell had a list and when they'd all got down she called out names and billets. Kate, Evvie and Agnes were all thankful that they'd be together. A soldier escorted them to what they took to be little more than a pile of stones with a roof on.

'It ain't much. It certainly ain't a palace, but at least you'll be dry and fairly warm.'

'In the name of God, why is there so much flaming mud in this country?' Kate asked, struggling to keep her coat and skirt out of it while clutching her small suitcase.

'Because it's always flaming raining and the roads have been blasted so many times, they're filled with holes and the holes are filled with water so you get mud. They're still being used, as you can see, so things won't get better until spring. You'll get used to it – you'll have to – and you'll have plenty of work to do.'

His words were drowned by a noise not unlike that of thunder. The three girls jumped and a few of the others cried out in fear.

'Oh Mary, Mother of God! What the hell was that?' Kate cried, while Evvie stood stock-still.

'It's artillery fire. We're shelling their trenches. Don't let it worry you. It's way ahead.'

'Way ahead! It sounds as though it's about five miles away down the road.'

'There's fighting going on at Fonquevillers. The front line trenches are up there.'

'Where is the hospital?' Kate asked, unnerved by the sound of the heavy guns.

'Just over there, on the corner of what used to be the village square. I think it was a public building of some kind, maybe for the Mayor.' Their eyes all followed his outstretched arm and then they all looked at each other in horror.

'It's a ruin!'

'So is everywhere else. It's not as bad as it looks.' He tried to sound optimistic. God help them, he thought. They'd probably never been away from their own homes before but they were now facing something as close to hell as you could get on earth.

They unpacked in the small stone room with its tiny window, from which the glass was missing, and which contained three camp beds and a washstand. Then having tried to make themselves understood to the stocky woman dressed completely in black who appeared to be the housekeeper, they decided to go over and look at the hospital.

'The first thing I'm going to do is get a pair of flaming boots, army issue if necessary. I'm sick of this mud already.'

'Honestly, Kate, how do they expect us to keep our uniform dresses clean, never mind our aprons, caps and sleeves? There's nowhere, nowhere at all, to wash them, let alone starch them,' Agnes wondered aloud.

'God knows. Maybe Sister Caldwell can tell us.'

The hallway of the building was small and dark and had pieces of tarpaulin covering part of the roof where a large section of the tiles were missing. The girls stood looking around them.

'Where are the wards?'

'Where are the operating theatres and sink rooms and —'

'We don't have the luxury of sink rooms or sluice rooms, and as for operating theatres, we have one small and not too badly damaged room.' Sister had come up behind them.

'You'll find no scrubbed floors or tables, and the place is almost impossible to keep clean. We patch the patients up and then they are shipped back down the line to Boulogne, if they're lucky. Follow me,' she instructed curtly.

They followed her into a larger room, which had windows and a tiled floor. There were rows of beds crowded into it and all were occupied by soldiers, all of them wounded. At the end of the room was a small desk on which there was a lamp and an assortment of bottles. A nurse sat writing into a book.

Another burst of gunfire broke the silence and one man began to scream. Sister went to him immediately and calmed him down.

'You'll see a lot of this. It's shell-shock. Some of them cry out, or scream hysterically, some don't utter a single word. Officially shell-shock doesn't exist but I can assure you it does.' She spoke directly to Kate, who had followed her and had bent to assist the man, plumping up his pillow and saying, 'Hush. Hush, now. It's only thunder.'

Sister Caldwell looked on approvingly. This one would be no trouble at all. Instantly she recognised in Kate all the characteristics of a good, dedicated nurse. She just wished to God she had more like her. The other two looked to be like some of the rest of her staff: little better than useless when under shell-fire. It was hard work not only to supervise them but keep them under control.

Kate looked down at her apron, beneath her half-open coat. 'Sister, do we *have* to wear these?'

'No you don't. It's impossible to keep them clean. You wear your dress and a calico apron, a tin hat like the soldiers, and in winter your army greatcoat.'

'But I . . . I . . . thought we . . .' Evvie stammered.

'Oh, I know what you thought and what you've been told, but we are almost in range of enemy artillery. Better safe than sorry.'

'And boots?' Kate added.

'And boots. See if you can scrounge a pair from the quartermaster or one of the lads. The only problem you'll have is that most soldiers have flaming big feet!' There was a spark of amusement in her eyes and Kate managed to smile back.

'When you've done that, report for duty. Your shift starts at six. That's when our day begins and we never know what it's going to bring. The shift system is completely abandoned when there's a battle going on.'

Kate nodded. 'Sister, what do we do about food?'

Sister's expression became grim. 'You demand to be fed. Madame over there has been paid for it but I think you'll find she's not very keen to part with it. They are a peculiar lot. I still haven't fathomed them out yet. Go on now and get settled in.'

When they'd managed to get a bowl of some kind of oatmeal and a slice of black bread plus a mug of terrible coffee out of 'Madame' they all huddled together on one of the beds, wrapped in blankets and still wearing their coats.

'Well, we've certainly had our eyes opened today,' Kate said.

'I'm beginning to think that working in munitions would have been better than this. At least we had some food and warmth and clean clothes and we'd be better paid too,' Agnes said morosely.

Kate could feel that there was something wrong with her sister.

'What's the matter, Evvie?'

'I think I agree with Agnes. I . . . I never expected it to be anything like this, Kate.'

'None of us did. But we've got to get on with it.'

'But it's not even a proper hospital.'

'Agnes Hawkins, didn't you use your eyes on our way here? Did you imagine that a building like Walton would be here waiting for us, untouched by shells or grenades?'

'Of course I didn't, but . . . but . . . it's awful.'

'I know it's awful but it's the best they have, and for God's sake don't either of you forget just why we're here: to nurse wounded men. Oh, it's freezing in here. We'll end up with pneumonia. I'm going to ask Madame if we can light a bit of a fire.'

'What with?'

'Anything I can find. There's all kinds of rubbish out there.'

'And it's all soaking wet and covered in mud and we've got to report for duty. She hasn't given us a day off.'

'I think the mud is something we're going to have to get used to,' Kate said sharply as she went in search of Madame, a woman with whom she was to have many arguments in the future.

The day proved to be fairly quiet and they concentrated on cleaning, learning the doctors', surgeons' and chaplain's names – as well as those of the soldiers who were able to speak. All the routine tasks were carried out until the girls were dismissed, being reminded that they started at six the following day.

They got little sleep, even though they were tired out. All night the artillery barrage continued, and Kate went to the small window in the wall and watched the bright orange flashes that lit up the dark sky. This was a world gone mad and she was worried about how Evvie would stand up to it.

They were on duty in good time. There wasn't much preparation needed except to get a wash in the freezing cold water that Madame had brought them, get dressed, tidy their hair and walk across the shell-pitted square, surrounded by what was left of the trees that bounded it.

From the quartermaster Kate had wheedled three pair of boots and three tin hats.

'Sure, they'll do you fine. Just put some cardboard inside them and remember you'll be after wearing stockings too.'

'Thanks. How did you get here? You're Irish.'

'I am so. The Dublin Fusiliers, and I came with the rest of them. Our boys are up the line and are giving them the bells of Shannon.'

'Well, thanks.' She smiled at him. 'I suppose we'll get used to the mud in time.'

'Ah, you will. But it's grand in the summer, except for the flies. They're desperate. They'd have you destroyed altogether.'

'I think I'd sooner cope with them and be warm.'

Charlie Wilson would have agreed with her as he stood knee-deep in water. Conditions were atrocious. God knows how they were supposed to fight surrounded on every side by the thick, glutinous slime. Going up the line with supplies was virtually impossible.

He was exhausted. His company had been here in Fonquevillers for a week now, and for a week it had poured down. There was no shelter in the trenches and day after day they'd had to try to eat and sleep standing up in conditions that were worse than a sewer. Even now the rain crept inside the collar of his supposedly waterproof cape that only came down as far as his knees and dripped into the water he was already standing in. So far they'd had four men taken out with trench foot. Their feet, once released from their boots were so swollen that they often jumped from a shoe size of nine to ten or even eleven. Charlie couldn't feel his feet at all. He just wished they were out of it.

No one seemed to know what the hell they were doing. Communications were far from good – in fact often nonexistent – and the morale of the men was very low. He hoped the bombardment would cease. That meant it was only a matter of minutes before the whistle blew and up they went, over the top. You couldn't think about it otherwise it would drive you mad. He'd lost six men yesterday. A mortar had landed in the trench. There hadn't been much left for the stretcher bearers to carry away for burial, God knows where, and he'd have to write to their next of kin whenever he got the chance. It was something he seemed to have to do more and more frequently.

'Well at least their trenches are better than this, sir,' a young lad grinned at him, how young he didn't know. The boy's face was streaked with mud. So many of them had lied about their ages, he knew that. One of the lads he'd lost yesterday had only been fifteen. A bit of a kid who had wanted to play 'soldiers' in a real war. Well, you couldn't get much more realistic than this.

'Anything would be better than this, Wilkins.'

'I hear they've got proper rooms, they're dug in so deep. Our artillery will have softened them up by now. Don't you think so, sir?'

'Very probably. It shouldn't be too bad.' Charlie thought of the damage the artillery would have caused. Those trenches wouldn't exist after being pounded all night long. The British soldiers wouldn't benefit from the creature comforts left by the enemy because quite simply there just wouldn't be any left.

'Where do you come from, Wilkins?'

'Liverpool, sir.'

'I know that from your accent. Whereabouts?'

'Scottie Road, sir, top of Burlington Street, sir.'

'I knew a girl from around there. Kate, her name was. Kate Greenway.'

The lad grinned. 'You mean the Angels of Silvester Street, sir.'

Charlie nodded. He'd never stopped loving Kate. He went over and over in his mind the conversations they'd had, the fun, the laughter, the tenderness. It was a pain that would never go away and was almost as tangible as a physical pain.

There was no more time for conversation. The bombardment had ceased. It was raining still when the shrill sound of whistles ran down the line.

'Come on, Wilkins, show them what Derby's Pets can do!' he yelled as he himself led the charge which in reality was more like a scramble over the cloying mud that had already been churned up by the heavy howitzers. Hopefully they had cut the wire to ribbons, otherwise they were in real trouble.

He heard Wilkins scream just behind him but there wasn't time to think about the lad now, it was onward, onward, onward.

He didn't feel any pain as the shrapnel tore into his chest and stomach. He lay face down in the mud and heard the yells of 'Stretcher bearer! Stretcher bearer!' and then the agony became unbearable but he tried not to scream. He was an officer; it wasn't in keeping.

When the bombardment had ceased Sister Caldwell told her nurses to get ready for the wounded, who would be brought in from the field dressing stations where basic first aid was given.

'Have you enough bandages, slings, iodine?'

'I hope so, Sister,' a seasoned nurse answered.

Kate and Evvie were told to go to the operating room and assist with whatever could be done there to make the place as clean as possible under the circumstances.

They'd only just finished scrubbing down one of the big kitchen tables when the noises from outside the building told them that their day's work was about to begin.

It was bedlam, Evvie thought. One minute the hall was empty, the next it was full of men, all with terrible wounds. Blood was soon spattered on the walls, the floor, and on themselves, and the air was filled with the screams and moans of the wounded and the shouted instructions of nurses, doctors and army medical orderlies.

Kate was on her knees propping up a young soldier whose face was covered in a mask of blood and whose arm hung limply by his side. The uniform sleeve was shredded and white fragments of bone were exposed.

Evvie couldn't stand it. The noise battered against her ears and she held her hands over them in an attempt to shut it out. She was going to vomit, she knew she was. Pushing aside the stretcher bearers and some of the nurses who were assisting them, she dashed out of the front door, sank down on the cracked stone step of the building and covered her face with her hands.

'Nurse G2, pull yourself together!'

Evvie looked at Sister Caldwell.

'I . . . I . . . I'm going to faint.'

'You are not.' Sister pushed Evvie's head down until it was beneath her knees.

'Just breathe normally, it will pass.'

It did and at last Evvie looked up.

'I'm sorry. Oh, I feel such a . . . coward.'

'Don't. Many's the nurse I've seen pass out or vomit the first time they're faced with the aftermath of a battle. I did myself. I was as sick as a pig. None of us was prepared for carnage on a scale like this. Get up now.'

Slowly Evvie got to her feet. She felt much better. So, she wasn't on her own. Others had gone through this, even Sister herself. She squared her shoulders and went back inside.

The boy with the shattered arm and head wound was on the table, which was now covered in blood and dirt, and Evvie thought what a waste of time it had been scrubbing it. Kate had rolled up her sleeves and her apron and her hands were also covered with it. Where she had used a hand to brush back of strand of hair, there remained traces of blood on her forehead and cheeks.

She looked up as Sister appeared with Evvie but she had little time to think of her sister as another wounded man was being lifted on to the table from the canvas stretcher that was stiff with dried blood and dirt. How many died from the infections caused by the dirty bandages and stretchers she didn't know.

'This one's an officer,' another nurse called out.

'What rank? What regiment?' a male voice asked from the other end of the room.

'It doesn't bloody matter. Just get this damned tunic off him. Cut it off!' the surgeon roared.

'Rank – Captain. Regiment – Liverpool Pals, 18th Battalion. Name – Wilson,' the Nurse shouted back, peering closely at the green identification discs around the man's neck.

Kate uttered a cry and turned. Underneath the mask of blood and dirt she recognised him. His hair was matted and pain filled his eyes. The nurse had begun to cut the uniform tunic away from the wound.

'Leave him. I'll do it! I'll see to him!' Kate cried, bending over him and taking his hand.

'Charlie! Charlie!'

There was a glimmer of recognition in his eyes.

'Kate? Kate, is that you?'

'Yes, it's me, and I'll look after you. Once I get your tunic off then I'll clean you up before the surgeon starts.'

'This is a fine way . . . to . . . meet.' His words were laboured and the smile he tried to muster turned into a grimace.

'Don't try and talk, Charlie.' Her fingers were shaking as she hacked at the top of his tunic.

'Never . . . never . . . forgot . . . you.'

'Don't talk, Charlie! Save your strength!' she cried, but inwardly she groaned. It was a stomach wound, a bad one. She fought down the nausea for in her hands she held a large part of his intestines. He was going to die. It was a miracle he'd managed to get here at all. She looked up at the surgeon and he shook his head and helped her pull and fasten together the edges of his tunic.

'Do what you can, nurse.'

'I will, sir. I . . . I . . . know him.'

'Kate.'

She could barely hear him and she fought back tears as she gently raised his head and held him in her arms oblivious now to the noises and smells.

'Oh, Charlie! Charlie, I should have married you.'

'What . . . what difference would it have . . . made?'

She cradled him against her. 'Not much, I know, but . . . but I'll never forgive myself for leading you on.'

He made an attempt to raise his face from her shoulder.

'Kate . . . I . . . I . . . love you.' The last word was little more than a gurgle as a froth of bright red bubbles oozed from the corner of his mouth.

'Charlie, Charlie, God bless you and keep you.' She choked back the sobs. They would do no good now. He was dead, but his last words would always stay with her.

Suddenly she looked up and saw Evvie standing on the other side of the table.

'It's . . . it's Charlie. He . . . he's dead, Evvie.'

Evvie nodded and turned away. She didn't want to see Charlie Wilson's face. The bright scarlet stain that covered her sister's dress and apron was more than she could stand.

'Nurse!' a doctor called to her, and she pushed through the press of bodies.

'Shrapnel in right arm and shoulder. Get the ether ready, please.'

She nodded and applied the liquid, the smell of which she hated, on to a pad of cotton wool. Then she looked down at the man.

'It's you!'

'Aye, it's me. Tommy Ormesher. It'll take more than this to knock the smile off my face. I didn't think I'd be seeing you so soon. Reckon they'll send me home now, sir?' he asked the doctor.

'Oh, I think we can count on that, lad. Nurse, let's put him out.'

'You'll come and see me when you get back to Blighty, if you can?'

Evvie managed a smile. 'I'll try.'

'That's grand, lass. Fine, send me off to the land of nod now, eh?'

She pressed the pad over his nose and mouth.

'It doesn't do to be too familiar with them, Nurse. That's not part of your job.'

'I know, sir, but he was such a likeable lad.'

The doctor shook his head. 'So many of them are, and that's the pity of it.'

It was nearly dark before the tide of wounded had become just a trickle, and the nurses got a respite. Kate, Evvie and Agnes went outside and sat on the steps, grateful for the sharp, cold but clean-smelling air. They ached all over, they were exhausted, hungry and thirsty. There had been no time to stop for food or drink. They were also filthy dirty but knew that they'd have to give their clothes and aprons to Madame to wash in carbolic to get rid of the bugs. They'd also have to check each other's hair for lice; the place was riddled with every kind of bug you could think of.

'Holy Mother of God! I never thought it would be like this. All that rubbish Sister Williams told us was useless. How the hell can she know what it's like?'

'She can't, Agnes. No one can until they experience it.'

'Oh, Kate, I'm so sorry about Charlie. I really am,' Evvie said. 'I . . . I . . . didn't think I was going to stick it at all. When they started to come in like that – the noise, the smells, the chaos, the dreadful wounds, I felt as though I was going to faint or be sick or both. I just ran out, I didn't care where to, I just *had* to get out.'

Kate nodded. 'I know, Evvie. There wasn't much time to think about it all. And especially Charlie. He was in a terrible state. God knows how he didn't die on his way here, he'd lost so much blood. Poor, poor Charlie.' She stood up quickly. 'Oh God, I think I'm going to be sick.'

Evvie was instantly on her feet and led her to the nearest pothole that served as a gutter. When Kate at last stopped retching, Evvie wiped her mouth and forehead with the cleanest bit of her dress that she could find. She felt slightly sick herself, but they'd both come through this first awful day and that was what mattered most.

She wasn't to know that that day was just the beginning – the beginning of the nightmares and hallucinations. In every soldier she would nurse she would see the faces of the lads she knew: Charlie, Ben, Frank, Kieran and his brothers, Agnes's brothers. She told no one, not even Kate, but her sister knew there was something wrong, something very wrong.

Chapter Twenty-Three

It was amazing what a difference a year made, Maggie mused as she sat on the tram next to Josie. In April last year the casualties had been very heavy from the battle for Ypres and for the first time chlorine gas had been used on Canadian and French soldiers. Everyone had been horrified and the hatred for the Germans had grown. In May it had got even worse when the *Lusitania*, or the *Lucy* as she was known on Merseyside, had been sunk by a U-boat. The city had been in uproar and everyone was appalled by the fact that it was mainly women and children who had been killed. Since then the war had ground on – always yielding more casualties, more bad news, rarely any real progress. Another Christmas had passed, the second of the conflict. So much for it all being over by Christmas.

Although it was now the first of June, the weather wasn't good and they both wore jackets. Maggie's was plain blue, which picked out the blue in the tartan skirt she wore. Josie's was a small black and white check that looked well over her black working dress with its stiff white collar.

'You know you look really nice, Josie,' Maggie said, tucking her parcels more securely under her arm as they alighted on Scotland Road.

'Thanks, I feel just great. I love work. Everyone is so nice and Mr Jeffries has been very kind to me. He's a widower and he's got a limp. That's why he's not in the army,' she added before Maggie asked the inevitable question the sight of a man not in uniform prompted these days. The war was dragging on and men were being conscripted now.

'I'm so glad I'm working at Blacklers.'

'Yes, it's a damned sight better than working on the trams or the railways or even in munitions. Whoever would have thought that it would be women and girls who would be keeping things going?'

Josie nodded her agreement. 'I used to think all those suffragettes were mad, but they were right. Women *can* do men's jobs. Maybe we'll get the vote when the war's over.'

'Oh, for heaven's sake, Josie, don't you of all people start on that. I would have thought you've got enough to occupy your mind with Matthew, a job and this Mr Jeffries that I seem to hear so much about these days.'

'Maggie, there's nothing going on between me and Mr Jeffries. He's old enough to be my da,' Josie protested, although a faint flush of pink tinged her cheeks. 'He's been very kind . . . very nice to me, that's all.' It was true. He was a very considerate man. He often let her slip out a few minutes early, knowing she always liked to get home to see her son. Nor did he comment when she was a little late back from lunch. No, she'd not come across a man as considerate as Stanley Jeffries in her entire life, except maybe for Kieran. And Stanley always asked how Matthew was getting on. She decided to change the subject before Maggie got too curious.

'How is business?'

'Slow. Very slow, if I'm honest. It's mourning clothes I should be making, not wedding dresses.'

'Why don't you?'

'Because it's so depressing. No one really cares what the dress looks like, just as long as it's black. They're too upset to think straight, never mind decide how much material they want in the skirt. How is Frank?'

'All right, as far as I know. He writes a sort of letter to everyone – me, his mam and da and Dotty. He doesn't say much. I don't suppose they will let them give too much away.' She really didn't think much about Frank these days, except when someone asked about him or Flo said something to remind her that she had a husband.

They'd reached the corner of Latimer Street.

'I'd better get going, Matthew will be ready for bed. He's always been washed and had his tea by the time I get in. She's very good to us both.'

'Sometimes, Josie, I feel awful about Davie not being out there with the others.'

'It's not his fault. By the way, I heard that nearly all the MacNamaras have been conscripted, rounded up by the scuffers and sent packing with the army police.'

'I thought that Tommy had already joined up?' Since the day Tommy had arrived with the money they'd heard nothing more of the MacNamaras.

'He has. Poor little Lizzie O'Connor was so proud of him but upset too. Her da was terrified of Tommy Mac. Now everything Tommy bought Lizzie will get pawned,' Josie sighed, thinking of Lizzie's plight. 'It was the others who have been holding out. She must have enough white feathers to stuff a mattress, must Ma Mac. They've got no shame, any of them.'

'I hope a shell lands on top of that flaming Kevin. He deserves it.'

'Maggie, that's a terrible thing to say.'

Maggie shrugged. 'They say the devil looks after his own. They'll probably come through it without a scratch. Well, I'd best be off.'

'Bye, Maggie,' Josie replied and turned into Latimer Street. She was tired, having been on her feet all day, but she was happy. She had the best of both worlds now. Matthew was well cared for and he'd become used to her being away all day. She had money in her purse, her own money. The clothes she had were not expensive, but they were new and she did enjoy working at Blacklers. Often she forgot she had a husband and she felt like a single girl again. She was quite content to sit in in the evenings. Her relationship with her mother-in-law had improved, a fact she put down to her being out all day and to Flo's love for Matthew. She doted on him but she was also strict, so he wouldn't grow up wild.

Maggie was tired and also worried, so when she saw Davie sitting in the kitchen she felt irritable. Couldn't he even give her time to get home and have a cup of tea?

'You've forgotten, haven't you?'

'What?' she asked sharply.

'We're going out for some supper and a bit of a sail.'

'I'm too tired to go traipsing out and it'll be cold and miserable on the river. It's more like January than June out there and it's starting to rain.'

'Maggie, don't be such a misery,' said Hetty. 'You've nothing pressing to do.'

'Mam, don't remind me that there's hardly any business. Josie was asking why I didn't do mourning clothes.'

'Why don't you?'

'Because I don't want to. It's depressing.'

'It's even more depressing for the mothers who have lost sons, the wives who have lost husbands. Count your blessings, Maggie.'

'I'm sorry. It just seems to be going on and on. I don't see the sense in fighting over a few feet of useless ground. I don't understand any of it.'

'Go and get changed and go out. It will do you both good.'

'I'll just get a wash and change my blouse then,' Maggie replied without any real enthusiasm.

They couldn't decide where to go. Davie wanted to go to Reece's but Maggie said it was too expensive.

'Just because your orders have fallen, don't take it out on me, Maggie.'

'I'm not. I just don't see the point in wasting money. At the rate you're going, Davie, you will have spent all the MacNamaras' money.'

'I won't and I've finally found decent premises.'

'Where?'

'At the bottom of Tithebarn Street.'

'You're dead set on this, aren't you? Why don't you just wait? No one wants to buy cars now and they won't until this flaming war is over.'

'I'll do all right. It might be slow to start with.'

'It's not a good time to start a business, and especially selling cars. Can't you see what's happening to my business? Use your brains! You'll spend all your money and then you'll be stuck with a showroom, a couple of cars and no orders.'

'It will work.'

Maggie was getting angry. He was just being downright stupid and stubborn, and besides she had plans for that money. After all, she'd thought of blackmailing Big Kevin Mac. After Tommy had brought the money, thankfully Davie had heard nothing further from the MacNamaras. Without her help Davie would be on the Parish now. After the war she would really go to town. She'd expand; she'd have a large establishment that would cater for everything. But she would need money and he seemed hellbent on wasting it instead of saving it.

'It won't work, you'll lose the lot and all that pain will have been for nothing.'

'I'm going ahead with it, Maggie. I've waited years for this chance and you're not the only one who can make a go of things.'

'If you go ahead with this and it fails, don't come to me, Davie Higgins, looking for sympathy because you'll get none.'

'Don't be such a bloody dog in the manger. You don't want me to be successful, do you? You want to be the one who's always right.'

'Don't you swear at me. Go ahead, make a fool of yourself, I don't care. Oh, go to hell!' And with that she turned and walked rapidly down Scotland Road towards home.

'What's the matter with you?' Hetty cried as Maggie slammed the door behind her.

'Oh, I could murder him! It's finished, over! He's insisting on going ahead with that stupid idea of his.'

'His own business?'

'Yes. Who the hell is going to buy cars in the middle of a war? That's if he can even find any or anyone to supply him. Everyone's making weapons. Most of the shops are empty, food is being rationed, and even the ships bringing it in have to sail in convoys. I tell you, Mam, it's stupid.'

'What's all the yelling about? I could hear you halfway down the street, Maggie.' Alf looked concerned as he came into the kitchen. Working on the docks now for the war effort he was tired out and feeling his age.

'Oh, she and Davie have had a row about him opening his car place. Sit down while I get your tea.'

'He's mad. He's just stupid,' Maggie fumed.

'He's got his pride, girl.'

'Well, so have I.'

Ignoring her he thrust a copy of the *Echo* at her. 'You'd better read that, Maggie. It looks as if you'll have to shut up shop, too.'

She grabbed the paper from him and scanned the first few lines of print. 'They can't do that! They can't conscript women!'

'They're not calling it conscription. Any woman who isn't needed desperately at home will have to work in some capacity for the war effort and that includes you, Maggie.'

'I'm not working in munitions or on the trams or anything else.'

'Then you'd better get yourself down to Walton Hospital. Follow in your friends' footsteps.'

'What friends?'

'Kate, Evvie and Agnes. You'd better be prepared to go to France.'

'You mean join the VAD?'

'It's better than all the rest.'

'But Josie Lynch works in a shop, in Blacklers.'

'Aye, and she got in just in time. She'll be able to stay on there because she's replacing a man. They were the plum jobs, Maggie, but they've all been taken.'

Maggie sat down and shook her head in disbelief. It defied all reason, the world had gone mad. 'I don't know a thing about nursing.'

'Neither did those three. You'll learn. I think if I were you, I'd go and make it up with Davie. You don't know how long you'll be away.'

'I won't apologise to him. I don't care if he makes a mess of his life.'

'Maggie!'

'No, Mam. He can come to me, and don't you go sneaking off to see him to tell him I'm joining the others.'

'Well, I think you're being selfish and childish.'

'I don't care. I'm not going round to see him and that's that.'

Maggie was still upset as the last days of June slipped into the first days of July. She kept thinking about the future. Now it certainly wasn't the one she'd envisaged for herself. She'd fully expected Davie to come around but he hadn't and it hurt her. It hurt her a great deal. She couldn't envisage a life without Davie in it. It would be empty. Oh, she had her business, she'd done everything she'd set out to do – almost – but without him to encourage, congratulate, advise and help her through the difficult times, what was the point of it all? She loved him even with all his faults and failings. She knew she wasn't the easiest person to be around at times, but he had always been patient with her.

She sighed despondently. The future. There wasn't much choice now. She was a young, single girl and her parents didn't need constant care. She didn't much fancy nursing but it was far better than the alternatives. Women were driving carts, lorries and trams; delivering coal and a few were even slinging their hooks with the rest of the shore gang down at the docks. She thought of Josie's words about the suffragettes. Oh yes, they'd proved their point, but what a way to have to prove it.

She sat in her workroom staring at her order book. She'd sent her employees, Mrs Frazer and Mrs Wharton, home last night with a week's wages, great regret and a promise to contact them as soon as she was back in business. It was just as well that the book wasn't full for she'd have bitterly resented having to turn custom away. As it was now she'd just have to finish packing everything up and stick a note on the door saying 'Closed for the duration'. It was a notice that was beginning to appear everywhere and with great frequency of late. She wondered how long 'the duration' would be and what faced her now.

Eventually she pulled herself together and continued the packing.

Most of the boxes could be stored at home, but she'd have to find somewhere to put the sewing machines where they wouldn't go rusty.

As she left, locking the door behind her, she shivered. It was drizzling, the sky was a sullen grey. By the time she got home, had something to eat and arranged with her da for someone to collect the machines, it would be time to go and see them at Walton Hospital. At least that would give her mam no time to start going on and on about Davie again.

She was bitterly hurt by his lack of concern. He must have read the newspapers. He must have realised she'd have to close down. She'd expected him to have come round to see her. Well, if that's the way he wanted it, so be it.

She bent her head, opened her umbrella, and frowned as she hurried towards the tram stop. It had proved to be a dreadful summer, so far at least. She heard a news vendor shouting something about a disaster, somewhere over there with a foreign name – the Somme, or something like that – but she was too preoccupied to take any notice.

Ben Steadman leaned his forehead against the wall of the assembly trench down which the water streamed. The assembly trenches were east of Talus Bois below the German-held village of Montauban and the Glatz Redoubt. The bombardment had gone on for a week, day and night, and he felt that his head was about to explode. The air reeked with the smell of cordite. Smoke hung in clouds everywhere and stung your eyes, made your throat burn and got into your lungs. The first of July 1916, he thought. They'd come all this way together, the lads from Silvester Street and Athol Street. There weren't as many of them now. They lay in shallow graves, little white crosses marking the spot, if they were lucky. Many had been left to rot, becoming just so much carrion. There had been no one left to bury them. He remembered the day they'd marched to Lime Street Station. The regimental bands had been playing the old Boer War song 'Dolly Grey', and the crowds who had turned out in their thousands had joined in, singing. It was a different world now and had been since the day they'd first set foot in France.

For days supplies and armaments had been moved up the line. The constant coming and going made sure you didn't get much sleep. In addition there'd been the eternal explosions which, he fervently prayed, had had the desired effect of cutting the barbed wire to shreds, ready for 'the big push'.

He looked up. 'What's this?' he asked Pat Ryan who was standing next to him.

'Waterproof sheet, iron rations, ammo, two Mills bombs and field dressings,' Pat reeled off the items.

'What the hell for? It'll be bad enough trying to get out of this bloody trench without carrying all this stuff.'

'Stop bloody moaning, we've had our orders.'

With grim resolution Ben added the items to his already heavy kit. Just whose idea this had been, God alone knew, but it was bloody stupid. How could anyone move at any speed carrying this lot?

Over the past hours he'd thought about his father and Evvie. He'd heard that she was over here nursing. Frank Lynch had told him. Occasionally Frank got a letter from Kate. It must be pure hell for those girls. The worst violence they'd ever have seen at home were the 'Lusitania Riots' when protests over the sinking of the *Lusitania* had erupted into violence against anyone suspected of German connections. Now they were not far behind the lines and were suffering all the privations the soldiers themselves were. Sometimes shells would land close to the hospital. He'd heard that the nurses wore helmets just like their own.

The first streaks of dawn were stealing across the sky but the sunrise was completely obliterated by the smoke from the shells. He just couldn't stop thinking of Evvie and his father. If anything happened to him the old man would be lonely, and as for Evvie . . . He shook himself. He was getting morbid and that wouldn't help him.

Frank was shaking uncontrollably. It was something he always did when he knew he was going into battle. He also felt sick and hoped he wouldn't vomit this time, the way he'd done after Fonquevillers. He gripped his rifle so hard that his knuckles showed white through the grime. He had no coherent thoughts. Disjointed words and images flashed through his mind: Kate, Matthew, his mam and Dad. He didn't dare stop to think what the next few hours were going to be like. If he did, he knew he'd start screaming and wouldn't be able to stop.

Kieran was standing on the fire step with his brothers either side of him. When they were together like this he felt somehow safer. So far they'd all been lucky. He knew from experience what would happen when the bombardment stopped. The flag would drop and then it would be time . . . He tried to fight down the panic. He wanted to be hundreds of miles away from here, back in Silvester Street with his mam and dad and Evvie. He knew that even now she wasn't far from him – just a few miles back behind the lines. He tried to pray, but all he seemed to be able to remember of a prayer familiar since childhood were the words 'Hail Mary, full of grace'. He repeated them over and over again in his mind. It couldn't be long now. It was daylight, or what passed for it. He turned quickly, bayonet fixed, only to find Ben Steadman standing in the trench behind him.

'What the bloody hell do you want?' he roared to make himself heard over the din.

'Look after Evvie for me, Kieran!' Ben shouted back. He just hadn't been able to shake off his morbid fears. In his heart he knew that this would be the last battle he'd fight.

Kieran's shoulders slumped and he let his rifle drop to his side.

'She's here, Kieran,' Ben told him. 'Just a few miles back. Did you know that?'

Kieran nodded and for the first time looked Ben Steadman squarely in the eyes. He saw fear and sadness in those dark eyes; he was superstitious enough to think that Steadman knew he wasn't going to make it this time.

Ben held out his hand. 'Promise!'

Kieran took it. Both their hands were shaking.

'I promise! On Mam's life, I promise!'

'Will you tell her that I was thinking of her this morning?'

Again Kieran nodded.

'Thanks.' Ben turned away.

'Ben!' Kieran yelled.

Ben turned back.

'May your God bless you.'

'May yours keep you safe, Kieran.'

Kieran could only stare back, tears pricking his eyes. He'd misjudged Steadman. He really loved Evvie as much as he did himself. Ben Steadman knew he could never support or marry Evvie so he'd bequeathed that love to the one man he knew who *would* love and care for her – himself.

Ben moved away and Kieran dropped his cigarette butt on to the muddy floor of the trench and ground it out with the heel of his boot. It would have gone out anyway in the mud but the gesture made him feel more determined to get through yet another bloody awful day.

'What the hell was all that about?' Pat shouted to his brother as Kieran climbed back on to the fire step.

'He knows, Pat. He knows he's for it today.'

'For Christ's sake, don't bloody start that or we'll have a mass panic on our hands.'

At seven twenty-five the scaling ladders were in place. At seven thirty the flag fell. The waiting was over.

Gunsmoke swirled around them like a heavy but patchy mist. All Kieran could see ahead of him were flashes of fire and columns of smoke that erupted like small volcanoes. Running was impossible; the weight of his kit had him doubled over. There were smaller flashes and he knew they were machine-gun bullets but he couldn't stop, he had to go on and on, even though he heard the screams and yells of the men behind him falling. He stumbled on, not even knowing where he was supposed to be going. He saw Lieutenant Mayberry fall just ahead of him and then there was a terrific explosion and he was hurled to the ground. He lay there stunned until he recovered his breath.

Through the gunsmoke and the clouds of lyddite shrapnel he could just see figures moving forward. He shook his head to clear his vision and ran his hands over his tunic. They were covered with a warm sticky substance – blood, he thought. He must have been hit. But no, there was no pain and it wasn't just blood; it had more texture, it was thicker. It was skin, with fragments of bone attached to it. He became frantic. It seemed to be all over him. He was trapped in a nightmare and he began to scream, for as well as the skin there were scraps of material and bits of paper. He had just made out the first letters on a small piece of green cardboard: 'P-a-t-r-i-c'. It was Pat. It was his brother Patrick. It was too horrendous even to think about. He didn't want to know. He wanted to get away.

He got to his feet and struggled after the moving figures, watching them go down one after another until he had to stop, shaking his head in disbelief. There were bodies piled two and three deep, with broken, twisted limbs and sightless eyes. He was too shocked and too exhausted to care now; he dragged himself the rest of the way into what was left of Montauban.

His knees buckled and he sprawled on the floor of what had been a German trench. A lad from Athol Street, whose name he couldn't remember, bent down and shook him.

'Are yer hit?'

Keiran pulled himself up into a sitting position and shook his head. He wished to God he had been.

'You are. Look at the state of yer leg and yer coat's all ripped away at the shoulder.'

He hadn't felt anything. He'd been too shocked. But now his leg hurt like hell and his shoulder, when he tried to move, felt as though it was on fire.

'How . . . how many of us are left?'

The lad passed him a lighted cigarette and shrugged. 'About one hundred and fifty.'

Keiran dropped his head in his hands. One hundred and fifty from so many. Both his brothers and God alone knew how many of his mates. He sat and cried like a baby for all the lads he'd grown up with and the horror of the last hours.

The girls had been moved up to Maricourt, which was marginally in a better state than Hébuterne. Again the hospital was a public building, or what was left of it. Over that year Evvie had coped but each time it got worse and she felt weaker and weaker. Kate knew about the nightmares but not the terrible hallucinations. She could get through the day by determinedly not looking at the faces of the men she tended but at night they filled her dreams. It was Kate who woke her and who held her and soothed her until she would at last fall into a troubled asleep again.

There had been little sleep for everyone, for the bombardment had lasted a whole week and subsequently nerves and tempers were frayed. Both Kate and Evvie had lost weight and there were dark circles around their eyes. But nearly everyone was in the same state, Sister Caldwell included.

They knew by the extended length of the shelling that there was something big coming up and when the guns at last fell silent it was that very silence that woke them.

Kate threw back the blankets. 'Come on, Evvie, get up and get dressed. The shelling has stopped. We'll best get over to the hospital as soon as we can.'

Evvie dressed mechanically. 'Oh God, just let me get through for another day!' she prayed. 'Just one more day, please.'

Sister Caldwell was already discussing arrangements with the doctors and surgeons.

She turned to the nurses. 'You all know the procedure. Start on your allotted tasks and don't dawdle.' Her voice was clipped and devoid of emotion.

They worked in silence until it was half-past eight. Then the first casualties began to arrive. By ten o'clock the hospital was packed. Men were lying on the floor, in the corridors in the hallway, and even on the steps of the building itself.

The scenes inside were chaotic and everyone was working frantically.

Evvie was coping, just. They'd never had to deal with such numbers, and she carried out her duties, her lips firmly compressed, her eyes riveted on the hands and wounds of the soldiers she tended. She had even learned how to cocoon herself from the noise by repeating the words of songs inside her head. When she sang 'It's a Long Way to Tipperary', she wondered would she ever go there and what would it be like? Green and fresh and peaceful. Yes, that's what it would be like. When she sang 'Pack Up Your Troubles', she wished she could. How *would* you 'pack' them? Would you mentally put the worst ones in first and then the others? Shove them all in a suitcase, close the lid and snap the locks shut so tightly that they could never be opened again? Such silly thoughts somehow kept her going.

Kate had stood beside doctors, picking fragments of bone from gaping holes, cleaning yellow pus from infected wounds. She'd helped move men with mangled, mutilated limbs from the stretchers. She'd bitten hard into her bottom lip as she'd passed the instruments for amputation to the surgeons. But what affected her most were the labels. They seemed to reduce the men to mere parcels – parcels covered in bloody mud-stained bandages. It was in the atrocious conditions of the field dressing stations that these labels were attached: a brief scrawled description of the injury, name, rank and regiment of the man, then the card was slipped inside a waxed envelope and tied with string to a button or belt. Some of these man had walked or even crawled here from the battlefields.

'Nurse, see to that man there.' Sister pointed to a young soldier who was sitting on the floor in the corridor, leaning against the wall.

Evvie weaved her way through the broken and bleeding bodies and bent down, her eyes fixed on the small hole in his chest. She cleaned it and covered it with a clean pad of lint, but his breath was coming in short bubbling gasps and she knew there was something very wrong. Gently she turned him towards her and inwardly groaned. In his back there was a gaping wound that she could have put her fist into, and the lung was torn and collapsed. She reached for a long swab and packed it into the hole, then bandaged it as tightly as she could. It was all she could do until a doctor finally got to see him and by then he'd probably be dead.

As she stood up she caught sight of his face and then the nightmare descended on her. The soldiers surrounded her and she couldn't shut out the sight of their faces. They were all here: Ben, Kieran, Frank, Pat and Niall. Something exploded in her head and she began to scream hysterically.

Kate was instantly beside her and caught her by the shoulders, shaking her.

'Evvie, Evvie! Stop it! Stop it!'

'They're here, Kate! All of them! They're here and they're all going to die!' she screamed, beating her clenched fists against Kate's chest.

Sister Caldwell was now beside them. She slapped Evvie hard across the face and Evvie collapsed against Kate, her body racked by sobs.

'Get her out of here and make it quick before we have mass hysteria!' Sister snapped.

Kate dragged Evvie towards the hall and picked her way through the bodies on the floor. She pushed Evvie into the tiny cubbyhole that was Sister's office.

'Just sit there, Evvie. I'll be back as soon as I can, I promise.'

'No! No! I don't want to be in here, Kate.'

Kate racked her brains, then pulled her sister to her feet and dragged her out of the building. The road outside was packed with men and ambulances. In the name of God, what was going on out here? she thought. This was sheer slaughter. She'd never seen anything like it. She pulled Evvie across the road to their billet and wrapped her in all the blankets they possessed. Evvie was still shaking and crying.

'Evvie, I've got to go back. Do you understand me?'

Evvie nodded, her eyes blank and staring. Kate didn't want to leave her but she had no choice

'Kate, is she all right?' Agnes asked as Kate went back to her work.

'She is. At least I think so for now. When is this ever going to end? It's as bad outside in the road.'

'I heard one of the lads say it's so bad up there that it will be hours, days even, before we get all the casualties in.'

'Oh, God help us!'

'And them!' Sister Caldwell said grimly as she passed.

It was eight o'clock before it slackened and they were allowed a break. They sank on to the front steps, cold, filthy dirty, hungry, thirsty and exhausted. They knew that they would have to go and strip everything off for Madame to wash with carbolic soap. There was every kind of bug here. They'd change into their spare set of clothes then they would have to go and find something to eat and drink.

'I'm aching all over,' Agnes said.

'I know, and I should go and see Evvie, but I'll have to rest for just a few minutes.'

'What will they do with her, Kate?'

'I don't know. She's just a nervous wreck. You know that she's been having nightmares ever since we left Hébuterne. God knows what she's thinking about in the day. I *know* it's something bad because it makes me uneasy.'

Kate shoved her hands into the pockets of her apron. Her fingers touched a piece of paper and she drew it out.

'What's that?'

'I can't remember. Let's sit further over, near to the light on the porch.'

When they'd settled themselves she began to scan the lines of a scribbled address and then she remembered how she'd come to have it.

'A lad gave me this. He asked me to write home to his mother for him.'

'Will you?'

Kate nodded.

'What happened to him?'

There was an awful inevitability about her answer. 'He died.'

'Oh God, Kate, can't an officer do it?' Agnes asked.

'No, I promised. I . . . I won't tell her that he died in terrible pain. I couldn't do that, but she might take some comfort from the words of a nurse, rather than of an officer who wasn't with him and probably didn't even know his name.'

Agnes nodded. Writing to a heart-broken mother was just another terrible task none of them had expected ever to have to do.

'There won't be many of them left after today, Kate. They were nearly all from the 17th and 18th Battalions.' Agnes shook her head sadly.

Kate stood up and stretched her aching limbs. She'd have to go and see Evvie now.

'Come on, Agnes, let's go home.'

'Some flaming "home". That hovel. I bet it wasn't much better before the war.'

'Silvester Street's hardly Buckingham Palace,' said Kate, trying valiantly not to let herself sink into self-pity.

Before they had taken a few steps a roll of thunder, louder than any gunfire, rent the air. The sky was greenish black and the forked lightning was so bright it lit up the high ground towards La Boisselle. Summoning their meagre reserve of energy, they ran back to the hospital to get out of the sheeting rain.

A doctor was on the porch, smoking a cigarette.

'Heaven's artillery,' he said quietly, looking up. 'More powerful than any gun or mortar that will ever be invented by man. Look at heaven's anger and marvel.'

The guns were still firing. Orange flashes lit the sky and they could see the figures of men moving slowly across the battlefield.

'Get something to eat and drink, you're likely to be called back to work soon.' Suddenly anger blazed in his eyes. 'Where's the sense in it all? Where's the bloody sense? They're cannon fodder. They're dying like cattle out there – worse than that, for you'd shoot an animal and put it out of its misery.' His voice was filled with bitterness as he cursed the stupidity of all mankind.

Evvie was lying on her bed, still swathed in blankets. Every few minutes a sob would shake her yet there were no tears in her eyes. They were bloodshot and swollen from the tears she'd shed earlier that day.

Worried sick, Kate tried to talk to her, to get her to eat and drink but she refused. To her relief, it wasn't long before Sister Caldwell came over to see them, accompanied by a doctor.

Kate helped Evvie to sit up.

'Now, Nurse Greenway, what's all this about? I can't have such behaviour. It upsets the men and your fellow nurses.'

Evvie couldn't answer, just kept looking at her tightly clenched hands.

'Sir, may I answer for her?'

The doctor nodded his assent to Kate.

'She's had nightmares ever since we arrived in Hébuterne and I know, even though she's not said much, she's been in a terrible state ever since we got here. I . . . I . . . can feel it, sir. I know it sounds stupid, but it's the truth. She's been just hanging on to her wits and there's nothing I could do.'

'And that performance this morning?'

'I think, sir, it was the last straw. There were so many of them, so much blood and dirt, so much noise and chaos, that she just snapped.'

The doctor exchanged glances with Sister Caldwell, who was sympathetic to a degree.

'Could she be suffering from the malady that doesn't exist, Sister?'

Kate knew he meant shell-shock.

'I don't know, sir. All I do know is that I just can't have behaviour like that on my wards.'

He bent down and drew Evvie to her feet. The striking blue eyes were vacant, devoid of any emotion.

'Give her a few days, Sister. If she's no better send her back down the line to Albert. I'll give you a letter to take to the Medical CO there. He can make a decision, just for a change,' he added sarcastically before leaving.

'Well, that's that, I suppose. I can't spare you to go with her, Kate, you're too good a nurse.' Sister Caldwell looked at her appraisingly. 'Had this been any hospital at home you'd have been a staff nurse by now.'

'I'll go, Sister,' Agnes volunteered.

Sister nodded slowly. 'You'll have to come straight back from Albert but maybe you'll get a lift. If you do, for God's sake, bring some supplies with you, as much as you can get. We need everything!'

As the woman turned to leave, Kate caught her arm.

'Sister, will she be going home?'

'I very much think so – on sick or compassionate leave, whichever they think is the more plausible. In my opinion it should be both. She's been a good worker, despite everything.'

Kate sank down on the bed, pulling Evvie down beside her. 'They'll send you home, Evvie. Away from all the noise, the blood, the dirt and the lice.'

Evvie turned to look at her with the first glimmer of expression in her eyes Kate had seen all day.

'Home. Home,' she repeated, and silent tears slid one by one down her cheeks.

Chapter Twenty-Four

Peg answered the door and found old Harry on the doorstep. These days he delivered milk as well as lighting the lamps.

'Just a jug today, Harry. It's not going off quickly the way it usually does in summer.'

'It's not much of a summer so far, Mrs Greenway.'

Peg passed him a jug and he filled it from one of the churns on the cart. The bay horse waited patiently. It had a nosebag on and was only interested in its food.

'Pay me at the end of the week, Mrs G.'

Peg didn't answer. She just stared beyond him and he turned to see what had attracted her attention.

'Oh God Almighty!'

They both stood in silence as the telegraph boy appeared at the end of the street. In horrified disbelief they watched him stop at almost every house. Panic rose in Peg. He must have got them mixed up! It couldn't possibly be everyone. The Ryans, the Hawkinses, the Gillans, the O'Learys, the Duffys, the Steadmans. There was hardly a house missed out down the length of the street.

The lamplighter shook his head. 'Oh, they all wanted to go, didn't they? It must be mass slaughter . . . I'm sorry, luv, I didn't think.'

'I lost my lad at sea, Harry.'

They stood rooted to the spot, just watching in silence as the lad wheeled his bike on towards the bottom of the street, but neither of them saw his tears.

Young Liam Hawkins flew out of his front door and ran towards them.

'Oh God! Oh God, Mrs Greenway! You've got to come. It's . . . it's our Fred and Georgie! Me mam's in a terrible state.'

Peg had started to cross the road when Mary Ryan stumbled from her hallway, followed by Josie. Both were sobbing uncontrollably.

Peg drew in her breath. Oh, she knew only too well how they were feeling, but someone had to be strong in the face of what looked like a terrible disaster.

'Liam, go and get your mam over here. I'll get Mrs Ryan and Josie inside.'

The lad ran back and emerged with a shocked and haggard-looking Vi.

Peg got them all inside her kitchen.

'Josie, luv, put the kettle on,' she instructed. Mary couldn't speak, and Peg gently eased her down on the sofa. Josie's face was white – even her lips looked bloodless.

'It's . . . it's . . . all of them,' she stammered. 'Kieran's been wounded, but Niall . . . and Pat . . .'

'What about Frank, Josie?'

Josie shook her head. 'Frank's . . . dead.'

Peg felt she was living a nightmare, but she was the calmest. As she'd said, she *knew* what they were feeling and she seemed to draw strength from their communal loss and grief. 'There's some aspirin in the drawer. Give one to Mary and one to Vi, then take one yourself, Josie, if you need it.'

Then her voice dropped to a hushed whisper. 'Dear merciful God! Vi's boys, Fred and Georgie; Frank Lynch; Mary's sons Niall and Pat, and Kieran wounded; Ben Steadman from the pawnbroker's, the two Gillan boys who lived further down the street. Ellen Murphy's eldest son . . .' Hardly a family had escaped.

No one had any heart to drink tea and talk. Friends and neighbours for years, they were all grieving, their families decimated on a scale that was unimaginable. When Bill Greenway, Ernie Hawkins and Matty Ryan at last came home nothing could be heard in Peg's kitchen except the sound of sobbing.

Five hundred telegrams were delivered in Liverpool as the sheer carnage of the Somme offensive unfolded. Five hundred families were plunged into grief and the City Fathers demanded answers. There were none. The whole country was reeling at the casualties, over one hundred thousand on the first day alone.

'Oh, Mam, even if people ask, I couldn't make dresses for them. I just couldn't! It's everyone we know, everyone,' Maggie said pitifully to Hetty the next day.

Mary Ryan was in a state of shock and, but for Josie rallying round, the entire household would have fallen apart. As Josie said to Peg when they met outside Ivy Holder's shop, 'Someone has to be fit to see to Kieran when he gets home.'

Peg had nodded in sympathy.

'Mam just sits there staring into space, Da's drunk most of the time and our Mickey keeps swearing and going on about wanting to join up, at his age. All our Rose, Sall and Maureen do is yell at him, Da and me. That's when they're not crying. I've lost a husband as well as two brothers, they forget that.'

With Peg's help, Vi was coping, but only just. Hetty McGee was also helping as many of her neighbours as she could, in and out all day, making tea, cooking meals, shopping and just listening to the outpourings of grief from demented wives and mothers.

When Hetty returned home briefly that afternoon she decided to tell Maggie what had been troubling her since the tragedy had struck their neighbours. 'This is no time for quarrels. Go and see Davie. He'll have lost friends and you'll be leaving in September. Go and see him, please, before you go? Don't part in anger, Maggie, you'll regret it.'

'I'll go later, I promise. I told Josie I'd sit in with her mam while she goes and gets some shopping. Frank's mam has taken it badly too.'

'Oh, where will it all end? Go on and see to Mary, poor soul. I'm going to Lily Gillan's for an hour.'

Maggie hadn't needed to go and see Davie; he'd come later that afternoon. As soon as she saw him she threw her arms around his neck.

'Maggie, I'm sorry.'

'No. It was my fault. I'm so glad you've come, Davie.'

'Oh, Maggie, it's terrible. I felt awful just walking down our street. There's so many of them dead, I just can't take it all in.'

'I know. It's the same here and in every street in the neighbourhood. Kieran Ryan is the only one to come through it alive, and he's wounded, quite badly I believe. Oh, why did they all have to join up together? Why didn't they choose different regiments?'

'It's not just the "Pals" and the Lancashire Fusiliers, Maggie, it's all regiments. They can't go on like this. There won't be anyone left soon. I heard that four of the MacNamaras were on the casualty list, including Tommy and Big Kev.'

'I shouldn't say it, but they're no loss.'

'I heard that Tommy's going to be given a medal, posthumously, they call it. He led the attack on a Lewis gun after the officer in charge of his lot was killed. They'll give the medal to his mam.'

'And she'll pawn it and drink the money. They should give

it to little Lizzie O'Connor. She was proud of him, she loved him.'

'That was the root of the trouble with Tommy. His mam didn't care a fig for him, nor for any of them. He'd have been all right with a decent family. Well, he died better than he lived.'

For the first time in that dreadful week Maggie broke down and sobbed. There was something so pathetic about poor Tommy MacNamara. Dragged up, shown no love, encouragement or example, yet he died bravely, leading the attack and no one in that family would even care. Only Lizzie, the product of a heartless, violent, poverty-stricken background herself, would mourn him.

'Oh, Davie, it's been a terrible week. And now I don't know what I'm facing. I'm due to go to France in September. I don't know if I can cope with it.'

He kissed her gently on the forehead. 'Don't cry, Maggie, luv. It won't be so bad. It just might be over before they have to send you.'

'It won't be. It *can't* be.'

'I know, I was just trying to help. I wanted to ask you something.'

She looked up at him, her eyes still swimming with tears.

'I know we always talked about what we'd do in the future, but I really never got around to asking you, properly, that is. Will you marry me, Maggie?'

'Yes. Oh yes, of course I will.'

'When?'

'I don't know.'

'In two weeks?'

Maggie nodded.

'Do you think your mam will mind if I come to live here? It's murder in our house; they're always rowing.'

'She'd love it, she really would.'

'Let's ask her first. There's no point in waiting any longer, Maggie, we might as well grasp some happiness now.'

She leaned her head against his shoulder. He was right: no one could possibly know what lay ahead for any of them. This week had taught her that. What were her ambitions for the success of her business worth compared to being with the man she loved? So many of her friends and neighbours had lost that chance.

'I'd set my heart on a very grand wedding, but now it's not important any more. Things have changed so much and I've changed, too.'

'Don't worry, you'll have your big day, leave it to me.'

She smiled wryly. 'I'll have to buy my own wedding dress – me, who's made everyone else's. I might even go to Sloan's.'

'Everyone needs something to look forward to around here, especially now. You'll have your day, Maggie. Call it a legacy from Big Kevin Mac.'

A week later Peg was dumbfounded as Evvie walked into the kitchen.

'Jesus, Mary and Joseph! You gave me a terrible fright! Where's our Kate? I didn't expect you! And you look terrible . . .'

'I'm on my own, Mam. They sent me home on leave for . . . well, for a rest. There wasn't time to write and I wouldn't send you a telegram. It's taken me nearly two days to get here.'

'No wonder you look worn out, girl. Take your coat and hat off and—' Peg fell silent as Evvie's shoulders started to shake with sobs. She gathered Evvie into her arms.

'Oh, Mam! Mam! I can't stand it any more. I'm crying all the time. I can't help it and I went hysterical on the first day. I just stood and screamed and screamed and screamed. I can't forget about anyone and you've no idea what it's like over there. I'm upsetting everyone, so they've sent me home on extended sick leave.'

Peg suddenly thought of Ben Steadman. It had been her misfortune to have to write to Evvie to tell her of Ben's death and that of all the other lads, for she'd insisted on doing it herself. It had been the hardest thing she'd ever had to do. When, after an hour and a half, the letter was finished she'd felt so mentally and emotionally drained that she'd dropped her head in her hands and cried. 'You've seen the casualty lists?'

Evvie nodded. 'So many of them, Mam, so many and . . . Ben . . . and we were only a few miles away from them. If I . . . we could have got to them at least we could have helped. But we didn't *know*, Mam. We just didn't *know*.'

Peg gathered her into her arms again and held her close. The girl was a bag of bones. You could count her ribs.

'What about Kate?'

'She's always been stronger than me, Mam. She's the one who always faced life head on. She knows about Frank Lynch.'

'Oh, Evvie, you'll feel better soon. We'll never really get over it, but maybe it's for the best that you've come home. I can look after you properly. Time is a great healer, that's what Nelly used to say, God rest her. Give things time, Evvie.'

* * *

Levi had sent for Evvie and, heartbroken though she was, she was shocked at the change in Ben's father. He'd aged so much and he looked haggard and broken.

'Mr Steadman . . . I . . . I don't know what to say.'

'Oh, Evvie, Evvie, child. I am to blame. God has punished me for being so bitter, so bigoted. We have the same God, all of us. I'm sorry.'

Evvie put her arms around him, pity for this broken old man, who could have been her father-in-law, making her eyes sting and her heart ache even more. 'Don't blame yourself, please. It wouldn't have worked, you know that.'

'I didn't even give you a chance, child.'

'It doesn't matter now, nothing matters now.'

Levi sat down in his old armchair and she sat at his feet, holding his hand tightly. 'There are so many . . . so many of them.'

'What use is the life of an old man when so many young lives have been ended? I would willingly have died in place of Ben. How are Mrs Ryan and Mrs Hawkins? Mrs McGee is fortunate she has no sons.'

'Mrs Hawkins is not doing too badly, considering, but poor Mrs Ryan is bad.'

'They will send him home, Kieran?'

'Yes, when he's well enough to travel.'

'She'll be better then, his mother. When she can see him, touch him, care for him. He is the one who loves you, Evvie, isn't he?'

She nodded, unable to speak. She felt Ben's presence very strongly in this room. There were memories, reminders of him all around her.

'Then marry him, child. You must have some happiness in your life.'

'I . . . I loved Ben so much.'

He patted her head. 'I know, but he has gone, Evvie. You must look to your future. Ben would have wanted it.'

'Not yet, not yet.'

'But one day?'

'Maybe . . . one day.'

Levi got to his feet and went over to the dresser. He opened a drawer and handed her an envelope before he slumped into the chair again.

'I want you to have this, Evvie. What point is there in going on saving now? I have no one else. I came to Liverpool with my zayde; everyone else was dead. My Ada was an only child. Ben would have wanted it this way, Evvie. You won't go to your Kieran without a nadan – a dowry.'

Evvie's tears fell on the envelope, staining the stiff white paper. She didn't want money. She would walk barefoot to hell and back if only she could have Ben with her again. But he'd never come back.

She nodded, trying not to think of the hospital in Maricourt.

'Thank you, I'll keep it.'

'When you go back there, Evvie, will you write to me? Will you humour this old and foolish man?'

'Of course I'll write to you, and when I'm home I'll come and see you.'

He nodded slowly. 'Only until you marry your Kieran, Evvie.'

Evvie knocked quietly on the Ryans' door. She'd only been home a day but she *had* to talk to Josie for Kate's sake. She wanted to know what Frank had said in his last letter to his wife and family.

'How is your mam, Josie?' she asked as Josie opened the door.

'Come in, Evvie. She's just the same. It's no use you talking to her, she won't answer. I don't think she knows where she is.'

'Oh, Josie, I'm so sorry.'

Josie sighed wearily. 'She always used to say God never gives you a cross your shoulders can't bear. He's given her enough of them in the past, but this time it's too much for her. She's going to end up in the asylum if she's not careful.'

She sank down on the bottom stair and Evvie sat beside her.

'Oh, Josie, I don't know what to say to you.'

'You don't need to say anything.'

'And what about Frank? You know how Kate loved him. She's always loved him.'

'I did too, once – or I thought I did. I grew to hate him in the end, God forgive me. I was a stupid little fool and I paid for it, but I made his life a misery too. The only good thing to come out of the whole mess was Matthew.'

Evvie groped for Josie's hand and squeezed it tightly. 'Did he . . . how did he seem . . . before?'

'Quite cheerful. All his letters were cheerful. He was glad to be away from me. He didn't write directly to me. The letters were for us all. He was glad to be with his mates again. Oh, I feel so old and tired. I'm worried sick about Mam and Flo and Matthew. I don't know what to do about anything.'

'Is Mrs Lynch as bad as your mam?'

'No. Lizzie comes in and she's got Dotty and she idolises Matthew, but I can't leave Mam. Maggie has been sitting with her for the odd hour, but I'm going to have to go back to work soon. I'm going to have to work all my life, Evvie, to keep Matthew and me. I've thought about moving back here, but if I take Matthew away from Flo it will break her heart, and anyway Mam's not fit to look after him in the day. Oh God, what am I going to do? Everywhere I look there are worries and problems.'

Evvie was surprised to find that suddenly she could think clearly.

'Leave him with Mrs Lynch all day, pick him up and bring him here to sleep, just until she's better. I know Mam and Mrs Hawkins and Mrs McGee will keep an eye on your mam while you're at work. She won't be like this for ever, Josie.'

Josie looked at her gratefully then put her hand despairingly over her eyes, her head bent. 'Evvie, we're only twenty-one; we've got so much to cope with. All the boys . . .' Josie began to sob quietly and Evvie put her arm around her.

'We're not alone. There's girls like us all over the country, though I know that doesn't help much.'

'I wish it was all over; I wish to God it was all over.'

'It will be one day, Josie.'

'When they're all dead, Evvie? When they've all killed each other? Oh, they went off so cheerfully, do you remember? What has it all been for, Evvie? What?'

'I don't know. I just wish I did, Josie.'

Josie managed a smile. 'At least we've got something to look forward to.'

'What?'

'Maggie's wedding.'

'She's marrying Davie at last? Then they're doing the right thing. You've got to grab real happiness when you find it – that's one lesson we've all learned.'

The prospect of the wedding at least took Davie and Hetty's minds off the terrible tragedy surrounding them. They had arranged everything, the Mass at St Anthony's and the reception at Reece's. That had been one of the things Davie had wanted to talk to Maggie about when he'd gone to see her.

'I know it's unusual, Maggie, but too many people are still upset, and to have the reception at home or in a church hall would only make things worse for them. If we have it somewhere formal, and away from the neighbourhood, it will be better. Well, no one's going to expect a knees-up, are they?'

'You're right. It's best to get people away from the area. There are too many painful memories, especially for anyone who was married at St Anthony's. Will it be expensive to have it at Reece's?'

'Not really. We won't have to supply a lot of drink, just a drop of something when we arrive and something for the toast.'

'Well, that's fine. We don't want to be putting on a great show now, Davie, you're right. We'll do it properly, but we'll respect our neighbours and do it seemly, too.'

She had gone to Sloan's for her dress, which gave her some satisfaction. But she didn't choose the traditional white with a train, neither did she have a headdress and veil. The dress was pale oyster pink, with broad insets of oyster lace set into the bodice and skirt. The bodice was softly pleated into the high waist, the skirt just on her ankle. She'd bought her hat from Millicent's in Bold Street. It was Bangkok straw in oyster pink with two huge silk roses on one side of the wide brim. She wore short white gloves and high-heeled white kid boots fastened with pearl buttons.

'It's as lovely as anything you've ever made, Maggie,' said her mother when they went for the final fitting. 'It all matches so well. It's elegant and very tasteful, bearing in mind the circumstances.'

'You are going to get on well with Davie? You won't mind him being under your feet all day?'

'No, luv, he'll be no trouble. He was telling me he's going to look for work now. His bad leg won't stop him from driving a lorry or a tram. Hold still while I untwist this sleeve.'

'I hope he settles for a lorry. You know what people are like, Mam, about any young man who isn't in uniform. I don't blame them but he'll get the height of abuse from some people on a tram.'

'But it'll be obvious he's not fit.'

'Not right away, and by the time they realise, the damage will be done. No, try and talk him into driving a lorry.'

At first Maggie had agonised over her decision to ask Josie to be her bridesmaid. 'It might be too upsetting for her,' she told Hetty one evening when they were checking the progress of the wedding plans.

'I don't think so. There was nothing but bitterness between her and

Frank at the end,' Hetty had replied, crossing off items on various lists strewn around the kitchen table.

As the others were away in France and there was no one else she felt close enough to, she'd asked Josie.

Josie was delighted. 'Oh, Maggie, I'll be pleased to be Matron of Honour. You've been so good to me, lending me clothes so I could get my job. It only seems like yesterday since you were my bridesmaid.'

'What did you do with your dress, Josie?'

'I sold it. I wish I hadn't but I needed the money then. One of the Murphy girls from Taliesin Street bought it. Before you say anything else, Maggie, I'm not having green. Everyone said it was unlucky and well, it was. Not for you, for me, and I don't want anything to go wrong between you and Davie.'

'So, what colour would you like?' Maggie asked, remembering how she'd brushed aside Josie's comments about wearing green at a wedding.

'We've not a lot of choice, Maggie, I'm in mourning. It will have to be either purple, or lilac. No one will expect black.'

'Not much of a choice really. We'll have to go for lilac.'

The first of September 1916 dawned clear and bright. It was a fine early autumn morning with a crispness in the air that heralded the colder weather to come. The church was quite crowded for it made such a change to attend a Nuptial Mass instead of a Requiem or memorial, as one of Flo Lynch's neighbours remarked.

'Josie looks well,' the woman commented.

'Aye, she's not a bad girl really. She works hard all day then goes round to her mam's to get her da's tea and tidy up.'

'Is Mary Ryan no better then?'

'A bit. She gets out now and then,' Flo sniffed. 'Mind, she never was a one for housework and those girls do absolutely nothing. I'd shift them all right if they were mine. Matty Ryan's never known what it's like to come home to a tidy house and a meal on the table, until recently.'

'Well, I suppose now he's got good reason to get paralytic.'

'He did hit the bottle to start with but strangely enough he doesn't now. I don't say he's signed the pledge but . . . Oh, I'd better hush, they're about to start . . .'

Only about a dozen people sat down to the meal in Reece's

Restaurant. Neither Hetty nor Alf had many relations, just a cousin of Hetty's and an aunt of Alf's. Davie's parents were there but none of his younger brothers and sisters. Peg and Bill Greenway, Vi and Ernie Hawkins attended, as did Matty and Mary Ryan, who still looked pale and withdrawn. Everyone except the bridal party was in mourning.

'It was a good idea of Davie's, coming here.' Hetty smiled at the new Mrs Higgins. 'Look at them, I've not seen anyone so . . . so . . . interested in things for months.'

'It even seems to have brought poor Mrs Ryan out of herself a bit. I hope she's going to get better. Josie's worn out and she was telling me that Stanley Jeffries, who she works with, has been kindness itself. She's been seeing quite a lot of him over the months. He takes her for lunch, nothing fancy, not here or anywhere like this. Just Lyons but well . . .' Maggie shrugged and looked knowingly at her mother.

Hetty nodded approvingly. 'That girl deserves a bit of good luck, a bit of care and attention. She's had a rotten time these last years. It's aged her.'

Maggie pulled a face. 'But, Mam, he's old, he's forty. That's old enough to be her da.'

'As long as he's good to her and Matthew it doesn't really matter how old he is and as I said, these last years have aged her. She's far more mature than the rest of you.'

Maggie shrugged her shoulders. She could see the attractions of security. 'Well, don't say anything; she told me in confidence about him. Nothing may come of it in the end.' Smiling, like the hostess she was, Maggie turned her attention to Father Foreshaw who had joined them for an hour.

As September and then October progressed the army moved forward along the Albert to Peronne highway. Then came Mametz, Carnoy, then turning north, they marched to Longueval, Flers and Bapaume, still in German hands. These were towns and villages in ruins, fought over bitterly and bloodily only a few months before. The casualty lists grew longer by the day, the mood at home sombre and dark.

For Kieran Ryan the war was over. He'd been wounded in the leg and chest by shrapnel and from the field hospital he'd been taken to a military hospital near Dover and then sent home to Liverpool. The army had no further use for him: he was invalided out. The hospitals were having a hard time coping with the neverending, always increasing, stream of wounded and dying men and couldn't find space to nurse those such as Kieran.

It was a very different man that Josie, Matty, Mary and Evvie went to meet at Lime Street Station. The train was full of wounded, and they had to wait until Kieran, in a Bath chair pushed by a nurse, came through the barrier.

As she saw him Mary Ryan burst into tears and sobbed on Josie's shoulder. Pushing forward, Matty took Kieran's hand. 'Welcome home, son. We're glad you're back, an' we're proud of yer. Yer mam'll be all right in a minute; she's had a bad time.'

Evvie released the nurse from her duties and took control of the Bath chair. She bent forward and leaned over Kieran's shoulder.

'We're so glad to see you, Kieran. We've all been worried about your mam, but maybe she'll get better now. Josie's been great the way she's coped with everything. God knows what they would all have done without her.'

He looked up at her, his eyes haunted. 'I'm sorry, Evvie, about . . . about them all.'

She nodded, forcing back the tears. 'Let's get you home. This station has always been a draughty hole. If we don't get a move on we'll be catching pneumonia.'

A week later it was clear that for Mary Ryan Kieran's presence was a tonic, a tangible reason to carry on with life. She'd become brighter, more like the mam she used to be, Josie confided to Evvie.

'She keeps patting him, every time she passes him. She just has to touch him to reassure herself. He won't talk about it, any of it. He just won't answer questions and he has nightmares. He wakes up screaming every night, shouting – names, places. Oh, Evvie, it's awful. He's frightening Matthew but I can't tell him that. I'm going to have to leave Matthew with Flo all night as well as during the day, if it goes on. I hate the thought, but I won't have him scared.'

'Oh, Josie, it's all so difficult for you, so hard to know what to do for the best,' said Evvie kindly. But her real sympathies were with Kieran. She knew all about nightmares herself.

Chapter Twenty-Five

It was Peg who first thought of the idea that would maybe help them all. She'd mentioned it to Josie who often called in to see Evvie, who was still very down. Her depression wasn't helped by seeing Levi failing fast. True to her word, Evvie went in to see him every day.

'Josie, hasn't your mam got a cousin or an aunt or someone over in Ireland?'

'Yes, our Oona, she's Mam's first cousin.'

'Whereabouts, exactly, does she live?'

'In a village, I suppose you'd call it. Kilmara, in Cork. It's about ten miles from the town of Cork. A proper one-horse place, Mam always said it was. It's where all Mam's family came from, in the Great Hunger, I think. Da's lot came from Sligo and he says they were lucky to get here.'

'Aye, nearly everyone's family came over then. Why don't your mam and Kieran go over and stay for a while? It would do them both the world of good.'

'I don't think she could manage on her own yet, and I can't go.'

'Then our Evvie can. She's a trained nurse and she needs a bit of peace and quiet too before they recall her to the front. And a change of scene. All this traipsing in and out to see Levi, good as it is for him, it's not doing anything for her at all.'

Peg had good reason to want Evvie away from Silvester Street. In Ireland with Kieran, but with Mary as a chaperone, she might just come to see that Kieran not only loved her but needed her now. Besides, she was very worried about Evvie. Kate was strong, she always had been, but Evvie couldn't go on living on her nerves. Eventually something would snap and that was what she feared most. She'd come very close to it once. All Peg could do for Tom was to pray for his soul; she had to take care of Joe and her girls.

'Do you think she will go?'

'I'll persuade her, Josie. It would be good for all three of them – time in the country with fresh air, decent food, away from the damned newspapers. You write to Oona. It will give you a bit of a break, too, Josie. Let those three useless sisters of yours see to Matty and Mickey. You've carried the burden of all of them for too long, girl. You've been a brick but they don't appreciate it. They'll all have to manage without you to lean on. It will do them good.'

So Josie had written and the reply came back quickly. Oona and her family would be delighted to have them stay for as long as they liked. Mary and Evvie could stay with her but Kieran would have to stay with Miss Gilhooley, her neighbour. Theresa Gilhooley was well into her sixties and would be glad of the company. She would be well able to attend to Kieran, she being retired from her job as schoolmistress. It wouldn't do for him to be stuck in a house full of desperate children.

The weather wasn't good. The day before the ferry, the *Cavan*, had been delayed due to the gales which had eased a bit by the time they boarded. But even so, it was going to be a night-mare of a crossing, Evvie could see that. Still, she had paid for cabins, so they might get a bit of sleep, unless they were all sick. She gripped the rail, looking unhappily at the churn-ing sea.

She hadn't really wanted to come but both Mam and Josie had pleaded long and hard.

'Evvie, you know how much good it will do Mary and she can't look after Kieran properly. You're the one who is trained – don't put more pressure on poor Mary. Don't give her something else to worry about.'

'You'll enjoy it, I know you will.' Josie had added her bit of persuasion to Peg's, looking so tired and anxious that Evvie hadn't been able to refuse.

But even now they were aboard she wondered if she was doing the right thing.

Mary was sick, but the rolling and pitching didn't affect either Evvie or Kieran, though when they tied up in Kingstown harbour the following morning, there were many passengers who looked tired and ill and who were giving thanks that the ordeal was over and terra firma was in reach.

It was a long train journey to Cork and they had to change trains three times, all of which took its toll on Kieran. It was so difficult to manage him and the Bath chair. Evvie became infuriated with the slowness of the railways and the lackadaisical manner of its employees. It was with sheer relief and exhaustion that they arrived at Cork and were greeted by Oona, who'd been patiently waiting with a pony and trap.

'We're all worn out, it's taken so long to get here,' Evvie said wearily when they'd got Kieran and Mary into the trap. She asked that they take the last leg of the journey slowly as Kieran had been jolted around for too long as it was, in her opinion.

'Oh, it's a desperate long journey. That's why we've never seen Mary for donkey's years. I expect the boat was tossed around like a bit of matchwood? I heard the winds were terrible, an' all.'

'It was rough. Mrs Ryan was very sick but Kieran and I were fine. I'm a bit bruised on the shoulder, I think – I was thrown out of the bunk. After that I decided it would be safer to sleep on the floor.'

'Jesus, Mary an' Joseph! Was it that bad?'

Evvie nodded. All she wanted now was a cup of tea and to lay her head on a pillow and sleep.

'Ah, well, we'll be home soon enough now.' Oona dropped her voice to a whisper. 'Himself's very quiet.'

Evvie answered her in a whisper. 'He's exhausted and I think he's got some type of shock. I saw a lot of it in the field hospital: men who couldn't speak, just staring at nothing for hours on end. Some would mutter words over and over again. It was almost as bad as seeing those with shattered legs and arms, or gaping chest wounds so deep you could see the bones of their ribs. By the time many of them got to us from the field dressing stations it was too late.'

'Ah, wouldn't it break your heart, the state of things? Did you lose anyone yourself, Evvie?'

'My brother and . . . and a close friend.'

'God have mercy on them.'

Evvie grimaced. 'There's no mercy over there. Mortars and machine guns and stick grenades have no feelings, no pity. I . . . I couldn't stand it. I couldn't cope, so they sent me home for a bit. I feel so ashamed and guilty.'

'Ah, don't be giving out like that. No young girl should have to be seeing such desperate things.'

Evvie looked away in shame. 'But my sister, my friends managed.'

'I don't know how you're all managing at all, both over the water and in France too, an' that's the truth of it. Sure, it's bad enough here – there's a lot of Irish lads been killed too. An' those eejits up in Dublin fighting an' carrying on last Easter. Stabbing the lads in France in the back is what I call it. Dancing on their graves. I'm all for Home Rule but not by murdering people and having half of the city left in ruins. Did you see the state of Dublin at all?'

Evvie thought briefly of the Easter Rising. At the time she had felt as outraged as everyone else; now she could hardly remember what had happened.

'There's a lot of unrest in the whole country, I can tell you. I just hope it doesn't get worse. Merciful Mother of God! Where's the sense in it all?'

Evvie didn't reply, she was too tired and heartsore even to think straight.

They reached Kilmara, which seemed to consist of one main street that ran downhill towards a river. There was a grocer's, a butcher's, a post office, a chandler's, a small dispensary and no less than five pubs, so Oona informed her. They were not like pubs at home, she noted; they seemed to double up as shops as well. The church was at the top of the hill, as was the small, grey stone school.

Their progress was slowed down considerably as people called out to them and Oona reined in the horse to introduce her visitors. Everyone was very pleasant and sympathetic and interested, but Evvie just wished they would get a move on.

Oona's cottage was the end one of a block of three that overlooked a pasture through which a small stream meandered. Cattle were grazing there and Evvie was amazed at how quiet it was. Only birdsong broke the stillness. It was a far cry from Silvester Street and the battlefields of France.

Inside the single-storey building it was cramped and cluttered. There was only one large room that served as a kitchen, dining room and sitting room, with the bedrooms leading off it. A peat fire burned in the range, giving off a pungent, unmistakable smell. There were statues and holy pictures, ornaments and utensils everywhere. The cushions were faded patchwork and the curtains sprigged cotton. The floor was flagged but bright rugs were scattered about and over everything pervaded the smell of soda bread baking.

'It's a bit on the small side but you'll get used to it. Now I'll show you where you're to sleep and then, Mary, would you be up to putting the kettle on, do you think? I'll just go and take the trap back to himself in the end house that was good enough to lend it to us. Then I'll wet the tea and then take Kieran in to meet Miss Gilhooley.'

'Mammy, there's no milk,' one of Oona Sullivan's younger girls informed her, eyeing the strangers with curiosity.

'Well, get yourself down to Flanagan's Farm, Kathleen Sullivan, and fetch some, like I was after telling you to do before I went to the station. Claire, will you set the table and show your Aunty Mary here where the crockery is kept? Aren't they a trial, Mary? No milk, an' us with our tongues hanging out for a cup of tea. I'll not be a few minutes,' she promised, pushing Kathleen out of the door in front of her.

Evvie went over to the window and gazed out at the peaceful scene. This was just what Kieran needed to help him get well – and, she admitted, it was what she needed, too.

Josie had found on her return to work that many of her companions had lost sons and husbands. She'd taken her sandwiches to eat in St John's Gardens at the back of St George's Hall, Stanley Jeffries accompanying her, ready to hear all the sad stories she had to tell.

'Oh, Stanley, it's been terrible. Thank you so much for your letter and card. I'd be a hypocrite though if I said I was heartbroken over Frank, but I am upset for Flo.'

'And how is your mother?'

'I'm at my wits' end. I don't know if she'll ever get over it. If it hadn't been for the neighbours and friends I couldn't have left her. I'd have had to give up my job and then God knows what would have happened to Matthew and me. She's gone to Ireland to stay with a cousin, and Kieran and Evvie have gone with her.'

'Josie, I don't want you to think I'm insensitive —'

'You could never be that,' she interrupted him with a sad smile.

'I . . . I want you to know that you can rely on me for help, sympathy, advice.'

'That's very kind of you.'

He felt he couldn't pursue matters. He couldn't say what was really in his mind. It *was* insensitive. It was too soon and she was so much younger than himself. 'Well, I mean it, Josie. Anything I can do, you only have to ask. Promise me you will do that?'

'I will. There's no one else whose opinion, whose advice, I value more.'

'Do you really mean that?'

'Of course. I'm so stupid. There's so much I don't know.'

'Josie, you're not stupid.'

She sighed, thinking it would be good to be able to have someone like him to take her troubles and worries to. He was patient, comfortable to be with, and capable. 'I worry so much.'

'About the future?'

'Yes. What's going to happen to Mam and me and Matthew?'

The words came rushing out, despite himself. 'I . . . I don't know what I can do about your mother but . . . but if you'd let me, I'll take care of you and Matthew.' He hadn't intended to say anything so he didn't wait for an answer but plunged on. 'I've got a house, some savings, you'd both have the best of everything. I know I'm a lot older than you and —'

'Oh, Stanley!'

Her words stopped him and he looked into her eyes.

'Are you asking me . . . to . . . marry you?'

'Yes.'

She reached for his hand. 'Then . . . yes, please. After a decent time for mourning.'

'Of course. I understand. After a decent interval.'

'I can't say anything to anyone at home yet. You do understand that? Mam and Flo would think —'

'I said I understand, Josie. I don't want you to worry about anything at all. When the time comes we'll do it properly. You'll have an engagement ring and we'll announce it.'

She smiled at him and slipped her arm through his, feeling relieved, secure and happy for the first time in months.

It soon became obvious that the change was doing Mary good. She became less withdrawn, more alert and interested in what was going on around her. She spent hours exploring the tortuously complicated family history with Oona's friends and neighbours. It appeared they were related to half of Kilmara and most of Cork too, Kieran remarked to Evvie one day in early November, as she pushed him slowly along the lane to the village. She'd insisted they make the most of the afternoon's unseasonably mild weather.

'Leave her to get on with it, Kieran. It's doing her good. It's giving her something else to think about.'

'The only trouble is we might never get her home.'

She pushed him on in silence for a few minutes before she spoke again. 'Would that be such a bad thing? Why can't they all come over here?'

'Could you see our Rose, Sall and Maureen settling here?'

'They could stay behind. Your da could come.'

Kieran laughed. 'Oh, aye, he's gone on for years about "Going Home". Going home! He was born in Liverpool and he's not set foot outside the place in his life.'

'There's Mickey to think of, and if this madness goes on much longer you'll have him joining up.'

Kieran thought about this. No, he didn't want Mickey to go through the hell that was the Western Front. He didn't want to risk losing the only brother he had left, for he missed Pat and Niall. Nor would his mam be able to stand it. It would kill her if Mickey were to go as well.

'What about our Josie?'

'Oh, don't worry about Josie. I think it's only going to be a matter of time before this Stanley Jeffries asks her to marry him.'

'But he's old.'

'Not that old. He has a nice house in Anfield, a decent job and she'd want for nothing and neither would Matthew. She's a good mother and a good housekeeper, very organised and practical. She learned that from Mrs Lynch.'

Keiran nodded. Organisation was a word his mam had never heard of, never mind knew what it meant.

'I suppose if you look at it like that . . .'

'There's not many men who would take on the responsibility of a child, another man's child.'

'There's not going to be many men left, Evvie,' he said bleakly, 'Rose, Sall and Maureen should come over here. There'll be no one left over there to marry them.'

She moved the Bath chair into a gateway to shield him from the wind and she sat down on a large boulder at his side.

'That's why I think you should get Mickey over here as soon as possible.'

'He'd hate it. He's a city kid. He's used to running the streets.'

'He'd get used to it here in time and your mam and da would be happy here. People are so good, so friendly, so easy to get on with, and it would be away from all the memories.'

'Is that why you came with me, Evvie?'

'Yes, that and Mam insisting I come. She stopped just short of blackmail. It would be too much for your mam, she said. You'd need expert care and I'm a nurse.' She turned her face away from him, thinking of all the others, wounded like he was, that she'd left behind, that she'd let down.

'Was it very bad for you, Evvie?'

'Yes, and now I feel so guilty. I just couldn't cope with it, Kieran. Maybe I went too soon. It was the neverending work, the exhaustion, the terrible wounds. The dirt and the lice and . . . and being able to hear the guns and the shells bursting and knowing there would be more and more and more casualties. And as they came streaming in I . . . I couldn't help but think of our Tom, your brothers, Frank Lynch and Ben . . . Ben Steadman. Each time a new wave of wounded came in I had to fight to keep from seeing their faces everywhere and in the end I just couldn't stand it. I'd just burst into tears and upset everyone and then on the first day of the Somme I . . . I just snapped; I went hysterical. Kate was good to me and Agnes, but they weren't like me. They coped and I just added to their burdens.'

'Kate was always more confident, more outspoken than you, Evvie.'

Guilt, shame, fear and sorrow all bubbled up and overwhelmed Evvie and she leaned her head against his shoulder, tears brimming in her eyes.

'Oh, Kieran, what's it all been for?'

He took her hand, no longer afraid, reticent or tongue-tied.

'God knows, Evvie. It's sheer madness. We thought it was going to be fun. Fun!' His laughter was hollow and bitter. 'All lads off to war together, off on the great adventure. Cheering, throwing our hats in the air! Oh God, Evvie! I saw those same lads die. I saw them cut down, blown to pieces, crucified on the bloody wire and crying, begging for someone to help them or shoot them to put them out of their agony. There were only one hundred and fifty of us left out of nearly eight hundred, and most of us were injured. I can't forget either, Evvie, not even when I'm asleep. They all come back to me. I . . . I see them and I see the rats in the trenches, the bloated bodies, the mud. Oh, Evvie, I'll never be able to forget it all. I'll never be able to forget how our Pat and Niall died. They were beside me. We all went over the top together. Everyone was shouting, the officers were yelling and shells were exploding.' He struggled to control his voice. 'The next time I looked they'd gone. They were blown to pieces. There was nothing left to bury, Evvie. All they could find were bits . . . tiny bits, and they weren't even sure that they belonged to them.' Again he struggled. 'I . . . I . . . had pieces . . . stuck . . . to . . . me. I have to live with that. I couldn't tell Mam that. I couldn't tell anyone about it and I was scared, too, Evvie. So scared.'

'Kieran, it's all right now, it's all right, I understand,' Evvie soothed, cradling his head, his tears soaking the front of her coat. 'I'm here, Kieran, and I can share it with you. I saw them too, the mangled bodies of the dead and dying.'

It was an hour before they stopped talking and crying together.

Everything they'd held back for so long had burst forth in an unstoppable torrent and when at last they were both calm, she wiped away their tears and pushed him home down the rapidly darkening lane. A new bond had been forged between them. A bond born in the sorrow they shared and the horror and the carnage they'd lived through which had swept away their youth, their innocence and the world they'd known.

Chapter Twenty-Six

Mary Ryan had seized on what she thought was Kieran's idea as though it were a life raft.

'I never want to go back there, Oona! If I stay, if Mickey and Matty come over too, I'll be as happy as I can ever hope to be. I can't go back. There's too many memories, too many people wearing black. Oh, you've no idea what it's like, Oona. Every house, every family, has been touched. It's peaceful here – well, peaceful enough – and there's Mickey, me baby. He'll be old enough soon and I won't let him go. I won't and they can't make me give him up. Two boys are enough.'

'What about those three fine beauties, Rose, Sall and Maureen?'

'They can please themselves. Selfish through and through, the lot of them. Our Josie's always telling me that. She's a great girl, is our Josie. I've waited on them hand and foot all their lives, but if they don't want to come over they can see to themselves.' Mary meant what she said: they were all old enough to get married, and without Matty's consent. Old enough to have their own homes where they'd have to make an effort.

Mary's letter, written by Kieran, arrived in Liverpool four days later.

'Is it from Mam?' Mickey asked as Matty struggled to read it. 'What does she say? When's she coming home?'

'She's not,' Matty announced.

'If she's not coming back why have you got that grin on your face, Da?' Maureen asked acidly.

'Because we're going over there.'

'What for?'

'To live, Mickey, that's what for.'

'I'm not going to up stakes and go and live in that Godforsaken hole!' Rose cried, aghast.

'We'll die of boredom. We'll go round the twist, Da!' Sall added, siding with her sister.

'They're about a hundred years behind everyone else,' Maureen added, exaggerating as always. 'We'll have to have you and Mam with us all the time when we go out. Can you imagine going to a dance and having to take Mam?'

'That might do yer all some good. It would have kept our Josie out of trouble,' Matty retorted.

'They probably only have dances on Holy Days of Obligation,' Rose said sarcastically. 'Da, I'm twenty-four, I'm not a kid.'

'Well then, you're old enough to see to yourself, an' so are you two. You can stop 'ere.' Matty had long harboured a dream – and until lately that's all it had been – a dream of going to the land his grandparents had fled to escape starvation and fever. Now that there was the chance of that dream becoming reality he had no intention of letting his daughters hold him back.

'There's only one of yer that's got any sense an' feeling for yer mam, an' that's our Josie. Fine bloody 'elp you three were when yer mam was bad. She'll be better off all round if yer stop here.'

'Well, that's nice, Da, I must say!'

'It's the flamin' truth, Rosie Ryan!'

'And where are yer going to live? What will yer do for a job?'

Matty waved the letter under Sall's nose. 'It's all been worked out. Yer mam's cousin is goin' to see someone about a house and she says that because so many of the lads have gone to fight, there's jobs to be had.'

'Da, I don't want to go! I want Mam to come back here, back home!' Mickey protested.

Having reduced his daughters to seething silence, Matty turned his attention to his son.

'Ah now, don't be saying that. Things are better there. You'll get used to it and then you'll love it.' Matty had taken to heart his wife's words about wanting to remove Mickey from any temptation he may have had to go and join up. Matty was getting old, too old to be fretting over another lad, wondering if another telegram would arrive. There seemed to be no likelihood of the carnage ending. He just wanted some peace in his old age and so did Mary. She'd said so and didn't she deserve it? Didn't they both? Aye, they'd grow old together in Kilmara, away from worry and everything that was bound up in city life, including those three idle selfish rossies who were giving him looks fit to kill. No more would poor Mary wear herself out running after those three.

'I don't want to go!' Mickey persisted.

Matty lost his temper. 'Well, you're goin' all the same, meladdo! An' until yer twenty-one you've got no say in the matter, an' I don't want ter hear any more about it!'

Evvie had been due to go home for Christmas but Kieran begged her to stay.

'This is the first Christmas without my brothers and my mates,' he reminded her.

'It's a wonder Mam isn't going to send our Joe over with Mickey. Da's watching him like a hawk.'

'Please stay, Evvie? I need you.'

So she'd written and explained and said if they really needed her then she'd come home.

Peg's reply had been prompt and firm. If Kieran wanted her to stay then she must stay. Peg had noted the change in tone of Evvie's letters lately. When she'd first gone to Kilmara in the middle of October, she had hardly mentioned Kieran, except to give brief reports on his health. It had been Mary and Oona, Miss Gilhooley, Bernadette Ryan, Maeve Slattery and Geraldine Brennan, all of them related in some way to Mary Ryan. Now it was mainly Kieran: what he did, what he said, where they went. Peg renewed her prayers to St Jude. She'd seen how close to the brink of despair and depression Evvie had come. Now it looked as though she might at last find happiness.

Mickey Ryan was far from happy at being uprooted from Silvester Street and dragged to the back of beyond, as he called Kilmara. But Matty had gone with Oona's husband to the surrounding farms and had found work for both himself and his son. There was a shortage of man-power in Cork as well, although nothing to compare with Liverpool.

Oona had managed to find them a house. 'It's only a bit of a cottage really, but as there's only the four of you, it won't be bad once it's done up.'

Mary had been delighted and showed more enthusiasm over the low, single-storey house than Evvie had ever seen her display in number eight Silvester Street.

'Ah, she'll be her old self again now that himself is with her and Mickey's out of harm's reach and she has Kieran, too. Those three selfish amadons back there will manage just fine an' if they don't, then it's the back of me hand to them,' Oona said with feeling.

* * *

They all exchanged small, token gifts on Christmas morning and then went to Mass in the little stone church that nestled into the hillside, as though sheltering from the winds that often swept this corner of Ireland. It was a bitterly cold day. A heavy hoarfrost made the hedgerows and fields sparkle in the pale sunlight. Everything was so white that it looked as though it had snowed overnight.

Evvie held Kieran's arm tightly. He insisted on walking and she was afraid that he would slip. She'd received cards and gifts from home in the mail, and a card and letter from Kate, apologising for not having got her a gift of some sort. She had a qualm of guilt, knowing Kate had neither the time nor opportunity to look for gifts. But she was delighted to learn that both Kate and Agnes were due for home leave at the end of February though she really wasn't overjoyed that her own leave would be over the same month. After Christmas she'd have to go home. She had to see everyone before she was shipped out again. She knew from Kate's letter that they were due to move up to Agny after Christmas. This last piece of news worried her a bit. Agny was near the Hindenburg Line where there was fierce fighting. But she knew that the nurses followed the troops. After all, they were fighting a war too.

After a good Christmas lunch Kieran suggested he and Evvie go for a walk.

'I think you've done enough walking for one day. You've to take it slowly, that's my professional opinion.'

'Only as far as the shrine at the top of the lane. To walk off all those potatoes.'

So she agreed and, well wrapped up in coats, scarves, hats and gloves, they walked slowly up the lane towards the little wayside shrine that someone had decorated with holly.

'That's far enough, we'll turn back now,' she said briskly.

'Not yet, Evvie. I want to talk to you.' Kieran had a fleeting memory of his painfully rehearsed words to her on other occasions in the past, but today he was able to ignore it.

'Evvie, you know the way I've always felt about you and since we came over here you've been so good, so patient, so understanding.'

'That's because I do understand, Kieran, as no one else here possibly can.'

'Evvie, will you marry me, when the war's over?'

She plucked at a piece of rough tweed on the lapel of his jacket, her eyes downcast. She was fond of him, she always had been. But she had to admit that over the last two months that affection had grown, fuelled ironically by the experiences they'd both shared. It still hurt her to think of Ben; if Kieran had asked her to marry him next week, or next month, she knew she would have had to refuse. But how long would it be before that wound healed? If she was honest she knew it would probably be years. 'Kieran . . . when it's all over, when I've had time to forget . . . to get used to . . . my loss . . .'

'I don't expect you to forget Ben Steadman, Evvie, but I don't mind.'

'Kieran, you've always been so . . . patient . . . so loyal.' She paused. 'Yes, I'll marry you when the war is over.'

'I'll have work then, Evvie. I'll be strong. The leg will get better.' He frowned. 'I know Levi gave you quite a bit of money. Your mam told my mam in confidence, but you know my mam. She couldn't keep a secret to save her life.'

'That doesn't matter, Kieran. Money is not that important.'

'It's important to me. I don't want to be living off their money.'

'Let's not talk about that yet, Kieran,' she pleaded.

He nodded. 'It's enough that you'll marry me, Evvie. I love you so much.'

She smiled and touched his cheek gently. 'I know someone who'll be so delighted: Mam. She's had her prayers answered at last.'

Peg was overjoyed. 'Oh, thank God, Bill! Thank God!'

'Now what?' Bill asked from behind his newspaper.

'Evvie. She's coming home but the best part is she's going to marry Kieran. After the war, she says, but you never know.'

Bill grinned at his wife. 'So your dream's come true. I suppose Mary is over the moon, too?'

'Apparently everyone over there is, except Mickey who still hates the place and his job —'

'I don't blame him. It must be dead boring,' Joe interrupted, remembering how Mickey had carried on to him when his da had first told him about the move.

'Well, dead boring's a damned sight better than just being dead, Joe Greenway! You've got a short memory, you and that thicko Mickey Ryan. You've forgotten your brothers already.'

Joe was instantly contrite. 'No I haven't, Mam, honestly.'

'And don't you dare to slope off to the army and tell them

you're eighteen. We've had enough misery in this family. More than enough.'

Joe said nothing. He wasn't even sure he wanted to join the army now.

Kate sat at her small table on which was an oil lamp that gave out soft but flickering light. Next to it was a battered but still serviceable clock and in front of her lay the book in which she wrote her notes concerning the events of the night.

She didn't mind night duty, it was quiet compared to the frenetic hours of the day. She glanced up and down the rows of beds that were placed as near to each other as possible. Space was a luxury they didn't have.

In the few weeks she'd been at Number 23 General Camp Hospital at Zillebeke there had been little time to stop and just think. Casualties came in all the time, but thankfully not in the hundreds as had happened at Maricourt.

She sighed and drew Peg's letter from the pocket of her dress. She smiled. She was so glad Evvie seemed to be recovering, as was Kieran. Maybe something good would come out of this bloody war and soon she would be going home on leave. Oh, after all this time she couldn't believe it. Of course she was looking forward to it, yet in a way she was dreading it.

It wouldn't be the same place she'd left. People would ask her questions. They were bound to want to know what things were like here, and she didn't want wounds that had only just begun to heal to be ripped open again. So many of the lads in the street, in the entire neighbourhood, were dead.

She covered her face with her hands and fought back her tears – tears for them all but especially Charlie and Frank. At least she'd been able to make Charlie's last moments happy for he'd died in her arms. But Frank . . . she didn't even know where Frank had died, on the battlefield or in another hospital. They had both been close to her heart, but especially Frank. What was there left in life now? In the past she'd pushed this question, and the memories, to the back of her mind, but now she had to face them.

When it was all over, what would she do with her life? Sister Caldwell had said she was an excellent nurse, high praise indeed from someone who was regarded as a dragon. What else could she do? What else did she want to do – go back and work in Silcock's? Suddenly she remembered Cecile Chapman's words:

'You've nothing to be ashamed of. Our day will come, Kate.' Cecile had been proved right. Women who had worked, and worked damned hard, doing men's jobs had proved themselves. Girls like herself had suffered all the horror, grief and atrocious conditions the soldiers had endured. At times they'd come into range of enemy gunfire and it had been frightening, but compared to what the men on the battlefields were suffering, it was nothing at all. No, Cecile and the others had never given up hope and neither must she.

She looked down the ward and suddenly she knew what she would do with the rest of her life. She would go on nursing. She would dedicate her life to the sick and the wounded, and there were thousands of them. Maybe in a way it would compensate for the loss of not only Frank and Charlie but her brother Tom and all the others, too.

Many of these men would go on suffering until the end of their days. There were men who had lost limbs; men whose lungs and eyesight had been destroyed by gas; men whose futures would always be blighted by injury and memories. She would do the best she could for them. All the energy, the compassion, the love that had died with Frank and Charlie she'd devote to those who were suffering. She wouldn't give up. Now she was so much stronger and she could almost laugh at the way she'd been so frightened and humiliated after that one night she'd spent in the Bridewell at Hatton Garden. She'd grown up and she must put all thoughts of Frank and Charlie behind her. It was the future that counted now and she was determined to make it successful. Maybe one day she would even aspire to the position of Matron.

She looked at her watch. It was time to do her rounds again but she felt infinitely better now.

Evvie at last arrived home and Peg beamed at her daughter. 'You look great, girl. You really do!'

'I feel it too, Mam. That was the best idea you ever had, sending us all over there.'

'Aye, Mary was a bit worried about Josie, but it looks like Josie has found herself another husband. Oh, he's a lot older than her, but he's a good, kind man. She'll be secure and happy. That little lad will have a da now and a good start in life. Flo is taking it hard, but Josie's promised she can have Matthew to stay at weekends and that she can come at any time to see him. She won't need to be invited. She's been good to Josie, has Flo, and it's not done Josie any harm living in Athol Street either.'

'Has Mrs McGee heard from Maggie lately?'

'Yes, she's in Amiens. Hetty said she doesn't know what she did without Davie. He's such a good help. Alf's not been too good lately. He's too old to be working down at the docks and so is your da, but they won't give it up. The country needs them. The ships have to be unloaded and turned around as quickly as possible. That's all I can get out of him and Alf McGee's the same.'

'What does Davie do now?'

'Drives a coal lorry for Alsop's. He has a lad and a girl to help him heave the coal about. A girl, I ask you! Mind you, she's a strapping one.'

Evvie frowned. 'Mam, when Kate's leave starts I've got to go back. I'm fine now, I've been off long enough. My leave's up and I feel as though I'm not pulling my weight. There are so many women working now, I can't waste my training.'

Peg sighed. 'I suppose you're right, Evvie, but at least I'll have you both home together for a few days. It will be the first time in years. We'll have a bit of a do, if I can scrounge enough stuff together. You can't even get enough to make a decent pan of scouse now. Most of the time it's blind scouse – just potatoes, carrots and anything else you can throw in, but no meat.'

'Oh, don't be fussing about having a do. Kate'll be so worn out all she'll want to do is sleep. I know, Mam, because that's how I felt when I came home.'

'We'll see, Evvie. We'll see,' Peg replied with the hint of a smile.

'Oh, I've never been so flaming cold in my entire life!' Kate said to Agnes as they shivered in the tiny attic room in their billet. She'd heard it said that it was the coldest winter in living memory. The wind still howled and the snow was banked up against the sides of the buildings. Long icicles hung from the eaves and the water in the jug had frozen solid. They were both wearing everything they possessed, layer over layer.

'It's got to be better in the hospital. At least there'll be a fire on the ward.'

'It won't be much of a fire and we'll have to take half of this lot off or we won't be able to work.'

Agnes tucked her hair up under her tin hat. 'Oh, roll on the end of this month. Mam will have a fire up the chimney and the kitchen will be as warm as toast. Oh, to be warm again, really warm. And to have a bed, a proper bed. How many days have we got left here now?'

Kate peered at the marks scratched into the bare wood on the windowsill. 'Only ten more days and then it's home to Blighty and no flaming work. I suppose the best thing you can say for the cold is it's killed off most of the lice.'

They nodded curtly to the owner of the house, a small, dumpy women dressed in black. Her hair was pulled back into a bun and her dark, birdlike eyes noted everything. When they were outside Agnes pulled a face.

'She'll be glad to see us go, will Madame in there, and I'll be glad to see the back of her. I hope we get a better billet when we get back. I hate this country. I sometimes wonder if we're fighting the right people. Most of this lot wouldn't give you the time of day, never mind any help. They charge for everything. I heard one of the lads say they were even charged for a drink of water. Flaming water, I ask you! And the lad was wounded doing his best to keep the Hun off their backs. No gratitude at all, no flaming thanks.'

'Oh, stop moaning, we'll be home soon.'

Agnes suddenly stopped halfway across the frozen rutted road as a high-pitched whine came to her ears. The thin, screeching wail of a *Minenwerfer*. The trench mortar, fired from the enemy lines by specially trained troops, was particularly hated. You could see them, you could hear them, but no one ever knew where they were going to land.

'Oh hell! They're off again. It's a flaming moaning Minnie.'

As they ran the sound became louder. Then there was a tremendous explosion and Agnes was hurled against the side wall of the hospital building. When she at last recovered her senses, caught her breath and rubbed the dust from her eyes, she couldn't see Kate. There was just an enormous mound of rubble that a few seconds ago had been a house.

Evvie had finished doing the potatoes and she gathered up the peelings and threw them on the fire, then picking up the dish she turned towards the scullery. She never reached it. The bowl clattered to the ground, potatoes rolled across the floor and she screamed and bent over, clutching her chest, gasping for air.

'Evvie! Dear God! Evvie, what's the matter with you?' Peg screamed.

'Mam, I . . . I . . . can't . . . breathe . . .' Evvie gasped, clutching Peg's hand tightly.

'I'll get the doctor. I'll send someone for the doctor.'

Evvie was bent double, then she suddenly slumped forward into Peg's arms, breathing deeply and normally, but she was shaking.

'Oh, Mam, I don't know what happened. I don't know what came over me.'

'Has it gone? Are you all right now?'

'Yes. Suddenly there was a terrible pain and I just couldn't breathe. I was choking, being crushed and then . . . nothing.'

The fit had frightened Peg, for that's what it undoubtedly was, a fit of some kind. 'I think you should sit down for a bit, I'll send for the doctor.'

'No, Mam. There's no need for the doctor.' She suddenly shivered.

Peg snatched up her shawl. 'Is it starting again?'

'No. No . . . but . . . it's Kate. Oh, Mam, there's something wrong with Kate, I know there is!'

Epilogue

They brought Kate Greenway home. The soldiers they buried where they fell, but she was only the second nurse to die; the first, Edith Cavell, had been shot as a spy in 1915. As Kate was the first Liverpool nurse to be killed St Anthony's Church was packed.

The war would go on for another twenty-one months but the crowds that stood three and four deep along Scotland Road were mercifully unaware of that fact. Later there would be monuments and memorials. Now there was just a coffin covered with flowers, and memories.

The traffic was at a standstill from the Rotunda to Byrom Street. Her family and friends sat in the front pews, behind them the civic dignitaries, and behind them the neighbours and parishioners.

It was Kieran who supported Evvie for she felt that part of her was also dead. She knew now the exact minute her sister had died and part of her heart had withered too. But she was going back to the front and she knew this time she would cope: she had Kieran's love and Kate's example to help her through. And Kieran knew he had strength enough for them both. It couldn't go on for ever. Something had to be done before more girls like Kate were killed, he thought sadly.

Josie bowed her head and leaned against Stanley's shoulder for support. They'd been friends, she and Kate, close friends until – Frank. Well, Kate was with Frank now and they would never be parted. She sighed and wiped her eyes. It seemed as though she'd come through these awful years with some good fortune. Now she'd have a good, kind husband, a nice home and a future for Matthew. Her parents were happier than they'd been for years and Mickey was beginning to settle down.

Agnes, home on compassionate leave, was weeping quietly. Vi had her arm around her daughter's shoulder, for Agnes was shocked and dazed and every night she awoke screaming Kate's name. But she was determined to go back. To stay at home would somehow diminish Kate's bravery and sacrifice. She wouldn't be alone, she'd be with Evvie and Maggie, and she knew Kate's spirit would be with them all.

Maggie couldn't come home on leave but Davie was there beside Hetty and Alf, and all three were imploring God not to put them through what Peg and Bill were going through now. Hetty prayed hard for Peg, for surely no woman, no mother, should ever have to suffer as Peg had done.

Peg and Bill sat close together. Bill held Peg's hand and his other arm was around Joe. Bill was remembering them all at Maggie's birthday party – a lifetime ago it seemed now and part of a lost world. Tom, Kate and Evvie, and Joe. Now only Evvie and Joe were left, and soon Evvie was going back over there. Both he and Peg tried to push their worries for her safety to the back of their minds. There was only so much one family could bear at a time. The worry and fear, for now, was in the future. He'd been a devout man all his life, but his faith was shaken and he wondered if it would survive.

As she sat, surrounded by her diminished family, Peg drew some comfort from Evvie and Joe. Over and over like a refrain, she repeated the words: 'We'll manage. Just leave me Evvie and Joe, Lord. Don't take Evvie too, please. If I have her and Joe, I can cope.'

Davie, his head bent, looked sideways at his in-laws and added his prayers to theirs. Before Maggie had gone they'd talked about the future. He'd given up the idea of the garage. He told himself it had only been a pipe dream, a fantasy. Maybe if war hadn't come, in time, the dream *may* have become reality, but then again it might not. Maggie *had* established her business. Maggie with her clever and novel ideas. His priorities had changed. It was Maggie herself who mattered to him most of all now. Maggie who was nursing at the front, just as Kate had been. They'd decided that when the war was over they would buy part of a building and Maggie would renew her business with his help. He would do the paperwork, deal with suppliers of materials, millinery, shoes and gloves. He would supervise all the departments and deal with the day-to-day problems of running a business. It would leave Maggie free to design and eventually to run their own home. They were grand plans and they would succeed, if only Maggie would come home safely.

Father Foreshaw was attended by the priests from all the surrounding churches, and at the end of the Mass he came to the foot of the altar steps and laid a hand on the coffin. At first he struggled, clearing his throat, but then his voice became stronger, the deep, well-modulated voice they all knew so well but filled now with great sadness.

'I baptised Katherine – Kate Greenway and her twin sister, Evangeline. Through God's mercy I was not to know that just twenty-one years later I would be called upon to lay Kate to rest. She went to nurse the wounded. To bring comfort and hope to our young men, and she died returning to her duties.

'Because of the gift of beauty that God bestowed on Kate and Evvie, many of you knew them as the Angels of Silvester Street. But Kate, like her sister and her friends here today, was more than that. Like them, she was an Angel of Mercy.

'So many of our young men, sons, husbands, fathers, brothers, have died for their Country and their King, but never have we asked or expected any of our young women to lay down their lives too.

'In so doing, Kate Greenway has immortalised herself in all our memories, in the memory of Liverpool itself, as one of the Angels who gave herself up for the love of others. We will never forget her; as we will never forget the rest of her like, for so many of us here owe so much to our Angels, our Angels of Mercy.'